ROGUE WARRIOR®

Dictator's Ransom

ALSO BY RICHARD MARCINKO

FICTION

Violence of Action

With John Weisman

Red Cell
Green Team
Task Force Blue
Designation Gold
Seal Force Alpha
Option Delta
The Real Team
Echo Platoon
Detachment Bravo

With Jim DeFelice

Vengeance
Holy Terror

NONFICTION

Rogue Warrior (with John Weisman)
Leadership Secrets of the Rogue Warrior: A Commando's Guide to Success
The Rogue Warrior's Strategy for Success

ROGUE WARRIOR®

Dictator's Ransom

RICHARD MARCINKO
AND
JIM DEFELICE

A Tom Doherty Associates Book
New York

This is a work of fiction. All of the characters, organizations, and events portrayed in this novel are either products of the authors' imaginations or are used fictitiously.

ROGUE WARRIOR®: DICTATOR'S RANSOM

Copyright © 2008 by Richard Marcinko and Jim DeFelice

All rights reserved.

Book design by Spring Hoteling

A Forge Book
Published by Tom Doherty Associates, LLC
175 Fifth Avenue
New York, NY 10010

www.tor-forge.com

Forge® is a registered trademark of Tom Doherty Associates, LLC.

Library of Congress Cataloging-in-Publication Data

Marcinko, Richard.
Rogue warrior—dictator's ransom / Richard Marcinko and Jim DeFelice.—1st ed.
p. cm.
"A Tom Doherty Associates Book."
ISBN-13: 978-0-7653-1793-3
ISBN-10: 0-7653-1793-1
1. Kim, Jong-Il—Fiction. 2. Rogue Warrior (Fictitious character)—Fiction. 3. Special forces (military science)—Fiction. 4. Nuclear terrorism—Prevention—Fiction. 5. Korea (North)—Fiction. I. Title.
PS3563.A6362 R6375 2008
813'.54—dc22

2008031732

First Edition: October 2008

Printed in the United States of America

0 9 8 7 6 5 4 3 2 1

DEDICATION

This book is dedicated to the memory of **SEAL Lt. Michael P. Murphy,** who died in Afghanistan during Operation Redwing on June 28, 2005. Details of the mission remain highly classified.

Ambushed and under heavy fire from a superior enemy force, Murphy maintained radio contact with his headquarters unit to obtain aerial support for his men. The lieutenant, who lived in Patchogue, New York, later died of his wounds.

Two other SEALs, Petty Officer Mathew Axelson and Petty Officer Second Class Danny Dietz, were also killed in the engagement. The lone survivor, Petty Officer Marcus Luttrell, undertook an incredible odyssey to freedom, finally escaping with the aid of Afghan tribesmen. He wrote an account of the battle and his subsequent fight to survive in *Lone Survivor: The Eyewitness Account of Operation Redwing and the Lost Heroes of SEAL Team 10.*

In the attempt to rescue Murphy and his men, an Army Special Operations Chinook was also lost, along with its crew and a number of Navy SEALs en route to help their brothers:

Army

Maj. Stephen C. Reich, Chief Warrant Officer Chris J. Scherkenbach, Chief Warrant Officer Corey J. Goodnature, Master Sgt. James W. Ponder III, Sgt. 1st Class Michael L. Russell, Sgt. 1st Class Marcus V. Muralles, Staff Sgt. Shamus O. Goare, Sgt. Kip A. Jacoby

SEALs

Lt. Cmdr. Erik S. Kristensen, Lt. Michael M. McGreevy, Jr., Senior Chief Petty Officer Daniel R. Healy, Chief Petty Officer Jacques J. Fontan, Petty Officer 1st Class Jeffrey A. Lucas, Petty Officer 1st Class Jeffrey S. Taylor, Petty Officer 2nd Class James E. Suh, Petty Officer Second Class Eric Shane Patton

SpecOp operators live and die for each other regardless of service affiliation. The "shooters code" goes beyond services and even nations. It's the true "good ol' boys network," and these men selflessly fulfilled the code with their own blood.

"A revolution is not a dinner party . . ."

—Mao Tse-tung

PART ONE

SNAFU

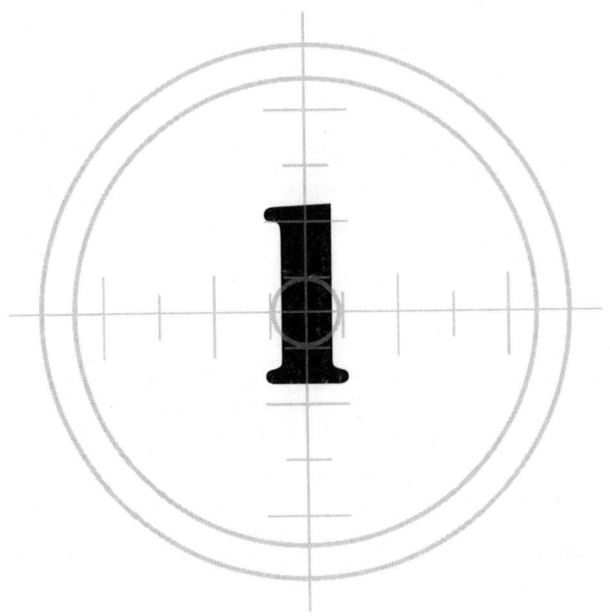
1

[I][1]

Impressions of North Korea:

Cold. Crappy food. Cheap booze.

Great place to hunt. Especially if you're with the world's cruelest dictator.

Not a good place to be shot, especially by said dictator.

But let me start at the beginning . . .

It was springtime at Rogue Manor:

The snow had melted, the crocuses and whatnot were pushing their pointy buds up through the turf, and there was a lovely scent in the air.

Gunpowder, that is.

It was the first week of April. Trace Dahlgren had just finished working with some new recruits for Red Cell International—the security company I run with a little help from my friends. Trace had spent the morning running the kids through a makeshift obstacle course on the back forty, trying to separate the wheat from the chaff. This was just a preliminary trial, so we gave them a nugget break—there were only two sections of live-fire exercise involved, and in both cases the shooters were instructed to keep their aim a *good* six inches from anything moving.

Any recruit who stopped, of course, was fair game.

"No casualties," said Trace, reporting in at lunchtime. She sounded disappointed.

Red Cell is an equal opportunity employer—we hire ex-army as well as ex-SEALs, and I think we even have an old air farcer on the payroll. As a former blanket hugger and a member of the female persuasion herself, Trace Dahlgren gives the company that well-rounded culture the human resources department

---

[1] You like these Roman numerals and mini-chapter breaks? Yeah, neither do I, but it was the editor's idea. We have to do *something* he wants, or he won't spring for drinks next time we see him.

would love to brag about, if we had a HR department. She learned how to break in new recruits while working with Delta Force, the army's counter-terror unit. (If you're a faithful reader—and you sure as hell better be—you'll recall that Trace was a member of Delta's female squadron.[2]) At five-eight and 130 pounds, Trace has assets male shooters don't, which makes her deadly in the field as well as undercover, both literally and figuratively. Her real love, though, is busting humps during training—even I have trouble keeping up with her PT routines—which is why she's in charge of what we call prerecruitment month at Red Cell.

The participants call it hell, along with some other choice terms of endearment—high compliments from guys and gals who have survived SEAL training and the like. Basically, if you make it through the month at Rogue Manor with all of your limbs intact, we offer you a job. The pay's great and the bennies can't be beat, though rumor has it that the boss is one mean son of a bitch.

We were in the process of gearing up for some new business ventures in Eastern Europe, and I was more than a little interested in finding out about what the new crop of recruits looked like. But before I could ask for a detailed report, Rogue Manor's early-warning radar began sounding an intruder alert.

No, it wasn't a high-tech burglar alarm—my dogs were hounding a black Lexus LS 460L as it sped up the driveway. Yappy, being male, took up the lead, with Macey and Rosie right behind him. Abbey hung back a bit, surveying the scene; she was the oldest, and had to present a dignified demeanor. I went out on the porch and watched the car fishtail around the curves and then slam to a stop in the muddy gravel in front of the house. The driver jumped from the front of the car as it stopped and tried to run around to open the rear passenger door. The

---

[2] Officially, Delta's "funny squadron" doesn't exist, and hasn't since it was created in 1993. Then again neither does Delta.

dogs intercepted him, pinning him against the car. They weren't being malicious, nor were they hungry; they hadn't had a chance to play all day.

"*Meomcheseyo!*" shouted the man, and right there I had a feeling that the day was going to be more interesting than usual. Because not only was he speaking Korean—loosely translated, "*Meomcheseyo!*" means "God damn it, stop this bullshit right now!"—but he had a North Korean accent.

The problem was, in dog speak "*Meomcheseyo!*" means something like *Come on and jump on my car, sniff my crotch, and hump my leg.* The dogs were happy to comply. They were so excited I had to whistle three times before they remembered who kept their food dishes filled.

"Inside, now," I told them when they finally looked in my direction.

They gave the air a sniff, decided they didn't like what they smelled, and retreated.

With the dogs gone, a gorgeous woman emerged from the car. When I say gorgeous, I don't mean drop-dead gorgeous—I mean kick you in the throat, douse you with kerosene, burn you to a crisp with no trace of remorse gorgeous. She was Asian, and as I gathered, Korean. Black hair, red skirt—short, short skirt—and a figure that demanded you do politically incorrect things in public.

"*Annyeonghaseyo,*" I told her, bowing my head, both in respect and to get a closer look at her legs.

"Enough with the Korean," she said sharply. "Your accent is terrible. You are Richard Marcinko, Mr. Rogue Warrior?"

"Dick to you," I said. "I love a woman who gets to the point."

Not to mention one who was holding a Smith & Wesson revolver six inches from my head. I can't imagine where she'd been hiding it; there sure wasn't any extra room in the dress.

"Nice pistol," I said.

"It's loaded, Dick."

"So are you."

"You are a very funny man, Mr. Marcinko."

The gun was a nice little S&W Chief's Special, a Model 37 I believe, with the blued J frame. Manufactured by S&W back in the day, it was a .38 caliber snub-nose, still a nasty little customer if you're not expecting it.

The chauffeur, meanwhile, had recovered from his encounter with the dogs and was reaching into his jacket.

"You can point anything you want at me," I told the woman. "But if he takes a gun out of his pocket he's going to eat it. And then the dogs are going to eat him."

She said something to him in Korean. The chauffeur frowned, but kept whatever weapon he had holstered.

"So, Mr. Marcinko, you do not seem as brilliant in real life as you are on the page," said the woman, returning to English. "There is a little bit of fiction in your accounts, no?"

Everybody's a critic these days.

"Why don't you come inside and we can discuss that. My study is always open."

"You want to get me in bed, is that it?"

"If that's what it will take."

She moved the Smith & Wesson so that it was no longer aimed at my head, though I've often been accused of having my brains where she pointed it.

"I am not here to sleep with you," she told me.

"Who said anything about sleeping?"

She finally smiled. But that was the extent of our budding romance—Trace interrupted our tête-à-tête with a flying jump from the side roof, landing on my Korean guest. I grabbed the Smith & Wesson as it flew into the air.

"*Meomcheseyo!*" I told the chauffeur as he started to reach for his gun. "One more inch and you'll have a new hole to eat kimchi out of."

Red Skirt was beautiful, tough, and highly skilled in Korean kickboxing. Trace is just as beautiful, twice as tough, and is an expert in Jeet Kune Do, the martial art that Bruce Lee made famous.

Wasn't much of a match. Trace had her pinned inside of ten seconds.

"All right, let her up," I said as the dust settled. "It's not every day the most hated dictator in the universe sends a personal representative to visit Rogue Manor."

Trace and Red Skirt gave me a funny look, but it was pretty obvious who she worked for. The only other people who would have been so rude were members of the Christians in Action—otherwise known as the CIA—and no intelligence officer was going to drive a Lexus limo this close to the Langley accounting staff.

"I am here to deliver an invitation," said Red Skirt.

"At the point of a gun?" asked Trace.

"In America, doesn't everyone travel with guns?" asked Red Skirt. "It is required by your Constitution."

She reached back into the limo and pulled out a leather briefcase. Trace tensed behind her as she opened it, but all she produced was an envelope. It was made of thick, fancy paper and had a wax seal at the back. It looked like the invitations I get when one of the great-aunt's grandchildren decides to get hitched.

"*Mr. Rogue Warrior, hand-deliver*" was written on the outside.

"Sealed with a kiss?" I asked, turning it over.

"Maybe we should check it for a bomb," said Trace.

I broke the fancy seal on the back and slipped open the envelope. There was an invitation inside, engraved of course, written in both English and Hangul, the Korean script.

At least I assume that's what those squiggly characters were about.

Dear Mister Marcinko:

Your honorable presence for drinks and dinner is humbly requested by the great one, Kim Jong Il.

Ms. Chimdae will make the arrangements.

There's something about being called "Mister"—especially when it's spelled out—that always gets me in a special place.

Usually my wallet.

"Thanks, but no thanks," I told Red Skirt, handing back the invitation. "Have a pleasant day."

Ms. Chimdae gave me a blank look. Obviously no one in her experience turned down a request from the Great Dictator.

I cracked open her pistol and slipped the bullets out, giving the cylinder a good spin before handing the gun back. "The dogs will be back out in a minute. Your chauffeur will probably feel more comfortable if you're off the property by then."

"You do not understand, Mr. Marcinko. This is a great honor," said Chimdae.

"No doubt."

"You be sorry for this, Rogue Warrior," chirped the chauffeur. "Very sorry."

"Words to live by," I said, turning around and heading for the door.

[II]

Possibly I was a little hasty. It's not every day that the world's sleaziest dictator asks me over for dinner. Nor should the fact that someone is a slimebag prevent me from hoisting a few at the bar with him. If that were the case, I'd have to remain sober every time I went to New York to meet with my agent.

But I'd been to North Korea once—you can read about it in *Red Cell*—and had no desire to go back, with or without Kim Jong Il's invitation. And I had plenty to do, both at home and in Europe with the company. So I didn't second guess my decision until the next morning when a black Lincoln Town Car made its way up the drive, the squeal of brakes accompanied by the howling of my dogs. The Town Car was not traveling alone—it was in the middle of a procession of black Chevy Suburbans, each packed with six or seven plainclothes security types, who fanned out along the drive as the Lincoln came to a stop. The sunglasses were Wal-Mart; the radio earplugs government issue. I whistled to the dogs, who circled the caravan, growling.

The door to the Lincoln popped open and a rotund man in a blue pin-striped suit emerged. It wasn't more than sixty degrees out, but the man was already perspiring heavily. He wore thick, wire-rimmed glasses, which teetered at the edge of his nose. The briefcase in his hand looked as if it had been through a war.

"Marcinko?"

"That's right. And you are?"

"Ambassador at large, Asia, Roderick Kant Fogglebottom[3]," he said. "State Department. May we talk inside?"

"It's a free country."

"The secretary of state sent me," he said once we reached the kitchen. He put his briefcase down on the table and snapped it

---

3 The publishers' lawyers have recommended I not use Fogglebottom's real name, which is William Yarkowski, for fear of pissing off the administration. This is what happens when lawyers are allowed to make contributions to political campaigns.

open. "He wants you to reconsider this invitation from Kim Jong Il."

"The secretary of state wants me to go to North Korea and have dinner with this scumbag?"

"I'm told the monkey brains are a delight," said Fogglebottom.

I'll spare you the rest of the conversation, which included a lively discussion of Korean culinary highlights such as rotted cabbage and fried dog innards. The bottom line was this: the U.S., with the help of South Korea, Japan, and China, was negotiating a deal with Kim Jong Il. North Korea's Great Leader had very generously (cough, cough) offered to forgo further development of nuclear weapons, and in fact to get rid of those that he had already made, in exchange for the release of several billion dollars in assets, two nuclear power plants, and a lifetime pass to Tokyo Disney. The talks had evidently reached a very delicate stage, and the administration was worried that any little upset would throw them off.

"Including indigestion?" I asked.

Fogglebottom curled his lip.

"Given the fact that your company has extensive contracts with the government," he said, "I don't believe you're in a position to argue."

"That's right," I told him. "So I'm not going to argue. Get the hell off my property now."

I emphasized my desire to see him gone by tossing him in the direction of the limo. Seeing him bounce, the dogs mistook him for one of their rag-doll playthings and bounded after him. He made it to the car with most of his flesh intact, if not his clothes. By the time the dogs answered my whistles, the Lincoln and its escorts had disappeared in a cloud of dust down the driveway.

Under ordinary circumstances, that would have been the end of my North Korean adventure. But just around dinnertime, the phone rang at Rogue Manor. I picked it up and heard a sweet young thing ask if I was Richard Marcinko.

"My friends call me Dick," I told her.

"Please hold for the director."

I was hoping the director in question was a movie director interested in bringing Rogue Warrior® to the screen. Instead, I found myself talking to the DCI—Director, CIA—or as I like to put it, Dunce in Charge of Imbeciles.

"Dick, this is Ken Jones. How the hell are you?"

"Admiral. Just fine. What can I do for you?"

"Can you be at the Riverside Bar in Tysons Corner at nine o'clock?"

Rear Admiral Kenneth Jones—he's retired from the navy, but once an admiral always an admiral—and I go back a bit. We'd been in Vietnam around the same time, and put in time on the same river—Bassac, which is one of the tributaries of the Mekong. Our careers took different paths; he was always a lot more political than me, for better and sometimes worse. But there's always been an unspoken bond between us. You tend to respect a guy who risked his butt to save your people.

Kenny commanded a PBR—Patrol Boat/River—on the Bassac and Mekong Rivers back in 1967. If memory serves—and it may not—he was an ensign, but he already had the look of weathered command in his face. Kenny may not have been fearless, but he was close, and the guys who served under him thought he was a god.

The PBRs were fiberglass gunboats about thirty-two feet long, armed with recoilless rifles, mortars, flamethrowers, MK19 grenade launchers, .50 caliber machine guns, smaller M-60 machine guns, and as many rifles as the four-man crew could carry. Among other things, the gunboats worked with SEAL units, covering insertions and various operations.[4] PBR commanders were a mixed bag. Having balls was just one requirement; you had to have some sense to go along with them. Kenny had both. He and his boat provided support and taxi service for me several times when I was

[4] I wrote about some of my experiences with PBRs and their commanders in the original *Rogue Warrior*.

out with a group of my guys on a "Mar-chinko"—an extended stay in Charlie country designed to wreak as much havoc as possible. He was always where he was supposed to be, except when we needed him to be somewhere else. He never let me down once.

After I left Vietnam, Ken got his boat shot to shit rescuing a pair of SEALs who'd been stranded at the tail end of a reconnaissance mission. Everyone on board that boat was hit two, three, four times by VC fire, but they still managed to get the SEALs the hell out of there alive. The bow of the boat looked like splintered glass when they reached home; I think the navy stripped it down and towed it out to sea for proper burial because it was so far gone. Ken got a bronze star with combat V for the operation. The "V" stands for valor and means Ken put his fanny on the line to earn it.

I don't put too much store in medals, even though I've been granted a few. Real honor to me is when someone recounts a story about a man with awe in his voice. That's how SEALs talked about Kenny Jones.

Which isn't to say that we always got along. After the war, Ken spent a lot of time at the Pentagon. Somehow he wound up in Naval Intelligence, though his war experience prevented him from becoming a true dip-dunk. Our paths crossed several times. At one point, he worked for my most senior sea daddy and mentor, Admiral William Crowe[5], who headed the Joint Chiefs of Staff. Kenny was very helpful to me during my early days in Red Cell, but then left the service to start a new career as a high-level bureaucrat at the Defense Intelligence Agency or DIA, also known as the Don't-know-nothing Intelligence Agency.

"High-level bureaucrat" is generally a synonym for "guy with head up his ass," but Kenny defied stereotypes and actually did a

[5] Admiral Crowe passed away while I was in Korea. He was one of the finest leaders I've ever known. He had a brilliant mind and he used it instead of his rank to show the way. The admiral was instrumental in having CNO pick me to commission Seal Six. I'm proud to say he was also a friend. He'll be sorely missed by his family, and his country.

bit of good there, mostly by working around the system. From the DIA he'd gone over to the CIA. I lost contact with him there, but from mutual friends had heard he'd retired again after a stint as the agency's number three man. Then, barely six months before this story takes place, the president found it necessary to appoint a new DCI, one who came from within the agency ranks but could work with the military as well. Ken was an obvious choice.

We hadn't spoken in at least three years, and that conversation had been about the weather. It was obvious that something big was up, and I doubted it was a coincidence that he was calling me right after I'd turned down Kim Jong Il's invitation.

"I'd like to talk over old times," added Ken as I hesitated. "When can you make it?"

"Nine o'clock," I told him. While I didn't owe him anything personally—and I owed the CIA even less—Ken Jones is one of the few people in Washington who deserves the respect his office generally affords him, and I decided I had to at least listen to what he had to say.

I canceled my evening plans—regrettably, since I had a movie date with Karen Fairchild, the lovely proprietress of my heart—threw a steak on the grill for dinner, then got out of my sweats and into my jeans. Depending on the traffic and time of day, Tysons Corner is maybe forty-five minutes away from Rogue Manor. I did it in a half hour, and Kenny still beat me. He was sitting in a corner of the bar, sipping a double Manhattan classic when I came in.

I suppose I should set the scene. Tysons Corner, Virginia, is a sprawling suburb just down the road from CIA headquarters at Langley. As far as I know, no river has ever flowed through there, so how the Riverside Bar got its name will have to remain an unanswered mystery, at least here. There are a lot of subdivisions in the area, though—miles and miles of them—along with office complexes and shopping malls. The town supposedly has more retail space than just about any city in the U.S., short of New York.

The Riverside was a small, square building shoe-horned into

a triangular lot off Route 7. Most of the cars in the lot were Toyotas and Hondas, with an occasional Chevy or Ford family sedan and a smattering of pickups. The outside walls were lined with planks of varnished wood. To get through the lobby I had to fight my way through a forest of ferns and hanging plants; once past them I stepped down into a long, L-shaped room decorated to look like a marina a bit past its prime. Or maybe the bar was past its prime; I wasn't sure. The place was about a quarter full, and most of the people in the place were watching the television sets tuned to a Bullets playoff game.

When he was younger, Ken's hair was bright, flaming red, which accounts for one of his nicknames. ("Indian." You can work out the etymology yourself.) Now it was mostly gone, with a thin haze around the sides that looked almost blond in the bar's dim light. His face looked thinner than I remembered, but he still had a boy's smile that puffed up his cheeks and made him look like a first-year cadet on leave when he saw me.

"Dick, come on and sit down." He half rose, gesturing at the chair across from him.

CIA directors tend to move with an entourage of security people and aides—George Tenet could have passed for a rap star with the size of his posse—but Kenny was here alone. He wore a college sweatshirt and a pair of raggy jeans; he looked like a plumber ducking his wife. I doubt anyone would have recognized who he was, much less guessed his profession. I shook his hand and pulled out the chair across from him.

"Still drinking Manhattans?" I asked, pointing at his drink.

"Stronger on the Vermouth as time goes on." He looked toward the bar, signaling a waitress. "Bombay Sapphire for my friend," he told her when she came over. "And I'll take a refill."

She gave me a big smile and walked away.

"Mmmmm," said Kenny, watching her go. "I wish I was twenty years younger."

"Don't let age stop you," I told him, laughing.

"It's not age. It's the job. Good thing I'm divorced already." Ken frowned, and temporarily turned his attention to the basketball game. I slid my chair back, scanning the bar.

"No, I'm alone. No security detail," he said. "No aides."

"No witnesses."

He smiled. "I take precautions. But here you and I are just old war buddies, shooting the shit. Right?"

I nodded. The waitress appeared with our drinks. She had a green and red dragon tattoo that ran up the side of her right arm; the tail circled above her cleavage.

"Where does the time go?" said Ken, holding his drink up. "It seems like only yesterday that I was going up the Mekong River, hunting for gooks."

I clicked his glass, but my BS detector was now pegged on high alert.

"Funny thing happened to me the other day," I said. "Kim Jong Il invited me to dinner."

"So I hear," said Ken, taking a sip of his drink. "You going?"

"I don't think so."

"He is a big fan of yours."

"I'll bet."

"No, on the level. There's a photo in one of our dossiers, showing him reading one of your books. I'd show it to you, but it's classified."

"You don't have to butter me up, Ken. What's the story?"

"I'd like you to accept Kim's invitation," said Ken, returning to point. "As a patriotic gesture."

"I'm supposed to be a goodwill ambassador to North Korea?"

"Not entirely. It would be helpful to us. Very helpful."

"Maybe you better explain."

Ken leaned back in his seat.

"What I am going to tell you is classified," said Ken. "It gets repeated nowhere."

"No shit."

"I wouldn't shit you, Dick. You're my favorite turd." Ken smiled, then told me what was going on.

North Korea's attempt to explode a nuclear warhead the year before—an attempt that did not quite succeed, but that's a tale for another time—had convinced China that its ally not only could not be trusted, but had become a significant liability. It was now in China's best interests for North Korea to disarm, and it had begun pressuring the North Koreans by withholding aid and shipments of food and oil. Reluctantly, Kim Jong Il had agreed to meet with China, the U.S., South Korea, and Japan to discuss disarmament.

Our eavesdropping friends at No Such Agency, also known as the National Security Agency or NSA, had intercepted communications indicating that Kim Jong Il had directed his negotiators to get the best deal they could. Low-level government representatives had approached American counterparts and indicated the country was prepared to agree to terms. In short, North Korea had decided to *really* get rid of its nukes; it was just a matter of coming up with a plan we could trust and a price they would accept.

All of this, at least in general detail, had been in the news. The columnists, talking heads, and bloggers all credited China and its naked blackmail for North Korea's willingness to disarm. Good China, good.

Of course if we'd threatened North Korea with starvation in the name of world peace, we'd be labeled pricks and worse.

I'm not one to underestimate the value of blackmail, but Kenny had a theory about what was really going on that made a hell of a lot more sense. According to Ken, North Korea was willing to get rid of its nukes because it wasn't.

At least not all of them. It was willing to get rid of the two that scientists had calculated it could produce—and which it had privately admitted to China it possessed—but not the four it didn't think anyone knew about.

"They have six nukes?" I asked.

"Seven and a half. Besides the two they've unofficially declared, there's one at their testing facility, where they're trying to figure out how to get it to blow up right. The half isn't a bomb but material for a bomb located at Yongbyon where the reactor is. We know where all of those are. It's the other four we're concerned about."

"You're sure there are four other weapons?" I asked.

"We're not sure of anything. But the information comes from someone who has been reliable. Obviously, we're interested in gathering whatever other intelligence we can."

"You think Kim has them in his house?"

"It's not just a house, Dick. It's a huge complex. Most of it's underground."

Ken reached into his pocket and took out a satellite photo of a complex. The quality wasn't fantastic—for security reasons it had come off a commercial satellite, not one of our military birds—but I could easily make out trucks and vehicles in the driveways.

"This is Kim Jong Il's new house north of the capital. The buildings that you can see are empty. The real house is underground. Deep underground—ordinary bombs wouldn't reach it."

The U.S. had watched the construction, but the North Koreans had managed to shield much of it from the overhead satellites. The bunker was beyond the reach of normal sensors, even from the ground-penetrating radar generally used to map bunkers.

"We have new technology coming online in two or three years which should be able to map it," said Jones, "but we'd really like to know what it looks like before then."

"And you want me to take a house tour?"

"Anything you can tell us would be useful," said Jones. "How big it is, what the security arrangements are, possible vulnerabilities, that sort of thing."

"And check the bathrooms for nukes."

"Absolutely."

Ken took a sip of his drink. Manhattans are made with Vermouth and whiskey or, in a classic, bourbon. They're usually topped off with a cherry, but Ken always asks the bartender to leave his out. He used to make a joke about having lost his cherry years before; now that he's head of the CIA he probably doesn't use the line anymore.

"I don't expect you to find them. I'm more interested in the size of the place, whether it's possible that they're there, that sort of thing. Now, if you did happen to find them . . ."

He reached into his pocket and pulled out a small pillbox.

"This little doodad will tell us where you are if there's trouble."

He flipped open the lid. Two very small, flesh-colored disks sat on a piece of black foam. I picked up the box and looked at them.

"They connect together. They send a very long-wave radio signal that can travel through the earth. We can use that to pinpoint the location of the bombs. The first broadcast lasts twelve seconds. From then on, it fires up at random intervals for only a few seconds. It takes about a week and a half for the battery to die, depending on how often it transmits. It's in that unit on the right."

He pointed to it, then described how the pieces were to be slipped together. Until they were connected, there was no power, no signal, and no way for the device to be detected.

"A doctor I know can implant them behind your earlobes tomorrow," said Jones, taking back the box. "They'll itch for a few hours, then you'll forget they're there."

"Why did Kim Jong Il invite me, Ken? Did you guys set it up?"

"No. We had nothing to do with it. I didn't even know about the invitation until the morning briefing was being prepared today. State brought it to our attention."

"I find that hard to believe."

"I'm sure we had information about it *somewhere*," said Ken. "But just because we gathered it doesn't mean the analysts looking at it thought it was significant. And it's not. Except to me."

"Why bring me here? Why not to Langley?"

Ken laughed. "And have a parade through the halls? Half the staff knows you. This isn't an agency assignment. No one else knows—not State, and not my operations people."

"Completely covert, huh?"

"Something like that."

I'd realized from the start that Ken was working around the CIA's normal chain of command; otherwise he would have brought me onto the headquarters campus. Meeting in a public place gave him absolute deniability—we were just two old war buddies knocking back drinks. He wouldn't have had that excuse if he'd come to Rogue Manor. There could have been a dozen reasons why he wanted to do this off the circuit—for one thing, even the DCI had to deal with the company lawyers, who would review everything to death for weeks if not months before giving even the most routine matter their imprimatur.

I didn't pry; I'm used to working off the books. And I wasn't sure whether Ken would give me a straight answer if I did.

"I can understand why you wouldn't want to do it," said Ken. His voice was suddenly philosophical. "You're famous, right? Getting out toward retirement age. Maybe past it, if truth be told. You're past the point of taking risks."

"Don't try to get me going with that reverse psychology crap."

"No, I'm being serious. Spying, covert action, war fighting—it's a young man's game. All us old farts have too much to live for. We can't afford to be expendable. Too many people depend on us. Right?"

I shrugged. Even back in the days when Ken and I were running around in Vietnam, people depended on us—he had a crew, I had a platoon. But we were still expendable. It came with the territory.

"Because if you did this, you'd be expendable," said Ken. "Absolutely expendable."

"What happens to the weapons when you find them?"

"The president's call." Ken shrugged. "I don't blame you, Dick."

"Blame me for what?"

"For getting old."

I laughed.

"But the thing that keeps pushing me," he said slowly, "is the thought that Kim will sell one of these nukes down the road to somebody like Bin Laden. If I don't find them and New York blows up, I'll never be able to live with myself."

Ken Jones had lost a lot of hair since I first met him, but he had the same conscience. And it was infectious.

Unfortunately.

"Didn't Bill Casey get in trouble for personally running ops through the back alleys of the government?" I asked. Casey was CIA director under President Reagan. Many people in the agency and SpecWar community felt he was a hell of a director, but he'd also managed to provoke Congress to the point that his successors had had their hands tied.

Not that Congress didn't generally deserve provoking.

"Who's running an op?" replied Ken. "I'm just having drinks with an old friend."

"Since it's drinks, I better have a refill," I said.

(III)

Yes, I did contact Kim Jong Il's minion the next afternoon and tell her that I would accept the invitation. Yes, I realized there was a hell of a lot more going on here than anyone, including Ken, had told me. No, I wasn't sure what it was, though my suspicions at that point leaned heavily toward a possible plan by the CIA to get rid of Kim Jong Il as well as his weapons.

Hating scumbag commie dictators is all well and good, but that wasn't my only motivation for going to North Korea. I was curious about who he was, and why he wanted to see me. I didn't buy the fan bullshit, but I was curious about what was going on.

"So who will your date be?" asked Ms. Chimdae.

"My date?"

"It is customary to bring an escort to dinner."

"I'm a stag kind of guy."

She hesitated for a moment. "We can arrange for an escort."

"Blonde or brunette?"

"Which would you prefer?"

"Who's easier?"

I glanced across the room. Trace Dahlgren had her arms crossed in front of her chest, scowling at me.

"That's all right," I told my would-be Korean pimp. "My escort will be Ms. Trace Dahlgren. You want me to spell that?"

"Please."

Now if this had been a *true* social situation, my escort would have been Karen Fairchild. Karen and I had been seeing a great deal of each other over the past several months. Our relationship had begun as strictly business—Karen worked for the Department of Homeland Security, where she'd been hired as one of the agency's token competents. Every government agency has a few of them, generally so spread out in the bureaucracy that they can't actually get anything accomplished.

Taking Karen with me to North Korea, however, wasn't an

option. She was heavily involved in a project involving preparations against biological warfare attacks, an assignment that had her working nearly to seven every night—which in the government world is the equivalent of around the clock. Besides, while Karen has proven her mettle in difficult situations before—most recently by batting a live grenade out the window of a NATO meeting—she's not a trained shooter. If I was going into the lion's den, I needed someone to watch my back.

Trace Dahlgren and I had a brief though highly enjoyable encounter of the romantic kind some time back.[6] But our relationship now is strictly professional and platonic. Of late, her heart had been stolen by a good-looking helicopter pilot named Ike Polorski. They'd met six weeks before when she'd ventured over to the local flight school to fill in some gaps in her education. Somewhere between the cyclic and the stick, romance had bloomed, and they were soon pulling each other's yokes. Trace was head over calloused heels in love with Polorski, or "Tall, Dark, and Polack," as I called him.

This was a more politically correct description than "that f'in' Polack," which also described him perfectly. Being Slovak myself, I was qualified to know.

I bring up Trace's love life because Trace had planned a hot weekend with TD&P. She expressed extreme reluctance to exchange it for a trip to bucolic North Korea. Not that she refused to go or even argued against the assignment. Either would have been far easier to deal with. Instead she pouted. Even I felt sorry for the recruits the next day. We had three cases of heat exhaustion, two sprained ankles, and a broken nose by lunch.

Just when I was debating whether to get another escort for Korea or relocate training to the local hospital grounds, Trace received a text message from Tall, Dark, and Polack, explaining that he had been hired for an absurdly well-paying gig in Japan and had to leave as soon as possible. He'd be there for about a week.

---

6 See *Violence of Action.*

Why don't you join me? he asked.

Trace arranged a rendezvous in Kyoto, to take place after our dinner with the dictator. Her attitude did an immediate one-eighty, and the afternoon session saw seven cases of heat exhaustion and one broken leg. I sent her home to pack before the early evening live-fire exercise, figuring that if I didn't, I'd feel obliged to hang around for the funeral services of half my recruiting class.

(IV)

North Korea has a long and intriguing history. In past centuries, the Koreans have had encounters of the violent kind with China and Japan; though it pisses the Japanese off when you say this, it's likely that the present emperor has Korean ancestors back in the family tree.

Japan eyed the Korean peninsula in the nineteenth century for all the usual imperial reasons, and its occupation and influence took various forms. Japanese agents assassinated the Korean empress in 1895; in 1905 the country was declared a Japanese protectorate, thanks to a treaty the Koreans signed basically at gunpoint. Korean resistance grew steadily, though it wasn't able to do much against the Japanese. The March 1st Movement of 1919 is a landmark in passive resistance, though we don't hear much about it in the West. World War II and the defeat of Japan brought both the U.S. and the Soviet Union to the country; the occupying forces more or less split the peninsula in two into North and South around the thirty-eighth parallel. Originally there was a plan for a combined government under the administration of the UN, but that got shoved aside after North Korea styled itself as the Democratic People's Republic of Korea (DPRK) on September 9, 1948.

The U.S. withdrawal from the South in 1949 brought the true benefits of democracy to the fledgling country—political chaos and confusion. The South Koreans took hold of the gifts with great enthusiasm as they elected and then rebelled against their chosen government at close and regular intervals.

In 1950, the North Korean government decided communism was so much fun the South should enjoy it, too, and sent a few million bodies south as traveling salesmen. The Russians supplied the weapons.

MacArthur had something to say about that, and with the (generally uncredited but critical) help of some early proto-SEALs, reversed the order of things with a landing at

Inchon. Worried about the effect on real estate prices when the Americans rolled the North Korean army up toward the Yalu River, the Chinese "volunteered" every military age male in their country to go south for winter break. Things were shaky for the next few months, until the Americans learned that the Chinese had a severe weakness for glazed duck, and subsequently cooked enough Chinese goose to force a stalemate back more or less at the thirty-eighth parallel, the original boundary between the two Koreas.

The North Korean leader—or Russian puppet, depending on your point of view—who caused all this fuss was Prime Minister Kim Il Sung. Kim proved marvelously incompetent as a war leader, but being a dictator means never having to say "*joesong-hajiman andwaeyo.*" He already understood that the number one characteristic of a successful dictatorship is to kill every possible rival, something he did with great vigor after the war. Eventually, he declared himself *The Great Leader* and proceeded to run North Korea as far into the ground as possible.

Or so it seemed until he died and his son, my erstwhile host Kim Jong Il, took over. Kim Jong Il pushed North Korea even further into debt and over the edge of sanity. But let's give credit where credit is due: he introduced such welcome reforms as changing the calendar so that the years began with Kim Il Sung's birth.

Kim Jong Il's great claims to fame are his nuclear program and unbroken string of record crop failures and famine, but he's no slouch in the areas where despots are traditionally judged. Whether you consider his concentration camps—the largest, Camp 22, holds something on the order of fifty thousand people, though the population is regularly trimmed by killing any children born to inmates—or his annual Hennessy cognac budget ($700,000 a year for moldy French wine), the man is a master of fascist nuance.

While today China bears the closest resemblance to an ally the North Koreans have, there's still a pretty strong undercurrent of distrust and even outright animosity between the people of the two countries. Some of the best North Korean insults refer to the Chinese. Of course, attitudes toward the Chinese are absolutely tame compared to the officially sanctioned loathing of America. According to the North Korean government, in fact, the Korean War is still going on. According to the official media, victory is just around the corner.

The State Department provided me with a thick binder of background on Kim, along with an even thicker binder on something called "diplomatic etiquette." I'm not sure what was in it, but since I had my suspicions I put it to its best possible use, rolling the pages into a log and burning it in the fireplace to ward off the midnight chill.

More useful was the special Navy Gulfstream the State Department procured to take Trace and me to Korea. Not only was the aircraft fast and well piloted, but a bright lieutenant had stocked it with Bombay Sapphire in advance of my flight.

The good Dr. Bombay made the patter of the Gulfstream's third passenger tolerable. The passenger was a short, nervous fellow named Lee Kamere whom Fogglebottom had sent along as a Korean translator and protocol expert. Lee himself was actually a bit better than most State Department flunkies I've met; he didn't have the snotty airs or bespoke suits of the worst of the breed. But he had an unfortunate nasal quality to his voice that under the best circumstances was grating. And his laugh sounded like the squeal of a hyena with its tail caught in a meat grinder.

It took us three stops and roughly twenty hours to reach Japan. The military base at Hamamatsu had been alerted to give us the VIP treatment, and there was barely enough time to stretch my legs on the tarmac or wax nostalgic about past visits before we were taking off and heading toward North Korean airspace. Local time was now 1010 hours military, 10:10 A.M. civilian, and there was not a cloud in the sky.

To this point, the trip was long and boring, a situation that can only be truly appreciated after you've experienced the opposite. Mr. Murphy—the proprietor of the infamous rule that whatever can go wrong will go wrong at the worst possible time—seemed to have missed the plane. The implanted locator devices behind my ears had stopped itching, and I was actually becoming curious about Kim Jong Il. Right up until the point where we neared their border, the trip looked like it was going to be as dull as a visit to Safeway, or maybe Safeway without the food.

As we approached the border, the North Koreans sent a welcoming committee to speed our landing. The committee consisted of four MiG-29 jet fighters, which announced their presence with a high-speed get-to-know-you dash at our nose.

Playing chicken with North Korean pilots is not highly recommended, since the North Koreans are unfortunately well known for their lack of flying skill. Our pilot flicked the Gulfstream hard to port, and one of the MiGs still managed to pass so close that its wing nearly grazed the window near my seat.

I was picking myself up off the floor when the pilot announced that one of the planes had just turned his targeting radar on. Given that we were unarmed, this was not a good sign.

"They're not answering our radio calls, Commander," the pilot told me when I went up front to see if I could help. "I don't know what's up their ass."

"Let me see if I can talk to them," I said. "I speak their language."

"Begging your pardon, sir, but I know Korean," said the copilot.

"I'm not talking about Korean," I told him.

I took the copilot's headset, and made sure I was on the interceptors' frequency.

"*Annyeonghaseyeo*," I said. "Hello."

There was no reply. Which was fine by me.

"Listen, you worm shits," I said in English. "This is Dick Marcinko. I'm on my way to chow down with your boss's boss's boss, Kim Jong Il himself. This flight has been approved by more people than live in Delaware. If you make me late for the soup course, I'm going to be pissed off. And so is he. Now turn off your bleeping missile radars and back away, or I'm going to grab my submachine gun and do some wing walking."

How much of the words they understood may have been debatable, but the tone was all they really had to decipher. In less than a minute, the radars were off and the planes had backed away. I gave the copilot his radio set back and went to finish off my drink.

[V]

The Koreans rolled out the red carpet for us at Pyongyang. There were three different bands, which brought tears to Trace's eyes—that's how bad they were. The official welcoming committee consisted of two navy officers and an army general, along with a short, fat fellow who was the Korean equivalent of our translator, Lee Kamere. I'm not saying he was ugly, but he reminded me of a dog my first wife once owned.

Everybody started bowing deeply as I ambled down the steps. I joined in, and we spent the next few minutes bullshitting each other on how happy we were to make our mutual acquaintances. Trace stood to the side, rolling her eyes in between bows. Kamere and his Korean cousin began jabbering away, half in English, half in Korean. When everyone had stretched their trunk muscles to the max, we were led to three waiting Mercedes, with each of us consigned to a separate car.

A ragtag selection of military and civilian vehicles joined us. The motorcade began slowly, the limos pulling out one by one and heading across the wide cement expanse to the terminal building, a structure that would have looked as if it were a 1950s cigarette factory except for the mammoth photograph of the Great Leader, Kim Jong Il, who stared down from the edge of the roof. Yet another high school band stoked up as the cars pulled up. A fresh contingent of officers came out of the doors and lined up at the edge of a yellow silk carpet. They nodded as we were ushered inside the building to an arrivals area several times as big as those at JFK International Airport in New York.

People milled around the far end of the hall. Most carried suitcases, apparently intended as props to fool us into thinking the airport was extremely busy. (In fact, the next outgoing flight was three days away.) A long table was set up in the middle of the space; six different customs officials sat there waiting for us. The special passports the State Department had issued for the trip were confiscated; in their place we were handed leather wallets. These contained a variety of official papers written in Korean. The customs officers then took turns inspecting these papers, stamping and in at least one case sniffing them. Finally we were declared legal and waved toward a crowd of small children holding flowers.

"Welcome—Demo Dick," said the kids as I approached. "We—very honored—to see you."

A few of the kids stepped forward holding out copies of my last book. Naturally, I began signing them. They may be commies in training, but they have good literary taste.

"Don't let this go to your head," muttered Trace as the authorities began to disperse the autograph seekers. "I'm sure Kim arranged the entire show."

"Oh, no, they really do admire Rogue Warrior books here," said Kamere. "The books are studied for insight into the Western mind. The Rogue Warrior ethos touches something very Korean at its core."

"That would be sickness," said Trace.

We were led out through the front of the terminal, where to the strains of yet another out-of-tune band we boarded a fresh trio of limos. The procession proceeded to downtown Pyongyang. The trip would have moved LA freeway drivers to tears: we traveled down highways wide enough to land a jumbo jet[7] but utterly devoid of traffic.

Pyongyang is a strange mix of Workers' Paradise (circa 1955) and Asian squalor. The city's skyline is dominated by a massive triangular building called the Ryugyong Hotel, a 105-story building that was abandoned in 1992 after Kim's father spent about two percent of the country's gross domestic product building it. From the distance, it looks like a landing dock for a UFO; up close it looks like the world's biggest derelict building, with crumbling cement and open, glassless spaces.

Then there's the Korean Arc de Triomphe, which honors

---

[7] The width of the highways is not a coincidence. They're intended to be used as runways during a war.

the Koreans who ended World War II by single-handedly defeating the Japanese. A little farther along is the massive statue to the Great Leader, Kim Jong Il's father, a bright bronze mannequin over sixty feet tall.

The cars stopped at the plaza near the statue.

"What we want to do here," said Kamere, gesturing to me after we got out of the cars, "is buy one of those flower displays the girls are selling. Then we place it at the statue's feet, and bow."

"I don't want to do that," I said. "Trace, do you want to do that?"

"I'd rather be gored by a bull."

"It's protocol," insisted Kamere.

"It's more like bullshit," said Trace.

"Please. Don't create an incident," hissed Kamere. "You're supposed to pay your respects to the Great Leader."

He pulled out a few five-dollar bills and walked over to the vendors. Actually, the entire transaction had been worked out in advance, and before Kamere could give the girls any money, one of our escorts came over and slipped the girl a few won for the flowers.

"I ain't bowing in front of any statue," said Trace.

"It doesn't mean anything," said Kamere. "It's just diplomacy. It's a meaningless ceremony."

"I'll do it," I said.

I took my wreath and walked up to the statue.

"Here you go, O Great Dog Breath," I said in a loud reverent tone. "I bow to your superior infertility."

Our Korean escorts were only a few feet away, but their English was too limited for them to understand what I said. I smiled at them. They smiled at me. Then I walked back, took Trace's flowers, and returned to the statue.

"The Great Leader is a dickless wonder," I said, bowing again. "He is a zit on the ass of imbecility."

More smiles.

It was so much fun that I considered sending Kamere over to buy out the rest of the flowers.

We spent the afternoon touring monuments around Pyongyang. These were all pretty much devoted to the Great Leader, except for those that were devoted to the *first* Great Leader. Sometimes it was hard to tell which was who. Generally, it didn't much matter.

Finally around four, we were brought to Yanggakdo International Hotel. Yanggakdo is pretty much *the* international hotel in Pyongyang, and as far as I know the only building in the city that has both hot water and electricity, often at the same time.

"We leave for dinner at five," said Kamere as we were shown to our rooms. "Be ready."

Our rooms were all in a row. Kamere and Trace went to take showers—not together—and I amused myself by checking the room for bugs. There were only three, but one had to date to at least 1960 and would have made a good addition to the CIA's historical collection. I made a mental note to grab it and some of the bath towels at checkout.

Trace Dahlgren looks ravishing in basic black ninja wear, so you can imagine how she looks in a black dress that stops about mid-thigh. Men snapped to attention in the lobby as we walked out with Kamere and our Korean escort, a Korean general whose name I think was Yu Stin Ki Pu. The general took personal charge of making sure we had no weapons, though he stopped short of personally frisking us. We were taken to a room off the lobby, made to empty our pockets and cummerbunds, and then wanded.

"Beeeeeeep," went the unit as it was swung up near the side of my head.

Everybody in the room tensed. The soldier working the wand stepped back, adjusted something on it, and tried again.

"Beeeeeeep."

Kamere looked like he was about to throw up. Trace glanced around, undoubtedly trying to figure out who to hit first.

I had passed through several metal detectors with the implants already. I couldn't imagine that the North Koreans had developed a stronger metal detector than the ones our military was using, but the device began sounding a third time as the soldier brought it up to my head. I reached over and grabbed it; the two guards and the general reached for their guns. Smiling, I lowered the wand to my clip-on tie. The volume of the alarm increased.

"It's not loaded," I told them, unclasping it so they could check it out.

The general started to laugh. Color returned to Kamere's face. All was well again and we were led out of the room, back through the lobby, and out front to a single large limo. The three of us slid in the back. There was a slight Korean woman of perhaps twenty or twenty-one, whose stiff blue worker's suit looked to be about two sizes too big. General Yu Stin Ki Pu got in the front, then turned around and handed us blindfolds and hoods.

"You will please put them on," he said in English.

"No handcuffs?" asked Trace.

There was a twinkle in Yu Stin Ki Pu's eyes as he worked out what she said.

"It's a joke," said Trace, pulling down the hood and clamping her arms over her chest.

The ride from the hotel to the compound took roughly an hour and followed a route circuitous enough to make an otter dizzy. When we finally arrived, we were left in the backseat of the car for a few minutes.

"What do you think they're doing?" asked Kamere nervously.

"Shooting our escorts," snapped Trace.

Kamere began gasping for air.

"Relax," I told him. "If they wanted to kill us, they would have done it at the airport when we landed. They wouldn't have gone through all the expense of flying us here."

"Are you sure?" asked Kamere.

"Reasonably sure."

The car door opened. Some soldiers helped us out. Yu Stin Ki Pu had us take off the hoods and remove the blindfolds.

When you're the absolute ruler of a country, even one at the brink of bankruptcy, you don't live in a tar-paper shack. Because Kim Jong Il's palace was actually underground, the compound was almost modest—fairly plain stone buildings stood in various locations around the grounds, and the whole thing was surrounded by two rows of fence. A small stone building near the gate housed the guards, and was also a gateway to part of the underground complex. At the center of the compound sat a massive slab of granite—the roof to Kim's house.

We walked across a road made of pink and white marble. The rock, a giant tombstone with a set of steps under one side, sat just over the walkway. As we approached, I saw that it had a set of stairs extending along its entire length, which I estimated at about fifty yards. A second granite slab supported the first, inset ten yards or so; a third and then a fourth lay under that, so that as you went down the stairs the ceiling also stepped down. The offset seemed calculated to make it difficult for a cruise missile to navigate into the opening at the center of the structure.

Two full companies of Korean soldiers were stationed on the narrow patio at the base of the steps. They wore dress uniforms, complete with white gloves, and their Kalashnikovs gleamed despite the dim light. You could smell the oil they used on the guns' wood furniture. As we reached their level, the men snapped to, dropped to one knee, and pointed their guns at us.

An elderly man in a colonel's uniform stepped up from near the doorway, barking in Korean that we were vermin and must submit ourselves to the will of the people.

"I thought you said they wouldn't kill us," said Kamere after giving me the gist of what he'd said.

"This is just Kim's way of saying, 'My house is your house,'" I told him.

We weren't in any danger. Kim was just having a little fun—and reminding us who was boss. There was a video camera inset in the stone near the doorway; undoubtedly we'd been watched the whole way down.

"It would be appropriate to bow as a sign of your subservience," said Yu Stin Ki Pu.

"Subservience I don't do," I said. "But I do bow to a superior terminal ileum."

You call it *asshole*, I call it *ileum*—Yu Stin Ki Pu saw only that I was doing what he thought was the right thing.

The door opened. A fresh set of guards stood with a pair of weapons detectors just inside. Behind them were four other men, armed with Chinese Type 64 submachine guns. H&K fanciers will turn up their noses at the Type 64, but at close range and in sufficient numbers, it certainly can get the job done. Among its features is an integral silencer as part of its business end. Clearly, the man in charge of selecting armaments for the security detail had the peace and tranquility of the palace occupants in mind.

Two more soldiers, these dressed in black pajamas, appeared. Trace frowned when Yu Stin Ki Pu informed us that they were going to frisk us.

"Ms. Lee is very professional," said Yu Stin Ki Pu, referring to one of the soldiers who despite the flat chest and short hair turned out to be a woman. "Nothing improper will be done, and the men will not look."

I suggested that Ms. Lee could do me first to put Trace's mind at rest.

"That won't be necessary," said Trace, who went with the Korean behind a small screen at the side of the hall. Kamere and I, meanwhile, were checked right out in the open, Kamere chirping as his guard came a little too close to the family jewels.

"That happens to me," I told the guard when he was done, "and your hands are going to be where your asshole is."

"He doesn't speak English," Yu Stin Ki Pu said.

"He has about five seconds to learn."

The frisk was uneventful, and Yu Stin Ki Pu led us down the hall, through a Z-shaped corridor—more protection against cruise missiles—and into a large room dominated by a pool of water. The rest of the room had been constructed to make the water appear as if it were in an underground cavern. We crossed at the side, where a rail gave the illusion that we were using a wooden bridge. An elevator was waiting, doors open.

We shot downward for five or six seconds. The elevator doors opened into a small vestibule whose walls were made of rose-colored marble. A second elevator sat right next to the first. Once we were inside, it began to descend. This trip lasted about thirty seconds, though because the car was moving more deliberately it was impossible to say whether the distance we traveled was farther than we'd gone in the first elevator.

A butler, dressed entirely in white, met us in the elevator foyer. He bowed very low, then gestured to a velvet-covered cushion on the right where we were supposed to leave our shoes.

The hall was lined with classical marble statues. There were silk Oriental rugs on the floor and elaborate tapestries on the walls. The floor, walls, and ceilings were all made of massive sheets of marble.

"I wonder how much of the artwork is stolen," muttered Trace. "Doesn't look like he grabbed this from the local Pier 1."

She wasn't kidding. The next hallway we entered was lined with paintings, most of them hundreds of years old. I'm not exactly an art expert, but even I recognized the Picasso and the Monet. Maybe they were knockoffs, but I'm guessing that Interpol ought to put Kim on their must-interview list anytime a famous painting is reported stolen.

Finally we reached the intersection of a large hallway. We turned right, then were shown into a large eight-sided room paneled in fine wood.

"The Rogue Warrior," bellowed a voice.

Two middle-aged Korean army generals appeared in the doorway across from us. The men stepped into the room and parted, each to one side. Two more generals entered, followed by a tall man in civilian dress. Kim came through behind him.

Followed by Kim.

And then Kim.

Nothing like a paranoid absolute dictator with a sense of humor.

The three Kims appeared nearly identical, dressed in blue denim proletarian suits, wire-rimmed glasses, and terrible haircuts. Their cheeks were round and red. All wore a self-satisfied smirk.

No one spoke, obviously waiting for me to make my selection in the human Three-Card Monte game. I took a step back, bowed at the waist, and said what any red-blooded American would say under the circumstances, "Fuck you very much for inviting me."

The three Kims nodded, more or less in unison.

"Which of us your host?" asked Kim Number 1. "Do you care to guess?"

"The answer's obvious." I turned to the video camera near the door. "The real Kim is back in the control room down the hall, watching."

A peal of laughter came from somewhere down the hall. The ersatz Kims looked at each other nervously, probably wondering if the penalty for failing to fool me was death or just exile. A few seconds later, the real dictator walked through the door with a large grin on his face.

"I should have known that the Rogue Warrior would catch on to my little joke," said Kim.

"Well fuck you very much, your scumbagship," I said, bowing deeply.[8]

The room suddenly became so quiet you could hear the sweat breaking through the pores of the DPRK generals.

"And fuck you, too, Demo Dick." Kim laughed. It wasn't a fake-polite diplomat's laugh, either—it was a belly-shaker, and within seconds the rest of the room was laughing with him. "This is an exchange of mutual endearments, yes?"

"As endearing as a turd in a soup bowl," I told him.

"I have admired your books for a very long time," said Kim. "You are my kind of man."

"And you're my kind of commie slime," I told him, shaking his hand. I meant it—eliminate people like Kim from the world, and I'd have to spend my days sitting around a pool sipping drinks with tiny umbrellas in them while watching the latest in dental floss walk past. Say whatever else you want about him; Kim Jong Il is a role model for the rest of the world's slimers.

Kim turned to Trace, bowing stiffly and taking her hand.

"You are Trace Dahlgren, of course," he said. "I recognize you by your lovely eyes—though you look lovelier than your boss ever describes in his books. Perhaps you should write your own."

"Careful," I told him, "flattery will get you everywhere."

Trace shot me a dirty look.

Kim led us through the door he had just used into another long hallway. This one was also lined with paintings; he ticked off the names of their creators as we passed.

"Rubens, Rembrandt, Da Vinci, Da Vinci."

"You like the old masters," said Kamere, trying to be polite.

"I like naked women," said Kim, laughing so hard I thought the paintings would vibrate off the walls.

---

[8] Should I confess here that Kim had used a variety of the stand-in trick on the Chinese the year before? Nah. Better you think I'm omniscient rather than well read.

You'd never know that his country was facing a severe famine by the spread Kim put on for us. Dinner began with eels so fresh they were squirming in the tureen. The server picked each one up and swiftly lopped off its head with a knife the size of a battle-ax after laying it in a plate.

The next dish was fresh monkey brains. I'll spare you the description of how those were prepared if you'll trust me when I say they were as fresh as the eels.

Kamere went into a state of semishock about the time the eels were presented, and didn't say a word for the rest of dinner. Trace kept rolling her eyes but picked through the courses, her stomach genetically toughened by the hardships Apaches had endured for centuries.

I liked the food, but in most cases it could have used a little more salt.

We worked our way through twenty-seven courses. Each course was separated by a toast of some vile-tasting Korean liquor; French wine matched each individual dish. About halfway through, General Yu Stin Ki Pu began to turn purple. He eventually passed out, falling to the floor; two of the Great Leader's waiters picked him up and carried him off. As far as I know, they may have sent him to a work camp somewhere, because I never saw him again.

The generals Kim had dine with us had clearly been chosen for their ability to drink, but they, too, started slowing as the night went on. Even Trace, who is no slouch when it comes to liquor, was wearing down as we finished dessert. So I wasn't surprised that she begged out when Kim suggested that we retire into his "drinking room."

"As you wish, Ms. Dahlgren." He snapped his fingers and two women attendants appeared to show her to her bedroom.

"I didn't know we were spending the night," said Trace.

"I hope you're not refusing my hospitality," answered Kim.

Kamere started to say something, then found it necessary to

close his mouth very quickly as his stomach threatened to erupt. Another pair of attendants appeared with a bowl and towels, helping him out. Kim was greatly amused.

"I can send them back to the hotel if you wish," he said to me. "They will be more comfortable here, however."

"Let them stay," I told him.

"Good. Come with me and we will have a nice game of snooker."

Kim led me out a side passage and down a wide hallway to a room decorated like an old English gentleman's club, complete with two waiters. A large snooker table sat at the side.

"Drink?" he asked. And then without waiting for an answer, he nodded to one of the waiters. The man went to a bar at the side and returned with two large tumblers of Dr. Bombay's finest.

"To your continued success," he said, nodding in my direction.

"To your demise," I answered.

Some of Kim's good humor had drained away. "Always joking. But I would not expect anything different. You are lucky that my people do not speak very much English."

"How is it that you speak English?" I said.

"Your CIA has not made a study of this?"

"If they have, they didn't tell me."

He wagged his finger as if I were a naughty boy. "You do not get along with the Christians in Action, do you?"

"Sometimes yes, sometimes no."

Kim had studied English as a young man during visits to Malta, and he spoke with a slight British accent. He had a surprisingly good command of vocabulary, and either he had genuinely read my books or been briefed very closely by someone who had, for he now proceeded to quiz me on them. He began by asking which I liked best. Of course I answered that they were all my children, and that choosing a favorite would be out of the question.

"A most judicious answer. My favorite is your first. There is more fiction there than all the rest combined."

I told him I'd heard that joke before.

He pointed at the snooker table nearby. "Do you play?"

"Only under duress."

Kim put his glass down and chose a cue stick from the wall. The dictator slapped his cue ball into the pile of reds, sending one careening into a pocket. He proceeded to run the table in a few minutes. For those of you who don't play—a snooker table looks like a very large pool table. There are fifteen red balls, a cue ball, and a yellow, green, brown, blue, pink, and black ball. You sink one of the red balls, then put one of the colored balls into a pocket. And on and on and on.

When it was finally my turn, I chalked up, potted a red, and made my way through the colored balls. I wasn't keeping score, but I was apparently doing very well—Kim was frowning long before I finally missed a shot.

"You practiced snooker before you came to Korea, yes?" he asked.

"Haven't played in years."

"We will talk," he said sharply, gesturing toward a pair of chairs at the far side of the room.

"Talk away."

"You think of your books as children," said Kim. "But children are not like books, I think."

Kim drained his glass, then called in Korean for a fresh round. The waiter immediately hopped to, returning with a bottle in each hand.

"A book can be depended on," said Kim, his tone philosophical. "Children have minds of their own."

I felt like I'd suddenly stepped into the middle of a Dr. Phil show.

"Why don't you just leave the bottle?" I told the waiter as he finished pouring. He nodded and set mine down on the small end table near the chair.

"You are a very practical man, Rogue Warrior," said Kim.

"Call me Dick."

"And you will simply call me Great."

I smiled. He smiled. We both knew that wasn't going to happen.

"You hold your liquor very well," said Kim.

"So do you. Considering you've been drinking water all night."

Kim gave me a dirty look, then started to laugh.

"I am glad to find that in person, you are even more clever than on the page." He rose. "Mr. Sun will speak to you."

And with that, Kim departed. I sat in the chair, sipping my gin very slowly. A video camera sat in the corner of the ceiling opposite me, obviously watching.

The complex was certainly large enough to house weapons somewhere, but so far I hadn't seen any indication of where they might be. Staying the night—or whatever was left of it—would give me a chance to wander around, so I yawned for the camera, preparing my cover story. As I stretched my arms back, a burly Korean dressed in a Western business suit entered the room and strutted over to me, his face screwed into a frown.

To this point, the dinner had seemed almost innocuous—as if it were, just as Kim's people had said, a chance for the Great Dictator to meet someone he admired. But I wasn't counting on that, and Sun's manner would have cured any misconception if I had.

"You are an enemy of the people," said Sun. "Your country and my country are at war."

"That war ended decades ago."

"The war will not be over until Korea is reunited and the people are free of Western imperialism."

"Your people are free of a lot of things," I told him. "Especially food."

"You have insulted the Korean people. Your presence itself

is an insult," said Sun. "Only by the grace of the Great Leader have you been tolerated. Do not forget this."

"I'll try not to."

"You are an American, and that is despicable," said Sun. "But you have one very important quality—you can get into places that others cannot."

"Such as?"

Sun frowned. "The Great Leader wishes you to locate his son, Yong Shin Jong. You have two weeks to bring him here."

"Two weeks?"

"The leader believes you can do it in one. You will be escorted off the premises now."

"I thought I'd grab a catnap before I left."

"Your friends are already waiting in the car. There will be no delay."

Six soldiers had entered while we were talking, and came toward my chair. I rose. Sun took a business card from his pocket. It was extremely simple—just his name, with a international phone number and a Google e-mail address.

Good to see our enemies making the best use of our technology.

"You will contact me when you have completed your task," said Sun. "The Great Leader will see to it that you are paid for your efforts. $64 million. The sum is not negotiable. If it were up to me, you would receive nothing but your life."

He turned and started toward the door.

"Hold on, cowboy," I told Sun. "Where is Yong Shin Jong?"

"I was told you were smart enough to figure this out. We last heard that he was in China. Two weeks. Or the Great Leader will not agree to your government's treaty. And I will have the very great pleasure of seeing that you do not have an opportunity to insult the Korean people any longer."

2

[1]

Yong Shin Jong, only son of a woman named Jeong Eun Kyung," explained Fogglebottom a few hours later in Tokyo. "She and the Great Leader had a hookup in the late 1970s and early eighties while he was on Malta. She's probably one reason he speaks English so well—she was one of his tutors."

"He likes older women?" I asked.

"He likes all women."

"A man after my own heart."

I paged through the photos Fogglebottom had brought. They showed a slightly pudgy Korean in his mid-twenties. He had a serious face, even in the two candid photos. He had dark buzz-cut hair and a dimple in his chin that looked like an upside-down triangle. He resembled his father as a young man, though unlike Kim Jong Il he didn't need glasses.

Fogglebottom and I were sitting in a secure room in the embassy, which included metal shielding in the walls—a Faraday Cage for the technically minded—to prevent eavesdropping. Kim's goons had marched me out of the complex the same way I'd come in, depositing me in the Mercedes where Trace and the translator were waiting. We'd been driven directly to the airport and returned to Tokyo.

"If he's looking for his son, it's very possible that he does have cancer," said Fogglebottom. "Two of Russia's top oncology experts have been flown to Pyongyang in the past month. Until now, we've had nothing connecting them to Kim, but it would make a lot of sense. Pancreatic cancer cannot be cured once it has spread beyond a certain point," he added. "So it's understandable that Kim is looking to reconcile with his bastard son before he dies."

Except that Kim didn't strike me as the touchy-feely type. Obviously there was more to the "request" than met the eye; it was just a question of how much more. I leaned back in my chair, listening as Foggy told me everything he knew about Yong Shin

Jong. Unlike Kim's acknowledged sons, who had reputations as eccentric ne'er-do-wells—or just plain psychos—Yong Shin Jong was not only normal but reputed to be fairly bright. He had been raised far from the capital until he was twelve. At that point he was taken to a private school in China, and later to Germany. He went to college in Hong Kong, studying economics. Upon graduation, he'd gone to work for Daddy, helping administer the Kaesong Industrial Region, a small area near South Korea where companies from the South can use cheap northern workers.

How cheap? The most recent estimates put North Korean wages—which are mostly paid to the state, not the workers—at about half the average Chinese worker's. And Chinese laborers get about a tenth of what a South Korean factory worker is typically paid.

Not a bad deal for the companies, which is one reason so many South Korean capitalists want to normalize relations with the North. But of course, nothing in North Korea works very well, even when Kim himself is behind it, and the Kaesong Industrial Region hasn't come close to its potential.

"According to the CIA, Yong Shin Jong disappeared three months ago," said Fogglebottom. "There was some thinking that he was on vacation in Europe, traveling under an assumed name—something Kim's other sons tend to do a lot."

"Did you look for him in Disneyland?"

"They did. And in many other places."

Disneyland wasn't a joke. Kim's oldest son—and onetime heir apparent, Kim Jong Nam—had been arrested in 2001 trying to sneak into Tokyo Disneyland. Kim Jong Nam has since fallen out of favor and last I heard was trying to sell condos in Macau, a tiny region of China once populated by Portuguese traders now best known for its casinos.

Son number two, Kim Jong Chul, was once considered a favorite of the army. (He was also a very big Eric Clapton fan.) But in the past few years Jong Chul was criticized by his father for being too weak and "girl-like"—the ultimate put-down in male-dominated North Korea.

The latest intelligence estimates listed Kim's youngest legitimate son, Kim Jon Woon, as the dictator's favorite. But Kim's interest in Yong Shin Jong was sure to cause a reevaluation.

"So how soon do you think you can locate Yong?" asked Fogglebottom.

"Who says I'm going to locate him?"

"You're not?"

Foggy looked like I had hit him in the gut.

"Why should we help North Korea?"

A long dissertation on the need for "patriotic Americans to stand up to the plate" followed. But patriotism wasn't the question here. I'd only gone to Kim's drinking party because of Admiral Jones; I hadn't had a chance to locate the bombs, but what I had seen would be of use, so I'd done my patriotic bit.

Fogglebottom pointed out that finding Yong Shin Jong might mean he would end up in power after Kim died—which in turn might help us win friends and influence enemies after the regime change.

"I would think if your government asked for your assistance, you would help gladly," said Fogglebottom.

"You'd think that, wouldn't you?" I got up. "See you back in Washington sometime."

"But, Dick—"

"Having dinner with him was bad enough. I'm not going to work for him."

"You'd really be working for us," said Foggy.

"Well that just cinches it, doesn't it?"

"Wait, Dick. Don't go. Someone from the CIA wants to talk to you. He wants to debrief you about Kim's palace."

"Where is he?"

"He must be running late," said Fogglebottom. "I expected him before you arrived."

"Tell him I'll meet him after lunch. I have to go see a friend of mine and if I don't go now, I'll be late."

"But—"

"If he's got something better to do, we can always discuss it when I get back to the States."

[II]

There's no way I can ever visit Tokyo without calling on Toshiro Okinaga. Tosho supervises a Kunika team, working on counterterrorism. Kunika is a special unit of the Japanese police force; they shut down the Japanese Red Army in the 1980s, and have played an important role in fighting a variety of terrorists, foreign and homegrown, in the years since. They're every bit as efficient and relentless as you would expect the descendants of samurai warriors to be.

I first met Tosho and friends back in my SEAL days, when Red Cell ran some exercises at a U.S-Japanese base at Yokosuka. He's a hell of a shot and a seventh degree black belt; he can also put away the Kirin like there's no tomorrow, a truly important quality for a SpecWarrior.

We'd arranged to meet in a quiet noodle restaurant at the edge of Akasaka, which is Tokyo's main business district. The restaurant caters almost exclusively to high-powered Japanese businessmen. Had we eaten there at night, Tosho would have had to mortgage his wife as well as his house to afford the meal. (Custom dictates that the host pay, and I would have insulted him severely had I even offered to do so.) Lunch, though, was very reasonable, with nothing on the menu more than a thousand yen—roughly eight and a half bucks.

Tosho was already waiting when I arrived; his loud voice carried across the room.

"Kusotare!"

"Shithead!" I replied, translating the term.

"It's about time you got here, sturgeon breath."

"I lost your scent out back by the garbage cans."

Every eye followed me across the room as we continued to exchange terms of mutual endearment. They probably would have anyway. I was the only gaijin or non-Japanese in the place. When I reached the table, we one-upped each other with expletives and then toasted each other's health with sake. Tosho ordered some sort of spiced octopus with noodles made of seaweed for me, then bragged about the pending addition to his family: a grandchild, due to be born in a few months.

"So why were you in North Korea?" he asked finally.

"How did you know I was in North Korea?"

Tosho frowned. The North Koreans and Japanese have an exceedingly testy relationship, and a good part of Kunika's resources are spent tracking developments in their dysfunctional neighbor across the Sea of Japan.

"Your flight was recorded," said Tosho. "And we received notification. It's routine."

"And you knew I was on it?"

"I can add two plus two. A flight comes from Pyongyang early in the morning. A short time later my old friend calls me for lunch. That's not exactly calculus."

I gave Tosho a rundown, leaving out the fact that the meeting had taken place at Kim's new palace, and that the real purpose of my visit had been to get a good peek at the inside. But I did tell him about Kim's request that I find his son.

"You're going to do it?" Tosho asked.

"Hell no."

"Good bit of money, Dick."

I laughed.

"You're not curious?" he added.

"Curious about what?"

"About what's going on behind the scenes. I think I'd do it just for the giggles."

"You're welcome to."

Tosho didn't know much about Yong Shin Jong. So far as he knew, Kim's illegitimate son hadn't been part of any of North Korea's operations in Japan.

Sun, on the other hand, had an entire building of Kunika files devoted to him.

"General Sun Sang Min—a Chinese-Korean who is one of Kim's secret police officials. He's the number two man in the

State Safety and Security Agency—Kim himself is number one," said Tosho.

State Safety is the Korean equivalent of the Gestapo, without the cool cars but with bigger cattle prods. State Safety has incredible power in North Korea; even the military is afraid of them. Which is why Kim Jong Il heads the agency personally.

"Sun is a very nasty customer," added Tosho as he slurped his noodles. "Killed his own brother to get ahead. And that's just for starters."

The North Korean secret service had run a variety of operations in Japan. For a while one of their favorite pastimes was kidnapping Japanese citizens. Though the entire operation was something of a mystery, it was believed to have been aimed at obtaining Japanese language teachers for North Korean spies. Sun, then a young operative, had been involved in at least one of the kidnappings. A few years later, he returned to Japan and lived there for at least three years, posing as a Singapore citizen. It was believed that he had helped beef up the North Korean spy network. Escaping just as the Japanese closed in, he had surfaced in Pyongyang as the director of a program to exterminate North Korean defectors living in South Korea. His excellent track record there led to his promotion to section director for internal affairs; there he consolidated his grip on the organization and moved up the ladder quickly.

"He is still very close to the Red Army," said Tosho, referring to the Japanese Red Army, or JRA. The JRA's heyday had long passed—the high point came in Israel in 1972 when they struck Lod airport. Since then, all the members have managed to do is get arrested, thanks largely to the efforts of Kunika. "He has many sources in Japan. He may even be watching you now."

"If State Safety is so powerful, why wouldn't he be looking for Yong Shin Jong himself?"

"You assume he wants to find him."

"Why wouldn't he?"

"Wouldn't he be a rival for power?"

"A puppet maybe. If he was a rival, wouldn't he just kill him?"

"He will feel more constrained to act in China, because they are North Korea's only ally," said Tosho. "But if I were you I would not think I had been given the entire story. More than likely there is much more here than meets the eye."

"Well, I'm not involved in it, so I don't care."

"Not at all?"

"No."

"You went just for dinner?"

"And the booze. I also expected women, but there weren't any."

"Ah."

"Ah" is one of those little words that means absolutely nothing on its own, but gains almost cosmic meaning depending on how it is said. This "ah" meant "I realize you have another reason but don't want to say, therefore being Japanese I will not press you for it."

"Stepping back from the business?" asked Tosho.

"No."

"I think of retirement myself," said Tosho. "I want to devote myself to my family."

"That's not it, Tosh."

"You're not thinking of retiring?"

"Not that I know of."

"You're just like the rest of us, you know. Age will catch up."

Nothing like an old friend telling you to your face that the gray hairs are starting to show. But Tosho has earned the right to say anything he wants.

"You watch out for Sun," he told me as we left the restaurant.

"Don't worry, I'm not getting involved in this."

Tosho laughed. "Watch out for him anyway."

(III)

While I was having lunch, Trace was riding a bullet train down to Kyoto, where she met Polorski and began exploring the sights.

Kyoto is the ancient capital of Japan, and there are over two thousand Buddhist and Shinto shrines there. Some are magnificent works of art; others are basically falling down shacks with donation bins out front. Trace saw none of them. Her devotions were of a much more personal nature.

As for my love life, being thousands of miles from Karen made me cranky and cantankerous. No different than normal, at least when I'm not blowing things up. But I did miss her.

Karen was staying at Rogue Manor in my absence, and despite the late hour I decided to call. Sometimes she stays up late, catching up on her reading—she's always reading some mystery book or another—and I thought I'd take the chance. The plan was that I'd let the phone ring twice and if she picked it up, great. If she didn't—well I'd probably let it ring a few more times. Then if the answering machine picked up, I'd leave her a message.

She got it on the second ring.

"I was hoping you'd call," she said. "We had a computer meltdown, and it's still going on."

I guess it was better than being told the lawn needed mowing.

"I missed you, too," I said. "What's the problem?"

The computer in question turned out to be the mainframe at Homeland Security, not the PCs at Red Cell. The situation was not without its lighter moments—hackers had apparently planted robotic programs that sent spam for feminine hygiene products coursing through the Homeland Insecurity Network.

"Give Shunt a call," I told her. "He'll be able to fix it."

Shunt is my self-anointed "computer dude" and all-around tech expert. His birth certificate claims his name is Paul Guido

Falcone, but we call him "Shunt" because he has several in his head. They're some sort of metal inserts placed into his skull because he was born with water in his skull. I think of them as brain gutters. He's loads of fun in an airport, especially when you're trying to make a plane.

"Shunt is on vacation in Iceland," Karen told me. "He recommended some guy named Matthew Loring. You know him?"

"Not at all. But if Shunt says he's okay, you can trust him. Whether you'll be able to understand a word he says is another matter."

We decided Karen would talk to Matthew in the morning, after running a preliminary backgrounder on him with the help of some of our police contacts. Business concluded, we talked about how much we missed each other and what we would be doing if we were together. She was planning on taking a nice warm bath as soon as we got off the phone; I had to take a cold shower.

[IV]

I remembered Tosho's warning about Sun having someone watching me as I headed back to the embassy for my meeting with the CIA debriefer. If you're ever looking to become paranoid, go to Tokyo. The crowded, narrow streets feel like they're closing in, and there's always someone right behind you.

On the other hand, the crowds make it easy to give someone the slip. I didn't see a tail, but I backtracked my way across town anyway, sliding in and out of two large stores and a train station before grabbing a taxi. Then just to be sure, I got out of the cab in the middle of the street while we were stuck in traffic and hopped in one going the other way. I suppose it's still possible I was followed, but if so my tail was damn good.

Most CIA officers don't have much of a sense of humor, and the man who met me at the embassy was no exception. Jimmy Zim was also about as nondescript as they come: somewhere between twenty and fifty, of average build and height for someone of Asian descent, with a face you could forget while you stared at it. Perfect spy material.

Like most CIA officers, Zim was good with languages; he spoke fluent Korean, Japanese, and several Chinese dialects. He'd obviously seen some difficult times: the backs of his hands and lower arms had hash marks on them, tiny scars that I guessed had been made by a razor—undoubtedly souvenirs from a torture session. He was vague about his job but very specific about his desires: he wanted me to describe what Kim's palace was like, and wanted to know everything that had happened while I was there. I gave him a full briefing.

If Jimmy Zim knew that Ken Jones's real goal in urging me to visit Kim had been finding the nuclear weapons, he didn't let on. They weren't mentioned or hinted at. I didn't bring them up either—there was no reason to, since I hadn't seen them.

Zim was a patient man, listening without comment as I described Kim Jong Il's underground palace. He took no notes, but I got the impression that he could repeat everything I'd said word for word if asked. I mapped the area out on a satellite photo he'd brought, approximating where Kim's underground rooms were. There were a lot of places left where the nukes could be. Given the depth of the facility, an air attack aimed at the warheads would need a specific location. A ground assault would also be difficult. But those weren't my problems.

"Well, that's it. That's what I know," I told him, getting up. "Pleasure meeting you."

"You didn't tell me about Yong Shin Jong and Kim's request that you find him."

"I didn't think that's what you were here for. Besides, didn't Fogglebottom tell you?"

"Your account would be more precise."

He had me there. I sat down and told him what I knew, which wasn't much. When I was done, he nodded.

"And you're taking the job?" he asked.

"No."

Jimmy Zim put his lips together. It was the first emotion he'd shown, if that's what it was.

"The director would like you to," said Jimmy Zim.

"You've spoken to him?"

"I got this." He reached into his pocket and took out an orange piece of paper. There was an e-mail on it.

```
Zim: State comm'ed NK-Kim request for
Marcinko. Meet. Render all assistance.
Remind Marcinko of my best wishes, one
old sailor to another.
—Adm Jones
```

Nowhere in that e-mail did it say that Ken wanted me to pursue Yong Shin Jong, but it was as obvious to me as it was to Jimmy Zim that he did. Hell, he wouldn't have bothered sending it if he didn't.

He knew I hadn't found the nukes—I hadn't activated the locating device he'd given me. Was he asking me to go back? Or did he figure we could worm the information out of Yong Shin Jong?

"Aren't you supposed to destroy this?" I said to Zim, handing it back. "That's why it's on colored paper, right?"

"I intend to as soon as our meeting is over. I didn't know if you'd take my word for it. You have a reputation for not believing people you don't know."

"Why don't you go and get Yong Shin Jong back? You have more resources than I do."

"If he's in China, the involvement of the CIA could be embarrassing," said Jimmy Zim. "I can provide background information on Yong Shin Jong. It may be that the task is not as daunting as it seems."

"Who says it's daunting?"

"Your reluctance speaks for itself."

Jimmy Zim had several photos of Yong Shin Jong. The CIA had last seen him in Singapore, where he traveled about once or twice a month. Like a lot of Asian millionaires, Kim's family stashed money in Singapore banks because of favorable tax laws and an emphasis on discretion that made Swiss bankers look like gossipmongers. North Koreans typically passed through Beijing on their way to Singapore, sometimes staying a day or two. Jimmy Zim believed that Yong Shin Jong had disappeared on the return trip, probably after arriving in Beijing.

American intelligence agencies routinely gather tons of information—humint, elint, comint, and every other *-int* you can think of. Humint is human intelligence, the stuff you read about in spy novels, though in real life it tends to be more along the lines of the bullshit and gossip you pick up at a bar after hours than microdot blueprints for blowing up the world. Elint is electronic intelligence, which includes signals gathered from the air freely—say a transmission of telemetry from a satellite—and not so freely—say electronic signals gathered in a manner that if I told you about I'd have to kill you. Comint is intelligence gathered by stealing communications transmissions. You get the general idea.

The problem for any intelligence agency isn't so much gathering the goods, but realizing they have the goods when they get them. There's so much information out there that the real heroes—unsung of course—are the guys and gals who can separate the one slim grain of wheat from the silo of chaff. Germany had all sorts of information about D-day, but they still couldn't figure out where the allies were landing. And don't even get me started about Pearl Harbor.

But I digress. Once the Christians in Action take an interest in you, it's amazing what they can dig up. So the fact that the CIA had found nothing on Yong Shin Jong in the past three months spoke volumes.

Volumes of what, I had no idea.

"He was booked on a flight from Singapore to Beijing, but we're not sure that he boarded the plane," said Zim. "He did not take a state airline out of China. He did not use his own name flying from Singapore following that date. We have also found that a Korean airliner was in Beijing when Yong should have been, but returned home without any passengers. He has not gone back via any flight that we could discover."

"Maybe he took the train."

Jimmy Zim shook his head so solemnly I thought it best not to ask how he knew.

"He could have walked across the border," I said. "Or gone into Russia."

"Unlikely," said Jimmy Zim. "Possible. Unlikely."

"But you think he's still in China."

"Yes."

"The Koreans haven't asked about him?"

"We're reexamining communications traffic. But from what you say, if they have, the Chinese haven't been forthcoming.

Maybe they are covering up a murder. Or maybe Yong Shin Jong doesn't want to be found, and has paid off the right authorities. With your abilities, it shouldn't take long to find out. And there's much at stake."

"Like what?"

"The treaty. And for you, $64 million."

CIA officers are used to dealing with people who would kill their own mothers for a counterfeit nickel, so Jimmy Zim couldn't quite get his head around the fact that I didn't care for the loot. Not that you should get the wrong idea—$64 million *is* a lot of money to me. But even if I put aside the fact that I'd be working for a slimebag, I doubted I'd be able to collect.

On the other hand, Jones clearly wanted me to take a shot. And now that I knew the general layout of Kim's palace, I'd have a better chance of finding the warheads if I went back.

"What should I tell the director?" Jimmy Zim asked.

"Tell him to screw himself," I said. "And maybe I'll poke around to see what I can find out."

Deciding that my first step would be to trace Yong Shin Jong's journey, I used an embassy phone to arrange a flight to Beijing. I also contacted a friend of mine named Lo Po who has a private detective agency headquartered in Shanghai, and asked him if he could arrange to meet me there.

Lo Po's father was an American citizen who moved to Hong Kong to do business soon after Nixon visited the mainland in the seventies. The family thrived. Among their many interests is a "research bureau" that aids overseas businesspeople. The company is a cross between a detective agency and a security firm, and it's Lo Po's baby. We've had occasion to work together several times, but I actually knew him as a friend well before we developed a business relationship. We met six or seven years ago when I was giving a terrorism seminar in D.C.; Lo Po asked so many damn questions during the Q&A that I had to invite him for drinks afterward to get him to shut up. He'd never had Bombay Sapphire before, and after his first sip he professed undying gratitude and friendship for life.

Lo Po has a large number of contacts in the Chinese Communist Party, which he claims is now about as Communist as your typical Iowa Rotary Club. True or not, if anyone could show me around the labyrinthine Chinese government, he could. He wasn't particularly happy about working for my "client," however. Kim had arranged for the execution of one of Lo Po's uncle's operatives some years before when he ran the firm. The man had been investigating a heroin smuggling operation apparently subsidized by the North Korean government when he met his demise.

"For you, I'll do this," said Lo Po. "For anyone else, in no way, Jose."

I didn't bother correcting his English.

Last but not least, I sent a text message for Al "Doc" Tremblay—aka Cockbreath and other assorted terms of endearment—asking him to give me a call. Faithful readers will recall that Doc was one of the original plank holders of Red Cell. He had been helping me out a lot lately as a troubleshooter, especially in Asia, and it happened that he was in the Philippines looking after some of our associates. I told him that if he could wrap that up, his assistance would be useful in China.

I noticed the scooter while I was on my way back to the hotel for a nap. It was one of those fancy Japanese rigs, black, streamlined, and absurdly expensive. Its driver was also completely dressed in black, wearing a thickly padded bodysuit with a dark windscreen on his helmet.

The scooter followed my cab as we neared the hotel. I decided to have a little fun, and told the driver to take me into northern Tokyo. We twisted around a bit, Scooter staying with us, until finally I had the cabbie let me out near Ameyoko Market. Back in the day, Ameyoko was the place to get all sorts of black-market bargains; you probably could have outfitted an army there. These days it's considerably more upscale, but just as crowded.

Walking west, I squeezed through the throng near the Inarico elevated subway line. Scooter had a bit of trouble with the traffic. I had to work to make sure he could keep up while not tipping him off that he'd been made. I tracked up and down through the small side streets, pretending to be a curious visitor looking for an unusual bargain.

A half hour of wandering between discontinued Nikes and unboxed Chanel No. 5 convinced me that Scooter was alone. Finally I looped back toward an alley off the main drag. I took up a spot near a corner fish market, pretending to be mesmerized by the hundreds of eyes staring up at me while waiting for Scooter to appear. When he came down the street and saw me gazing in his direction, he turned his head the other way, as if he'd suddenly developed an unnatural fascination with the iced octopus tentacles on display there.

I made my move just after he passed me. With a hop, skip, and a jump I landed on the back of the scooter, wrapping my arms around his chest and pressing close.

Did I say *his*? The chest in question was decidedly un-he-like.

"*Konniciwa,*" I told Scooter. "*Nihongo wa hanasemasen.* Good afternoon. I don't speak Japanese worth shit. So let's use English—what the hell are you following me for?"

Scooter responded by hitting the gas.

The people in the street dove out of the way as we whipped forward. The motorbike jumped the curb and took out a large display of vegetables, but still stayed upright. Cabbage and cucumbers sailed through the air as we careened back into the street, bowling over a group of British tourists along the way. I lifted my left hand up to Scooter's neck and pressed hard enough to get her attention. She rammed her head backward, bouncing her helmet against my chest several times until my grip on her neck tightened sufficiently to make her stop. In the meantime, we shot up onto the opposite curb, which was high enough to separate us from the bike. We tumbled to the right. The bike flew to the left, crashing through the thin wooden facade of a candle shop that had probably stood here for decades if not hundreds of years—long enough for the wood to dry out so completely that the building ignited moments after the scooter upset some of the candles set out and lit for display. Gas poured from the bike's ruptured fuel tank, and within seconds Tokyo had an impromptu fireworks display.

Meanwhile, the scooter's driver and I crashed through a table of women's handbags and sprawled onto the sidewalk. I dragged her away from the sudden burst of flames, pulling her down the street to a nearby alley. Her body had gone limp and I thought the accident had knocked her out, but as soon as I pried off her helmet she erupted in a frenzy, kicking and punching crazily.

Nothing warms my heart more than a woman with spunk, but there's only so much spunk I can take. In this case, I reached my fill with her first kick, and retaliated by belting her in the stomach with the helmet. She fell back against the side of the building, dazed but not completely out of it.

She looked very familiar, though it took me a second to place her.

"You drove us to Kim's palace," I said, grabbing her by the shoulders and holding her down as she tried to get up. "You're North Korean."

"You are most rude, Richard Marcinko," said the girl. "You no touch chest, understand? Keep hands self."

"Why were you following me?"

"Mr. Sun sent me. I have information for you. I help. But you no touch."

"You no kick, I no touch," I said.

She frowned, but then nodded. I let go and got up. Fire engines were racing down the nearby street, and policemen were flooding into the area. I suggested we find a quieter place to talk.

Her name was Cho Lim. (She actually said Lim Cho, in the Korean style placing her last name first, but the copy editor told me to anglicize it to make it less confusing and I'm too tired to argue. The "l" is silent in her last name, so it sounds like "im.") Cho claimed that Sun had assigned her to help me, but that I had left North Korea too quickly for her to properly introduce herself. She'd had to catch a flight to Beijing and then Japan, finally staking out the embassy until she spotted me.

North Korea isn't known for being big on equal employment, even in the spy business, but there was no reason not to trust her story. Her English was excellent, with almost no accent. Clearly, she worked for Sun and thus couldn't really be trusted, but she at least came with data: coordinates of a villa outside Beijing where she claimed Yong Shin Jong was being held.

"Why is Yong Shin Jong there?" I asked.

"The Chinese know that the Great Leader will soon join his father," said Cho Lim. "They do not wish him to succeed as leader."

"Who do they back?"

Cho Lim claimed not to know. She also didn't have much information about the layout of the villa or what sort of security arrangements it might have.

"Well, thank you for the information."

I started walking toward the elevated subway entrance about a block away. I was just about to go up the stairs when I realized Cho Lim was tagging along.

"What are you doing?" I asked.

"I am going to help you."

"You already have. Thanks."

"You will need more help in China," she said. "You will have to talk to Yong Shin Jong. He won't trust you."

"You know him?"

"We've met."

"How?"

"From distance."

"You're friends?"

"I have met him. From distance."

Cho's English had a habit of getting worse as soon as she was pressed on a topic she didn't feel like speaking about. If you're thinking there was a bit more to the relationship than she was willing to let on, go to the head of the class.

"I can be of great help," Cho Lim added. "I speak Chinese fluently. I can pass for Chinese. You cannot."

I furled my fingers through my beard and squinted at her.

"Maybe a little," she conceded. "I am still big help."

"Let me discuss your information with someone I know," I told her. "If it checks out, then you can come to China with me. If not . . ." I shrugged.

"It will check out."

"Then I'll meet you at Tokyo airport Monday morning at eight."

She frowned.

"You will be there?" Cho Lim asked.

"Have I ever lied to you?"

She frowned again, but didn't follow me into the train station.

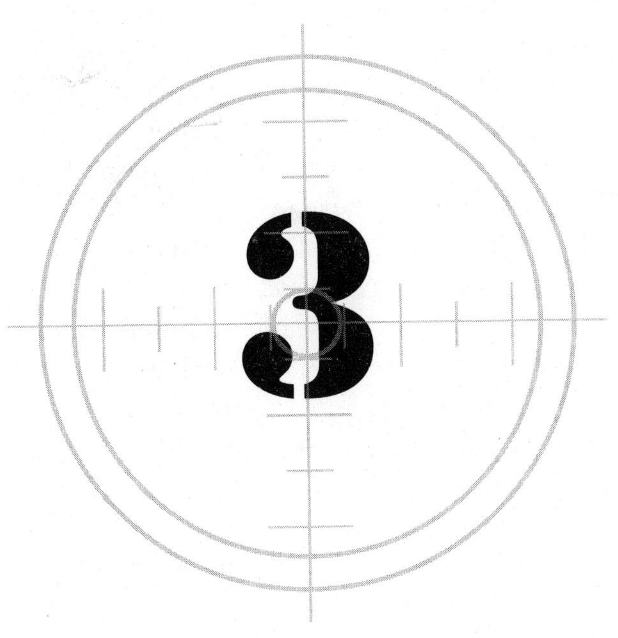
3

{ 1 }

There was no way to properly vet Cho Lim. Neither Kunika nor the CIA had ever heard of her, but given her age and nationality that wasn't surprising. She apparently had used a South Korean passport to enter the country; the address she'd given the customs people was in Seoul.

It was highly unlikely that she could have come from North Korea on her own. And while it bothered both my friend Tosho and Jimmy Zim that Sun hadn't told me about the China villa himself, I knew that our brief conversation in Kim's palace hadn't been entirely private—everything had been recorded by the video camera in the corner of the room. Sun might have many reasons for not letting anyone know that he was helping me, or that he already knew where Yong Shin Jong was.

Logically, I had two choices—either take Cho Lim's information at face value and check out the villa, or pretend I hadn't received it and track Yong Shin Jong's path. It was a coin flip either way, so I decided I'd do both.

I got up early Sunday morning and worked out, doing a five-mile run through Tokyo to sweat out some of the rust that had accumulated in my system over the past few days. Then I hit the hotel gym, pumping iron and breathing hard for about an hour and a half before finding my way back upstairs. My butt was dragging, but I was glad I could say that when Trace called from Kyoto to check in.

She and lover boy were having a great time.

"How many Shinto temples have you been to?" I asked.

"There are temples here?"

That pretty much summed up our conversation, not to mention her priorities. I wasn't surprised when she barely made the plane the next day, arriving at the gate about five minutes before boarding was announced.

Cho Lim, on the other hand, had gotten there before me. She glanced up when I passed by but kept her distance, pretending to read a Japanese paperback. As far as I could tell, no one else in the gate area was watching us.

We landed in Beijing a few hours later. Doc Tremblay and his handlebar mustache were waiting for us when we cleared passport control.

"Glad you could make it," I told him.

"Fuck you very much," he grumbled. "Lo Po's outside with the car. Who's the shadow?"

"She claims she knows where Yong Shin Jong is," I said. "She works for Sun."

"We trust her?" asked Doc.

"About as far as you can throw her with one hand."

By the time we reached the parking lot, Cho Lim had closed the distance between us. She followed silently as we made our way to the car Lo Po had rented. I introduced her to the others. She sat between Trace and me, mouth shut, gaze blank.

Lo Po took us south, bypassing the capital and its rings of nonstop traffic as we swung through Daxing. Several miles south of the suburb we came to a country house owned by a family Lo Po had done work for. The family was on an extended vacation and had kindly let him use it while they were away; when you save the life of their only son, people tend to be thankful.

The house was more a villa, set up on a hill away from what had once been a tiny, sleepy village. It was now an overgrown little city, where factories crowded up against housing developments and old stone buildings. Two of Lo Po's men were waiting on the front portico, handguns discreetly concealed beneath their jackets.

"I'm afraid we're going to have to search you and your bag," I told Cho Lim as we pulled into the driveway. "I hope you don't mind."

Cho Lim barely shrugged. Trace went inside with her and did the honors. Meanwhile, I brought Lo Po and Doc up-to-date. It was hard to say which one of them was more skeptical.

"Are you sure this isn't a Chinese plot to capture you?" asked

Lo Po. "Maybe Kim is delivering you to the government. He'd do anything for a trainload of diesel oil these days."

"Or onions," said Doc.

"Obviously, there's more here than meets the eye," I told them. "But that's not it. If the Chinese wanted to get me, they would have done it themselves."

Lo Po and Doc remained skeptical, even after Trace announced that our friend was carrying neither a weapon nor any electronic device capable of giving her location away. Cho Lim remained quiet as I laid out the agenda—Doc, Lo Po, and Trace would go into Beijing, find the hotel where Yong Shin Jong customarily stayed during his visits, and see if they could discover any useful information. Such information would more than likely be found in the hotel's records, which they would have to acquire by whatever means came to hand.

Cho Lim and I, meanwhile, would locate the compound she had identified and, if the opportunity presented itself, conduct a sneak and peek.

"What is sneak and peek?" asked Cho Lim.

"Kind of like playing peek-a-boo," I told her. "Except we get shot if we get caught."

Yong Shin Jong always stayed at the Beijing Guoji Julebu Fandian—better known as St. Regis Beijing—the number one choice for heavy hitters and world leaders, no matter who they were related to. The first step in tracing his footsteps was to confirm that he'd been there two months before. The only way to do that was to have a look at the hotel's computers, where the registrations were kept.

Like all top hotels, the Regis is known for its discretion, and part of that discretion involves keeping its databases from prying eyes. The system was protected against outside intruders by state-of-the-art firewalls, and used thumbprint readers as well as passwords to keep uninvited eyes from accessing the records. So obviously we needed to be invited to have a look.

Trace began the operation with the cheapest trick in the book. She entered the lobby with a slip of a dress that stopped midthigh, highlighting the legs she used to kick our new trainees' butts. She marched up to the reception desk, removing a wad of yuan notes as she went. Then just as she reached the desk, she stumbled. The notes flew out of her hand and scattered on the floor. Within seconds, she had a dozen hotel employees and passersby helping her pick them up—and another dozen, all male, trying to grab a peek up her skirt.

Doc Tremblay had been at the counter when Trace came in, trying to reserve a room for next week. Concealed in his palm was a computer dongle, a small device that would freeze the computer and render it unusable—a necessary precursor to our breaking into it. The dongle had a USB plug at one end; all Doc had to do was slip it into one of the computer's ports and we'd be ready for the next step in the plan.

With everyone's eyes on Trace, Doc had no problem leaning over the counter and pushing the dongle into the port at the rear of the computer. Or rather, he would have, if there'd been a USB port to plug into.

USB stands for *universal serial bus*. It lets computers use a variety of peripherals, everything from disk drives to mice. It's been included on even the most basic computers for at least ten years. You would assume that a high-class hotel like the Regis would have a computer no older than that, wouldn't you?

We certainly did.

What had Ev Barrett, sainted chief and my first sea daddy, said about *ass*-u-me back when I was a tadpole?

Doc slipped the gizmo back in his pocket and tried to figure out some other way of messing up the computer. All he could think of was the old standby—pulling the plug.

With Trace's money recovered and her dress safely covering her legs, she proceeded to the reservation desk. The clerk came over and saw that something had happened to his machine.

Unfortunately, it took him all of five seconds to look in the back and figure out that the monitor plug had somehow come out of its receptacle. He had it rebooted and working a few minutes later.

Which explains why he gave Lo Po a puzzled expression when he walked in and announced that he was there to fix the computer.

"The computer's fine," said the man.

"Not what they told me," said Lo Po. He set his tool case down and snapped the locks open. "I'll only be a few minutes."

"It's not broken," protested the man. They were speaking in Chinese, of course.

"You're from Hong Kong, I can tell."

"What's that supposed to mean?"

Lo Po smirked.

"Nothing wrong with Hong Kong, brother," insisted the clerk.

"Hong Kong, no," said Lo Po, removing a large screwdriver from his toolbox. "But everyone knows, people in Hong Kong are cheap."

"This is the hotel's computer. I don't have to pay."

"Exactly. So let me do my work."

Exasperated, the clerk retreated toward the office for reinforcements. Lo Po quickly turned off the unit and opened the box. By the time the clerk reappeared with the manager in tow, he had the machine in several pieces.

"It's not broke! There's nothing wrong with it!" said the manager.

"Then why did you call?"

"No one called," insisted the manager.

While they were discussing this very loudly, Trace returned from the room she'd just been given to complain that its view of the Forbidden City was blocked.

The truth is, no room in the hotel has a view of the Forbidden

City, but no one wants to disappoint a guest, especially one with ample cash and assets. The manager and clerk went to another computer to find a room; Lo Po pulled the hard drive, swapping it with a blank one he'd brought with him. Meanwhile, Doc ambled back over, picked up the old drive, and walked out the door with it, nodding at the doorman as he went.

[11]

While Trace, Doc, and Lo Po played who's got the computer repairman, Cho Lim and I grabbed some light backpacks and took a leisurely bicycle ride around the neighborhood about five miles away where Yong Shin Jong was supposedly being kept.

You probably think palatial estates don't exist in China, since the country is communist and the "people" own the land. But then you probably believed in Santa Claus once, too.

Even under Mao, China followed a complicated system of usage rights that effectively gave certain people rights that looked to an outside world a lot like traditional ownership. The Property Law passed in 2007 formalized some of the ownership arrangements, though like most laws adopted in the U.S., the legal code is so complicated only lawyers can make sense of it.[9]

This property had been used by a prominent family in the nearby village for decades. Surrounded by woods and backing onto a steep hillside, the property contained a three-story main house barely visible from the road. It, along with two smaller buildings, were all made of red brick; they had curved bamboo roofs that made them look more like temples than personal homes.

Two eight-foot chain-link fences ran around the perimeter; the space between the fences was nine or ten feet wide, and rutted with tire tracks. Beyond the fences grew prickle bushes. Botany not being one of my specialties, I can't tell you what genus the plants belonged to, but I can say their prickles were large enough to be seen from the road a good twenty yards away.

We cycled past slowly, following the road into a small community of brand-new town homes a half mile down the hill. Except for the roofs, whose clay tiles were accented by Asian-style curves, the concrete-sided houses would not have looked out of place in Arizona or New Mexico. Dust and grit swirled through

---

[9] Think of it this way: they give us cheap manufactured goods, we give them legalese and bullshit. Fair exchange.

the place as large earth-moving machines cut a new road and prepared foundations for a new set of buildings. Not far from a bulldozer, a middle-aged man used a long, thin stick to herd a pig toward one of the older houses clinging to the road at the side of the hill.

Cho Lim held her bike silently. She seemed to be seeing all of this for the first time.

A good sign? Or a good actress's flourish?

We turned the bikes around and rode back. This time I paid more attention to the area near the fence, trying to see if there were detection devices: motion sensors, video cameras, trip wires. I couldn't spot any, but there was so much vegetation nearby that they would be easy to hide.

I was just considering where to stash the bicycle when I heard something running through the vegetation. A brown wedge flew against the inner fence, barking ferociously. The dog was a Chinese Shar-Pei, reputed to be one of the best watchdogs in the world. A second came running up behind the first; then, from the other direction, came a third, this one in the path between the two perimeter fences.

Good thing we have the fence between us, I thought.

Just then I heard a fourth dog approaching, this one barking louder than the others.

And, unfortunately, coming from the field opposite the compound, where there was no fence to stop him. I bared my teeth and did my best imitation of a junkyard dog growl. Whether this warned off the dog or not, it changed direction and sprinted after Cho Lim.

Just as the dog reached for her leg, Cho Lim flew into the air. She came down on the animal's back. Stunned, the Shar-Pei tried to reach back and snap her, but with Cho Lim's two hands around her throat the animal had no way of doing any damage. Cho Lim jumped to her feet, raising the dog up high enough to deliver a quick heel kick to its midsection. Then she dropped it, leaving it whimpering at the side of the road as she retrieved her bike.

"Animal lover, huh?" I said. "You should have snapped its neck."

"It is not right to harm a dumb animal," said Cho Lim. "I use only force necessary."

"I'll remember that if I decide to ask you for a date," I told her.

One of the great things about China's rapid commercialization is that it is really very easy to get a Coke. Not only is it sold in a wide variety of stores and restaurants, but you find machines in the strangest places—including on a dusty road about a mile down the hill from the estate.

"Thirsty?" I asked Cho Lim as I studied the machine, puzzling out the coins.

She shook her head.

I bought two bottles anyway, tucked them into my pockets, then rode back up the hill, stopping a good fifty yards from the compound. We pulled our bikes into the scrub near the road, then began hiking up the hill. The compound sat on higher ground, but there was enough brush and ground cover to make it difficult to see us.

The first thing I wanted to do was find out where the dog that had attacked Cho Lim had come from. I hadn't seen a hole in the fence, and besides, the dog had come from the opposite side of the road. I thought maybe there might be a lookout post or even a barracks in the property across from the estate, but a slow, careful sweep with my binoculars failed to pick it up. The scrub-filled field backed into a swamp, and the nearest buildings were on the other side of a small pond maybe a mile away.

After staring at them for several minutes, I realized that a pile of rocks near the road didn't really belong there; the stones were a different color than the others scattered nearby. Though at first glance—and second and third for that matter—they seemed haphazardly placed, they'd been carefully arranged to form a kind of pyramid just high enough to hide something on the other side.

It took us nearly an hour to backtrack and circle around through the swamp to get close enough to verify my hunch. The rocks concealed an opening about a foot high and a foot and a half wide—big enough for a dog. The rocks were angled so that it was impossible to look inside from a distance. Even up close I couldn't see more than a few feet down, as the tunnel turned sharply in the direction of the compound.

Above the tunnel, a thick wire snaked through the rocks, connecting to a small video camera that faced the road. Obviously, we'd been watched by the security people in the compound; they'd loosed the dog to convince us not to hang around. Or maybe it was just their idea of fun.

The trip through the swamp had left me cold and wet. I was wearing good boots—no way I would compromise on footwear—but in the interests of blending in, the rest of my clothes were tourist fare, which translated into wet and chilly pants and a muddy shirt. I've been much wetter and a hell of a lot colder, but I was still cranky by the time I satisfied myself that the video camera and tunnel entrance were the only parts of the compound's defenses on that side of the road.

Our next task was to set up our own video cameras so we could keep the compound under surveillance without having to physically be there. There are so many remote surveillance cameras available these days that it's a buyer's market; we probably could have picked up some cheap Chinese models in town. But quality pays, and so I stuck with units manufactured by Law Enforcement Technologies, Inc., a little company out in Colorado Springs that had the bad judgment of appointing me to its board. The cameras in the units covered a 270-degree arc, had daylight and night-time modes, and combined a 10X mechanical zoom with an electronic zoom that gave a virtual 150X—pretty standard stuff these days. They were very small, which was notable, but their real asset was the fact that they connected via a thin wire to a transmitter that could be as far as a half mile away.

What? Connecting cameras via a wire? Dickie, that is *so* twentieth century. Why not go wireless?

The fact of the matter is, wireless technology is relatively easy to detect and even easier to defeat, especially in an application where the transmission has to be constant. Encrypting the signal doesn't help much—as soon as the subject realizes there's a radio wave there, he knows he's under surveillance. In a city where there are literally hundreds of radio signals traveling through every cubic foot of air, a few more may not seem out of the ordinary. But here, a radio transmission would stick out like the proverbial sore dick.

Which is what I got trying to wedge one of the cameras into the crook of a bush. The damn prickles shredded my fingers. I stifled my curses, sucked up the blood, and continued laying the wire, stringing it back to a sending unit about four hundred yards away from the camera. The small dishlike device sent a focused microwave to a satellite above; from there the signal would be beamed back to Lo Po's house.[10] The unit, which included a set of batteries to power not only the microwave but the cameras, was about the size of two bricks and weighed twice as much; my ruck felt empty without it.

I then laid out two small scanner receivers, connecting them via hard wire to the sending unit. These would allow us to hear any nearby radio transmissions, including those made by cell and sat phones. The scanner allowed the receiver to zip through literally hundreds of possible frequencies, stopping only if it heard something.

I've worked with some pretty quiet shooters in my day, but Cho Lim put them all to shame. She didn't say a word while we worked through the swamp; when I told her to conceal the wires, all she did was nod. Returning across the road and working our way toward the house, she was so quiet I had to check every so often to make sure she was still there, and breathing.

---

[10] Unlike "ordinary" microwaves, this one could only be detected by someone standing—or flying—directly in its path. My technical description leaves something to be desired because parts of the unit have not yet been cleared for patent.

Even when I took out the Coke and began shaking the bottles, she just gave me a puzzled look.

"Take it and throw it between the fences, about thirty meters to my left," I told her. "Then slip back and we'll see what happens."

Cho Lim took the bottle and quietly began walking through the woods, sliding between the low scrub and trees like a cat creeping up on an unsuspecting mouse. I crawled forward as well, waiting until I heard her bottle plop and explode. Then I tossed mine and sat and watched.

It took the dogs nearly a full minute to arrive, and it was another minute before two ninja types wearing helmets and body armor drove around the fence on motorcycles. The dogs ran to the first bottle and started lapping up the soda; the ninja drove past them, then looped back, driving up and down a few times. They scanned the general area, then kept moving.

So what do we figure from that, gentle reader?

A silent alarm had been set off, probably by some sort of motion detector. The alarm had released the dogs from a kennel somewhere, and alerted a guard or a supervisor, who sent the ninjas.

We sat in the woods for another hour, waiting to see what else the security people would do. The answer was nothing—typical, actually. The quick check by the ninjas was considered sufficient. While the exploding soda bottles may have put the compound on a higher state of alert, that didn't translate into any meaningful measures on the perimeter. Among other things, that told me that the security team was relatively small, if not complacent.

Our initial survey of the property complete, we returned to Lo Po's house for a little rest and refreshment. When we got there, Trace, Doc, and Lo Po were just pulling up with the hard drive they'd stolen from the hotel. Lo Po gave the drive to a computer expert he'd brought along for the mission. The man installed it in one of his computers and began poking at it with whatever software sticks he had in his magic black bag.

Meanwhile, I reviewed the satellite photos of the site, comparing them with what I'd seen from the road and the nearby property. Before we could plan a rescue operation, we needed to know more about the internal layout, other defenses and forces they had. And it wouldn't hurt to make sure that Yong Shin Jong was actually there.

I sketched out a sneak and peek with the others. We'd lure the dogs out, drug them, kill the detectors, then go over the fence. Survey the grounds, find the house, see what was inside. Depending on what we saw, we'd leave open the option of taking Yong Shin Jong out with us.

Wham, bam, thank you, ma'am.

Trace, of course, objected. To the plan, not the phrase—she had long ago given up trying to make me politically correct.

"They'll realize something is up as soon as the dogs fall asleep," she said. "And what makes you think they haven't figured out what the Coke bottles were all about?"

"Not much vandalism in China," said Lo Po. "No kids throwing bottles. It's bound to be suspicious, especially if you do it again."

"Don't worry," I told them. "I never make love the same way twice."

Trace said something in Apache that I couldn't understand, which was probably just as well.

Their points were valid. Our first visit had alerted the compound to the fact that something was going on. But I didn't mind that. If anything, I was counting on it. I wanted them to be at full alert. My primary goal was to find out what the defenses were, so that I could defeat them. If, by luck—sometimes Murphy actually plays on my side of the field—their defenses were *so* weak that taking Yong Shin Jong was child's play, then I'd play along. But I wasn't counting on that.

Give me enough information, and I can break into anywhere, including Fort Knox. Hell, Fort Knox is easy. I've done it several times.

(III)

As much as I liked Lo Po and the people he hired, I felt we were a little light on shooters; we'd need more muscle for a snatch operation. I wanted a couple of our people in place so I wouldn't have to struggle with the language barrier if things got tight.

We had two operators in Japan, taking a well-deserved break from the operation in the Philippines that Doc had been checking on. One of them—Thomas "Mongoose" Yamya—spoke decent Mandarin, so it was natural that we enlist him. And we never sent Mongoose anywhere without Paul "Shotgun" Fox along as well. They were almost like a matched set, though they were as different as salt and pepper. They razzed each other so badly that there were plenty of times I debated whether it was OK to give either a loaded weapon.

Mongoose is Philippine-American; he looks vaguely Hispanic, vaguely Asian. He's on the short side at five-six, with a pretty average build. But that's his secret weapon. People are always underestimating him.

Like a fair number of Red Cell International's employees, Mongoose is a former SEAL, only recently separated from the service. He has a good story about being in an airplane en route to a mission to grab Bin Laden when the plane was called back by the secretary of defense.[11] That was pretty much the point where Mongoose decided he'd had enough of the military life. Eight or nine months after he left the navy, he showed up on my doorstep. I wasted maybe three seconds before hiring him.

Shotgun is a different story. Not that I wasted too much time hiring him either. A six-foot-eight guy who weighs three hundred pounds, can run the forty-yard dash in 4.1 seconds, and bench-press close to seven hundred pounds is not somebody you piss off, especially when his résumé includes a stint in the Rangers. The man is

---

[11] I believe the mission remains classified. Mongoose has vowed one day to tell the story himself, so I won't steal his thunder.

a giant. And he is always eating—always. Mostly junk food. He's always got a Twinkie or a Doodle-Dad or some other little pie or something in his hand.

He is also the most good-natured summuva bitch going. I've never seen him frown, which is why he's an antidote to Mongoose. Together they cancel each other out.

Shotgun's as white as white gets and still remains a skin color. You may think from his nickname that he grew up somewhere rural and learned to handle weapons at a young age, maybe specializing in handling a shotgun while hunting. The truth is he didn't: Shotgun grew up in a white-bread suburb in Connecticut, and never came close to a weapon of any sort until he enlisted in the army two days after graduating high school. The nickname came from the fact that when he played center on the high school football team as a freshman, he only entered the game when the offense was using the shotgun formation. (By the time he was a senior, Shotgun was not only in on every play, offense and defense, but he was basically the entire line.)

Wherever it came from, the nickname fits, because there's no one better at riding shotgun or watching someone's back. And though it's not his weapon of choice, he is pretty handy with a scattergun.

Lo Po picked the boys up at Beijing airport. Mongoose grouched about the flight, Shotgun laughing at how he crowded out the other person sitting next to him in coach. We had a decent meal—Doc cooked—then got changed into black clothes and saddled up around midnight, dividing ourselves between the two *Geely Merries*, Chinese-made Mercedes knockoffs that Lo Po had rented.

Our first stop was in a village about five miles south of us. There I procured two local chickens from a villager's coop, leaving about twice the number of yuan notes that the chickens would have fetched in the local market. I wrung their necks and stuffed them into a bag.

Lo Po's people back at the house were watching the feed

from the video cameras we'd placed earlier. No one had gone into or out of the compound since we'd set up the cameras, and the place was dark.

Doc dropped me, Trace, and Cho Lim off down the road, then drove past the compound, proceeding to the housing development on the other side, where he and Shotgun would wait and watch our flank. Lo Po, who had Mongoose and one of his men with him, took a position off the road behind us, positioning his car for a quick getaway.

I led the way up the hill; Trace was the tailgunner, with Cho Lim in the middle. We each had a pair of Gen 3 night-vision goggles. For communications, we used a discreet-burst radio system whose only drawback was the fact that it had to be used in line-of-sight mode. And of course we were armed—MP5s, pistols, and Rogue Warrior Strider knives, both folders and straight blade.

Cho Lim had a pistol and knives, but no submachine gun. I trusted her, but not quite *that* much.

Under our tac vests we wore lightweight body armor Doc had brought with him. These were vests about the thickness of a wool sweater made of a Teflon-type material over a honeycombed carbon skeleton filled with inert gas. They wouldn't stop a rifle bullet at close range, but would slow down most anything else enough to limit injuries. The vests were intended to shield the body from shrapnel injuries, the sort of thing you get from IEDs[12] when they go off in the neighborhood. There were no trauma plates inserted to mitigate possible internal hemorrhaging without our immediate knowledge. But their light weight meant they could be used on operations like this one where ordinarily the weight of a bulletproof vest made it impractical to wear any protection at all. These were so light that you really forgot you were wearing them, though in hot weather the fact that they didn't breathe made them extremely hot. Red

[12] IEDs=Improvised explosive devices, also known as bombs.

Cell International had used them with some success in the Philippines, and we had the company working on a new version we hoped would provide even more protection.

Cho Lim's was so big it looked almost like a dress on her, coming down to the top of her thighs. The ruck strapped above it looked like a flat purse in comparison.

I'd expected that the dogs would be given free rein at night, but I was wrong; there was no sign of them as we approached the fence. What I did see were a pair of motion detectors, mounted on tree limbs about chest-high and arranged so their detection fields overlapped. The devices were similar to the sort of thing you'd find on a garage back in the States, actually detecting infrared radiation—heat—rather than motion.

I prepared the chickens, smearing the carcasses with sedative-laced honey. Then over they went.

I followed, scrambling over the outer and then the inner fence. Pulling a small spray bottle from my vest, I soaped the eye of the sensor, neutralizing the detection mechanism.[13] Then I jumped up and raced to the other.

Almost.

Murphy stuck his foot out about ten feet from my target. (Others may say I tripped over a large tree root, but I know Murphy's foot when I fall over it.) I sprawled face-first on the ground, eating a good bunch of dirt in the process. I could hear the dogs running toward me; I rolled back into the bushes, hoping they were hungry.

The dogs exploded down the raceway. They pounced on the first chicken, wrestling with it for a second. Neither would give way to the other, nor did there seem to be time to—they had the carcass down to feathers and feet in maybe thirty seconds. Then it was on to the second. By the time the bikers appeared, all that remained were feathers.

---

[13] I'd explain the physics of that, but there's really no time to here. The technique is an old one.

Wham . . .

The bikers stopped. One of them took out a night-vision device and scanned the terrain near the fence, looking to see if anything was nearby. Of course, since he was looking for intruders, he searched only the outside of the fence line—a common error.

Being dumb animals, the Shar-Peis didn't make the same mistake. They sniffed the air and growled. But the doggie sedative was already starting to have an effect; they snapped at the air, then at each other. One of the bikers looked at them for a moment, then shook his head and gunned his bike away, starting a circuit of the estate's perimeter. The other guard yelled at the dogs in Chinese, then took off after his companion. The animals decided the hell with the humans, and trotted drunkenly back in the direction they had come.

I crawled behind the second motion detector and sprayed it, then gave the all-clear. Trace and Cho Lim were over the fence in seconds.

We worked our way up the hill toward the main building, looking for other detection devices and booby traps. After about fifty or sixty yards, the wood gave way to a rocky, level stretch of ground that surrounded the compound. The area was actually a large Chinese cup garden, a pseudo-natural garden complete with dirt and gravel paths that wound past plantings deliberately arranged to make miniature arrangements.

More interesting to me than the arrangements were the video cameras hidden in the foliage. Some of these were hard to spot, and it took me nearly fifteen minutes before I was sure that the cameras were focused only on the paths.

An eight-foot wall separated the main house from the rock garden. Cho Lim, silent as ever, followed as I picked my way across the rocks and through a grouping of ferns. Just as I reached a niche in the wall, she whirled and dropped to her knee.

I had to strain to see what she was staring at. Two eyes appeared in the vegetation, low to the ground. They were followed by a distinct *meow.*

Cho Lim ducked forward and scooped the cat out of the bush. She held it close to her face and whispered something, then stuffed it into her ruck.

"It promised to stay quiet, Mr. Dick," she said softly.

Trace shot me a look, but it was too late to do anything about it. The cat seemed docile enough; it stuck its head out of the side of the ruck, full of curiosity but silent.

I unfolded a telescoping spy scope and held it up over the wall. There was a garden and a pond on the other side; beyond it, a patio and the back of the house. A pair of video cameras covered the inside grounds.

One of them swiveled in the direction of the spy scope, paused a moment, then continued. The pattern was preprogrammed; it did a wide-area sweep back and forth, then stopped about halfway through, focusing on the east wall before swinging around to the north. The other camera followed a similar pattern from the other side.

Whoever had designed the system intended to provide a full view of the backyard. But the cameras were slightly out of synch, and they left part of the wall and the doorway uncovered for about thirty seconds every four and a half minutes—more than enough time for someone to get over the wall and to the house.

The problem was what to do when I got there. There was no way of telling if the doors and windows were alarmed. Even if they weren't, it was likely to take me more than thirty seconds to get past the locks.

But that was a problem I'd have to deal with once I got there. The alignment of the cameras left a narrow spot not far from the door where I could hide while waiting for them to sweep away. It looked as if I'd fit if I held my breath.

I had to go over a six-foot wall topped by shards of glass as sharp as razor spikes, drop down into some sticker bushes—worse than the glass—and then clear a small wire fence that I suspected was electrified to keep out animals. It should have taken me twenty-five seconds tops—and it would have, if I hadn't tripped after I cleared the electric critter fence.

Had I had time to think about it, I might have considered myself lucky—two more feet and I would have fallen head-first into the small pond at the center of the back patio. Instead, I pushed up, barely avoiding the fence before getting my balance and hurling myself toward the wall. I landed with a soft thud with about a half second to spare. Fortunately, the house was made of stone; if it had been wood I probably would have gone right through the wall.

Which would have been one way in.

I caught my breath. My MP5 was tied to my back in a custom-made rig. As small as the gun is, it would still be a bit clumsy to wield if it wasn't needed, so I left it there and checked my PK instead. The pistol sat at the front of my hip, ready to slide out of its holster if necessary.

"Get ready," warned Trace. "I'll count off the seconds."

"Ready."

"One second, two seconds . . ."

I slipped over to the window. The room inside was lit and appeared empty; it looked like a living room or a lounge, with Western-style chairs arranged in a semicircle and a pair of passages at the far wall.

Metal alarm tape circled the glass panels. It wouldn't be hard to defeat, but anything I did would be easily spotted. I've always been big on zipless penetrations.

"Twenty-eight, twenty-nine . . ."

I slipped back to my hiding place, working hard to control my breathing. No matter how much you work out—and I work out a great deal—there's a huge distance between exercise and a real operation. It couldn't have been more than a few feet between my hiding spot and the window, but I was as winded as if I'd run ten miles.

"Get ready," Trace warned.

The door was a four-panel French-style door. It appeared from the hinges and metal flanges at the base that only the middle two opened. The alarm was set by a magnetic contact, visible from the side panel. Defeating that was no big deal, even if there was a second one toward the bottom that I couldn't see. The door, of course, was locked when I tried it. You never know when you're going to hit the lottery.

"Twenty-five, twenty-six . . ."

I ducked back with about two seconds to spare. While I was waiting, I looked up at the video camera above me. It was housed in a metal case, not quite tamperproof but enough of a pain in the ass to make it not worth fooling with. I got my burglar tools and small roll of tape out and ready.

"One second . . ." started Trace.

I slipped back to the door and used my burglar tools to undo the lock. I heard a good click at fifteen seconds; I eased the door out ever so slightly, being careful not to break the lock contact. I slipped a piece of plastic and tape over the latch, then put more tape over the edges of the door panel to keep it from opening until I got back.

That took me to twenty-eight seconds.

I got a stitch in my side hustling back. There wasn't enough room to squat down or even twist to relieve it; the best I could do was try and work it out with my thumb while I waited. Massaging my muscle, I closed my eyes and forced the rest of my body to relax, lowering my breathing and pulse rate. By the time I reopened my eyes, I had only about another minute to wait. I turned my head toward the door, and noticed it was straining against the tape. Something inside, a fan or an air conditioner maybe, was pushing air against the panels, trying to spring the doors open.

"Trace?"

"Not yet," she hissed.

The doors moved back inward. Just as I started to take a breath in relief, they surged back out again.

Then the tape broke.

"One . . ."

I'd already jumped out to the door, putting my hand over it and just barely keeping it closed. I dropped to my knees and took out my "alarm extenders"—thin pieces of metal connected by a long wire, allowing the alarm circuit to remain unbroken even though the door was open.

". . . Twenty-eight, twenty-nine, thirty."

On thirty-one, I had the door closed—and I was inside the house.

Classical music was playing somewhere inside. A standing fan in the corner swung back and forth, sending its draft across the room. There were a dozen chairs arranged in a haphazard circle, as if they'd been used for a conference and then left there. A pair of sofas were pushed against the wall on the left; a long, empty table sat in the middle of the wall on the right. The wall opposite the doors was framed by a pair of archways, which led to separate halls into the rest of the house. Large Chinese paintings of winter scenes hung on the walls.

I bent down to brush the crumbs of dirt I'd tracked onto the floor from the tiles, dispersing it under the chairs. I'd just finished when I heard the sound of footsteps coming from one of the halls. I dropped to my haunches, hiding behind an upholstered chair and holding my breath as they continued toward me.

A shadow appeared in the right doorway.

If it was Yong Shin Jong, I could grab him and go—no need for an elaborate assault.

If it wasn't, and I showed myself, I might not live to mount an escape mission.

The only way to find out was to look. I leaned over slowly, peeking around the chair.

It wasn't Yong Shin Jong, unless he'd taken to wearing a red print dress.

And carrying a submachine gun.

[IV]

Take a breath, Dickie.
And lean back behind the chair.

The woman took a few steps into the room, walking to my left. She pushed one and then another of the chairs, moving it slightly to adjust its position in the circle. She began working her way around the room counterclockwise. I was at five o'clock; she started at one and moved toward twelve.

I slipped my hand to my pistol. I'd shoot her before she shot me.

She was at nine, just about in view, when someone called to her from inside. She said something I couldn't understand; the male responded harshly, and she left the room.

I was just considering whether to follow when Lo Po reported that two Mercedes sedans had stopped in front of the property and were waiting for the gates to be opened. The chairs hadn't been left from a conference—one was about to take place.

"Trace—I'm coming out," I said over the radio. "Tell me when the cameras are on. Lo Po, can you bring the parabolic up?"

"On the way."

I moved to the doors, waiting for the "go" signal from Trace. Meanwhile, the male voice I'd heard earlier began barking again. Other voices answered, and within moments a whole troop of footsteps were echoing loudly down the hall.

"One . . ." said Trace finally.

I went through the doors, closed them, and hustled back to the spot below the video camera, just in time to beat the sweep.

The only problem was that I'd left my alarm extenders against the door.

Great time for premature Alzheimer's to kick in. I waited for the cameras to swing around, then slipped back to the door. There was a person in the archway, his back facing the doors. I reached up and pulled the wire for the top alarm out, then dropped to my knees and tugged at the second. It stuck for a moment, then came loose—and pulled the door with it.

The shriek of the alarm vibrated the stone wall as I threw myself back against it. I held my breath.

"Dick?" asked Trace.

"Tell me when the cameras are clear," I whispered, my eyes fixed on the half-open door nearby.

"Wait—wait—wait."

On the third "wait," someone pushed through the doors and stuck his head outside. The alarm continued to ring.

"Go!" said Trace, but at that moment I was doing my best to pretend I was part of the wall. The man didn't see me, and closed the doors.

"Thirty," hissed Trace. "Wait. Wait."

I did. The alarm stopped ringing. Finally, Trace gave the all-clear sign and I raced to the wall, ignoring the prickles and sharp glass as I vaulted back over, collapsing in a heap in the comparative safety of the rock garden.

Cho Lim, standing a few feet away, glanced down at me.

"Let's back out and meet Lo Po," I said, getting up. "We'll put the mike into one of those trees and aim it at the glass on the doors."

The microphone worked by detecting vibrations in the glass and translating them into sound. The technique was first used during the Cold War. The results vary widely depending on the room and the vocal qualities of the people talking, but the mike has the advantage of being virtually undetectable by the subjects, at least as long as they stay put.

We were on our way back through the rock garden when a thin glimmer caught my eye near Cho Lim's leg. A straight line ran across the garden. At first glance it looked like a spider's string, but the moonlight revealed it was just a bit too thick.

"Trip wire!" I yelled.

I'm fairly sure I yelled it. I had to, to be heard over the explosion.

11

Bam . . .

We landed in a heap, more or less together, at the edge of the rock garden near the perimeter fences. I'd say that all hell broke loose, but I'm not given to understatement. Sirens were sounding, dogs were barking, and motorcycles were revving. Flares went off, and the dark night turned into a sick but bright yellow glow. My nostrils were filled with the comforting smell of burning gunpowder and tungsten. We had reached the blissful state of SNAFU—situation normal, all fucked up.

I pushed myself to my feet and looked around for Trace and Cho Lim.

"Thick way, Dick," said Cho Lim in the radio. Thick or this—my ears were ringing. She was standing about ten feet away, almost directly ahead of me. Trace was squatting against the fence, her submachine gun out.

"Here come the bikers," said Trace.

"Move back behind that rock," I told her. "Let's see what they do."

There were four of them this time, riding in single file, a lot slower than before. They passed us by, then came back and congregated around the spot where I'd thrown the hens earlier. They didn't seem to know we were there, but there was no way for us to move from where we were without being seen. One of them peeled off and returned in the direction they'd come; the others stood around talking.

"Lo Po, where are you?" I whispered over the radio.

He didn't answer.

"Dick, he went up to bring you that mike," said Mongoose. "You want backup?"

"Stay where you are. Get the car ready."

"Roger that."

The biker returned and began gesturing at the fence. Two

of the men got off their bikes—they'd obviously decided they were going to climb over and have a look.

I'd brought up my submachine gun and was just about to tell Trace I'd take the two on the left when I saw Cho Lim starting down the hill to my right.

"Cho Lim, what are you doing?"

The answer came in the form of a meow, followed by the pitter-patter of little feet crashing through the brush.

Which was followed by the pitter-patter of submachine guns, fired in the direction of the cat.

The gunfire lasted for only a few seconds. The man who'd pointed toward the fence began yelling insanely, probably telling them I guess that they'd just wasted the kitty. We hunkered down while they ran over and peered through the chain links.

The curses turned to laughs. Finally, the men got back on their bikes and rode off.

Thank you, ma'am.

Trace and I jumped up and started for the fence. Cho Lim went over and crouched down near the dead cat. Her face was as pained as I've ever seen.

"Come on," I told her. "They'll be sending somebody through to pick it up and make sure there's nothing else. *Come on.*"

She sniffled, then got up and followed me.

Whether they were fooled by the cat or not, the men who'd come for the meeting didn't stay very long. Their Mercedes left the compound about ten minutes after we did. Doc and Shotgun followed them as far as the highway, but once there they had too much of a lead for Doc to keep up without being obvious. He lost them in a maze of heavily laden tractor-trailers heading for Beijing—some parts of China never sleep.

"I don't know if they were businessmen or officials or what," he said when we rendezvoused back at the house. "The windows were all darkened. We couldn't see inside. There were no markings or plates on the car that I could see."

"We need X-ray vision, boss," said Shotgun brightly. He was stuffing Twinkies into his mouth. "You should get your friends to invent that."

"Oughta get them to make something to feed you intravenous," said Mongoose.

"They got that," answered Shotgun brightly. He barely paused to unwrap another of the little cakes before gulping it down. "Thing is, what's the sense of eating if you're not biting, right?"

"You don't eat, you swallow," said Trace.

I'll spare your tender ears and eyes the locker-room humor that followed. Doc and I went into the other room, trying to figure out what else we could do to verify that Yong Shin Jong was in the compound. So far we hadn't seen him, and while something was going on there, there was no way of knowing whether it should interest us or not.

Lo Po's computer expert, meanwhile, was having trouble with the hard drive Doc and the others had stolen from the hotel. I put in a call to Shunt, Red Cell's resident computer genius, forgetting that he was on vacation. There were some clicks on the line, and then someone picked up and asked me what the hell I wanted.

"I'm looking for Shunt. This is Dick Marcinko."

There was a pause.

"I know who you are," said the young man on the other end of the line. He sounded just a hair less sure of himself as he continued. "What do you want?"

I explained that we were having some technical problems getting a hard drive to work, and asked if he was willing to help out. When he said sure, I got Lo Po's computer expert on the line, and let them talk geek to geek.

That was my first conversation with Matthew Loring.

Loring and Lo Po's computer guy talked through the problem for about an hour. They finally figured out that the problem was some sort of quirk in the Linux operating system the hotel used instead of Windows. A half hour later we were looking at the hotel's registration form.

But that was all we were looking at—the registration data itself was kept on another computer in the hotel.

Using the information they shared over an Internet connection, Loring spent the next two hours working out a way to break into the hotel system and download all the information without being detected. Because the hotel system wasn't connected to the Internet, however, the program would have to be imitated from within the system itself, either from one of the hotel computers or by plugging into the network.

"I don't know if we can get away with the computer repairman gag twice in a row," said Doc. "They'll realize something's up."

"You can plug directly into the server," suggested Loring. "Look for a switch box similar to your Ethernet router at Rogue Manor. They probably have it in a closet in the basement or something."

I rousted Mongoose from bed, planning to take him and one of Lo Po's men into the hotel to look for the server closet. Lo Po brought up the hotel's Web site so I could get a rough idea of the place's layout before going in. He stopped when we got to the fourth photo, which showed the hallway just off reception.

"Problem with the Internet?" I asked.

"No." He pointed to a door in the right-hand corner of the screen. "That's what you're looking for."

"You sure?"

"It says computer room," said Lo Po, magnifying the screen so we could see the Chinese characters on the plate next to the door.

"No way you're sneaking through that door without being seen," said Mongoose sourly. "You got the video camera and the front desk."

"You're a very negative thinker, Mongoose," I told him. "We'll just create a diversion."

"It would be easier to break right through the side wall," suggested Lo Po. "Go through the back and hook in."

"That's a ladies' restroom," said Mongoose. "Even in China, men aren't allowed in."

"They are if they're plumbers," said Lo Po.

[11]

Overalls, work cap, a bit of dye to my beard, a slight nurturing of my eyebrows: Richard Marcinko, Rogue Warrior, became Number One Plumber.

Even Cho Lim was impressed, blinking two or three times before opening her mouth wide in surprise.

"You look like a plumber, Mr. Dick."

"*Shie-shie*," I said, bowing. "Thank you."

"Until you open your mouth."

"She's right. You don't sound very Chinese, Dick," said Lo Po. "But I have an idea."

And so was born Number One Plumbing, Father & Daughter, Best Plumbing Beijing. You drip, we make the trip. No job too big or small.

Trace reprised her role as hotel guest, in this case a particularly dull-headed one who screwed up the plumbing. She did a damn good job of it, too—I was nearly bowled over by the flood of water when Cho Lim opened the door to the restroom.

The hotel manager followed me as I waded into the bathroom. Water was spurting from two of the toilets. (This was a high-class Western-style restroom; no squatting, and each commode had its own stall.) The manager began saying something in very fast Chinese. I didn't understand anything but the curse words, which there were a lot of.

"Errgh," I grunted.

"My father fix. No worry," said Cho Lim in Chinese.

The manager looked at me. I folded my arms and kept my Asian squint.

"Father is *very* temperamental," explained Cho Lim. "He does not work while people are watching. You can stay if you close your eyes."

"Just tell him to fix it," said the manager. "I am not paying him to stand around."

The manager left. I reached into my bag of tools and found

a large pipe wrench to turn the water off with. Then I took out a small RotoZip and started cutting through the Sheetrock near the computer closet.

The sound of the tool brought the manager running. I had just enough time to slosh over to the toilet area before he came in.

"What are you cutting? What are you cutting?" he demanded.

I curled my lip at him.

Cho Lim glanced over at me, then back at the manager.

"Do you speak English?" she asked in English.

"English? Why?" he answered in Chinese.

"Because he doesn't," she said in English. "My father is very temperamental. If you question him, he may just leave. Last week, he was working for Premier Zhu, and one of the men wanted to stand with him in the kitchen as he fixed the pipe. He was at the other side of the room. This was very reasonable, for security, but my father—"

"He worked for the premier?" asked the manager in Chinese.

"Speak English," hissed Cho Lim, "or he will know what we are saying."

"He does work for Premier Zhu?"

"No, that is just it—he walked out. Premier wanted to watch. My father said, 'Fix your own damn sink,' and handed him the wrench. He has not gone back. The premier himself called to apologize, but he would not change his mind. My father is very stubborn."

The manager turned white.

"Isn't he worried that the premier will become angry?"

"Have you tried to get a good plumber in Beijing?"

The manager nodded solemnly.

As he did, Cho Lim slapped him across the face.

"What was that for?"

"I will tell my father you asked for a date. Otherwise he will be suspicious."

"Yes, yes, thank you, thank you. Please carry on," he said, bowing and backing out of the restroom.

Five minutes later, I had a hole large enough to see into the back of the computer closet. I located the network connections, plugged in, and fired up the laptop I'd brought in the other case. Within a few minutes, I was looking at a screen showing Yong Shin Jong's account.

He had, it turned out, been here three months before: twice, with two days in between.

His account also had several credit card numbers, as well as phone numbers of people he'd called from his room. I saved them all, disconnected the laptop, and taped the hole I'd cut in the wall.

Cho Lim, meanwhile, was clanging away at the toilet. I thought she was just making noise to make it seem as if we were working hard, but as I packed up she looked over and smiled.

"Toilet is fixed, Mr. Dick."

"Great, Cho Lim," I told her. "Maybe you and I will go into business someday."

[III]

While we were playing plumber, Doc and the others added to our reconnaissance capabilities near the compound. They set up the parabolic mike in the trees, aiming it at one of the second story windows. Then they tapped the telephone wire running up the street, giving us a way to listen in to any landline phone calls made from the compound—and, unfortunately, the small housing complex down the road, which meant Lo Po's people had to do a lot of extra work trying to isolate the proper circuits.

Mongoose crawled through the brush on the hill behind the compound, trying to find a place where we could set up a long-range camera to watch the rear courtyard that I'd traipsed back and forth through the night before. But the compound had been arranged so that this was impossible. The only way to watch the patio would be to put a camera on the wall, and after all our adventures, the risk didn't seem worth it.

"We can take the place down, no sweat," said Doc that evening as we reviewed the situation. "It's the only way we can be sure Yong Shin Jong is or isn't there, short of staying here indefinitely."

"The problem is, once we do that, we'll have to leave Beijing for a while," said Trace. "So it's a Catch-22."

"More a coin flip," said Doc.

"Whatever. If we're wrong, we're screwed."

"I'd like to know who the people in the Mercedes last night were," said Lo Po. "That would tell us a lot."

I got up from the table where we were sitting and walked into the other room, where Cho Lim and one of Lo Po's people were monitoring the video and audio from near the estate. The microphone was picking up ambient noises—people moving around the house—but no conversations; the compound was simply too big for us to hear much unless the conversation was in or very close to the room the mike was aimed at. There hadn't been any traffic on the road, let alone visitors, in the past two hours.

I took out my sat phone and called home. The twelve-hour time difference meant it was just going on 8:00 A.M.—Karen would be getting ready to leave for work.

"Hi, lover, I really miss you," she said, picking up.

Love that caller ID. I'll spare you the gushy stuff, of which there was plenty, and concentrate on business.

"Matthew has some information for you on the credit card numbers," Karen told me. "I think you'll be interested."

"Already?"

"He's been working the whole night. I think he's even more committed than Shunt."

Committed is a dangerous word to use in connection with Shunt. In Matthew Loring's case, however, it was only a compliment. I'd sent the data we'd taken from the hotel in an encrypted file via e-mail just a few hours before. Loring, apparently working through the night, had used it to obtain a list of all the transactions the credit cards had made over the past six months.[14] In and of itself that information was useful, but Loring managed to use the account data to ferret out three other credit cards, including an American Express Black Sapphire, which also belonged to Yong Shin Jong. His probe turned up an alias we didn't know about, which yielded a little more information as well.

Kim's Korean son hadn't used the cards in the last three weeks; the last transactions were all in Singapore. There was a charge for the first-class ticket for an air flight there besides the one that the CIA knew about. He had registered as a Mr. Wong on another flight. A Wong had apparently flown on the plane, though it was impossible to tell if Yong Shin Jong had actually been the person on the plane.

"Possibly, there are other cards and more identities," added

[14] The possibility exists that he obtained this information using means that would not meet the approval of the U.S. justice system. But since I wasn't there, I am convinced that the data simply fell from the sky, and you should be, too.

Karen, who'd gone through the data as she had her morning coffee. "But this almost looks as if Yong Shin Jong or someone wanted to give the impression that he left Singapore, yet really didn't. You say he didn't stay at the hotel when he came back."

"Not according to the records. He was there before Singapore, not after. At least not as Yong Shin Jong."

"He wouldn't use an assumed name there. They know him," said Karen. "Easier to stay somewhere else."

You see why I love her. Plus she's beautiful, and she comes the closest anyone ever has to keeping me in line. Those are a few of the reasons I call her "Pocket Rocket!" We theorized some more, talked mushy again, then returned to business, this time to the people who had been tying up my computer network by bombarding my server with port scan attacks, among other things.

"Matthew has tracked the Web attack back to the source," Karen told me. "Guess where it originates?"

"Pyongyang."

"Not quite. Alexandria."

"Virginia?"

"That's right. He hasn't found out who's paid for the accounts yet, but he's working on it. We should have it by the end of the day. Our day, not yours."

Across the room, Cho Lim suddenly sat straight up.

"Karen, I'm going to have to call you back," I said.

I hung up and went across the room to see what Cho Lim had heard. She had her hands pressed hard against the earphones, as if she wanted to push the tiny speakers into her ear canals. When she turned around to look at me, she had a painful expression on her face, as if she'd just been punched in the stomach. She handed me the headset without a word, then hit the control to replay the audio.

A man's voice, cursing. A loud noise, maybe of someone falling against furniture. A crash. Shouts and then a kind of whimpering noise, followed by shuffling and silence.

"Yong Shin Jong," she said softly.

[IV]

We needed two helicopters for the operation. Lo Po could fly one. Even though Trace was far enough along in her training to take the other, I preferred to have her on the ground with me. That meant we needed another pilot—I couldn't trust a Chinese rental, since nearly all Chinese pilots are also members or former members of the military, sometimes moonlighting while actually on duty. Lo Po knew a man he trusted in Hong Kong, but the man had been hired for another gig and wouldn't be available until the following week. I didn't intend on waiting that long.

"We'll have to bring someone in from Japan," said Doc. "Maybe Tosho can get us someone."

"What about Ike?" said Trace, volunteering her boyfriend.

"What about him?"

Trace's usual response to that kind of question would feature a string of four-letter words. But she got a real sincere, almost dopey look in her eyes, and proceeded to tell me what a great pilot he was. She'd spoken to him just a few hours ago via satellite phone; his job had finished early and he was waiting in Kyoto for her.

"He's volunteered to help any number of times," she said. "He'd do it."

"What about our no fraternization rules," said Doc.

"What rule is that?" shot back Trace, glaring at him.

Doc glared back. The two of them have a generally close relationship; in some ways Trace is like the daughter he never had. But there was definitely an edge in his voice.

"I think we can count on Trace to keep things professional," I said. "All right?"

"Absolutely," said Trace.

Doc frowned, but nodded.

I left Lo Po and Doc to lease the helicopters and make the other logistical arrangements while I took Shotgun and Mongoose toy shopping.

When I told them, they thought I meant we were going in search of weapons, and practically knocked each other over heading for the car. But I meant it literally—I had one of Lo Po's drivers take us over to Honggiao, a big manufacturing district in Beijing (what isn't?). Beijing is basically Toys "R" Us east; pretty much every toy sold in America these days comes from China, and the toy market near Honggiao has samples of everything. Mongoose looked at me as if I were crazy as I started examining displays. Shotgun was in heaven.

"Dick, look at this—Boba Fett *Legos*!"

"It's a toy, Shotgun," sneered Mongoose.

"Geez, no shit," answered Shotgun. "You think the real Boba Fett is made out of plastic?"

"Boba Fett is not real. I can't believe I'm having this conversation."

"You think it's a knockoff?"

"Probably."

"Hey, Dick, action figures!" said Shotgun, moving over to another display. "You think there's a Rogue Warrior doll here somewhere?"

There probably was, especially since Blue Box Toys in Hong Kong produced three versions of the Rogue Warrior Collector figures a few years ago, marketing them under the *Legend* series. The figures were twelve inches tall, with weapons, etc., all to scale. As I frequently jest, now every woman can have a twelve-inch Dick.

But I hadn't come to indulge my inner child—or Shotgun's outer one. We bought a pair of radio-controlled toy airplanes, picked up a few more useful items—and a Boba Fett for Shotgun—then found a field outside the city where we could practice until nightfall. After grabbing something to eat, Shotgun and I engaged in a midnight dogfight over Yong Shin Jong's compound. It was a fierce but brief battle—both of our planes ended up crashing into the drink.

Upon which, we returned to the house and consoled ourselves

by crashing into our own drinks, straight from the medicine cabinet of the good Dr. Bombay.

"Something's up at the compound," said Lo Po when I went in to check on the monitoring team the next morning. "They just called a fish expert. Their carp are dying."

Copper-sulfate will do that to a fish, especially when the pond they're in has been dive-bombed by a remote control toy airplane the night before.

Lo Po canceled the emergency call, calling the vet and pretending to be Yong Shin Jong's valet. Meanwhile I took a long shower, emerging with a white beard and hair.

"You get older every time I look at you," said Lo Po, amused.

I bowed solemnly.

A half hour later, I used the same bow as Lo Po and I presented ourselves to the video camera at the main gate to Yong Shin's compound. A road crew had set up shop on the roadway nearby, and their jackhammers made it difficult to hear through the tinny intercom speaker attached to the gate. But Lo Po's gestures, along with the sign on the front of the truck, featuring a large fish, apparently was sufficient: the gates swung open.

Lo Po and I drove the panel van up the driveway. We were escorted by the dogs, who yapped and growled as we drove up the cutbacks to the main house. Two women appeared at the front door; both wore red dresses similar to those I'd seen on the woman the other night. I'm pretty confident these women didn't have machine guns with them, however; there would have been no place to hide them. A whistle from one of the women sent the dogs running to a small concrete shed near the side of the yard. The other woman was holding a metal-detector wand in her hand.

"Ready, Dick?" whispered Lo Po.

"Let's do it," I said, opening my door.

I was beginning to like playing the role of grouchy ancient.

With the help of a Chinese work cap pulled low over my face and a pronounced slouch, I shuffled to the back of our truck, where I donned a long white lab coat embroidered with our company motto on the back. ("The best swim with us." In Chinese, of course.) Then I retrieved a fishnet and a small toolbox filled with jars of potions. Lo Po put on a similar coat, then took out a large coil of rope from the truck.

"*Dsao-shang,*" Lo Po told the women. "Good morning. We're here for the fish."

"Yes," one of them replied. "You will be searched first, please."

She nodded to the other woman, who approached us with the metal detector. I frowned, but said nothing as she wanded me. I was clean, but the wand beeped twice as she waved it near Lo Po's pocket.

"Metal detector?" he asked, reaching into his pocket. "It must have gotten my paint and car keys."

He held out the small spray can and keys.

"Why do you have paint?" asked the woman, examining the can.

"To mark the fish, if necessary. It doesn't hurt them."

She gave it back.

"And the rope?"

"In case my father has to go into the water," explained Lo Po. "For his safety."

"What is in his box?" said the woman.

"My father's medicine," explained Lo Po. "For the fish."

"We will inspect it."

"That's not necessary."

"It is necessary. We will look in it."

"He is very sensitive," said Lo Po. "If he thinks you don't trust him, he won't do the work."

"Trust is not the issue. We will inspect the box," answered the woman.

Of course, they were doing all this talking in Chinese. I stood behind Lo Po, frowning as cantankerously as I could.

Finally, Lo Po told the woman that he would smooth things over for her first.

"They want to look in your box," whispered Lo Po.

I grunted menacingly, then handed it over. Lo Po opened the box and let the woman look inside.

"These look like kitchen herbs," she said.

"They are ancient medicines that my father uses in his work," said Lo Po, bowing deeply as he mentioned me.

I think the bow was a nice touch. Maybe I'll have everyone do it from now on.

"You can go," said the woman, handing it back. "Li will take you through the house."

The woman was right about the herbs—I'd grabbed them from the kitchen just before we came over. But that accounted for only about half of the bottles. The others were small grenades. Under them in the toolbox's false bottom was a pair of PK pistols, one for Lo Po and one for yours truly, along with some explosive charges and assorted other goodies.

As we walked up the path, I spotted a woman in an upstairs bedroom covering us with an ancient Type 67 machine gun, a weapon I had first become acquainted with in Vietnam. There's nothing like a belt of 7.62mm bullets to evoke the warm feeling of nostalgia in my chest, but at that moment at least I wasn't thinking about the past or the future, just the immediate present.

The front door opened to a set of steps that took us down about two feet to a small vestibule. The main hallway opened directly opposite the door, and ran to the back of the house, through the room I had snuck into two nights before and from there out to the garden.

"You must save the fish," said the woman leading us through. "They are very precious."

"We'll do what we can," said Lo Po.

Lo Po and I went to the pond, where no less than a dozen fish were floating belly-up. I knelt down slowly, staring at the water as if I were communicating with the souls of the departed.

Or carp, as the case may be.

"Two guards," whispered Lo Po. "Maybe more upstairs."

"At least one more. Probably two or three."

"Think they're all women?"

I grunted noncommittally. Their sex didn't matter; I was interested in their competence and weapons, which seemed fairly formidable. We hadn't seen the motorcyclists, but the only other building on the property large enough to house them was in the northwestern corner. Foliage blocked the satellite view of that part of the property, but it was likely there was a small path connecting it to the racetrack between the fences.

Lo Po bent over my box and took out the top tray. I swatted at his arm and we began a mock argument over which potions to use. Our backs were blocking the video cameras so they couldn't see what we were really doing: pulling the guns out of the bottom of the case and hiding them under our long lab coats. Ready, Lo Po rose, shaking his head as if disgusted with his pigheaded father. He waved at me, then walked over toward the house, saying in a loud voice that he was going to check the electrical connections. He slipped his toolbox down and crouched next to the house, just out of view of the cameras, waiting for them to move so he could jump back out and over the wall.

Shaking my head, I rose slowly, using the net to help me balance. I went to the water and poked at one of the fish, taking its carcass out of the pond. I leaned over and examined it—and caught a glimpse of one of the women watching me from inside the room.

She didn't stay there for long. The door soon opened and she came out, speaking in rapid Chinese.

Guessing that she was asking where number one son had gone to wasn't very hard. What was difficult was answering. I turned to her slowly, cocking my head at her as if I believed she was insane. This only increased the speed of the words flying from her mouth.

Obviously, some sort of response was required on my part. I rose slowly, shuffled to the toolbox, and retrieved two sticks of incense. These I brought to the water's edge.

Even *faster* Chinese ensued.

"My father believes your water is not in balance," said Lo Po, slipping back over the wall. "His methods are old-fashioned."

"Where were you?"

"I am looking for the electrical conduit. We must check out the power supply."

"The wires are underground."

"Precisely." Lo Po held up a small volt meter. "It must be examined."

The volt meter would be about as much use checking for underground current as a flashlight, but the guard apparently didn't know that. She turned back toward me.

"Why does he not answer me when I speak to him?"

Lo Po sidled up to her and lowered his voice.

"He's a little deaf. Also, he—he is very old-fashioned. Women . . ." He shook his head. "He is not a modern man, my father. Very old-fashioned."

"Hmmmph."

"Also, he is very touchy. You should not question him."

"We are paying for his services!" said the woman.

Lo Po nodded solemnly. "I try to get him to change, but with the older generation . . ."

The woman frowned. Lo Po changed the subject, saying that while other causes would have to first be ruled out, he suspected that there was a very grave problem with her water owing to pollution. Pollutants were coming from somewhere on the property; until they were discovered, the fish would continue to die.

"Your father believes this?"

"My father uses ancient methods," said Lo Po. "I have science. I must take more tests. Do you have water inside? I will examine your drinking water first."

Though puzzled by the request, the woman showed Lo Po inside. As soon as she was gone, I reached inside the toolbox and took out a shortwave radio unit disguised to look like an Apple iPod. Lo Po checked in a few minutes later, saying he was downstairs.

"Three of them, one in front of the stairs," he whispered. "Haven't gone upstairs. They say it's not possible. So that must be where he is."

"Very perceptive, honorable son."

I glanced at my watch: H hour was five minutes away. I looped the rope around my shoulder, then picked up the can of spray paint Lo Po had left behind. Slowly, I began to shuffle over to the house, right under one of the video cameras. I went slowly, gesturing and pretending to talk to myself. When I got there, it was H hour minus thirty seconds.

I pulled a small straw from my pocket and attached it to the nozzle on the spray paint. Then I removed the stiff belt I'd been wearing, removed the small bolts that held it together, and refashioned it as a carbon-fiber grappling hook.

Twenty seconds. The alarm was set on the watch; I could see the tiny little indicator blinking, telling me to get ready.

The plan was simple. At five seconds to H hour, I'd reach up and spray paint the video lens. Then I'd hit the second one. While Lo and I had already been videoed, the less of the operation on tape the better. Lenses blocked, I'd step back and toss the rope up into the window, haul myself upstairs PK in hand, and start looking for Yong Shin Jong.

Outside, Trace would lead a small team through the front of the building, rendezvousing with me upstairs. Doc and Lo Po's men would take care of the motorcycle people and any reinforcements, while Mongoose and Shotgun watched the road. You can't keep Mr. Murphy from inviting himself to a party, but the plan was flexible enough to accommodate him if and when he showed up.

Fifteen seconds. An eternity when you're waiting for something to happen, especially since the only thing that can happen in those fifteen seconds is a visit from Mr. Murphy.

At about nine seconds, the back door flew open and a tall, pudgy man with a remarkably bad haircut came out of the building. He walked out the door to the pond where I had left the toolbox, stopped, then turned and looked at me in astonishment.

It was Yong Shin Jong. Which wouldn't have been a bad thing, except that the toolbox was about to explode.

[V]

The human body is not really designed for flight. We don't have wings, and our muscles are not strong enough to flap any of the limbs that we do have quickly enough to supply lift. Our bone structure is altogether too heavy to overcome the most basic law on earth: gravity.

And yet, under the proper circumstances and with the proper motivation, flight is indeed possible for the human body, as I proved at that instant, throwing myself toward the box with the rigged grenades and hoping to knock it into the pond. But Yong Shin Jong inadvertently ducked into my path, diverting me toward the water rather than the box.

I grabbed him as I fell. We tumbled together into the pond, and his weight combined with my momentum was enough to take us to the bottom of the shallow pool as the tool case exploded. By the time we surfaced, there had been plenty more explosions, and a heavy cover of smoke was wafting around the building. At the front, Doc and the road workers—actually men who worked for Lo Po—had used smoke grenades to temporarily defeat the machine-gun nest on the top story and make a rush at the building. (Since Yong Shin Jong was supposed to be upstairs, a real grenade would have been too dangerous.) There were shouts and screams, punctuated by the lively music of gunfire.

Yong Shin Jong coughed, then started to sink back into the pond. I grabbed hold of him and hauled him out of the water.

"Yong Shin Jong, I am here to rescue you," I said, using the Korean I had carefully rehearsed. "My name is Dick Marcinko. I am your friend."

Yong Shin Jong shook his head.

"Do you speak English?" I asked. "I am your friend."

"Who are you? You're Chinese? You speak English?"

"I'm American. Your father wanted you rescued, and he hired me."

Yong Shin Jong shook his head again. He started to say something, but a series of loud explosions coming from the northwest drowned him out: the motorcyclists had discovered the grenades and trip wire Lo Po had set.

The back door to the house flew open. I wheeled around and pumped two slugs into the female guard just before she could demonstrate how easily her submachine gun carved up the human torso.

"We're getting out of here!" I told Yong Shin Jong.

"What?"

"Listen." I held up my hand, then pointed in the direction of the thump of the approaching helicopters.

"We're rescuing you," I told Yong Shin Jong. "We have everything planned."

"Why are you rescuing me?"

"Because I'm a nice guy."

"I don't need to be rescued," said Yong Shin Jong. "What is going on?"

"You *are* Yong Shin Jong, aren't you? The son of Kim Jong Il, North Korea's leader."

"Don't say that name in my presence."

"Your father's?"

Yong Shin Jong spat. "I hate that son of a bitch."

Technically, that would have made him a grandson of a bitch, but this wasn't the time for exploring the family tree.

"I'm not going," insisted Yong.

"You're a prisoner here. At least come with me and we'll find a place where you can be safe."

"I'm not a prisoner. I came here for my own safety. My father and his people want to kill me."

One of the helicopters popped over the hill, skimming low over the courtyard and spraying the building with machine-gun fire. The other came in to pick us up. I wasn't inclined to argue with Yong Shin Jong, but as I took a step to grab him and toss him into the helo, he reached beneath his shirt and pulled out a pistol.

A small caliber peashooter, not that size is important.

"I'm not going," said Yong Shin Jong.

"Now listen, Jong. I'm not a big fan of your father's either. But even if you're not a prisoner here, you're not safe. The Chinese will sell you out as soon as the price is right. Come with me and I'll get you to a place where you'll be okay."

"Why should I trust you?"

"I have a friend with me." I pointed up at the helicopter, where Cho Lim was standing in the doorway.

If you've been reading along carefully, gentle reader, you've noticed the averted eyes, sighs, and quickness of breath every time Cho Lim heard Yong Shin Jong's name. More than likely, you're expecting some big Hallmark scene here. Yong Shin Jong will see his erstwhile lover standing in the doorway of the helicopter, drop his weapon, and raise his arms to her. Cho Lim will bend down and scoop him up with one hand—maybe two; she's kind of small—and together they will fly off into the sunset. Meanwhile, I'll jump up on the wall and leap toward the helicopter skids, barely managing to hold on as Polorski—aka Tall, Dark, and Polack—flies us over to the secluded airstrip we carefully staked out, where our fully fueled Embraer EMB-120 is waiting to whisk us away, not to Pyongyang but a small airport in Japan, where there will be leisure for the love birds to enjoy their reunion in bliss—and for me to pump Yong Shin Jong for information about Kim's underground palace.

But neither Yong Shin Jong nor Cho Lim had read this book. Instead of the neat little story arc that I laid out, they went completely off rail, improvising their own plot twist: both took aim at each other and fired, Yong Shin Jong with his small pistol, Cho Lim with her considerably more potent submachine gun.

Cursing in two languages, I dove at Yong Shin Jong. Once again we fell back into the pond. As we did, Cho Lim fell as well. Yong apparently hadn't won his trophies for target shooting just because he was the dictator's bastard son. If the bullet didn't kill her—though it was a small caliber round, it was probably aimed at her head—the fall probably did.

I was too busy trying to get Yong Shin Jong out of the water to figure out exactly what had happened to her. The gunfire at the front of the house had increased—two battalions of Chinese army regulars were now arriving via truck and armored personnel carriers.

We had gone well beyond the SNAFU stage, directly to FUBAR—fucked up beyond all repair.

Trace had heard what was going on over the radio, and after neutralizing the machine gunner on the top floor she came downstairs and out the back. She and the three men with her immediately got into a firefight with two of the motorcycle riders, who'd skipped around into the rock garden after being ambushed by our booby trap and Doc's men.

Out on the road, Shotgun and Mongoose had ambushed the arriving Chinese army, hitting them with flash-bang grenades and then submachine-gun fire as they started to get out of their trucks. Stunned or at least slowed by the grenades, the soldiers were promptly pinned down. But my guys were outnumbered and outgunned—the biggest weapons they had were the MP5s—and at best they could supply only a short diversion.

"It's time to go, Dick!" yelled Trace from the other side of the pond. "Let's go! In the helo!"

A pair of Chinese jets streaked overhead, emphasizing the point.

"I don't have time to argue," I told Yong Shin Jong. "Grab the line from the helicopter and we'll talk about this later."

"No." Yong Shin Jong still had his gun in his hand. He raised it—and pointed at his head. "I'd rather die here than go back to my father."

"We can do it that way if you want," I said.

"No bluff," he said, pushing the gun next to his skull.

I held up my hand, trying to think of something to say that would not only persuade him to come but could be heard over the explosions and gunfire. I've never been good with the touchy-feely stuff, and the best I could do was to tell him we'd work it out. That convinced him so completely he put the gun in his mouth.

"Yong. I'm your friend. Take the gun out of your mouth."

Out front, the Chinese were regrouping for a counterattack. Our forces were split up—Doc and a few of Lo Po's men who'd been watching the perimeter headed toward their designated pickup down the road, while Mongoose and Shotgun came through the house. They ran for the helicopter, which was now so low that I thought I was going to get a haircut any second.

"Dick! Time to go!" yelled Mongoose. "We're the last ones through."

"Chinese are behind us, Dick!" Shotgun sounded happy as he leaped for the chopper's door.

The jets passed overhead again. The boys had sprinkled some booby traps on their way through the house, but the Chinese soldiers were already in the back room.

"It's your call, Jong," I said, sidling toward the helicopter.

He stared at me, the gun still in his mouth. Finally I decided I had no choice. I jumped up and grabbed the chopper skid as it whirled around, trying to duck the approach of another Chinese jet. At the same time, Shotgun started firing his submachine gun from the door of the helo, sending the two soldiers who'd come into the patio back into the house.

Yong Shin Jong threw down his pistol and put up his hands, trying to tell the Chinese not to hurt him.

Finally, I thought, leaping from the chopper. For the third time, I knocked him into the pond. But three was the charm—he was so surprised that he couldn't struggle, and I managed to hook my left arm under his without a problem. Mongoose tossed a rope down from the interior of the helicopter. I grabbed it with my right arm and held on as the helicopter jerked upward. We just barely cleared the wall of the garden—something I was thankful for, as the masonry began splintering from rifle fire. But my arm felt like it was about to fall off.

"Pull us up, pull us up!" I yelled, but as the rope began edging upward, the helicopter pitched sharply on its side. Yong Shin Jong and I spun so violently I lost my grip. We fell into the low brush outside the compound's double fence. Head spinning, I grabbed my reluctant rescuee and dragged him with me down the hill toward the road. The helo circled, ducking another pass by the fighter jets, then came back, dropping until its wheels were practically on the pavement. I pushed Yong Shin Jong into the belly of the aircraft and dove in behind him as the chopper took off. Mongoose grabbed my shirt as we pitched once again; if not for that I would have rolled out onto the ground.

"I thought you knew how to fly helicopters!" I yelled into the cockpit.

Polorski was too busy cursing to answer. The Chinese jets were Shenyang J-7s—rebranded MiG-21s, not state of the art, but more than enough to take down our Aerospatiale Cougar.

The Chinese pilots were flashing by us, but not firing, maybe because they realized that we had Yong Shin Jong, or maybe because they knew China is a really big country and there was no way the helicopter could fly far enough to get away.

"Take us to the backup site," I told Polorski. "Don't go to the airport."

"Yeah, that's a good idea. Hang on."

"Hang on" apparently was Polish for "now I'm going to pull some really harsh maneuvers." He jerked the nose of the helicopter straight up and twisted the craft around, changing direction as the fighter came on. I can't say how successful he was at ducking them because I flew into the back of the bird, bouncing against Mongoose and landing on Yong Shin Jong. I managed to get back upright and pulled Korea's prodigal son to his feet, sitting him in the bench seat at the side of chopper cabin.

"What is going on?" he demanded.

"That's what I'm trying to figure out," I told him. "Are you a guest of the Chinese, or a prisoner?"

"Guest."

"Then why are they trying to shoot you down?"

He didn't have much of an answer for that.

"Why did you shoot Cho Lim?" I asked.

"Cho Lim bad news. Very bad news," said Yong Shin Jong.

"She wasn't your girlfriend?"

"Ancient history."

Another hard turn and spin sent me sprawling back against the seat. I have to admit, Polorski was an accomplished helicopter pilot. His maneuvers at treetop level had been enough to get us out of the sights of the fighter jets, and we were so low that neither their radars nor the local air traffic radars could see us. He sped along a rail line to our backup rendezvous point, a small garage south of Botu. Meanwhile, I tried questioning Yong Shin Jong again. But he answered my questions with one of his own:

"Did Sun send you?"

"You mean General Sun?"

That was all I said, but apparently it was enough for Yong Shin Jong, who smiled wryly and folded his arms, signaling he wouldn't be talking anymore. I decided I'd have plenty of time to change his mind under better circumstances later on; I got him a blanket to dry off with, then found one for myself.

I was lucky just to be wet. Two of Lo Po's men had been injured, one with a busted arm and the other with bullet wounds to his thigh and buttocks. Trace bandaged them up as best she could. The one with the bullet wounds had lost a good deal of blood and was light-headed, but his injuries didn't seem life threatening.

We landed in an empty field about ten minutes later, rendezvousing with Lo Po's helicopter, which was also just setting down. We'd parked a bus near the road. As far as I could tell, the jets had lost us somewhere to the north. I told Mongoose and Shotgun to go and watch the road while we loaded the wounded into the bus, then "volunteered" two of Lo Po's men to help me with the wounded and Yong Shin Jong. In the cockpit, Polorski was telling Trace to go with us while he got rid of the helicopter.

"What do you mean?" she said. "We're leaving the chopper. Come on."

"I'm afraid I can't."

Trace sensed he wasn't worried about losing his deposit when he pulled his pistol.

"What the hell is going on?" she said.

"Out, darlin'," snarled the Polack. "And don't try anything or I'll shoot you."

Trace was in a state of shock, but I doubt she would have left the helicopter voluntarily, even with the gun pointed at her. The door opened behind her and two arms reached in to pull her out. Trace, still stunned, began to fight back, but found her face filled with tear gas.

I was all choked up myself. Six men in black coveralls and gas masks had emerged from the garage on the other side of the field after we landed, firing the gas point-blank at and into the chopper. Instinctually, I tried to cover my face, then I realized that was the wrong thing to do.

But it was too late. One of the men had already grabbed Yong Shin Jong from my grip and thrown him to the back of the helicopter. Before I could turn around, the helo was airborne.

PART TWO

DEEPER & DEEPER

"We are opposed to the line of compromise with imperialism. At the same time, we cannot tolerate the practice of only shouting against imperialism, but in actual fact, being afraid to fight it."

—Kim Il Sung

5

[1]

Yong Shin Jong, Polorski, and the six ninjas were all gone. Tears streaming from my eyes, I yelled at Shotgun and Mongoose to shoot the damn helo down. Then I ran toward the other helicopter, hoping to go after them.

By the time Mongoose and Shotgun realized what was going on, Polorski had put two hundred yards between them and the helicopter. Just as Shotgun raised his gun to fire, the helo started banking back in his direction. He couldn't believe his good luck and started emptying his magazine at it.

Mongoose grabbed his friend's shirt and pulled him down just in time to avoid the RPG round that flew from the door of the helicopter. The rocket-propelled grenade exploded close enough to shower them with dirt, though fortunately far enough away not to hurt them.

I had just about reached the other helo when a second RPG round flew from Polorski's craft and struck the tail. At first, it looked as if the grenade had only passed through the metal and not exploded. Then there was a burst of light and the tail flew to the ground, the rotor still spinning. Lo Po, who'd been securing the cockpit, dove out headfirst, rolling on the ground as the grenade sparked a fire. Two of his employees, the last men in the chopper, jumped out as well. One of the men's pant legs was on fire, but he patted it out before it spread to the rest of his clothes.

Miraculously, Polorski's ambush hadn't cost us any serious injuries. What really hurt my pride was the fact that I had not seen this coming. I should have known better than to trust a dumb Polack. As a crazy-ass Slovak myself, I should have learned that long before.

But if I was mad, imagine what Trace Dahlgren felt. Her rage went beyond volcanic. Beyond nuclear. Beyond supernova.

"I am going to kill that motherfucker with my bare hands," she said softly when I caught up to her in the field.

And that was *all* she said on the subject, which is what really worried me. (Remember her artful performance on a SEAL turncoat in *Vengeance*? Imagine something worse . . .)

"Into the bus, into the bus," I told her.

"We can't let him go."

For the moment, though, we had to. I tugged Trace with me toward the bus. I've pissed off a lot of women in my life, but I've never seen one as angry as Trace was. The only sign of it, though, was in her eyes—they looked as if they could burn a hole through granite.

Despite the fact that he had caught a good dose of tear gas himself, Doc had taken the wheel of the bus. Not necessarily the best driver under good circumstances, Doc is even worse when he's having trouble seeing. We careened through the dust as he found the hard-packed road, bouncing through the ruts and scraping the stone fences on either side as we went. Lo Po stood up next to him, providing directions via his GPS device. We were about ten miles from the airport, but the roads we'd mapped out were narrow and mostly dirt, so it was going to be a long drive.

The jet that had harassed us earlier took another pass but seemed to lose interest. Doc's driving got progressively better as we went; finally we hit a macadam roadway.

"Two miles, straight on," said Lo Po.

Doc ground the gears and began to accelerate. I started to relax, thinking of how we might track Polorski, when I heard the sound of a jet streaking nearby.

Awful close, I thought.

"Watch out!" yelled Lo Po as the fighter appeared in front of us.

Whatever constraints he'd been under earlier not to use his weapons apparently no longer applied—he lit his cannon. The bullets tore through the road alongside us.

"Enough of this bullshit!" yelled Shotgun, jumping up from his seat.

He ran to the front of the bus, pushed open the door, and held his submachine gun up toward the sky. Doc swerved sharply as the plane came into view for another pass. Shotgun nearly flew out into the road but Mongoose, who'd trailed him to the front, leaped over the forward passenger rail and caught him, clinging to the restraining pole with his foot. Shotgun began firing, emptying a mag and slamming another in while halfway out of the bus.

You know and I know that Shotgun's gunfire was a wasted gesture; those 9mm bullets had about as much chance of hitting the plane as spit, and probably wouldn't have done much more damage. It's likely the pilot never even saw Shotgun firing at him. But I'll be damned if the plane didn't turn off and not come back.

Mongoose pulled Shotgun back into the bus, cursing at him for being a fool. Shotgun got a shit-eating grin on his face and asked for more bullets.

"Here we go again!" yelled Trace from the back of the bus as another plane came up from the rear, guns blazing. Doc pushed the bus right, out of the path of the bullets, but into a huge ditch, where we stalled out. The airport was a few hundred yards away.

"Out, everybody out!" I yelled. "Run for the plane!"

Pushing out through the doors and windows, we spread out across the field and sprinted in the direction of the airstrip. The ground had recently been plowed and fertilized; the fresh dung gave a sweet fragrance to the proceedings, mixing deliciously with the scent of burning gasoline and metal as the Chinese pilot doused the bus with more bullets. A red and black fireball shot upward, exploding with a pronounced crack.

They say there's a silver lining inside of every dark cloud. I've never been able to verify that myself, but this dark cloud was definitely an asset—the smoke made it hard for the J-7's pilot to aim his guns on the next pass. He fired anyway, which had a laudatory effect on our stragglers, the bullets just close enough to convince even Doc that the quarter mile was a sprint, not a jog.

The Embraer EMB-120 was owned by a friend of mine named Buzz Sawyer, who used to be a pilot for Air America—the CIA's favorite airline. Now based in Thailand, Buzz is an old hand at sticky situations, not to mention ducking J-7s. He'd apparently kicked his engines off as soon as he saw the Chinese fighters in the air, and was now idling at the end of the runway, impatiently waiting for us.

Not exactly idle. Buzz was hard at work, using his cell phone to set off a series of smoke grenades he had wired around the airport. They shrouded us in a fog thicker than the pea soup you can get at my local diner. This confused the Chinese pilot who was shooting at us, but it also made it harder to see the plane. I finally found it by running toward the turboprop's whine, stopping just before the engine's blades would have sliced me into chop suey.

"This way, this way," I yelled, ushering the troops toward the aircraft. I counted as they hustled in; Buzz was straining at the brakes when I realized we were one short.

Trace.

"Pilot says we gotta go!" yelled Mongoose as I leaned out the door, looking for her in the haze. "There are more fighters on the way."

No way I was leaving Trace. "Go without me," I told him. "I'll catch up."

"Dick!"

"Go. That's an order, asshole," I told him, adding several other terms of endearment to make sure he knew I was serious as I jumped.

The plane was already rolling forward. The fact that he couldn't see anything on the ground didn't stop the F-7 from firing anyway. The Chinese fighter pilot missed the Embraer by a good margin, but his bullets were close enough to me to send a hail of rock and asphalt against my back.

I was worried that Trace had decided to stay behind and somehow track Polorski to get revenge. It would have been understandable, though not particularly bright. In fact, she had simply tripped and become disoriented in the smoke. Finally recovering, she raced forward, going fast enough to bowl me over in the man-made fog. I landed on my back near the edge of the runway. The smoke cleared, and I had a perfect view of the airplane as it left the ground.

"Now what?" asked Trace.

"Looks like we'll have to pay your bill at the Regis after all," I told her.

(11)

Let's tie up a thread before it gets lost instead of loose . . .

The F-7 pursued the Embraer, trying to stay with it as it jinked hard to the south. The Chinese fighter pilot had spent most of his bullets and a good part of his fuel already, and had to turn away within five minutes. By the time reinforcements arrived, Buzz had pointed the airplane southwest and was flying at low altitude and top speed toward the water. With the Embraer off their radars because it was so low, the new fighters set up a time-consuming standard search pattern. They never did find the Embraer.

Buzz ran into trouble near the coast, though. By that time he'd climbed to a more reasonable altitude, trying to sneak into the Yellow Sea as a "real" passenger plane. Queried by a pair of Chinese air force Su-27s on patrol, Buzz's story began to fall apart with his lousy Chinese—he had a great vocabulary, but unfortunately his accent strayed closer to Brooklyn than Beijing when he got excited, and being in the bull's-eye of two Su-27s tends to make even the calmest pilot's heart race.

Especially when they fire heat-seeking missiles at you.

Buzz's business often brought him interesting assignments, and he was prepared for all possibilities. His Embraer was equipped with a variety of warning systems. It also had decoy flares and a laser detonating system to ward off IR missiles. He fired the flares, then pushed the plane hard to the right, hoping the decoys would suck the missiles away. That didn't work—these must have been the latest Russian Vempel heat-seekers—and Buzz quickly hit the lasers. By the time the missiles exploded, they were so close that they peppered the aircraft with shrapnel. The blast pushed the plane downward; Doc swore later that he could have grabbed a fish if he hadn't had his eyes closed.

Buzz pulled back on the stick and leveled off about five inches above the waves, give or take a spritz. Odds are, he and everyone aboard the plane would have been toast, except for the timely arrival of a flight of American F/A-18 Super Hornets, which just *happened* to be on a routine training mission in the northern China Sea off Korea.

We all know there's no such thing as a coincidence—Jimmy Zim had arranged for the flights and told me about them before I left Japan. But there was *one* coincidence, or at least a convenience—the carrier was the *Ronald Reagan*, and among its crew was a chief petty officer who'd had the misfortune of serving under yours truly when he was still young and virginal. I ruined him for life, and he's been grateful ever since, as have the aviators whom he trusts with his aircraft. I'd sent him an e-mail from Tokyo to make sure his planes were in top shape, and while I'm sure the pilots would have done a good job in any event, knowing we had a personal connection to the Hornet drivers helped Doc breathe a little easier.

While the Embraer flew south, Trace and I were making our way north to Beijing.

We smelled like all hell, thanks to our roll in the freshly manured fields, and our first order of business was to get cleaned up and changed. We found fresh clothes for Trace neatly displayed on a peasant's clothesline about two miles to the north. Trace pinned some yuan notes in their place, then took them over to a nearby pond, where after making me promise not to peek, she stripped down and took a bath.

Of course I peeked. Who keeps a promise like that?

I washed the makeup off my face but didn't have anything strong enough to remove the dye from my beard and hair. I dunked my head in anyway, and was doing my best to wash out the white when something bumped up against my hand, then slipped up my forearm, tickling me. I thought it was Trace, getting back at me for looking at her, so I grabbed it. As I pulled it out of the water, I realized it was too light and small to be attached to her. I opened my eyes and looked into the slimy green slits of a water snake.

I hurled it across the pond without thinking. A second later, I heard a shriek. Trace ran out of the water, grabbing for her clothes.

"What happened?" I asked, knowing that if I didn't play dumb my life would be in danger.

"Snake," she said.

"You're not afraid of snakes, are you?"

"The human kind I can handle," she said. Then she blushed, and turned around to get dressed.

Finding something that would fit was a bit harder for me than it had been for Trace, and it wasn't until very late afternoon that we were able to find some clothes at a small market in a village about ten miles northeast of the airfield. I had only a few yuan on me, but the proprietor's inclination to haggle was overpowered by my scent and a deal was quickly struck.

Our next problem was to get to Beijing. Between us we knew maybe a dozen words, none of them repeatable in polite company. We had a few yuan and might have tried puzzling out the arrangements for a bus, but we didn't see one. Bicycles, on the other hand, were in good supply, especially in the village, where people left them without locks. But when I started toward two I saw leaning up against the side of a building, Trace immediately objected.

"We can't steal their bikes. That's probably all they have."

"We're not stealing," I told her. "We're borrowing."

I got the Apache death stare in response.

"We'll send them back when we're done," I told her.

"How?"

"We'll use Western Union or something. UPS them. I don't know."

Trace gave me another stare, though this was less mortal. Her standards for fairness have become higher since she agreed to become a kind of godmother for a young girl in her Chihauhua Apache tribe, but it was obvious that we had to get to the city.

"How are you going to remember their address?" she asked.

Easy solution—just grab the nameplate next to the door. That done, we took the bikes and set out. Once we found a highway, figuring out the direction to Beijing was easy. Even before we saw the English language sign, we knew all we had to do was head for the smog and we'd get there.

There was no way of knowing how much of an alert the people guarding Yong Shin Jong had put out because of our picnic there. While I'd initially thought we would simply return to Trace's hotel, as I pedaled north, the more I thought better of the idea. The hotel wasn't exactly low-key. It would be better to stay in a smaller place, one not likely to host foreigners, and even less likely to ask questions. Fortunately Beijing, like all large cities, has plenty.

I suppose we could have gone directly to the U.S. Embassy and asked them to call Jimmy Zim for us, but that would have meant dealing with the officious State Department bureaucrats, and made me more beholden to Fogglebottom than I really cared to be. Besides, when faced with a choice of dealing with faceless bureaucrats or risking life and limb by weaseling past the Red Army, I'll take the Chinese every time.

Discretion is generally paid for in cash. With dusk falling as we arrived at the city, we headed for the Red Cell International version of an ATM—a hidden stash of cash, IDs, and bank cards secreted in a drop at the Lugou Qiao bridge. Known to us round eyes as the Marco Polo Bridge, it's located about ten miles from the center of town, on the southwestern side of the city. If you've ever been to Beijing, you've probably been over the bridge. The Lugou Qiao crosses the Yongding River—or the marshy field of grass the river turns into when it isn't flooding.

Forget the reference to Marco Polo that foreigners are fed. The bridge has a much more interesting, and tragic, history. Its eleven stone arches were built in the late seventeenth century and have withstood countless floods, revolutions, and wars. In 1937, the bridge was the scene of a battle between local troops and Japanese soldiers looking for a pretext to invade Beijing.

(Since they'd already taken over a good hunk of the country north of the city, they didn't need much of a pretext. Nevertheless they came up with one, saying they wanted to search for a deserter in a Beijing whorehouse.) The Chinese forces won the first battle for the bridge, but within a few days were overwhelmed; all of north China was soon in Japanese hands. The Japanese were not gracious in victory.

The bridge is made out of granite—something you may not realize because of the grime. It's guarded by stone lions, who are reputed to come to life at night. I hoped the legend wasn't true—our money was hidden under the paw of one of them.

The bridge is primarily a tourist attraction these days, and in the early evening there weren't many people around to ask us just what the hell we were doing. On the other hand, there wasn't much light, either. The lions are heavy—five or six hundred pounds, I'd guess, and most are carved or otherwise attached right into the posts of the walls. But number sixteen, counting from the western end, had a loose paw, and that's where the envelope with our money was.

Or so Doc said. The paw wouldn't budge when I pushed at it.

I went across to the other side, and checked that lion. But it seemed even more reluctant to move than the first.

"Maybe he counted from the east side," said Trace.

I was just about to send her to check when I realized that I had counted the creature at the start of the bridge, which was more elephant than lion. Before I could get to the beast in question, a group of kids swarmed over me, jabbering in Chinese. I tried to put them off by saying I was a tourist and only spoke English. That didn't even slow them down—they quickly switched to English, speaking better than most dishwashers and lawn guys back home.

"Hey, mister, you take picture with us. You be famous."

"Good for vacation, mister."

"You Number One Tourist, Joe. Give us five dollars."

"Listen, kids," said Trace loudly. "See that guy at the far end of the bridge? That guy owns a candy factory, and he's looking for some kids to test new candies. Tell him George sent you. I'm sure he'll hire you."

They were off in two seconds. The money, cards, and ID were under the paw, as promised. We grabbed a cab and went into town, where we bought some Western clothes. Then we went prowling outside the tourist area, looking for hotels. What we saw wasn't very appetizing—the better-looking places were brothels, and even they looked like they were crawling with cockroaches, insects as well as humans.

"Instead of hanging around town for the night, maybe we can catch a flight," said Trace finally. "It's still early. If they're looking for anyone, it'll be Yong Shin Jong and an ancient Chinese veterinarian, not you and me."

She had a point, and after a further survey of the seamier side of town, we made our way to a better section and grabbed a cab. Our false IDs had open tickets on Japan Airlines; we booked into a flight leaving for Tokyo in less than three hours.

After passing through the customs check—you have to smile to leave China—a stone-faced official appeared and waved us off the moving sidewalk.

"Doesn't look like he's directing traffic," whispered Trace.

"Yes."

"Should we run?"

"Nowhere to go."

"Bullshit then?"

"Absolutely."

The man walked over to us.

"You," he said, pointing at me. "Where is your passport?"

Two equally unsmiling men with submachine guns came over and stood behind him. I handed over my passport. He held it up close to my face, then pulled it back.

"Good forgery," he said.

"Think so?"

"Your name is not Harold Bishop."

"Most people call me Harry."

"I would say you are Richard Marcinko."

"Really? Richard Marcinko? Who's he?"

The man pulled a well-thumbed copy of *Red Cell* from his pocket, holding up the cover near my face as he had the passport. I wouldn't have minded so much if it hadn't been a cheap bootleg Chinese edition—no royalties.

"You got me," I told him.

"You sign for me?" asked the man.

"I need a pen."

He produced one, then told me how to draw his name in Chinese characters. Five minutes later, we were in the line at the departure gate.

It pays to have fans all across the world. A few fifty-dollar bills, American, tucked into the signature page of a personalized book don't hurt either.

[III]

Yong Shin Jong said the Chinese were protecting him," I told Fogglebottom when I arrived at our embassy in Tokyo the next day. "Why didn't your people know that?"

"The CIA is not 'my people,'" said Fogglebottom, looking over at Jimmy Zim, the CIA officer.

"I said it was a possibility," said Jimmy Zim.

"Who is Polorski working for?" I asked. "You?"

Jimmy Zim frowned. I frowned back.

"Polorski does not work for the CIA," said Jimmy Zim. "You should have checked his background."

If he'd been an employee, we certainly would have done an extensive check. But I didn't hire him blind either: before Trace started taking lessons from him, we had a friend in the FBI investigate his background. He was Polish, and in America legally. Interpol had nothing on him, and a contact in the Polish military confirmed that he had the equivalent of an honorable discharge.

That was a fair amount of checking for someone who was just teaching a friend to fly helicopters. The mistake had been trusting him beyond that.

"What is his real background?" I asked Zim.

"Maybe we should get a drink," Jimmy Zim suggested. It was the first intelligent thing he'd said since we met.

We didn't leave the embassy, just the floor. The ambassador had a private study, which the deputy ambassador was glad to make available after Jimmy Zim explained the situation to the CIA's chief of station. Fogglebottom was invited to find something else to do, an invitation he accepted with a frown. Zim and I settled into a pair of thickly padded leather chairs, the CIA officer with a Scotch, me with a double dose of Bombay Sapphire.

According to Jimmy Zim, Polorski was a member of a particularly nasty strain of the Russian mafiya—not that there are any strains that go around buying Barney dolls for your kids. The group included former Russian paratroopers, some special ops guys, and mixed in Georgians and Poles, an unusual feature that indicated its size. Organized along business as well as military lines, the group specialized in selling banned weapons and other items to African and Middle Eastern countries. There had apparently been contact between Pyongyang and members of the enterprise some months before.

"We think it's possible they've worked out a deal to trade Yong Shin Jong's life for one of Korea's nukes," said Jimmy Zim.

"Hmmmph," I said, sipping my drink. Zim claimed to have dug out the background in the past few hours, since hearing from me and Fogglebottom what had happened. But I had my own suspicions. One of them was that Polorski had come to America specifically with the idea of infiltrating my organization somehow. He might have tried getting into Yong Shin Jong's compound himself, then decided to let Dick do it, convincing Sun or even Kim Jong Il to hire me as bird dog.

The alternative was that he'd come over without any plan and just lucked into a jackpot. But I didn't believe in that much luck.

The real question was how much the CIA had known about Polorski beforehand. Zim hemmed and hawed when I asked, giving me some bullshit about late translations on intercepts, too many foreigners to track, human error—all the usual crap you hear from the Christians in Action when they're not playing straight with you, which is eighty percent of the time. Given the CIA's track record, it's entirely possible he was telling the truth—that they had had no idea who Polorski was until he screwed me. But it was certainly a question I'd've liked to ask my good friend Admiral Jones.

"We want the nuclear weapon that Polorski's going to trade for Yong Shin Jong," said Jimmy Zim. "If that's what they're up to."

"That's nice."

"Can we count on your help for this?"

"I wouldn't," I told him, putting my drink down and walking from the room.

(IV)

I wasn't walking into the sunset, or giving up on finding Yong Shin Jong. No way that was going to happen, if only because Trace was sure to want to observe the quaint Apache custom of castrating her lying lover, tying him to an anthill in the middle of the desert, and pouring honey on him while the buzzards circled above. She'd follow Tall, Dark, and Dogmeat to the ends of the earth if she had to, and frankly, so would I. But for the moment I didn't see any point in working too closely with Jimmy Zim. Not only didn't I trust him, I didn't like him. In fact, I was in a pretty pissed off mood at everybody, including Disney, whose outrageous admission prices to their Tokyo Park put a major dent in my operating budget when I arranged to meet my Russian friend Ivan[15] there.

Ivan is a member of the Russian FSB—that's the *Federal'naya Sluzhba Bezopasnosti*, the foreign spy service once known as the KGB. He's "covered" in Tokyo as a diplomat, a pretense that fools absolutely no one. He and I have had our various encounters over the years, and while I trust him as far as I can sneeze, he's an impeccable source of information about the Russian mafiya, a subject that he will discourse on for hours if he's in a good mood. And the best way to put Ivan in a good mood is to take him to Disney World.

There's probably something Freudian about his attraction to Mickey Mouse, but I've never analyzed it too carefully. When I met him on line to the Jolly Trolley, he was grinning from ear to ear—Goofy had just waved at him. I did my best to feign interest in animated characters and amusement rides, while gradually working the conversation around to Ike Polorski. Ivan recognized the name immediately—you could see the flicker in his eyes—but we boxed around for another half hour or so, riding the Jolly Trolley twice and even visiting Minnie's House, before

---

[15] Ivan is a pseudonym. I hope to have use for him in the future.

he finally admitted that the FSB had listed him as a "person of interest" within the past two months. This apparently translated as someone they would shoot first and interrogate later. Polorski had sold weapons to a Chechen group that had subsequently used them to blow up a school full of children in southern Russia.

"Very nasty human being," said Ivan. "Horrible man. Do not trust."

What a surprise. Usually you find Girl Scouts in his line of work.

"I put you in touch with Colonel Setrovich, antimafiya force," said Ivan.

"He likes Disney, too?"

Ivan frowned, then shook his head.

"Can I trust this colonel?"

Another frown.

"If your interests are similar, you may work in parallel," said Ivan. "But trust—that is something I would be surprised to find anywhere in Russia these days."

While I was having fun in Tokyo, Doc and the others were resting up and getting their bearings in South Korea. After escaping the Chinese fighters, they had landed near Kunsan on the coast. After hearing that we were OK, Doc and Lo Po started working on tracing Polorski. But even with the help of our navy connections and Lo Po's friends in the Chinese military, the chopper's course and whereabouts remained a mystery. The U.S. uses a number of "platforms" to keep track of traffic in and out of North Korea via China, and at least according to everyone Doc spoke to, no helicopter or unscheduled truck traffic had made the crossing.

"He could have slipped into one of the food convoys," said Doc. "He's had plenty of time."

"Maybe. But if they're setting up some sort of swap, I doubt he'd trust Kim or Sun well enough to simply go over the border like that. He'd have a more elaborate plan."

I told Doc to see about tickling some of our South Korean friends and to keep working the phones. In the meantime, Lo Po and his people were returning to Shanghai, where he had other pressing business. I thanked him with the usual terms of endearment, as well as a promise to return the many favors I owed him as soon as possible.

"Remember old Chinese saying, Dick."

"What's that, Lo Po?"

"Payback is a bitch."

Back home, Karen was doing a fine job of handling Red Cell's business, with a little help from Danny Barrett, my vice president in charge of kicking ass. Matthew Loring had determined that the computer e-mails we'd been bombarded with had been the result of an e-mail advertising campaign gone bad. The owners of the Chinese restaurant responsible for the campaign had pretended not to speak English when he called to ask them to do something about it, so he'd written a reverse computer virus that would attack the sender's servers and stop the attack.

And in his spare time, he'd tracked down some more of Yong Shin Jong's accounts—including two with hedge funds in Singapore that were not recorded in his name.

"Large accounts," said Karen. "Fifty million dollars apiece. They were opened about four months ago, and haven't been accessed since."

That gave Kim Jong Il one hundred million reasons to call his bastard a bastard.

It turned out that I had met Russian FSB Colonel Setrovich about a year and a half before, when I had traveled to St. Petersburg for a conference on international tourism. He'd been with a group of FSB officers who had tried to convince me that vodka was superior to gin; it was a losing battle, but they fought a good fight.

"I think I may still have that hangover," he confessed when I finally reached him. "But, enough fun. I understand you are interested in Ike Polorski."

"Very interested in him," I said.

"He is man I would personally like to cut open his stomach, pull out his liver, and force it down his throat," said the colonel. "I have real love for him."

Colonel Setrovich was busy trying to squeeze information from some former mafiya associates who were living in semi-exile in the cold Russian northeast. But he would be back in his office in Khabarousk, a city about a thousand miles from Tokyo, the next day, and suggested we meet there around five.

"We may be able to find this Polorski," said Setrovich. "Or his friends. We show him Rogue Warrior–style love, yes?"

"Sounds good to me."

"And then we will renew our debate," he said. "Vodka better than gin. You see."

As soon as he hung up, I dialed Karen.

"How do I get ahold of Matthew Loring?" I asked. "And how good do you think his Russian is?"

Matthew's Russian was nonexistent, but he was fluent in the language that counted: computerese. Colonel Setrovich might or might not be forthcoming when we met, but I figured his computer would be. The plan was simple—while the colonel and I traded drinking songs, Trace and Matthew would sneak into his office, fire up the computer, and see what they could find.

Ordinarily, I would have expected Trace to give Matthew a hard time. It wouldn't have been anything personal—she always puts newbies to the test. But something about Loring elicited her maternal instincts as soon as she saw him.

Maybe it was the fact that his suitcase looked to weigh more than he did.

"We gotta get Junior something to eat," she said after we spotted him coming out of the international arrivals area at Tokyo Narita Airport. "He's going to blow away in the wind."

Matthew was thin, though at six-four I wouldn't call him

small. He had a good frame, with wide shoulders and long lean legs; his problem was that he had no meat on his bones. Karen had e-mailed me a picture of him that made him look as if he were in middle school. In real life, he looked even younger. He had round cheeks, huge eyes, and peach fuzz. The background check Karen had done confirmed that he'd graduated college, but if it wasn't for his height I would have thought he was just entering his teens.

He spotted me and Trace across the hall and stopped. He blinked those owl eyes of his twice, then opened his mouth without saying anything for a minute. Finally, he managed to blurt, "Mr. Marcinko? Sir?"

"Call me Dick, kid."

"Yes, sir, Mr. Marcinko."

"Oh, that's cute," said Trace. She took his bag. "Come on, Junior. Let's get something to eat."

"Um, I'm not really hungry, Ms. Dahlgren. It's, um, a pleasure to meet you."

Trace grabbed his wrist and dragged him to the nearest noodle shop. She forced two full helpings down his throat—think mother bird feeding a baby—before we had to take off for the plane to eastern Russia.

The flight to Khabarousk (also spelled Kharovsk) took about three hours, counting the time we spent circling the city while the pilot looked for coins to throw into the parking meter at the airfield. During the Cold War, Khabarousk was the headquarters of the Soviet Union's Far Eastern Military Command, which made it a pretty happening place if you liked thick woolens and surface-to-air missiles. Now it's even more important as a gateway between China, Russia, and the rest of the world. Japanese and Korean businessmen have invested billions here over the past decade or so, and though the airport remains pretty primitive, the city bears Asia's most obvious sign of prosperity: it's perpetually covered by a thick haze of smog.

If you hold your breath long enough, Khabarousk can be

almost pleasant. The basic Cold War architecture of gray concrete has been supplemented by older and newer buildings with actual bricks; the main streets in the city center are lined with parks and very wide sidewalks. The sidewalks have to be wide to accommodate the foot traffic; many of the residents can't afford the inflated bus fare to get to work.

We found a hotel, swept the rooms for bugs—there were none—then mustered for a quick reconnoiter of the area. Colonel Setrovich's office was in a six-story 1950s-style cement-sided building a few blocks from the geographic center of town. A fat babushka sat at a desk in the lobby; the doors beyond her were keyed to open with swipe cards. We watched the place long enough to discover that the local employees' watering hole of choice was across the street, two blocks down.

"Come with me, Junior," Trace told Matthew Loring as the clock wound its way to five. "Let's go get a drink."

"I, um, I don't drink."

"Drinking is a job requirement in this company, Junior," she told him. "The sooner you learn, the better."

"American Bear! You are here!"

Colonel Setrovich's voice could have been heard over a sonic boom as I entered his office. I extended my arm; he grabbed me in a hug.

"You son of a bitch, yes?" said Setrovich.

"The biggest."

"You outdrink me last time. Not now. I have practiced." Setrovich patted his belly, as if its rotund shape was proof. "Come. We have dinner. You pick up tab."

He thought this was the funniest joke in the world, and laughed all the way down the back stairs to the parking lot.

Colonel Setrovich's black Lada looked about ten years old; the rear quarter panels were dimpled with rust and flaking paint that didn't quite match the original. Setrovich had to jiggle the key a bit to get it to start. When it did, the engine gave a double hiccup that shook the car as if we were experiencing a 5.3 earthquake. The shake disappeared until the vehicle warmed up, then came like clockwork every forty-five seconds.

Setrovich took me to what looked like a small house about two kilometers out of town. The place turned out to be a restaurant with two medium-sized dining rooms at the front and some smaller ones farther back. The colonel was apparently well known there; the woman who met us at the door simply nodded when we came in, then walked us silently through a zigzagging corridor to a room at the far back. It looked almost like a private study, with thick upholstered chairs and a table off to the side. Setrovich walked to the table, took off the sports coat he was wearing, and rolled up his shirtsleeve.

"Well?" he asked, putting his arm down in wrestling position.

"Loser pays," I told him, rolling up my sleeve.

"You already pay," he said.

"Double or nothing. I win, you pay. You win, I pay you and get the drinks."

"Dah!"

Setrovich's forearm was larger than a bull's thigh. I put my elbow down, looked toward the door, and caught Colonel Setrovich off balance with a posting toproll.

"You cheat!" he exclaimed.

I shrugged. "Best two out of three?"

"Dah. We go again."

Colonel Setrovich put down his arm. Now on his guard, he tested me gingerly; as soon as I started to push, he pushed back. I let him get some pressure on me for a few seconds, then started to press back. I could have taken him from there, but then I would never have gotten any information from him—I let him beat me back, then gave up with a bit of a flourish.

Setrovich grinned. His face was beet red.

"Let's leave it there," I suggested. "I'll pay for drinks."

"You very good man, American Bear," he said, slapping me on the back.

Several vodkas later—vodka was all they served—Colonel Setrovich got around to telling me what he knew about Ike Polorski. Polorski's military background was admirable—his paratrooper unit had been an elite within the elite, with every member trained to handle weapons ranging from knives to helicopter gunships. He had gone on to lead a special squad of soldiers dedicated to improving security at Polish facilities—now who does that remind you of?

They even stole a submarine.

Or tried to.

"That trick got him kicked out of the service," said Setrovich. The submarine was the *Orzel*, a Russian Kilo-class boat and the most advanced ship in the Polish navy. The admiral in charge of the fleet was ready to retire, and the embarrassment over the issue meant he couldn't be promoted before his retirement, which cost him much money. "Admiral very angry. He talked to people, called in favors. Polorski was . . ."

Setrovich ran his finger across his throat. I suddenly felt a lot of sympathy for Polorski—our military experiences had a number of parallels. But our career paths differed once we left the service. He moved to Russia, where he joined up with some former friends and went to work with or for—Setrovich wasn't sure which—the mafiya. At first, they had merely smuggled stolen prescription drugs from the West into Russia. But as the years went on, they had dabbled in art theft and counterfeiting. Then Polorski and friends had put their military backgrounds to better use. They began stealing weapons from Russian army bases and selling them in places like Somalia. I say stealing because Setrovich did, but it's more likely that they simply paid off starving members of the chronically underpaid Russian military to give them surplus weapons, a popular pastime in the mid and late 1990s. Their customer list grew quickly, eventually expanding to include the Chechen rebels who murdered the schoolchildren.

That incident had brought Polorski's gang notoriety, but it was small potato peelings as far as Polorski was concerned. The gang was now selling to African and Middle Eastern governments, and had made at least one attempt to steal a nuclear weapon out of a Russian arsenal. Setrovich didn't say exactly where, but from his description it was probably from the air base at Belaja, where the air force keeps a stockpile of nukes just in case the day comes when they find enough spare parts to get their Backfire bombers back in action.

"Very dangerous man," concluded Setrovich. "Here, have more vodka."

[V]

While the colonel and I were trading drinks, Trace was working her way through the crowd at a bar across the street from Setrovich's office, fishing for ID cards. It was a bump and grab routine—she bumped up against someone, then gently grabbed the key card clipped to their shirt or belt. She had already gotten three cards—it never hurt to have a spare—and was on her way back toward Matthew when a big, grouchy Russian got in her way.

"Let's dance, then fuck," said the Russian.

The only thing that saved him from being kneecapped was the fact that he was speaking Russian, and Trace didn't understand. She squinted at him, wondering if he had seen her lift the IDs.

"We'll dance," said the lug, reaching for her hand.

Had he succeeded in actually touching Trace's hand, it's more than likely that he would have found himself breaking the sound barrier along with the plate-glass window at the front of the place. But luckily for him Matthew had seen him approach and was already creating a diversion. Swinging his hand wildly as a waitress passed, he overturned her tray of glasses and vodka. The crash got everyone's attention—Russians hate to see good vodka go to waste. Realizing that hitting the idiot in front of her might complicate the mission, Trace took the opportunity to slip away, ducking into the crowd and then out the door, with Junior close behind.

Trace planned to use the magnetic strip on the cards to gain access to the building; once inside, they'd simply act as if they belonged, a time-honored and surprisingly effective technique. But as they crossed the street, she spotted a three-man cleaning crew unloading their gear from a van at the side of the building. She and Matthew followed them through a rear door, watching as they opened up a closet just off the back staircase and filled their wash buckets. After the janitors then took off on their respective assignments, Trace led the way to the closet, which was generously supplied with extra uniforms as well as more cleaning apparatus. The only complication came in the person of Mr. Murphy, who happened to be lurking down the hall. Just as Trace and Matthew were zipping up their blue jumpsuits, a foul-mouthed, cigar-puffing shift supervisor appeared and began yelling at them in Russian.

Matthew put his head down and slunk out the doorway. Trace started to follow, but the supervisor barred her way. He said something she didn't understand, but his leer made his meaning obvious enough. He blew a cloud of cigar smoke into her face—wooing by scent, I suppose—then tapped her chest with his hand.

Trace pushed him back with the handle of the broom. He smiled, threw his cigar down on the floor, and grabbed the broomstick. Trace flicked her wrist, breaking his grip, then whacked him in the face. A knee to the groin sent him back against the hallway wall; Trace finished him with a boot to the chin.

The commotion brought the guard from the front running. Trace squared to confront her, but it wasn't necessary: as soon as the security guard saw what had happened, she began nodding approvingly. Then she walked over to the supervisor, said something in Russian, and gave him two kicks of her own before spitting on him and returning to her post.

Trace and Matthew made their way to Colonel Setrovich's office upstairs without any further interruption. Getting past the lock on the inner office took Trace a few seconds. Setrovich's computer was on a low desk at the side of the room. Matthew knelt in front of it as if he were praying, then began looking around for a password, hoping that like most people the colonel had written it down somewhere nearby for easy reference. When he couldn't find one, he booted the computer into diagnostics mode and made an end run around the security protocols. The Russian characters made things difficult, but the database program was itself a slightly altered version of Oracle, standard software that Junior had learned to manipulate back in ninth grade. It took about half an hour, but after some trial and error he managed to find the classified folder Setrovich's unit kept on Polorski, dumping the information into a file on a USB memory key for translation back home.

I was working on my own database, using vodka as my software. The more it flowed, the freer Setrovich was with information about Polorski. The mobster had a good number of influential friends, thanks to his generous impulses; according to Setrovich they were to blame for Polorski's continued freedom. Several times, the colonel and his people had been closing in on Polorski, only to have him slip away at the last minute. The colonel suspected that someone in his own office tipped Polorski off whenever they were closing in.

"For him, when I find him, snap," said Colonel Setrovich, twisting his hands together as if wringing Polorski's neck.

Setrovich hinted that Polorski's dealing with "foreign criminals"—terrorists, tango, scumbags; use the term of your choice—was sanctioned by someone in the government itself. The government official hated America, and believed that any attack, large or small, helped Russia.

"Which official?" I asked. "Who?"

"No, no, no, theory only," protested Setrovich. "To put you down a peg, though—that would be aim."

"Put who down a peg?"

"America. Too big for his britches."

Actually, he said bitches. Setrovich's English got worse the more he drank. I struggled with the image as Setrovich continued. There are definitely Russians who wouldn't mind seeing the U.S. hit by another 9/11-style attack, or even a more devastating nuclear strike. The Cold War may be over, but the us-versus-them mentality continues. A larger number of Russian officials, in government and in the military, realize that we face a common threat—and that Moscow is an even more inviting target than New York for some Islamic crazies, especially those from Chechnya.

"So where is he?" Setrovich asked finally.

"Who?"

"Polorski. You have come to tell me."

"I thought you knew."

"Me?"

"That's why I'm here."

"*Nyet. Nyet.*"

Setrovich refilled our glasses and started a long rant in Russian. When he finished, he downed his vodka in one gulp, slapped the glass on the table, and said loudly in English that Ivan had promised I knew where he was.

"Ivan got it wrong. I'm trying to find him myself."

"You have wasted my time." Setrovich rose.

"Two days ago, he was in China," I said calmly, remaining in my seat. "He got away from me. The trail isn't cold yet, if you help."

"He escaped from you? From American Bear?"

I hate to puncture my image of infallibility, but Polorski certainly had gotten away from me. I nodded.

"Huh," said Setrovich.

"It's possible if we work together we can catch him," I said.

"If I know where he is, I catch him myself."

"I'm sure you could."

Setrovich looked down at the vodka bottle. "Why was he in China?"

"Are we working together? Or just talking?"

The Russian frowned, then pointed to the bottle. "Pour."

"Partners?"

"Partners? *Nyet.* But . . ." He sat down. "If we have a goal in common, we share information, like we share vodka."

That was as much of a commitment as I was going to get. I told Setrovich about Yong Shin Jong, and that Polorski had managed to snatch him from the Chinese.

"I've been told he's planning to turn Yong Shin Jong over to

Kim Jong Il for a nuclear weapon," I said. "And from what you've told me, it sounds very plausible."

Setrovich's face, not particularly ruddy to begin with, had turned several shades whiter.

"It will be very important to apprehend him as soon as possible," said the colonel. "His organization has recently acquired a Topol mobile missile launcher, and seems to be trying to sell it."

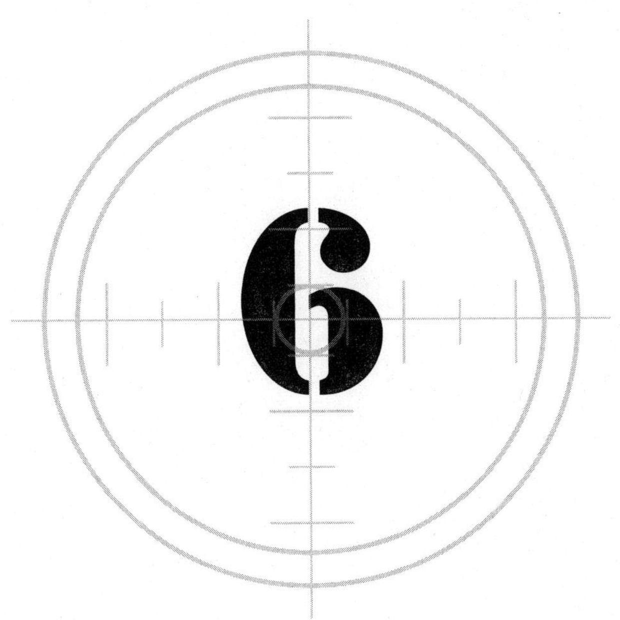

[1]

The Topol missile—officially the RT-2PM[16]—is a three-stage, solid booster rocket that is often compared to the American Minuteman, mostly because it's about the same size. Known to NATO as the SS-25 "Sickle," it's roughly ninety feet long, can carry a good-sized warhead (the Russians originally outfitted it with a thousand-kilogram payload before upgrading the missile for multiple warheads), and unlike North Korea's Taep'o-dong 2, can actually be counted on to hit a target in the U.S. that it was aimed at. The range varies depending on the size and configuration of the warhead, but during the SALT talks the Russians declared it could fly 10,500 kilometers—which by my arithmetic works out to roughly 6,500 miles . . . a bit less than the distance from Tehran to Washington, D.C.

The Topol would be considered just another run-of-the-mill weapon of mass destruction except for one quality: its size and fuel system not only allow it to be easily transported by truck, but it can be launched from one as well. I'm not saying it can be hauled around in the back of your pickup; the missile carrier is as long as two and a half school buses, or half again as long as your standard semi. It requires a trained crew to get the damn thing erect and fired at a target, and your local car mechanic can't do the maintenance. But compared to just about any other nuclear-capable missile, it's very easy to use and very hard to find. Park it someplace where it blends in with the scenery—say a train yard in North Korea, where with a minimum of fuss it can be disguised as a tanker car—and even a trained expert can miss it on the satellite photo.

The missiles were originally constructed and stationed in several different Soviet regions, including Belarus. In 1996, Belarus—by then an independent country—returned eighteen

---

[16] A newer version of this missile is still being manufactured in Russia, which has declared it is no longer bound by the START treaties.

missiles to Russia, accounting for the last of those officially stationed there. But what went unaccounted for was a spare unit and some associated parts, kept at the original factory. It was this missile, which lacked a warhead, that Polorski had obtained.

If you're wondering, gentle reader, why Polorski and company didn't just sell the missile and launcher to North Korea, you're in good company. I wondered the same thing. In fact, I wasn't convinced that he hadn't, though Setrovich believed that the missile was still in Russia somewhere. But I had to admit that this was a case where a whole was worth a hell of a lot more than the parts—supply a nuclear warhead with the missile, and the price would be exponentially greater. If Polorski could pick up the nuke relatively cheaply, his profit would shame an oil company executive.

Polorski's unit was not your typical small-time outfit filled with wannabes and rap hopefuls. They had a serious infrastructure and money in the bank. At least three banks, according to the file that Matthew had teased out of the computer. We had the file translated within an hour of our return to Japan, thanks to one of the Russian experts we have on retainer at Red Cell, a one-eyed professor at Virginia Tech. The professor lost his eye in a boating accident when he was thirteen; while he was recovering someone gave him a copy of Dostoyevsky's *Crime and Punishment* and he was hooked on Russian literature. From what I understand, he goes around telling cute-looking students that he lost the eye in a duel over a woman while spying in Odessa; they apparently find it hard to resist a one-eyed former spy.

"The organization uses three different banks to move its money around. They're all Russian, they all have numerous ties to the government and the mafiya, and none of them are known for cooperating with foreigners," the professor told us after reviewing the files. We were listening by speaker phone at the hotel. "They use Rigndael encryption, which can't be decrypted by anybody except the NSA—and maybe not even them."

"Except for Junior," I said, turning to Matthew.

"I wish," he said. "Only the No Suchers[17] can do it. Maybe."

Rigndael encryption is better known in the U.S. as AES or Advanced Encryption Standard. It uses a set of mathematical equations to change clear text—the message—into gobbledygook. Without going into the technical bs, defeating the encryption—"breaking the code" to us nonexperts—requires considerable computer power and generally requires invading the computer using it. As good as Matthew was, he didn't have the horsepower necessary for the job.

He did, however, suggest an alternative. Rather than looking at the banks in question, we find other banks that did business with them and look at what that business was. He fired up his laptop and began looking for transfers from the accounts in question to other banks. Electronic transfers generally passed through a third-party clearing house. These records were also secure—but we knew how to access them because of some work Red Cell had done a few months before ferrying hard data backups around Asia.[18]

"There's this HSBC bank account that's interesting," said Junior about an hour later. "It was used to put a down payment on a trawler a month or so ago."

He found about a dozen other transactions, all of which were suspicious and we checked out, but it was the trawler that turned out to be important. I contacted Jimmy Zim and told him that I would be willing to engage in some parallel play by exchanging information. He was nonplussed to hear from me, not surprised, not excited, not dismayed. Just, "Yes, Dick. We'll see what we can find."

A half hour later, he called back. The ship's name and regis-

---

17 "No Suchers," as in members of "No Such Agency," aka the National Security Agency, which as we all know doesn't exist and wouldn't if it did.

18 See *Rogue Warrior: Vengeance.*

try had been changed twice; it was now the *Shchi*, homeported at the far east Russian city of Kamenka.

"Is it still there?" I asked.

"I think we should continue this discussion face-to-face," said Jimmy Zim. "How long will it take you to get to the embassy?"

"Get the ice ready," I told him. "I'll be there before it starts to melt."

The CIA agent was better than average at following directions, and Dr. Bombay's finest was perfectly chilled when I reached the ambassador's study.

Unfortunately, so was Fogglebottom. The State Department pseudo-ambassador and his cuffed pants loomed in the corner, arms folded, scowling with disapproval as Jimmy Zim gave me my drink.

"Polorski hasn't made the deal yet," Zim told me as I sat down in an overstuffed leather chair. "Now it's even more critical to stop him."

"How do you know he hasn't made the deal yet?"

"Because of this." Zim took a piece of paper from his suit jacket and handed it to me. It was a copy of an e-mail sent to a Google account. Only the address and e-mail header were readable; everything else was in computer character gibberish. For all I knew it could have been an encrypted ad for penile implants.

"Sorry, I don't read geek," I told him, handing it back.

"The unencrypted message says 'Transaction is ready.' It gives a GPS reading for a port on the Somalia coast. It's set for four weeks from now—about the time it would take for your trawler to get there from Russia."

"That's easy then. Sink the damn thing."

Jimmy Zim smiled in a way that suggested he wished it were that easy.

"The trawler set sail from Kamenka a few hours ago. We want you to give the Russians the information about it and join them on the raid."

"I don't think that's a good idea. The Russians may have their own agenda. And frankly, I don't really trust them."

"The Cold War is over, Dick," intoned Fogglebottom solemnly.

That's right. We're all joining hands and dancing around the maypole now, one big happy family.

"Actually, there is a bit more to the plan," said Zim.

A lot more—a force of Navy SEALs would be made available to "assist" the Russians on the QT. They wouldn't be officially involved, of course, just available if something went wrong—say, for example, the Russian commander was paid to let the ship and its cargo continue on their way. Or if the Russians decided not to turn Yong Shin Jong over to me. Having me working with the Russians would accomplish several things. Number one, I'd be there to sound the alarm if there was a deviation in the plans. Number two, I'd be cover for anything the SEALs did—the U.S. could always claim that it was Demo Dick who was shooting up civilian ships on the open seas, not *real* Navy SEALs. I'd also be the fall guy if anything went wrong.

And then there was the matter of Yong Shin Jong. The State Department still wanted him returned to his father—not for the sake of family harmony, but the nuclear treaty. If he was aboard the trawler, which seemed like a good guess, I would come away with him and proceed to North Korea.

I'll spare you the back and forth "discussion" that ensued. I wanted to talk to Yong Shin Jong, believing that I could get more information about the bunker from him. And I definitely felt the Russian missile should be destroyed. But the operation violated several basic precepts, not least of all was the golden rule: KISS, or Keep It Simple, Stupid. Coordinating action between two different branches of the military is very difficult; coordinating an operation with another country, especially one like Russia that isn't even a member of NATO, is even harder. (Lest you think the task was so simple that even the Russians couldn't screw it up, in the past the U.S. has managed to lose track of several arms shipments that came out of North Korea via ships. Those "only" involved things like spare parts and guns and Scud missiles though, nothing too important.)

Let the SEALs take the ship and forget the Russians—that plan made sense. Or hell, let the Russians go in, screw it up, then sink the damn ship, diplomacy and public relations be damned. Doing it arm in arm, with me in the middle and the SEALs pretending not to be there, made about as much sense as letting a bunch of lawyers and congressmen write the tax code.

Obviously, I'm too dense to understand the finer points of geopolitics. In the end, I agreed to tip Colonel Setrovich off to the information and suggest that "assets" including the SEALs could be made available to help if things got nasty. Setrovich laughed and insisted that while things certainly would get nasty, neither the SEALs nor our navy was needed. Then, without me having to say anything else, he invited me along for the show.

(11)

Junior had given the NSA a copy of the data we'd gotten from Setrovich's office. But he kept a copy for himself, and while I was discussing things with Fogglebottom and Zim, Junior put on his hacker cap and waded through the Russian mob's web of bank accounts. He had a very distinct style: leaning closer and closer to the screen, he would type furiously for five or ten minutes. At some point he would lean so far forward that he would literally fall out of his chair, leaving it to roll behind him and crash into whatever was nearby, usually Trace. Oblivious, he would keep pounding the keyboard until suddenly he'd straighten, and with a big grin on his face announce the mobsters' bank balance.

He was getting such a kick out of his new role as Red Cell International's favorite dweeb that I felt like a heel telling him he was going to have to stay in Japan while Trace and I went on the operation with the Russkies.

"But don't you t-t-trust me?"

"Sure I trust you, Matt. But you're not trained for an assault."

"I've done skydiving. Three hundred jumps. Fifty-three at night."

"We're not parachuting," I told him.

"It's going to be a night assault from helicopters," said Trace. "It's not going to be a joyride."

His frown deepened. I think he thought she was rubbing it in.

"I need you to work with Doc," I said. "We need to set up a contingency plan in case something goes wrong here. And I'm still interested in what sort of accounts Yong Shin Jong has in Singapore. You have a lot of work ahead of you."

I can't say he was really happy, but within a few minutes he was pounding on the keyboard again.

"I have an address one of the companies used in Kamenka," he announced. "It looks like it's in the harbor area."

"Write it down for me, and keep checking."

"Maybe I can check it out myself?"

"You do and I'll personally put you over my knee and spank the living shit out of you," said Trace.

Junior opened his mouth to say something, saw from Trace's expression that she wasn't kidding, then reached for a piece of paper.

Colonel Setrovich met Trace and me at the airport in Khabarousk, Russia, late that evening. An elaborate assault plan had been worked out—two Russian Hind Mi-24P helicopters carrying a dozen Russian marines would be escorted by two Mi-28 Havoc gunships; the marines—and we—would board the trawler while the gunships provided cover. Two destroyers were steaming toward the trawler and would be about ten miles away when the assault began—close enough to get there quickly if there was trouble, but far enough away that they couldn't take the credit if things went smoothly. It was a classic FSB maneuver.

Two U.S. Navy surface ships, along with a submarine carrying the aforementioned SEALs, were also in the vicinity, though a little farther away. Setrovich didn't ask, and I didn't tell.

The "P" in Mi-24P stands for *pushka*, a Russian word for cannon, and refers to the double-barreled 30mm cannon in the Hind's nose, an upgrade over the not-all-that puny-in-itself four-barreled machine gun carried in the other versions. The *pushka* makes a very low *thud-thump* sound as it fires, and in the dark the flash from the muzzle is impressive, even when the gun is aimed harmlessly at the water.

"Just to let them know we mean business," Setrovich yelled over the whine of the helicopter's rotors. He put his hand to his ear, listening to something from the pilot attempting to communicate with the captain of the trawler. I turned around to the window, watching the floodlight beneath one of the gunships illuminate the forward deck of the trawler. The helicopter was hovering about twenty feet above the trawler. I couldn't see anyone aboard.

Nor could I see anything that looked remotely like it might be a missile.

The marines rose and lined up near the door, ready to fast rope down. Trace got up and moved to the head of the line, her MP5 cradled beneath her arm. I slipped in behind her.

"*Nazdaróvye!*" yelled the team's jumpmaster, and off we went. I grabbed the line and shot downward as if speeding down a fireman's pole. The ship looked like a sore prick in the night, easy to see, but the twenty or so feet between me and the forward deck was a *long* twenty feet, the chopper bucking with the wind and trawler rolling hard starboard as I hit the deck. I managed to land with the roll, keeping my balance as the trawler pitched back to port. I ran forward to the cargo hatch, then tucked around a winch assembly for one of the shipboard cranes. Working my way up the ship's starboard side, I reached a railing that separated a ladder off the deck to the superstructure; glancing behind me to make sure the marines were with me—they were—I jumped up and over, securing the catwalk as the rest of the small team followed.

To this point, there had been no sign of resistance aboard the ship—in fact, there was no sign that it was occupied at all. But that changed quickly: light flashed on the port side of the deck. A boom and a crash followed, topped off by a serenade of automatic rifle fire. I threw myself against the side of the catwalk, watching as a pair of Russians near the bow fired at a lifeboat, their tracers blazing across the night.

There was no answering fire. My guess is that the boarding party had used flash-bang grenades to enter the ship, and someone outside got a case of jitters. Once the genie's out of the bottle it can take quite a while to restore order, and gunfire erupted from several quarters at once. With adrenaline flowing like beer at Oktoberfest, the NCOs had a hell of a time calming things down. Curses and pleas to stop firing overran the radio circuit.

Just as the gunfire stopped, a figure climbed out of the forward cargo hatchway and made a beeline toward the ladder to my right. Realizing he'd be much more valuable alive than dead, I jumped up and ran for him, tackling him just as he reached the catwalk. Unfortunately, in the confusion it probably wasn't clear whose side I was on; bullets started whizzing overhead.

Trace's voice cut through the chaos over the radio.

"Stop shooting or I'm going to kick each one of you in the balls!"

Either the marines understood English or they'd run out of ammunition, because to a man they stopped firing.

I pulled the man I'd flattened up. In the dim light he didn't look like much of a mafioso, Russian or otherwise. And he wasn't Yong Shin Jong, either. He looked all of seventeen, weighed two pounds less than your average house cat, and spoke Vietnamese.

Very scared Vietnamese.

He jabbered something about being a seaman and papers lost at sea. One of the Russians who'd come up the catwalk behind me escorted us as I brought the kid to Setrovich's command post near the bow. My Vietnamese was a little rusty, but as near as I could tell the kid claimed the only cargo were tins of fish. He said that they were going to South Korea, not North. And he didn't know anything about missiles or passengers. He claimed all of the crewmen were Vietnamese, and had been hired within the last three weeks, during the ship's last visit to Haiphong, the North Vietnamese port not far from Hanoi.

Setrovich didn't believe him, and called him a liar in Russian. While the seaman didn't understand the words, he got the implied threat and began shaking, but stuck to his story. Personally, I didn't see much reason for him to lie, outside of the obvious fib about having lost nonexistent identity or work papers. Neither his nationality nor the cargo would be unusual.

The general outlines of his story were confirmed ten minutes later by the trawler's captain, a Russian who looked like Santa Claus with a black beard and smelled of sweat and stale vodka. Setrovich, frowning in my direction, ordered the marines to conduct a full inspection of the ship.

Trace and I conducted our own search. There were plenty of crates of canned fish in the hold, along with several stamped "bicycle parts" in Russian. These turned out to contain . . . bicycle parts.

Setrovich was looking cross when I found him on the bridge. He didn't blame me as much as give Polorski and company credit for outwitting us.

"He is always two steps ahead. Even of the great Rogue Warrior."

"More likely he's behind us," I said. "This ship was probably a decoy. He's probably still in Russia somewhere."

"Ah. First you tell me he is in Beijing, then you say Russia. You must be working with American CIA—always backward ass."

"Ass backward."

"Yes. I will call the helicopters for pickup."

"Why don't we look for him in Kamenka? If he sent the ship out as a decoy, he may still have the missile there."

"His hideout is not in the city."

"You're sure?"

Setrovich shrugged. "Where it is, who knows?"

"Let's look here." I gave him the address that Junior had found. A light seemed to go off in Setrovich's head—a dim one, but a light nonetheless.

"Yes. Yes. This might be useful," said the colonel. "Tomorrow morning, we will visit."

"Let's do it now," I told him. "This way no one can tip him off. The helicopters have to go back there anyway."

Setrovich frowned, which I expected. But then he nodded, which I hadn't.

"Rogue Warrior lives up to his expectations," he said, clapping me hard on the back. "Always thinking."

The address belonged to a building that was part of a storage depot near the port, with a rail spur and several warehouses, along with a good-sized yard. Assaulting a facility of that size usually calls for a lot of careful planning and, if possible, a rehearsal or two. It's also not the sort of thing you want to undertake with a unit that's just coming off another mission, especially a nighttime operation in the middle of the ocean. But if we were really going to surprise Polorski and his group, any raid against them had to be completely spontaneous. Someone was tipping these guys off, and the only way to get them was to hit them when they thought we were elsewhere.

Setrovich told the helicopter pilots that they were going on a second mission, and then instead of telling them where it was, ordered them to simply follow his craft. He decreed complete radio silence, saying that anyone caught making a transmission would be thrown from the helicopter without a parachute. That's my kind of punishment.

Setrovich's assistant had a good set of satellite maps with him that showed the port area of Kamenka where the *Shchi* had docked; the maps happened to include enough of the nearby area for us to spot Polorski's yard and the surroundings. It covered about two acres right along the water, separated from a long wharf by a set of train tracks. (The *Shchi* had sailed from a wharf about a half mile away, closer to the center of the port.) Two large steel buildings sat at the north end of the yard; there were two tractor-trailers, a pair of small tractors, and enough rusted steel drums to keep a calypso band in business for years. Setrovich and I worked out a plan with the captain of the marine detachment. We'd drop half a helo's worth of marines at the south end of the yard, near the gated entrance to the port's road network, sealing off access. The rest of the force would be divided up for assaults on the buildings. The gunships would make sure no one left via the water—there were two small speedboats tied up near the wharf—and provide whatever additional muscle was necessary.

My group consisted of six marines who could speak good enough English—they knew enough to nod if I said "listen up." We'd come in at the eastern side of the buildings, fast roping down and heading directly to the building. We'd go in with the help of flash-bangs and as many submachine-gun bullets as necessary.

Trace was in another group tasked to land on the other side of the buildings. She and her marines would move to the fence separating the yard from the railroad tracks and approach the buildings from there, positioning themselves to cut off anyone trying to escape us.

The sun had just come up, but there didn't seem to be any activity as the helos came in. We hit the ground in good shape, fanning out for our assignments.

The Russian marines were well trained, and used techniques for entering buildings that were very similar to what a U.S. force would have done. A runty-looking sergeant named Mikhail stepped up to the door with a shotgun loaded with special steel slugs, then waited as a companion threw a flash-bang grenade through the nearby window.

Whap! Crash—*ka-boom!*

Lock obliterated, the door flew open. The team barreled inside, weapons ready. We were in a small room, maybe ten by ten, completely empty except for a wooden bench against the northern wall. There was an open interior doorway in the wall facing us as we came in, offset by a few feet. The marines and I took up positions at the side of the door, and we did the flash-bang routine once again.

Bounce—bounce—*ka-boom!*

K-k-k-BOOOOOM! BOOM! BOOM! BOO-OOM!!!

The sound was a lot worse in person than it looks in print. The grenade had set something in the other room off, and the booms quickly crescendoed as secondary explosion begat secondary explosion. They may not have been the loudest explosions I've ever heard, nor the most powerful, but they were among the most inconvenient.

"Out!" I yelled. "Get the hell out of the building! Go!"

The marines ducked and ran past me as I waved them out. Tapped by the last man, I pitched myself toward daylight. I hit the dirt about twenty feet beyond where I'd been aiming, my flight assisted by a fresh round of explosions, which not so coincidentally pulverized a good portion of the building.

I didn't have time to check for injuries. The fire we'd inadvertently started with our grenade sent a ball of flame surging upward. Spitting dirt out of my mouth, I managed to scramble to my feet and yell to the rest of the squad to retreat. They were already two steps ahead of me; a few of them three. We regrouped behind some oil drums about fifty feet from the building as fire completely engulfed it. A second group of marines tasked to watch the front of the building retreated and hooked up with us. One of the men had been hit by shrapnel that had cut his arm below his bulletproof vest; otherwise, we had no casualties.

I know what you're thinking: Dick, you just found the missile. But I'm something of a connoisseur of explosions, and even as I crouched behind the barrels I realized they weren't coming from a rocket on fire. They were more like what you would expect if you threw a match into a room filled with kerosene fumes and large barrels filled with the fuel, with maybe a few grenades cooking off for good measure.

We weren't the only ones having fun. One of the gunships whirled above and began firing rockets into the southeast corner of the yard. And there was heavy gunfire near the second building. With our objective now covered in flames, I decided to put my Russians to work backing up the unit taking the second building. We circled back around a cluster of barrels to get a look at what was going on. As we did, we came under machine-gun fire from the northwestern corner of the yard. Mikhail and two other marines were pinned down.

"Cover me!" I yelled, turning and heading back in the direction I'd come in.

I planned to crawl up along the fence line and surprise the machine gunner from the flank. The plan wouldn't have been a bad one, either, except that the way was blocked off by a wall of barrels. There were two alternatives: frontal assault into the teeth of the machine-gun nest, or a sweeping attack from the flank. The latter meant I'd have to run to the back of the building we'd just set on fire, go up and over the fence, then sneak around behind the machine gunner's back.

I enjoy frontal assaults as much as anyone—which means not at all. Opting to climb the fence, I did my best wind sprint to the back of the building, gritting my teeth as a fresh round of explosions shook the ground. The flames were a good incentive to hit the fence, sending me up the chain links in four short pulls. Strung across the top were three rows of old-fashioned barbed wire, more a pain in the neck than a real hindrance—I pushed the rows down with my gloved hands and did a forward somersault over the top, spinning around and grabbing the fence with one hand as I started to fall.

Well, almost.

Mr. Murphy pushed one of the barbs up as I went over, grabbing my shirtsleeve and ruining my flip. My left hand slipped from the fence, and I slipped more or less straight down. I was lucky to hit the ground feetfirst, though I was so off-kilter I shot face-first into the weeds and rocks behind the yard. Dazed, I had to rest for a minute before getting up. I grabbed the AK74[19] Setrovich had loaned me and ran toward the back of the machine-gun nest, which was still firing in the direction of my men.

The machine gun was a *real* machine gun, a DshKM M1938/46 12.7mm weapon dating back to the time when bullets were bullets and machine guns were machine guns. There'll always be a special place in my heart for the "Ma Duce"—the Browning M2 heaving machine gun that first began supporting American troops in the 1930s—but the Russian "Dushka" is nearly as good a weapon. You really can't say you've come under heavy machine-gun fire until you've had the Dushka's half-inch bullets whizzing a few inches from your fanny. It's a

[19] Yes, AK74, not AK47. Among its alleged improvements is the fact that it fires a smaller, NATO-sized round. I greatly prefer my MP5.

feeling you'll never forget, though you'll probably wish you could.

I know I certainly wished I could as the barrel of the gun swung in my direction and lead started buzzing like a hive of angry bees around my head. I squeezed off a burst from my own weapon just for form's sake as I hit the dirt, burrowing into the scant cover behind the gun emplacement.

Scant as in nonexistent. The only thing that saved my butt from being perforated was the fact that I was so close to the gunner that he couldn't lower his weapon far enough to actually hit me. I could have waited until he went through his 250-bullet belt, but being the naturally rambunctious sort—and not trusting that he wouldn't take out a handgun—I rolled onto my back and took one of the flash-bangs from my vest. I tossed it over my head in the direction of the gunner. As the grenade went off, I rolled over and began firing, emptying the gun's magazine. Half my bullets found the sandbags they'd used to protect the rear of their position. The other half found the head of the son of a bitch who'd been firing at me.

Ugly. But a very pretty ugly.

I slammed a new box into the gun and jumped up, making sure there was no one else with the machine gun. Then I ran back to the spot where I'd come over the fence, not wanting to take the chance that one of the Russian marines might mistake me for a bad guy moving to take over the gun.

I was just about to put my hand onto the fence to climb up when I heard Trace yelling something along the lines of "Stop that son of a bitch!" I looked toward the railroad tracks and saw not one but two sons of a bitch running down the wharf.

Trace and her marines had been covering the side of the building near the water, waiting to grab anyone trying to get away from us. When the building first caught fire, she backed up a bit, still watching to make sure no one was inside. As the building continued to burn, she left two marines to hold the position and went back to the other building, intending to join the team clearing that building. Three men jumped from a window at the back around the time Trace arrived; one fired at her, slowing her down enough for the other two to jump the fence and run off.

Which is where I came in.

I started running after them, angling out in the direction they were going in an attempt to head them off. The field I was in was overgrown with grass, which partially hid a spiderweb of railroad tracks that made it hard to run through. There were dozens and dozens of empty vodka bottles, some intact, most shattered into large but sharp pieces. By the time I got past the tracks and other obstacles, the two men had disappeared somewhere along the wharf.

As I was trying to figure out where they'd gone, I heard the loud blast of a horn behind me. I whirled around and saw a small diesel engine chugging on the track to my right, pulling a row of flatcars behind it. The train was moving at a good clip, and I wasn't—it passed in front of me, cutting me off from the wharf.

It was a long train, and I wasn't in a patient mood, so I did what any normal red-blooded American would do when faced with an interminable wait—I cut in front of the line.

Or more precisely, I started jogging alongside the train car, then grabbed the small ladder at the end of the car as it came by. Flatcars are among the easiest train cars to hop, though easy or not I still had a tough time pulling myself against the ladder. I managed to get my right knee onto the rung and pushed upward, slapping my left foot onto the ladder and then sprawling across the deck of the flatcar. I got up and did a stutter-step toward the side, losing my balance and jumping before I was really ready to. I twisted in midair, flipping over like a bag of mail but at least clearing the tracks. I landed on my shoulder and lost my gun. By now my clothes were soaked with sweat; my left ankle hurt and my right knee was pulsing with a beat that would have made a salsa band jealous. It occurred to me that I might be getting too old for this sort of thing, but I did what I always do when that thought pops into my head: I grit my teeth and keep going.

As I made it to the wharf, I realized where the two men had disappeared to. There was a small dock below; they'd grabbed a small boat and were now sailing northward out of the harbor. Out of frustration, I fired a few rounds from the AK74, cursing and looking for the helicopter gunships that were supposed to be guarding against just this kind of escape. I was about halfway through my list of Russian curses when I noticed another speedboat coming up alongside the wharf. I turned, ready to fire, then realized Trace was at the wheel.

"Dick! Jump down!" she shouted.

I hung over the edge of the wharf, waiting until she was below. I jumped, hit the deck—and she hit the gas. By the time I managed to get back upright, she had pulled the boat to within two or three hundred yards of the escaping Russians.

"Careful!" she yelled as I raised my gun. "Setrovich wants them alive. They'll know where the missile launcher and Yong Shin Jong are."

Maybe they would and maybe they wouldn't, but trying to find out *was* a good idea. Especially since we were steadily catching up to them. I lowered my aim, sighting the outboard at the stern of their boat. Just as I started to push on the trigger, our boat abruptly slowed. Now I realized why the bad guys had left us the faster boat—we were out of fuel.

My shots at the outboard on the other boat missed, and as it rapidly pulled away I once more began exhausting my knowledge of curse words, this time in English as well as Russian. I got through only a small portion before Trace pointed skyward.

"The helicopter!"

"What?"

"Helicopter!"

The gunships had finally broken away from the firefight in the compound and were coming to see what was going on. But as the cannon beneath the closest helo rotated in our direction, we realized this wasn't necessarily a good thing.

"We're on your stinking side!" yelled Trace.

She still had her radio—I'd lost mine somewhere along the way—but they either didn't understand her English or weren't tuned to the right frequency. The helo did a slow turn above, then came back at us, cannon blasting.

"Out!" I yelled, jumping into the water about five seconds before the boat was demolished by cannon fire.

I swam away underwater as fast as I could, holding my breath for about a minute and a half before coming up for air. Trace popped up about ten yards away. Chewed-up fiberglass and boat parts filled the water where the boat had been. I'd taken about two strokes toward shore when I heard the sound of a helo approaching hot and heavy behind us.

"Duck!" I yelled, thinking it was the attack chopper, back for more. But when I surfaced, I saw it was the Hind, low to the waves and dangling a sling for us.

Trace went up first. I treaded water, fighting the wash of the propellers as the helo hovered directly overhead. Finally it was my turn: I grabbed on to the sling and hung on as it yanked my arm practically out of its socket, spinning me through the twelve or fifteen feet to the chopper's cabin.

"Very sorry about the boat," shouted Setrovich, who helped pull me in. "Mistake. Sorry."

Trace was standing in the corner with a blanket wrapped around her. She didn't say anything, but I knew what she was thinking—"sorry" didn't begin to cover it.

The helicopter spun around and headed out to sea, following the two gunships. The Havocs were crisscrossing ahead, buzzing the other boat like a pair of angry bees. The boat had stopped, apparently convinced that the gunships would blow it out of the water if it didn't.

Inside our chopper, two of the men had stripped to their shorts and were pulling on wet suits.

"We will take over the boat, take these men as prisoners," said Setrovich. "They will give us information."

"Did you find the missile at the yard?" I asked.

"Not yet," said Setrovich.

Since I was already wet, I volunteered to go with the marines who were jumping to take the boat.

"Not enough for one day?" Setrovich smiled, but put up his hand as if to restrain me. "No, no, these men will take care of the situation. You have time to rest. Then we have drinks, no? Vodka, not seawater."

Setrovich picked up a microphone as the helicopter reached the boat and began broadcasting a message, telling the men inside it they were under arrest and the only way out would be to surrender. He promised leniency if they gave themselves up.

The offer appealed to them so much they answered by peppering the side of the Hind with rifle fire. The helicopter jerked away, but not before a handful of bullets smacked through the open side door. One ricocheted off the pipe of the bench where I was sitting, missing me by a few inches. Another broke the top of a fire extinguisher strapped to the bulkhead, sending white spray through the cabin.

The Hind answered with cannon fire, turning the boat and its occupants into fish food—*little fish* food, the kind goldfish eat.

(III)

Setrovich was wearing a very long face when we returned to shore. Three of the marines had been killed in the raid, and two other men had been severely wounded. Worse, we'd found no trace of Polorski, a missile, or Yong Shin Jong. Twelve defenders had been killed at the yard, and the warehouse that didn't blow up contained enough rifles and grenade launchers to equip a small South American country. Three computers had been seized from the building, so there was some hope of getting more information on the gang. And here's another bright note: the barrels that I'd hidden behind during the battle turned out to hold rounds of small-arms ammunition. But Setrovich still figured the ledger strongly favored Polorski when he tallied it on the ground.

"We will find him." Setrovich pounded the desk in the office of the remaining warehouse. The marines were busy inventorying the weapons cache; it was far too big to move by helicopter. "I make solemn vow. I will get bastard. Crush him."

I pretended to be impressed, then slipped outside, looking for Trace. I found her in the field across from the yard, talking to one of the gunship pilots about how the bird was flown. I went over and got her attention.

"He's going to give me a ride," said Trace. "And I can drive. What do you think?"

She said it with enough of a smirk that made me think she might be interested in something more than just a helicopter ride. The pilot surely was—I could see his leer from where I was standing.

"Go to it," I told her.

The Russian was about six-six, but Trace already had him wrapped around her little finger. He not only showed her to the cockpit, but helped her into it. Then he scrambled into the forward seat. Trace had the rotors turning before he even had his hatch cinched. The helicopter took a few hops forward, then suddenly surged into the air. Trace took it into a wide orbit around the yard, then pushed its nose down and accelerated out to sea. I could just about hear her "yah-oos" as it whipped back in my direction.

I was waiting for her to try an invert when my sat phone began to ring. It was Matthew Loring.

"What's up, Junior?" I asked.

"Polorski and his people have another ship. That one's just a decoy."

"You think?"

"I've been tracking through their financial transactions," Matthew told me. "Dick, there's a lot more to this than it seems."

Duh.

"I'm pretty sure it was a decoy as well," I told him. "Where is the other ship?"

"About a day south of Vietnam. Doc got somebody he knows at the navy to check with—"

"That's all right, Junior. I don't need the details right now. What I need is transportation. I want to get back to Japan, and then I'll need an airplane that can get us to that ship."

"No, I don't think so," said Setrovich behind me. "Transportation is not what you need at all."

I turned around and saw Setrovich standing there with a very wide grin on his face.

The grin didn't bother me. The gun in his hand was an entirely different matter.

{ 1 }

There was a very good reason that Setrovich hadn't caught Polorski and the mafiya group he worked with—the FSB colonel was paid good rubles not to.

Or euros, or possibly even American dollars. But I digress.

"Who are you talking to, Marcinko?" asked Setrovich. His English had measurably improved, as had his snarl.

"Just getting the time to set my watch," I said.

"Hang up now."

I turned the phone off.

"Drop the phone."

I did so.

"Take the gun from your belt," said Setrovich.

"Tell me first, was this part a setup?" I asked. "Did these guys know we were coming?"

Setrovich didn't answer. My guess was that it wasn't—Setrovich knew that the raid would please his superiors, and would probably argue that to Polorski. Certainly it would let him take the heat off the mobsters while they got away with the missile. Dead bodies make wonderful trophies, even if the real heart of the operation is untouched. Knowing that I was interested in Polorski, and that the CIA was involved, even if at arm's length, Setrovich had probably decided that a little raid might divert me. But the fact that I had found the real ship changed everything.

"Where is your woman?" asked the colonel.

I probably should have had a snappy, in-your-face comeback for that, but I didn't. It would have been drowned out anyway: Trace, still showing off, flew her helicopter directly overhead at about eight feet off the ground.

Dirt and dust flew through the air. So did I. Setrovich fired, but by then he was already falling backward. I'd hit him square in the chest with a tackle that would have made an NFL linebacker proud. We wrestled around in the dirt as the helo circled above us. It wasn't exactly a match worthy of WrestleMania—I punched, squeezed, and shoved, while Setrovich mostly rolled and tried to get away. He hit me with the butt end of his gun, but since he was hitting my skull, there was little chance of damage.

He twisted around, his back to me and his belly on the ground. The gun was underneath him. Somehow, it went off.

Maybe my finger on the trigger helped.

He was dead when I pulled the gun out from under him and stood up. Our little fracas had attracted the attention of several nearby marines. They weren't sure what was going on, and I didn't trust my ability to explain. Nor did I think the little peashooter I'd taken from Setrovich—a Pistolet Makarov, aka PM, a dead ringer rip-off of the Walther PP—was going to hold them off for very long.

Fortunately, the marines had a great deal of respect for the 30mm cannon in the nose of the Havoc, which swooped down in front of me. They didn't realize that the cannon was controlled by the Russian in the forward compartment, who at that very moment was punching his dashboard in a vain attempt to figure out a way to override the controls Trace was using to fly the chopper, and I certainly wasn't going to tell them—I was too busy trying to figure out how to get the hell out of there.

A normal helicopter would have had a rear compartment, but the Havoc is basically a cannon with two seats strapped to it. If you've ever seen an Apache or a Cobra, you get the basic idea. So did the Russians, who shamelessly copied from those helos when designing it. Among other things they cribbed was the Apache's landing gear; rather than the more familiar and easy-to-grab-on-to skids used by most helicopters, the Havoc uses large planelike landing gear in a tricycle arrangement beneath the cockpit, two front, one back. Seeing no other way out, I grabbed on to the left wheel of the helicopter as it hovered above me. A second later, the chopper began moving sideways across the yard toward the field where it had taken off. I got ready to drop to the ground, but it didn't slow down. On the contrary, it not only sped up but rose another hundred feet in the air.

I had a hell of a view of Kamenka. And let me say this for Kamenka: it is truly a pit of ugly brown and gray feces spread in box form across a gray landscape, relieved only by urine-colored streams running to a puke-colored ocean. I expect a Lonely Planet guidebook on it to be published soon.

I hugged the wheel tighter, hoping that Trace knew what she was doing. Finally, we started to slow down and descend. The ground below me went from gray to black to green. I waited until I could just about count the blades of grass below me before letting go.

I hit the ground and rolled, got to my feet, and—though dizzy as hell—ran to the chopper, gun drawn to cover the pilot in the forward compartment as Trace set the chopper down. She hit a number of buttons before finding the master cockpit unlock, which forced the windscreen to open; once the Russian saw the pistol in my hand, it didn't take much to persuade him to give up his seat. He undid his seat belt, called me a cocksucker under his breath, then jumped out of the helo and ran away.

I pulled myself over the side, tangling my feet as I tried to get situated in the cramped cockpit. The windscreen started closing above me, smacking against my head and pushing me down into my seat. We rolled forward, then abruptly pitched upward. The chopper turned hard port, slamming me against the right instrument panel before I managed to get my fanny properly situated in the seat. The pilot's helmet had rolled to the floor; I picked it up and squeezed it over my ears.

"Dick, can you hear me?" asked Trace.

"Copy. Roger."

"Hang on."

By now the other helicopters that had been assigned to the mission had realized something had gone wrong and were pursuing us. Trace pushed us northward, throttle open. The two Hinds fell behind, but the other Havoc stayed with us, announcing its annoyance with a stream of 30mm rounds just to the right of our tail. Trace tucked hard left, turned in a tight bank, then slammed us out toward the water.

"Get us south," I told her. "Get us out near the navy destroyers that were shadowing the operation."

It wasn't a bad idea, except that the destroyers were at least two hundred miles away, and we had fuel for maybe a hundred.

We also had someone on our tail. Another burst of cannon fire let us know he wasn't going away anytime soon.

"Dick, can you figure out how to work that cannon?" asked Trace.

"Give me a minute," I told her, studying the controls. I knew the weapon had to be turned on from the main armament panel, but since all the writing was in Russian gibberish I had a difficult time figuring out what to do. I hit some toggles and got some lights to turn from red to yellow; one had the word "pushka" in tape next to it, so I figured I was in business once the light went yellow.

The next hurdle was figuring out what exactly fired the gun. Unlike in computer games, where all the Russians have weapons slaved to the eyepieces in their helmets and fire by saying "kill," the cannon in the Havoc was slaved to old-fashioned mechanical controls.[20] The cannon was aimed by looking through an ocular—think creaky old telescope—perched above a set of dials in front of me. Wheels at both sides of the device focused it and apparently worked various adjustments—like wind—but I didn't have time to get too fancy. I grabbed the stick in front of me, got something of a feel for how it swiveled, then started hunting for our adversary.

[20] One of our technical advisors says that I was actually looking at the backup controls, and that the helicopter did indeed have high-tech gear that would have worked with a whisper and a curse, had I properly plugged in the helmet I was wearing. All I can say is: where were you when I needed you?

Which was a bit like searching the beach for a tack with a straw.

"Trace?"

"Dick?"

"I'm ready with the gun. Where is that son of a bitch?"

"Behind us. Hang on."

Trace pulled the helo nearly onto its side. I lifted my head from the ocular and saw the other helicopter moving across the top part of my windscreen. I put my eye back on the gunsight, got the bull's-eye in the other helicopter's path, and fired. A black stream of bullets spit out of the gun beneath my seat, making a big smudge in the sky in front of me. I pushed the smudge in the direction of the other helicopter, managing to get the bullets close enough to force him to jink in front of us. Trace tried to get close for the kill, but the other pilot easily slipped off to the left. Trace spun around, trying to stay with him. I don't know where exactly he went, though—all I could see were tracers from the two Hinds, which had managed to catch up while we were playing tag with the other Havoc.

Shells streaming around us, I moved the gun stick up, trying to get the ship on the right. I bracketed the sucker, but couldn't manage to get him before Trace once more turned off, pushing the helicopter around to the east. She moved the throttle to full military power—or whatever the Russians call the get-the-hell-out-of-here-fast position—and we zipped out over the water, temporarily clear.

But they knew we'd be going south, and as soon as we turned they were on us again.

"They're coming for another pass!" shouted Trace, so loud I wouldn't have needed the interphone.

Her warning was followed quickly by a fresh stream of bullets. Several hit the side of the chopper and we fluttered a bit before Trace was able to get us turned away from our pursuer. She tucked us a little farther out to sea, then banked around, anticipating that the Havoc would be closing in again. I had the gun ready, but the other helo had turned back toward land.

"Now what?" said Trace. "I figure I have about ten minutes' more fuel left in the tanks."

"Take us north along the coast, see if you can find a boatyard," I told her. "I'll call home."

"North?"

"They'll be looking south."

"Good. Copy."

The far eastern shore of Russia is a lonely place, and we didn't see anything that even looked like it might float until nearly fifteen minutes later. By then, the cockpit was buzzing with warnings indicating we were about to run out of fuel, and Trace was trying to gauge how soft the waves would be if we plowed into them. I was on the sat phone with Doc. The good thing was that he knew where we were, thanks to the GPS locator in the sat phone. The bad thing was that he was several hundred miles away in Japan.

"Dick, I see a fishing boat down there. I'm going to land near it," said Trace. "I think we'll fit on the road."

We might have, if we'd had enough fuel to make it. We were still about a hundred yards from shore when the motor quit.

Airplanes can glide when they're out of fuel. Helicopters basically become bricks with useless pieces of metal waiting to chop off your head when they crash.

We hit the water at about forty knots, fast and hard enough to pop the forward windscreen. Water flooded into the compartment from every direction—beneath the seat, over the canopy window, through the ventilation system. By the time I managed to get the seat restraints off, the water was lapping at my chin. The center front panel was too narrow for me to squeeze through. That meant waiting another few seconds for the water inside the cabin to be roughly equal pressure-wise to the water outside so I could open the side panel door. By then I was underwater. I pushed open the door and squeezed out, snaking my legs out from under a piece of the control panel that had twisted upward after the crash.

I climbed up the side, looking into Trace's compartment, which was about halfway down into the water. She was still strapped into her seat, apparently stunned into unconsciousness by the crash. I reached for the handle to get her out, then realized that her door was on the other side of the craft.

As I worked myself around to the other side, I saw that the helicopter had stopped sinking. We had landed on a ledge about ten feet from shore, just high enough to keep the water from reaching Trace's head. Mr. Murphy had been kind.

Not. As I reached for the door, the helicopter shifted suddenly, sliding away from me into the deeper water.

[11]

One of the arguments that's always been raised against women in combat has been that men will drop everything to save a woman on his team if they're in distress, risking their own lives to help them.

True. But anyone who has been in combat knows that's true of *anyone* on the team, male as well as female. Real warriors fight for each other. They save each other. That's why they're there. Most soldiers will tell you that once they get into battle, they're not really fighting for the flag or their country—when the bullets are flying, those are abstractions that you don't have time to think about. What you do think about—or rather feel, since there's not too much time to think about anything—is saving your buddy, your fellow soldier.

If the person in the cockpit was anybody on my team, from Doc to Hiccup to Shotgun, from Junior to Mongoose—from plank holders to newbie nugget cannon fodder—I would have dove in to rescue them regardless. The fact that Trace had more curves than most of the rest of the people on my team made zero difference.

I'm the first to agree that if a woman can't pull her weight, can't kick her quota of butt, then she's got no place on the team. But that goes for a man as well. The standards don't change. You have to be one mean mother, willing to bite the head off of your enemy, chew, digest, and bite some more, if you want to run with Rogue. Not too many women can do that—but not too many guys can either.

Trace could bite with the best of them. And I was damn well going to save her ass from that Russian death trap.

Mud and crap swirled around the water. I pushed down, tugged by the current as I tried to follow the helicopter. I was seeing more shadows than lines when suddenly there was a new thick cloud around me. The next thing I knew, something brushed past me.

I thought shark—until it reached back and tugged my shirt.

Trace!

I pushed up with her. Not being a SEAL, she broke the water a little exuberantly, though under the circumstances I could hardly blame her.

"You okay?" she asked.

"I'm fine—are you?"

"I was knocked out. The water was up to my tits when I came to."

"Lucky for you they're good-sized."

She smirked at me and began stroking toward shore. The boat we'd spotted from the sky was a few hundred yards away, tied up to a battered concrete pier. Two small skiffs and a rowboat were tied nearby, and the half-rotted hull of an old wooden speedboat was beached on the rocks on the other side of the pier. A cluster of houses sat a few dozen yards away, arranged in a close jumble on the land.

The village inhabitants had apparently heard the helicopter crash. They were gathered near the pier, watching as we swam toward them. Wet, tired, and battered, the last thing we wanted at the moment was a fight. But we also wanted the fishing boat. And as the Bible says, those in need are best off taking first, and asking never.

That would be the Rogue Warrior version, of course.

"I'll get the ropes," I told Trace as we reached the boat. "Get the thing going."

"Aye-aye, Captain Bligh."

"Good to hear you joking."

"Who's joking?"

I got up on deck and hustled over to the stern. Ordinarily I'd've just cut the line, but there was nothing handy, so I had to jump onto the crumbling cement and untie it. By the time I reached the second line, Trace had the engine coughing.

I've coughed louder for the pecker inspector squeezing my balls to see exactly which hernia I've added to the collection.

The motor surged, spit, then died. Meanwhile, the crowd had begun moving in our direction.

"Get us going," I yelled.

Trace probably yelled something back along the lines of "no shit," but if so, it was drowned out by the angry Russian curses that were being hurled in my direction by the three old women coming down the pier. Their average age looked to be just under ninety, and while they may have been spry for their age, they looked to have about ten teeth between them.

I undid the last rope and jumped down into the boat. One of the women hurled her cane at me, catching me on the side of the temple.

You have to admire gumption in someone that old.

Unfortunately, I could admire it from close-up, because Trace still hadn't managed to get the damn engine restarted. The boat, which had been drifting away from the pier, changed its mind and started going back. The old women were spitting and flapping their arms at us. I was one happy son of a bitch when the engine finally started strong and we pulled away: I've done some terrible things in my life, but I have yet to stoop to smacking grandmas and confiscating their canes.

[III]

We set a course east, aiming to get out of Russian waters ASAP. The manufacturer's claims that my satellite phone was waterproof came up somewhat short, leaving me unable to call for help. But help was already on the way. Doc, knowing there was a problem because of the way our conversation had ended, used my last transmission to set up a search pattern for the navy. Not content with that, he contacted two helicopter companies based on Hokkaido and hired them to look for us. The first spotted us about four o'clock in the afternoon, and within fifteen minutes we were on our way to Hokkaido, which is that big island at the top of the Japanese chain where they make Sapporo beer.

The Havoc's crash may have helped us escape the Russian marines and anyone else Setrovich's people sent after us: the Russians were looking for a helicopter but couldn't find it. I didn't draw it up that way, but I was more than happy to take advantage of it. If you want to put that one in Murphy's column, go right ahead—he owes me a few.

Doc sent Shotgun and Mongoose up to meet us. Shotgun was so happy to see us it was kind of cute—he was waiting on the helipad as we landed, big-ass grin on his face, shirttails flapping in the breeze. Mongoose was Mongoose—all business, frowning like he'd just been foreclosed on, gripping his MP5 so hard his knuckles were white.

Yes, he did have his gun with him, and in plain sight. Ditto for Shotgun. Doc had told them to take no chances.

"Hey, Cap, how's it hangin'?" shouted Shotgun as Trace and I hopped from the helo.

"Low, Shotgun. How about yourself?"

"Tucked up tight like a bull going for a fight." Shotgun giggled like the schoolgirl that he is. "And how's the most beautiful woman in the world?"

"About an inch away from giving you a kick that will make you a member of the Mormon Tabernacle Choir for life," said Trace.

"Touchy," Shotgun said with a laugh. "Glad you're in a good mood."

"Doc says you wanna hustle, boss," said Mongoose. "We got a plane waiting for us. Taking us to Sado-ga-shima. There's food onboard."

"Is that like sado-masochism?" said Shotgun.

"Ha-ha," said Mongoose.

"Hey, you shouldn't name a place that if you don't want it made fun of."

"Maybe you should write a letter to the emperor and point that out."

"Since when did Shotgun learn to write?" Trace asked.

Sado-ga-shima is an island off the western coast of Japan. It's generally a quiet place, with a few fishing villages around the rocky shorelines. The medieval Japanese rulers used it as a place to send exiles; most notably Emperor Juntoku and the Buddhist priest Nichiren both called Sado home. Tourists generally don't get too much farther than Ryotsu on the east side of the island, or Ogi, which is on the southwest, where hydrofoils connect them to the mainland. There's a gold mine museum at Aikawa, which is on the west side of the island; if you go, try not to ask too many questions about the slaves who worked there during World War II.

Doc had set up shop in a small fishing village on the northwestern end of the island. It wasn't a casual choice—Toshiro Okinaga had once again come through with an assist, arranging on very short notice for us to use a rustic compound his unit occasionally used for training. When I say rustic, I mean rustic—there were no European-style bathrooms in any of the huts.

Which pleased Trace all to punch soon after we arrived. But she was cranky from the plane flight and boat ride anyway. Even the arrival of Sean Mako, her sometime partner in busting newbie recruits, didn't cheer her up.

Jimmy Zim had come over, too, and stalked through the situation room Doc had set up in one of the larger cottages we'd been given. He was talking on his sat phone when I came in, pausing every so often to look at a map taped to the wooden table. A cardboard cutout representing Polorski's ship was tacked to the map. It was 150 miles from the North Korean coast. A navy plane had flown over the ship a few hours earlier, just before sundown. We were expecting the photos within an hour, but the preliminary word was that nothing unusual had been seen on deck.

"A photo may not tell us," said Doc. "It could be below ship. Crated and in pieces."

"Or it could be somewhere else, in a cargo container, aboard any of a thousand other ships," I said, finishing his thought. Ships represent a vast security problem, and containerized shipping is especially difficult to police. The newest container ships can carry upward of twelve thousand containers; there are something like six million containers on the sea at any one moment. Imagine trying to inspect each one of them. The longest piece of the Topol missile was the first stage; it was roughly eight meters long—round it out a bit and say twenty-six feet. Containers come in five basic sizes; the first stage would fit in all but one of them. The launcher would have to be cut up and sectioned off, but welding steel back together is not a difficult skill.

Jimmy Zim was apparently debating what to do with his superiors back in Washington. The argument was essentially the same one that had taken place earlier. Under no circumstances did the CIA want the missile-launcher combo to escape. On the other hand, the State Department was screaming about the "delicacy" of the North Korean disarmament talks. Not seeing the missile on deck meant it might not be there, and the possibility of Yong Shin Jong being on the ship made everything more complicated.

Not in my opinion, of course. As far as I was concerned, there was no need to take chances: just nuke the ship and North Korea while we were at it. But no one in charge seemed ready to consider that one.

"Okay, this is the story," said Jimmy Zim, snapping off his phone. "We have a go for military action—our guys this time, not the Russians. We can use two platoons from SEAL Team 2 to stop the ship."

This is not the normal, assigned operational area for SEAL Team 2 but the op-tempo of combat in the Middle East and the worldwide expansion and franchising of terrorism have made the teams rotate assignments as they come up. I like it. No one is going to miss the action due to bureaucratic bullshit like primary AOs. Thank God. But it's not something new: when the fun happened in Cuba in the 1960s, SEAL Team 1 came east, and everyone was invited to play when Vietnam broke out. True *Team* spirit.

But I digress.

"You go with the SEALs," Jimmy Zim continued. "They get the missile, you get Yong Shin Jong."

"And we take the fall if something goes wrong?" said Trace.

"What could go wrong?"

"Maybe your information is screwed up."

"You gave us both leads," said Jimmy Zim. "Don't blame the CIA."

"We can work with SEAL Team 2," I said.

"That's not the point, Dick." Trace had her arms folded, and her lips pressed together in a pout.

Junior grunted from his workstation in the corner. I went and looked over his shoulder, observing what looked like a satellite image of a lone ship in the ocean.

Which was what it was.

"Russian system," said Junior. "Didn't think it would be polite to break into ours. Besides, this was easier, though there's a bit of a trade-off in detail."

"This is our target?"

"Yeah. Trawler, old fishing vessel."

The Russian vessel was a basic fishing trawler, roughly twenty-five years old, similar to ships used for cod fishing in the Barents Sea. The blocky bridge superstructure sat just forward of midship; a pair of stacks sat about a third of the way from the stern, between two large boom structures. There was a well below these booms, so large fishing nets could be pulled up from the stern. The booms looked like the lower half of the letter A; their main function was to hold two massive pulleys above the deck that made moving the large fishing nets considerably easier. A narrow deck ran across the top of the boom; there was a radio mast in the center.

A pair of lifeboats sat on raised cradles between the superstructure and the wedge-shaped smokestacks; a crane filled the space between them. Another crane sat above the ship's forecastle.

"They could have a whole missile in that factory section," said Doc, studying the photo. "This could be it."

"Hmmmm," said Trace. She was still skeptical, but no more than usual. The more we looked at the vessel, the more obvious it was that it wasn't an ordinary fishing boat.

"They have watches posted here, here, and here." Junior pointed to four spots around the ship. "There may be more. I think this is an infrared sensor here, but I can't get enough resolution out of the Russian system to tell. And check this out."

He slid the mouse cursor to the top of the screen, revealing a menu of tools. They were written in Cyrillic, of course, but thanks to trial and error our intrepid hacker had managed to figure out what most of them meant. He clicked on a tool that placed a magnifying glass on the screen, and selected a small area near the bow. Four or five clicks later, the fuzzy outline of a tarp with a long pencil sticking out the front filled a box on the screen.

"At least a machine gun," said Junior. "Maybe a cannon. And what do you think this is?"

He clicked away, zooming again on the flying bridge at the top of the superstructure. The image showed a boxy baseball bat on a box or maybe a table.

"Launch kit for an SA-16," said Doc.

"I think it's something like that," said Junior. "But I've never seen one."

I had, and though admittedly the image was on the blurry side, I thought Doc and the kid were right. Boarding the ship by helicopter would not be a simple operation.

As it happened, the SEALs had no intention of using helicopters. They planned a seaborne assault, launched from the USS *Greenville*, an attack submarine that had been on maneuvers off the coast of Korea near the DMZ and was at that moment hurrying to get into position to intercept the trawler.

SEAL Team 2 is the unit that yours truly served with in Vietnam. (And if you haven't read the story in *Rogue Warrior*, hie thee to the local bookstore or library and do so. *Now, grasshopper!*) I'll just mention again for the record that the unit continues to uphold the finest warrior traditions in the military. Today's SpecWar fighters are a breed apart, highly trained professionals who are the best in the world at what they do. A lot of them give me the aw-shucks routine when I meet them today, telling me how proud they are to meet me and all that BS; I can honestly say that I'm the one who's impressed. These young bucks have a lot of ability and are true professionals in every sense of the word. I'm proud to say I once served in the same unit they do.

The USS *Greenville* is a Los Angeles-class warship that has been modified to operate the Advanced SEAL Delivery System, or ASDS. The ASDS is a piece of metal shaped like an obese, rectangular torpedo. It does exactly what its name says it does: deliver SEALs, generally to dangerous places near shore. Why a submarine equipped with gear like that would be near North Korea—shucks, I have no idea.

The plan here was simple: the *Greenville* would locate the

trawler, then move into position nearby. It would surface out of sight during the night. The SEAL team would board high-speed rubber raiding craft, approach the target under the cover of darkness, get aboard, and take things from there.

While we were invited along, there was one caveat in the plan. SEALs wait for no man. Or men. Or women. Certainly not us. So if we wanted to be part of the party—and remember, it was supposed to be our party—we had to get out to the SEALs and their submarine, the *Greenville*, posthaste.

Our island was about 350 miles from the sub, too far for a helicopter without refueling. Jimmy Zim got us in touch with an air farcer who promised an MC-130 to pick us up at Niigata, the airport on the Japanese island of Honshu opposite Sado. From there, we would fly to South Korea, where another helicopter—this one belonging to the U.S. Navy—would take us out to the submarine. The schedule was going to be tight; we'd have maybe five minutes leeway to find the submarine or miss the adventure. In that case, we'd have to go back to Korea, refuel, and join the show in progress, missing all the fun.

The MC-130 is an excellent aircraft, a version of the venerable C-130 Hercules outfitted for spec warfare and flown by specially trained air farcers who coat their balls in bronze and take their aircraft into places where aircraft are not supposed to go, depositing warriors where they're least expected. Most of this depositing is done via parachute—which gave me an idea.

"If we have to go all the way to Korea to grab a helicopter, we may not make it back in time," I told Doc, who was helping Jimmy Zim with the arrangements. "Why don't we just use the plane."

"You finally figured out a way to walk on water, skipper?"

"No, but I can fall into it pretty well. We'll parachute and aim for the sub. Shouldn't be too difficult to find if they're on the surface."

"Like hell it won't," said Doc.

"Yo, Dick, screw all that," said Shotgun, who was standing

nearby and stuffing his face with some sort of Japanese egg roll. "Why don't we just, like, parachute onto the ship. KISS."

Trace smirked, but Shotgun wasn't getting homo on us. He was referring to one of the main precepts of special operations—KISS, or keep it simple, stupid. On the other hand, a night jump onto a ship is hardly simple. True, the ship is more of a target than you'd think; even if it's not all lit up—and we didn't expect this one to be—it sticks out like a sore dick with even minimal international nav lights. But seeing what you want to hit and actually hitting it can be two different things.

It would be easier than parachuting to the submarine, though.

To make sure the creeps in the trawler didn't see us, we planned the mission so the MC-130 would fly in a straight line nearby just before drop time. We also mapped a flight profile that would make the aircraft look as if it were a commercial flight—and would keep it above fifteen thousand feet, the ceiling of the Russian antiaircraft weapon we'd spotted. We'd jump a bit over five miles south of the ship, and swoop—you may call it parasailing if you prefer to be more accurate—onto our target, guided not only by guts and instinct but GPS units with big-ass, glow-in-the-dark faces that strapped onto our arms.

One of the things they never mention in movies and online games where guys parachute out of airplanes in the middle of the night is that it is F'in' cold. And "F" doesn't stand for freezing. The temperature in the back of the aircraft was bad enough; once we went out it would be below zero. As we waited for the plane to hit its last way marker, everyone on the team was moving around to try to stay warm.

Except Shotgun. He was eating Twinkies.

"Way marker reached," said the crewman assigned to shepherd us out the plane. "You have five minutes."

We checked our gear and got ready to jump. Besides thermal undies, we were equipped with jumpsuits, balaclavas, and some Nomex gloves Doc had "found" while we waited for the air farce to get its aircraft over to us. The oxygen—you go out at twenty-eight thousand feet, you need oxygen—had come courtesy of a jump school at the airport.

Courtesy might be too strong a word, as they had charged us twice the usual rental. Something in Mongoose's shifty eyes must have given him away as a poor risk to return them.

We made sure our watches were synched, the radios in our helmets were working, and the GPS units calibrated. We were ready. All we needed was word from the SEALs to proceed.

But the SEAL communications channel was uncomfortably silent.

"Maybe they don't want to invite us to their picnic after all," said Doc. "I don't think I'd've wanted any civilians screwing me up, even if they were you."

"Who says I'm a civilian?"

"Uncle Sam."

The thought had crossed my mind. But SEALs tend to be blunt—if they thought we were going to screw them up, they probably would have just said so.

"Maybe Mr. Murphy kicked them in the balls," suggested Sean. "Maybe they aren't going to make it."

"SEALs find a way," said Mongoose. He snapped it out angrily.

"Hey, I ain't putting them down," said Sean. "They're only human."

"No they're not," said Shotgun.

"Watch it, blankethugger," said Mongoose.

Shotgun started laughing. He put his hand on Mongoose's shoulder. "Relax, little brother."

"Fuck your little brother shit."

There's nothing like love and kisses in the air between team members before a mission. But they were only blowing off some excess testosterone before hitting the silk.

"I say we go out and the hell with them," said Trace. "We'll take the ship ourselves if we have to. There's six of us, for Christsake."

Trace's math was off. Yes, there were six shooters from Red Cell—Trace, Sean, Shotgun, Mongoose, myself, Doc—jumping despite a balky knee, I might add. But you can never forget the inestimable Mr. Murphy. Murph is along whatever you do, whatever lengths you go to to keep him from getting an invitation.

He was with the SEALs as well. In fact, he was having a hell of a time with them, goat-fucking their communications system so badly that they couldn't communicate with each other. Nor could they talk to their sub—or us, for that matter.

I didn't know that was the problem at the time, of course. As far as I was concerned, Trace was right—we could take the ship ourselves if we had to.

The rest of the team looked at me. I looked at my watch.

0100 hours on the dot. H hour.

"Let's go," I said.

[IV]

Black is black, but there is no black blacker than the ocean on a moonless night.

The chute gave me a good tug as it deployed, punching me in the family planning region hard enough to make me focus *very intently* on what I was doing. All things considered, though, it was better than the alternative. The altimeter on my left wrist told me I was falling at sixteen feet a second, about as perfect as you'd want. I had a good chute, and I was even heading in the right direction, as verified by the GPS.

One by one, the others checked in. Now that we were on our way, idle chatter dropped off. Even Shotgun was quiet.

I was only about a mile away from the ship as I fell through eight thousand feet. I could see it a bit to my left, a yellowish jag of lights bobbing into the murky ink. I tacked into a spiral to get closer to the bow of the ship, where I intended on landing.

"Something moving on the water near the ship," said Trace over the radio. "Away from it—northwest."

"Where?" I asked her. "Show me on the GPS."

Our GPS units had integrated wireless transmitters, making it possible for team members to track one another. The units had small cursors that could be used as pointers during transmission, showing direction or, in this case, where something was. (Gamin sells a civilian model nearly as powerful as the ones we used for a fraction of the price, so if you're planning on doing a night jump to take out a ship this weekend, check them out.)

Even with the GPS pointer, I couldn't see the boat. The location made me doubt it was part of the SEAL assault—they had briefed an approach from the south, and they were going in the wrong direction.

"Listen up," I told the others over the radio. "Looks like we have a motorboat trying to get away. Trace and I will check it out. The rest of you proceed as planned."

The chorus of "copy that"s was interrupted by a series of flashes that silhouetted the ship. The SEALS had arrived, right on schedule.

The official after-action report presented an executive summary of the action: the SEALs came, they saw, they kicked butt; same old, same old. Casualty count: good guys 0, bad guys 13 dead, no wounded.

The *actual* play-by-play was a hair more complicated, and I'm proud to say that my guys held up their end.

The submarine surfaced ahead of and parallel to the ship, which was moving at roughly twelve knots, your typical merchant vessel not-getting-too-crazy-with-the-fuel speed. The SEALs quickly launched and boarded their rubber rafts, revved their outboards, and went off in pursuit of their prey. There are a number of different methods for hostile boarding of a cargo ship under way; all entail enough bruises and general aggravation to make you one ornery son of a bitch by the time you get aboard.[21]

Consider first of all the fact that those rubber rafts are not built for comfort. You can get them up to forty knots, maybe even higher, but you feel every shock in every bone of your body as the craft smacks against the waves. They do have their pluses—the craft are very hard to see at night, since they and their occupants are low to the water and as black as black can be. Because of the typical ambient and not-so-ambient sounds aboard ship, they're also relatively hard to hear. Your basic merchant ship—hell, *any* ship—has a fairly loud engine, and then there's the water and all manner of other noisy distractions to render even large outboards virtually silent.

But getting back to my point. The real bumps and bruises

---

[21] At some point in the future, this sort of mission may be carried out by a high-tech carbon fiber inflatable like the Stiletto, whose M-shaped hull not only can take her over fifty knots but also is gentle on the back. For now though, the rubber met the waves.

come with the boarding itself. The method of choice involves telescoping poles that can be hooked on to the ship and unfolded into a primitive caving ladder. The contraptions are made of titanium; while light for what they do, they still weigh a ton when you're holding them up in the open sea. SEALs also use line firing guns—they look like mortars—that shoot lines over the railing. The problem is that the lines can easily go right through without catching. Using the telescoping rod/ladder in a boat moving twenty or so knots is like trying to hold up an extension ladder on the freeway while sitting on your car roof, but my feeling is it's much more reliable. Some things haven't changed much in forty-some years—although in this case I'll bet a lot of guys wish they had.

The SEALs weren't dealing with a warship, but the vessel was definitely of a hostile sort and had a full watch mounted—there was that gun at the bow and the antiaircraft missile up near the bridge. The invaders were getting real-time intelligence thanks to a small unmanned plane circling above the area. A direct data link—unlike the radios, this one was working—showed them where all the watch hands were. That helped cut down on the pucker factor as they climbed up the narrow ladder to the deck. The SEALs' image was crisper than the satellite view Junior had hacked for me earlier: not only did it show that the weapon up front—still tarped—had the barrel of a 12.7mm DShK—but it was sharp enough to show them how many of the men on watch were bald (two out of six).

That's one big difference between the SEALs today and what us "experienced" guys did back in the day: when I was their age, we had to guess about where the blind spots would be on the trawler; the young bloods' eye in the sky let them leave the guessing to the enemy. Their technology doesn't make them better SEALs—excuse me for sounding egotistical—because a SEAL is a SEAL is a SEAL, then, now, and forever. I might even argue that not having that intelligence gave those of us back in the day a certain advantage—we had to be naturally more flexible, an important asset when dealing with Mr. Murphy. But the pictures helped these young bloods narrow Mr. Murphy's all-important window of opportunity, making them, even in my prejudiced opinion, more efficient than we were.

Now that you've read that, burn this book, because I may never admit it again.

But Mr. Murphy long ago proved that even if you lock all the doors, he'll slip through the window. One of the groups assigned to get aboard on the starboard side had trouble getting the ladder to hook on to the railing so they could climb up. It wasn't *much* trouble—it just took them four or five tries, while the others were able to hook up in one or two. Not a big deal—except it gave Mr. Murphy a chance to tickle the ship's first mate's tobacco habit. The mate came out on deck and whether he heard the clank of a grappling hook nearby or just looked over the side to see if it was safe to pee, we'll never know. One of the SEALs below saw him look over the side, almost directly overhead. The Russian stood there stunned for only a moment, but it was long enough for the SEAL to cure the man's curiosity with a few rounds from his MP5N. A friend who'd been coming out to join him for a smoke saw him fall. He threw himself back inside and slammed home the lock on the door, then alerted the ship as the SEALs began their attack.

Knowing the locations of the men on deck made the shooters' job easier than it might have been, and within three minutes the two platoons of SEALs had successfully eliminated opposition on deck, killing all of the watch hands. That left the people inside the ship. And that's where things started to get interesting.

Generals often complain about how hard it is to fight in an urban environment—close quarters and all that. Imagine that same fight in a ship. Instead of roads, you have corridors and ladders. And it's at night. The ship is rolling ten degrees every few seconds, and stinks of fish that died twenty-five years before.

Not that the SEALs were complaining. Or even cursing. They were too busy working.

A trio of SEALs pushing up the starboard side of the superstructure came under fire, barely managing to duck fire from the bridge as the Russians began to rally. Meanwhile, another team approached from the other side. As the point man reached the railing at the deck outside the wheelhouse, a Russian emerged from the top of the superstructure and began firing down at him. The SEAL threw himself against the bulkhead only a few feet away from the bridge. He couldn't have been ten feet from the man who was firing at his companions on the other side. But he might as well have been ten miles away—the guy on the top of the ship had him pinned and unable to move.

Here's another difference between SEALs now and SEALs back in the day—the new guys have much better air support.

Doc, Sean, Shotgun, and Mongoose had been observing the situation as they descended. Mongoose was closest to the bridge, and began tugging on his guidelines to speed his descent even before Doc tasked him with the job of helping the SEAL. Knowing Mongoose, his preference would undoubtedly have been to land directly on the SOB, but the antenna mast made that impossible. And not even Mongoose is crazy enough to try shooting his machine gun during a descent.[22] Instead, he took one of the flash-bang grenades he'd prepared, slipped off the tape with his thumb, then tossed it down. He claims he got a bull's-eye; whether that's true or not, the grenade's strum and thrum was more than enough to give the Russian an immediate dry-cleaning emergency. The SEAL saw the flash, realized what must be happening, and jumped out of cover, taking down the man who had been firing at the team on the starboard side of the ship.

Mongoose, meanwhile, dipped his parachute's left "wing," trying to turn back quickly enough to land on the main deck near the bow. The sharp maneuver caused him to stall so close

[22] Shotgun, on the other hand, surely would have tried that.

to the water that there was no space or time to recover. He plopped unceremoniously into the sea, lucky that he hadn't slammed face-first into the side of the ship a few meters away. He cursed, shed his chute, then swam over to one of the SEALs' inflatable boats.

Shotgun had been tasked to take the high ground at the stern of the ship, and was aiming to land on the catwalk of the rear crossbar. But the catwalk was narrow; Shotgun is not. Even though he slowed the chute down considerably as he approached, there was simply not enough space to land properly. So he pretended he was a jet fighter—note that I'm talking about the aircraft, not the aviator—using the walkway's wire railing as an arrestor cable, bashing into it as if he were an F/A-18 stopping on a carrier.

That had to hurt. And if it didn't, tumbling over onto the steel-plated catwalk and bouncing a few times as the parachute tried pushing back with the wind almost certainly did. But Shotgun would never admit that it did, not even to himself. His response was to start laughing—a little chuckle at first, which grew to a pretty loud guffaw after he'd straightened himself out on the beam, unhooked his chute, and grabbed his gun. Three of the Russians made the mistake of running toward one of the lifeboats, probably hoping to escape; Shotgun promptly demonstrated that it was a supremely poor move.

Doc had a routine landing near the bow, rolling gently onto the deck to preserve his knee, all as planned. He hooked up with the SEAL lieutenant in charge of the op, and watched as the SEALs continued their demonstration of how to successfully take over a ship. Sean landed a few feet away and joined one of the search parties. Taller than anyone else on the team, he found himself at point—there was no sense staying back, he explained, since he was likely to get the ricochets anyway.

The Russian captain and a few crewmen tried to take a stand on the bridge, locking the doors and yelling incomprehensible curse words at the invaders, punctuating their oaths with automatic weapons fire.

"Looks like it's time to negotiate a surrender," said the SEAL lieutenant. He called in his chief negotiator, a young petty officer with an advanced degree in the LAW.

That's L-A-W, as in Light Antitank Weapon, officially known as an M72. It looks like a bazooka and can be fired by one man. As the initials suggest, the weapon is actually intended for tanks, but it can blow other things up as well.

Negotiations were quick and thorough. The weapon was aimed at the middle plate of glass on the bridge. The weapon was fired. The projectile penetrated the glass. The projectile detonated. The bridge was incinerated, as were its occupants.

Negotiations successful. Deal closed.

With the ship's captain eliminated, the remaining crew quickly surrendered. The SEALs began searching the ship. Mongoose went aft with the team tagged to look into the fish well; Shotgun stayed on top providing cover and stuffing Twinkies in his mouth.

The fish well looked exactly as it would if the trawler was still being used for fishing. Not only did it reek of dead-fish stink; it was rusted, bloody, and smeared with crushed fish gizzards. But the bulkhead on the end of the well below the bridge superstructure had been subtly altered, not only reinforced but enlarged and equipped with state-of-the-art locks.

Even the best lock won't stand up to C4, the ultimate lock pick. The SEALs were accommodating fellows; upon learning that Mongoose was a member of the fraternity, they bestowed upon him the honor of pushing the button that blew the locks. The charges blew out with so much enthusiasm that the entire panel flew downward into the well, revealing a large garagelike structure big enough to hold a rocket launcher and its missile. And, as a special added bonus, there was a spare next to it, resting on a set of wooden cradles and a pair of small trucks, which looked to have been fashioned from Gators, the ATV-like vehicles often used for ferrying supplies around military bases.

The basic ingredients of solid fuel are ammonium perchlorate (an oxidizer) and hydroxyl terminated polybutadene (the actual fuel), which is often spiked with PETN and other explosives to make it more potent. The ingredients are inert until brought together. Hydroxyl terminated polybutadene is comparatively safe and easy to handle *unless* you do something to make it burn. Once ignited, it gets extremely hot and very bright—so bright that I'm told it can be seen clearly from five miles away, which was where the *Greenville* picked up the team and our guys just as the timers the SEALs had set ignited.

Made a hell of a snapshot.

The SEALs hauled twelve sailors back to the sub with them, using the ship's lifeboats. None of the sailors were Yong Shin Jong, which disappointed Doc a great deal.

But I wasn't surprised at all.

(V)

I left myself dangling from my chute along with Trace as we tried following a small boat moving at a high rate of speed away from the trawler. For the first few seconds, I thought we might be able to drop in on them—from our angle and height, it looked as if we would be able to do just that. But that was an optical illusion, and after a minute passed it was obvious that we were falling behind. Trace and I each trimmed our chutes, trying to accelerate, but it was a losing battle, and by the time we hit the water we'd fallen behind by what I'd guess was a mile and a half. I spotted a low, dark silhouette on a dead run ahead, maybe three miles away. I made a mental note of it as I tucked my feet together and did my best side roll to ease the landing impact.

The water was not warm. My chute came in right over me, forming a soggy little tent as I surfaced. It felt as if I'd been swallowed by a jellyfish for a few seconds as I struggled to get my bearings in the darkness. I finally untangled myself from the nylon, got out from under the chute, and took a healthy breath of sea air.

"Dick!"

I growled in Trace's direction. She'd inflated her little raft and gotten herself squared away.

"Which direction?" she asked as I pulled myself onto the gunwale.

I pointed in the direction of the silhouette.

The tiny survival raft had not been designed as a transport vehicle, and was not particularly large. We shoved our knapsacks—waterproof, of course—and the rest of our gear on them. Then Trace and I lined up shoulder to shoulder on one side, kicking in the direction we wanted to go, guided by our GPS units. But it was very slow going, and more than an hour passed before we saw the shadow of a ship on the water ahead.

It turned out not to be a ship—it was the motorboat we'd been following. But at first the darkness and shadows and our own expectations played tricks on our eyes, and we had a hard time deciphering what we were seeing. It wasn't until we were less than fifty yards away that we finally realized it was the boat. From where we were we had no way of knowing whether it was occupied or not.

Trace took the bow; I took the stern.

The boat was a small pleasure craft, thirty or so feet long, much of that devoted to a cabin. She was powered by a pair of good-sized Mercury engines. None of her lights were lit.

Just because the boat seemed deserted didn't mean that it was. And if I was going to ass-u-me anything, I'd better ass-u-me there'd be trouble aboard.

A metal swimming ladder hung down off the starboard side. I put my left hand on it, pausing to listen. In my right hand I had my RW Strider knife.

I slipped upward, taking a peek.

Nothing.

Up and over.

Still nada. Knife away. Gun out. Ready for bear.

Something moved near the bow.

Trace.

But as I dropped to my knee, I saw a shadow near the opening to the cabin. I pointed my weapon there, waiting.

The shadow didn't move.

"Dick!" hissed Trace.

I hissed back, then rose and walked toward the shadow slowly. It grew into a head, and then the head grew into a body.

A dead body. Behind it were two more.

"There's a dozen bullet holes in the boat," said Trace.

"Yeah," I said, pulling out a flashlight to check the rest of the small cabin. When I was absolutely certain there was no else there, I shone the light on the first body.

It was Yong Shin Jong.

"Damn," I said, cursing as I snapped off the light and went topside.

"Since when are you so sentimental about dead scumbags?" asked Trace.

I ignored her question, inspecting the controls. The boat had an ignition key circuit; the key was missing.

"See if you can hotwire that," I told her. "I'll check the engine."

"Quicker to just find the key," said Trace, going back down the ladder to the cabin.

A line over the side near the stern held a small anchor. I pulled it up slowly, half expecting I might find another body attached. But it was just an old can filled with cement that had hardened into concrete.

"What the hell is this?" yelled Trace from the cabin. "Jesus."

"Since when are you so sentimental about dead scumbags?" I said mockingly.

"Since they're all Yong Shin Jong."

I let go of the rope and went down the ladder to the cabin. Trace had turned over the bodies and played her flashlight on their faces. Sure enough, she was right—three Yong Shin Jongs, each one deader than the other, lay on the deck of the small cabin.

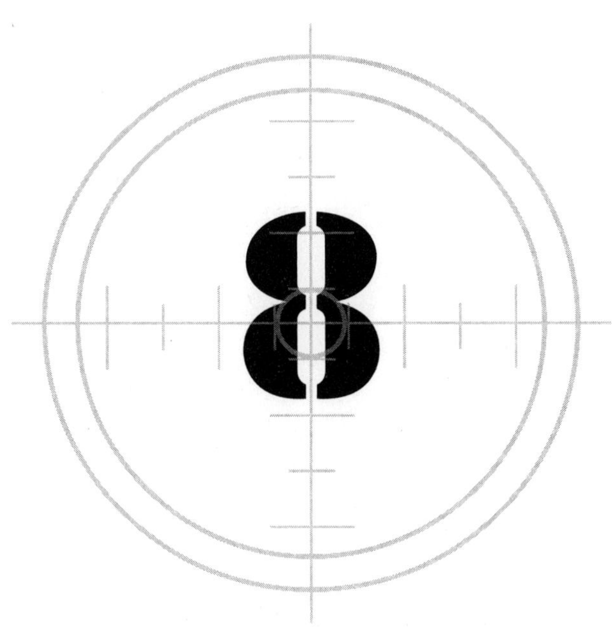

[I]

Three for the price of one?

"They have to be body doubles," insisted Trace. "Doesn't Kim do that?"

Kim was certainly notorious for using body doubles, but did his son do the same? And were all three doubles, or only two?

It was dark, they were dead—any one of them could be the dictator's bastard. Or none. One looked a little chubby, another too skinny, the third too tall. The more I stared, the more I questioned. They were definitely dressed like the man I had seen—and who knew if I had seen the real McCoy or one of these men?

I certainly didn't. I went back up to the wheel, ducked under the instrument panel, and with the help of my knife got the motors running. I set a course due west, toward North Korea—and, I hoped, the ship that I had seen earlier.

"Where have you been, pond scum?" asked Doc when I checked in, flattering me with his overwhelming affection.

"Trace and I went for a quick swim."

We traded sitreps. The SEALs had reestablished their link to the submarine, and I was able to give Doc our position and heading. According to the GPS, we were 120 miles off the Korean coast, well outside of North Korea's coastal waters—but tell that to the crew of the *Pueblo*.

For those of you who were still twinkles in your daddies' beer in 1968, the *Pueblo* was a navy "research" ship that went fishing for electronic signals off North Korea, only to be captured by the North Koreans. The crew was tortured by their gracious hosts, even more so after said hosts realized their guests were giving them the finger in the propaganda photos they'd taken. The ship's captain was eventually given the choice of apologizing for being in Korean territorial waters—which of course he wasn't—or watching his crew get shot one at a time. He opted to save his men, and thus wrote the first apology in the history of the world that peed on his captors. (The commander used the word "paean" in a sentence along the lines of "we paean the great leader of Korea." The Koreans looked up the word "paean" in the dictionary and figured they were being honored.)

The cabin cruiser's engines had been tweaked, and if the instruments were to be believed, were able to propel the boat to forty-two knots at the red line. The engine work was hardly the only modification made to the craft. Large auxiliary fuel tanks had been installed, and there was a GPS system on par with my mobile unit, and a radio sophisticated enough to pick up everything from standard military communications to old *I Love Lucy* reruns still circulating in the ionosphere. A computer hard-wired to the cabin desk was connected to the Internet via a satellite link. The browser's memory had been wiped clean.

"I know there are ways to look for deleted files," said Trace. "What if I give Junior a call and see if he can talk me through them?"

It was worth a shot, so I handed over the sat phone. In the meantime, I held a straight course and contemplated the $64 million question: *Was Yong Shin Jong one of the dead men below, or had he escaped to whatever ship it was I was following?*

I know what you're thinking: Dickie, you've gone about as far as you can with this one; pack up your tent and go home. There's not going to be any $64 million payoff at the end of this rainbow; there's not even going to be a rainbow. Even assuming that Yong Shin Jong is alive, and is aboard that ship, how are you going to get him?

Truth be told, I might have asked myself the same questions, if I hadn't seen a smudge on the horizon ahead to port.

Not just a smudge—a moving, ship-shaped smudge. I changed course to follow.

The ship looked like a coastal freighter, a bit smaller than the trawler that had held the missiles. It was making about sixteen or seventeen knots, moving diagonally to the North Korean coast, traveling south as well as westward.

I called Matthew back at Sado-ga-shima. Jimmy Zim had just left for Tokyo, but that was just as well. I told Junior to try and get some information on the ship we were following from our navy friends. He came back about fifteen minutes later with the news that it was registered in Myanmar, the country you and I used to call Burma.

"But I did some checking," added Junior. "I hope you don't mind."

"Tell me."

"It's been back and forth between a dozen South and North Korean ports over the last eighteen months. And before that it was in Russia," he said, a note of triumph in his voice. "Kamenka. Same place you just raided."

"Good work, Junior," I told him.

"Ask him about the computer," hissed Trace. "Tell him the files are erased. Isn't there a way to get them back?"

There was. Junior talked her through the procedure and came up with some interesting e-mails—interesting largely because they were encrypted and couldn't be read. There were also some Web porn sites he didn't know about.

"I can take the e-mail addresses and see if they mean anything to the No Suchers," said Junior.

"Good. Do it. And get yourself a milkshake. Call me if you find anything."

"Ike's on board that ship," said Trace as I disconnected. "What are we going to do?"

"Just follow for a while."

"What's the plan for going on board?"

"Who says we're going on board?"

"We can't just let him get away."

"We're not. We're following him."

"We have to stop him. We can sneak on and grab him."

"Polorski?"

"Yes."

"He's not necessarily on the ship, Trace. And it's Yong Shin Jong we're interested in."

"You know he is, Dick. He wasn't at the base, and he wasn't on the other ship—he took Yong Shin Jong with him. The real Yong Shin Jong. These were imposters—I'll bet backups that he was going to use if he couldn't get the real one. He's going to deliver him now."

"Or one of them was the real Yong Shin Jong and your love toy was told to kill him," I said.

"Why bring him all the way here if you're going to kill him?"

"Why bring the imposters?"

"In case someone on the ship's crew tried to get nasty. No one would know who was the genuine bastard."

"Maybe."

"We have to get him, Dick. Whether Yong Shin Jong is with him or not. Let's do it."

"Someday I'm going to sit down with you and give you a long lecture on not getting your emotions involved in an operation."

"I'm not letting my emotions get involved."

"You don't want to kill the son of a bitch?"

"I *do* want to kill the son of a bitch. With my bare hands. After I've dragged him under the hull of his ship a few times and fed his balls to the sharks."

"And you're not emotionally involved?"

"Of course not."

Apache logic. Hard to argue with.

I turned the wheel hard to port, setting my course parallel to hers. I took out the sat phone to call Doc—then noticed that Trace was rummaging through her gear.

"What are you doing?"

"I'm look for the pancakes."

"Pancakes" was her quaint term for the suction cup devices

we'd packed as backups to get aboard the trawler. While Navy SEALs do use the devices, they're really a last-ditch choice—they're literally suction cups, used to pull yourself up the side, arm length by sagging, cramping arm length. You press a button to release the grip, then smack it on the hull a little higher, moving up perhaps a few excruciating feet at a time.

"You're not thinking of boarding the ship, are you?" I asked her.

"Aren't you?"

I was in fact, but not without help. I called Doc back, but my timing was off—he'd just gotten aboard the submarine and for the moment couldn't receive the signal from the satellite.

Trace gave the vessel a good look-over with the night goggles from her pack, staring intently at the ship.

"This will be easier than I thought," she said suddenly. She handed the glasses to me. "Look."

The vessel was trailing a line near midship, possibly inadvertently left earlier when they had hooked up with the motorboat and made the exchange. Poor seamanship—but very common.

"We can use the line to get aboard," said Trace. "Easy as one, two, three."

Using the line to get aboard the ship was easier than using the pancakes, but ease was a relative concept. It was also easier than hiking up Mount Everest in my underwear while carrying a polar bear on my back.

"If we're going to get Yong Shin Jong, we're going to have to get aboard before daybreak," said Trace. "They're only a few hours outside of Korean waters."

"That's just it—we're going after Yong Shin Jong, not Tall, Dark, and Polack," I told her. "You have to keep your emotions in check. This isn't a lovers' quarrel we're involved in."

"Fuck you."

Isn't that just like a woman? Always trying to sweet talk you into something.

The sat phone buzzed; Jimmy Zim was returning my call.

"You've lived up to your reputation," said the CIA officer. "Washington is very pleased."

"Sorry to hear that."

"Excuse me? Our connection must be bad."

I'm not in the business of pleasing Washington, but I dropped the matter without further comment and explained our situation. Zim's tone changed abruptly.

"There's no way we're going to get any kind of okay to use the SEALs against that ship, Dick. Just zero. Less than zero."

"What if Yong Shin Jong is aboard?"

"Is he?"

"I don't know."

"Even if he is, it'll be a hard sell. A very, very hard sell. How close is the ship to Korean waters?"

Close enough that the *Greenville* would never reach it before it crossed over the line. It was no use arguing with Jimmy Zim; he was just the messenger.

But I argued with him anyway.

"You get on the line with Washington and tell them we have to stop that ship. Tell them Yong Shin Jong is aboard. Tell them the nuke is there. Tell the State Department to drop dead."

"Dick—"

"Just tell them. Call your boss, and tell him, too."

"Who?"

"Admiral Jones."

"I don't think the director—"

"Call him. And get our submarine moving. I'll be on the ship."

[11]

The truth is, I didn't think Jimmy Zim would pass along my "request" that the USS *Greenville* stop the ship, much less believe that he would actually win official permission to do so. But I did think the sub would respond to a distress call if the ship was floundering.

The merchant ship was doing just under twenty knots, much faster than a cargo vessel typically travels, especially in these fuel conscious days, but not so fast that we couldn't catch up in the cabin cruiser. As we approached, Trace locked her GPS unit on transmit and left it on the cruiser's bench so we'd be able to find it later. Then she grabbed her gear and walked out onto the bow. The closer we got, the more she leaned forward, until at last I thought she was going to fall in the drink. The line she'd spotted dangled off the side, slapping against the water, barely visible in the shadows as we pulled up.

Matching course and speed to another craft can be difficult at night, especially if you're trying to do it by mental telepathy. Despite the fact that I'd tied the wheel with my belt, the cabin cruiser veered starboard as soon as I reached for the rope to follow Trace upward. I bent back over the windscreen and corrected the rudder. Then I juiced the throttle for a moment before killing it completely.

The line stayed just out of reach. The cabin cruiser once more started to veer away from the ship. I started leaning back to get the wheel, then saw the rope shoot toward me.

It nearly knocked me over with a teasing love tap. I grabbed it backhanded as I fell, then hung on as the cabin cruiser veered off again. The screws driving the ship were making a sound like *KER-chunk, ker-gonnagetya-chunk, gonnachunkya, gonnachunkya.* They were meat grinders with suction, waiting to welcome me if I lost my grip. The sound chased away my fatigue and I pulled myself tight to the ship, scraping against the barnacles at the waterline.

By the time I neared the deck, I was more than a little wet. I was also pissed off enough that I didn't care. I grabbed one of the rail stanchions and hoisted myself up, reaching for my gun's waterproof cocoon at the same time.

"Trace?" I whispered.

No answer. I adjusted my radio—the clip-on microphone on my shirt had slipped down—then asked for her again without getting an answer.

The bridge superstructure sat over the stern; the rest of the ship was given over to cargo bays and a pair of booms for cranes. The ship may have been a few years younger than I was—but not many. It looked as if it hadn't been painted for at least a decade. A mossy smell mixed with the stench of oil and exhaust whenever the breeze died.

I got my bearings, sorting the shadows from the lines and machinery. Hearing voices, I moved in their direction, toward the bow. A pair of seamen were sharing a cigarette and a bottle near the anchor chain, complaining about something in Russian.

I'm guessing they were complaining because they were sailors, and because of the tones of their voices; I didn't understand most of the words. Under other circumstances, I might have been inclined to live and let live: not because I'm filled with the Christian spirit, but because eliminating two watchmen might indirectly raise an alarm when someone came looking for them. But I'd just taken a god-awful beating on the way up the side of the ship, and I was feeling even more ornery than normal. I stowed the submachine gun and took out my Strider.

The radio on the belt of one of the sailors chirped. He acknowledged it, then started aft. I waited until he was just passing me, then leaped up from behind the boom's winch machinery and gave him a boost off the side. He yelled all the way down.

His shout was enough to get the attention of the man who'd just shared his cigarette. The Russian came back cautiously, one hand on his radio. I came up behind him, and slipped one hand hard into his diaphragm while pulling the knife sharply across his neck. He made a gulping sound and dropped to the deck.

He followed his smoking buddy into the drink, after I grabbed the radio and keys from his pockets. I also relieved him of a Glock. There's no such thing as having too many weapons when you're crashing a party.

The radio crackled at me as I made my way back. Between the squelch and the noise of the ship, I'm not sure I would have understood what they were saying if they were speaking English. What I did understand was the movement of a pair of shadows over at the superstructure. I squeezed low to the deck, then slipped sideways to what looked like a metal gangplank secured nearby. One of the shadows disappeared back into the superstructure; the other went toward the stern. I started to rise, then saw something out of the corner of my eye—a figure jumped from halfway up the crane boom and trotted in my direction. Some sixth sense kept me from firing my gun.

"Trace," I hissed.

"Dick. Where the hell have you been?"

"Lowering the head count. Why didn't you answer the radio when I called you?"

"I didn't hear you," she said. "I was inside the ship."

The downside of burst transmission radios—they don't burst transmit too well through solid objects.

Trace had snuck inside and moved along a corridor to a metal stairway (or ladder, since we're on a ship) before hearing voices and taking cover in a cabin used as a storeroom. When the crewmen passed, she'd gone up the ladder far enough to see a guard standing in front of a doorway about halfway down the corridor. Before she could do anything else, she heard a sailor coming up from behind her; she ducked below, crouching in the shadows. Had the sailor been very attentive, he'd have seen her, but most of us don't look for things we don't think are there, and so he passed by without noticing her.

"Yong Shin Jong has to be in that cabin," she said.

"Maybe."

"Who else would they be guarding?"

"Maybe Polorski."

"I couldn't be that lucky."

Before checking it out, I decided to secure our escape route. Swimming back to the cabin cruiser was one option, but not an attractive one if we had to tow Yong Shin Jong, too. A better solution was to steal one of the lifeboats. Or rather *the* lifeboat—the merchant ship was equipped with only one, mounted on the starboard side near the stern.[23] To get there, we'd have to go all the way around the fantail.

We moved aft cautiously to reconnoiter. Lights were on in the cabins that lined the stern portion of the deck; it took us two or three minutes to crawl beneath the portals and get to the other side without being seen. Just as I turned the corner, I heard a watchman cursing. I froze, then slid out far enough to see a boot sticking over the edge of the deck above. His radio was squawking—very possibly they were looking for the crewmen I'd sent overboard.

Pressing myself against the bulkhead, I inched my way forward until I was parallel with the lifeboat. Light flooded out onto the deck from the cabins above. I could reach the davits easily enough—two quick steps across the deck—but there was the question of swinging the boat out without being seen, either from the cabins or the man who was still cursing above.

According to the GPS unit, the cabin cruiser was still relatively close. If we weren't seen aboard, it would make more sense to simply drop off into the water and swim for it.

I made my way back to the other side of the ship, where Trace was watching a pair of sailors barking orders at each other.

"They're looking for the guys you sent overboard," she said. "They were saying something about drinking. One's going below."

[23] It turned out that there was a collapsible raft lashed to the superstructure, but we didn't see it at the time.

"Since when do you speak Russian?"

"I understand the words 'vodka' and 'shit-faced.' "

The men split up. We waited until the first sailor went inside the ship, then snuck toward the second as he walked forward along the deck. Trace ducked behind the hatchway to the cargo hold. I positioned myself near the crane boom, leaned against it as if for support, and whistled.

The man turned, probably blinked, then came at me like a bull, aiming to give me a reaming I'd never forget. There was just enough light on the deck to see his eyes jump from their sockets in surprise and then shock—not so much at my ugly mug, but at the hard slap of Trace's blackjack against the base of his skull. Her first shot sent him crumbling to the deck; her second and third were icing on the cake. She grabbed his sweater and cap—neither would have fit me—then we sent him overboard where he'd have a better chance of finding his companions.

The man who'd gone below emerged from a hatchway on the cargo deck just as we were disposing of his companion. Trace saw his head pop up about ten feet away from us. Before he could react, she double-tapped her MP5N, putting a large hole in the top of his skull.

The H&K MP5N noise suppressor sounds a bit like an overanxious pellet gun, easy to miss over the constant hum of a ship's engines, especially if you're inside the ship. So I might have taken our chances had the Russian not been on the radio when he saw us.

"Let's get Yong," I yelled to Trace, sprinting toward the door. "Come on."[24]

I flew through the passageway and up the ladder. The guard Trace had seen earlier heard me coming and started to unhol-

---

24 One of my wise-ass editors just pointed out I should have called Doc around here somewhere. "Always communicate with your team," he said. "They should know where you are at all times."

Great advice. Fuck you very much.

ster his pistol, but before he could bring it to bear, it was bouncing on the deck. He'd dropped it as he ricocheted back against the bulkhead, propelled by the force of my bullets as they slammed against his bullet-resistant vest at close quarters.

That was the first pair of bullets, aimed at the center of his chest. My third bullet added a pretty red mark to his forehead.

I scrambled to the cabin, yelled, "Stand back," and blasted the lock. Then I did a one-two dance step, snapping the door back hard enough to knock it off one of its hinges.

Yong Shin Jong blinked at me from a chair at the far end of the room.

"Can you swim?" I asked.

"W-what?"

"Can you swim?" I grabbed his arm and pulled him to his feet.

"Yes."

There was a life jacket on the wall nearby. I grabbed it and pushed it into his hands.

"Dick!" Trace yelled in the hall.

I pulled Yong Shin Jong with me as the passageway outside began echoing with gunfire. There was a loud bang—Trace had tossed a grenade—then silence.

"Go!" yelled Trace.

I pulled Yong Shin Jong from the cabin and half dragged him down the ladder with me. Trace took up the rear.

"What's going on?" he asked as we ran.

"We're rescuing you. But you're going to have to swim for a bit."

I pushed him up against the side of the passageway as more gunfire sounded above us. I fired a burst behind Trace as she scrambled down, dropped my empty mag, and reloaded. She ran toward the door we'd used to get in.

"I got point," she said.

"Go!"

Yong Shin Jong had pulled the life jacket over his head, but was still moving in slow motion. I grabbed him and pushed him to follow Trace. Just as she reached the open door, there was a flash of light outside. Someone tried coming through the passageway and she cut them down. But bullets began swarming around us. I shoved Yong Shin Jong down, throwing myself on top of him as the gunfire continued. We were maybe ten yards from the railing, but the amount of lead pouring through the passageway made it clear that we weren't going that way without the help of a tank, and maybe not even then.

"Back up topside," I yelled to Trace. "Give us some smoke."

She waved the grenade at me. I grabbed one of my flash-bang grenades and tossed it toward the door. By the time it exploded, Yong Shin Jong and I were halfway up the ladder. Four sailors lay in the passageway between us and the cabin Yong Shin Jong had been in.

"Try not to trip over the dead bodies," I told the Korean, forging ahead.

The air inside the ship, not particularly fresh to begin with, turned sharply acrid as the smoke began furling from Trace's grenade. Another ladder started to the starboard at the end of the corridor. We ran up it, spotting a passageway that looked as if it would run to the other side of the ship. As soon as I stuck my head around the corner a fresh round of gunfire beat me back. I waited for Trace to reach us, then rolled out onto the deck, hosing the corridor. But whoever had fired had vanished; there was no answering fire. I led the way down the passageway, then out the door onto a catwalk that ran around the exterior of the ship's superstructure. The lifeboat I'd spotted earlier sat about ten yards to my right, and down two decks.

"Wait until I give the signal," I yelled to Trace and Yong Shin Jong inside. Then I ran down the narrow catwalk toward the stern, figuring that the man who'd been firing at me earlier had retreated outside and taken cover around the corner. I threw myself down as I reached the turn, landing on my shoulder in a skid. I meant to stop, but the deck was slipperier than I'd thought, and I slid out past the edge of the cabin area, just barely stopping myself by hooking my foot around one of the wire guardrails. I had my submachine gun ready, but there was no one there.

By the time I got back to my feet and retreated, Trace and Yong Shin Jong were out on the catwalk. Yong Shin Jong started over the rail, intending to climb down a ladder that ran down to the deck. I looked over at the lifeboat and realized that it was no longer tied down to the deck as it had been earlier—the davits had been pushed out so that it now hung over the water.

"Wait," I yelled, grabbing Yong.

A flare shot up from the area of the bridge.

"You're screwed, Marcinko," said a voice over the loudspeakers. "Time to give your ass up."

"You're a son of a bitch, Ike," yelled Trace. "When I catch you I'm going to cut your balls off and feed them to you."

Good thing she wasn't letting her emotions do the talking.

[III]

The situation was this: Polorski's men had pushed the lifeboat out, either thinking that we would head for it or intending to use it to follow us if we got away. They had then taken positions near the stern and the forward base of the superstructure behind the machinery and gear boxes, covering the routes to the boat. They were also inside the cabins behind us. We couldn't get to the deck, let alone the lifeboat, without getting shot. And unless we grew wings, there was no way to go over the side from where we were. Trace and I *might* have been able to jump it—emphasis on the word might—but pudgy Yong Shin Jong would go plop on the deck.

What we had was an old-fashioned stalemate—one which favored Polorski.

Temporarily. Because sooner or later, Doc and the SEALs would be heading in our direction, looking for us.

"Give me Yong Shin Jong, and I'll let you go," said Polorski. "I have nothing against you, Dick."

"I have something against you, Ike," yelled Trace.

Polorski clearly heard her.

"We had a great time, Trace. Too bad it couldn't last. Another time, maybe."

"Fuck you, asshole."

"We can try that."

Trace answered with a string of expletives notable in their creativity. As she and Tall, Dark, and Polack traded insults, I examined our position. We were a deck below bridge level; another catwalk ran back from the bridge above our heads.

The best defense is a good offense, and being naturally offensive, I decided our best bet was to take the initiative. Pointing at Yong Shin Jong to stay put, I hopped up on the railing and leaped for one of the stanchions above. I caught it and threw my legs to the right, hauling myself upward. My acrobatics did not go unnoticed—someone below shouted, and as I rolled onto the narrow gangway a burst of gunfire punctuated the metal just above me. This was followed by more shouts to cease fire, and the bullets soon stopped.

Polorski obviously didn't want Yong Shin Jong hit, which explained why he was wasting time haranguing us instead of pressing his advantage. I guessed that he was also undermanned—if he'd had more people, he would have posted some above us.

I moved toward the bridge. There was a curve in the outer passageway around the superstructure, an extension out toward the water that provided a clear view of the ship's forward machinery. As I rounded it, the door to the bridge flew open, and two Russians came charging out. They paused momentarily to look over the side in a vain attempt to see Trace and Yong Shin Jong, then started aft.

One of the things cranky NCOs emphasize when leading a group through small unit combat training is the importance of separation. A lot of times this is emphasized in the context of a mortar strike—one good shot can take out the guy next to you and the guy next to him if you're too close. But it has a general application, as frick and frack here found out. Tailgate your point man, and when he trips, so do you.

Point man had a little help tripping—a burst of bullets through the kneecap as he came around the bend set him right down. The tailgater flew over him so quickly I barely had time to adjust my aim.

With these two baboons out of the way, I thought the bridge would be undefended. But I thought wrong. I no sooner took a step forward than people started pouring out. I ran through the clip on my submachine gun, my finger glued to the trigger until I saw the flare of a tracer sparking against the darkened silhouettes, warning me I was about to empty the box. I retreated, dumping the magazine and reloading as I went.

Or rather, reaching for a fresh magazine to reload, and not finding it in the waterproof tac vest I was wearing. My various adventures had used up more ammunition than I'd thought. I wasn't out of ammo entirely. There were still four mags in the ruck, but this wasn't a convenient time to grab them. I reached to my belt and grabbed the Glock I'd taken off the sailor earlier. A pair of shots convinced the people following me to rethink their strategy.

Going up had worked once; I decided I'd try it again. I jumped up and grabbed the life raft, hoping to climb over it to the top of the superstructure. But the raft must have been held on by Velcro or something similarly lightweight—it pulled away as soon as I put my weight on it, and both it and I tumbled to the catwalk. Cursing, I threw the damn thing in the direction of the water and jumped on top of the rail, looking for something else to grab. A hail of bullets from above convinced me that wasn't going to work; I half jumped, half slipped, trying to swing down to the level where I'd started.

More slipped than jumped. More plummeted than fell.

The bullets didn't hit me, but as they tore through the railing, the metal, weakened by years of neglect, gave way. I fell almost straight downward, bouncing off one of the catwalk stanchions below and knocking the last rocks in my head loose as I hit the deck.

I got to my feet, battered and dazed. Trace and Yong Shin Jong were a few yards away to my left.

"What's our next move?" Trace asked.

We had two choices—try to continue our war of attrition, or get down in the water and swim for it. I didn't mind being outnumbered, but we were running low on ammunition; to keep up the battle we'd have to start using their weapons. And more importantly, they'd win if Yong Shin Jong got killed. He was a vulnerable target, whom I didn't quite trust with a gun.

"We'll go over the side," I told Trace. "Swim for the life raft."

"We're not going to get Polorski?"

"This isn't the time, Trace."

Her eyes were like two green disks of jade in the night. She wanted to get him; I'm sure that was the only reason she'd come aboard.

"Dick."

"We'll get him, Trace. You have my word. But right now, Yong Shin Jong is our priority."

Someone fired at us from the bow. Trace emptied her gun, then turned to me calmly.

"All right," she said. "It's a long jump from here. We'll have a better chance if we get down to the main deck."

"You have any more grenades?"

"Just one smoke grenade."

"Use it when I give the signal," I told her. I opened the ruck and took out the MP5 ammo, giving her two and stuffing the spares box in my vest. "I'll create a diversion. Take Yong Shin Jong down and get in the water. Yell when you're jumping. I'll follow."

Polorski was most likely marshaling his forces, possibly looking for the rest of the army they thought we'd brought with us. The ship's engines were still clanking away, but the gunfire had stopped, and the place was relatively quiet—the calm before the storm.

I moved toward the stern, leaning cautiously over the side as I tried to see where the gunner or gunners were. The ship's interior lighting had been shut off, and even the shadows had shadows. I saw one of them moving ahead and stopped, dropping to a knee, waiting.

I almost gave Trace the signal to go. But as the shadow fluttered back, something in the way it moved made me realize it wasn't a person—it was the shadow of a flag above.

Once more I started ahead. The outer passageway I was on ended at a bulkhead aft of the fantail. The superstructure cut off the view below, where I guessed one of the men who'd shot at us earlier must be holed up. If there hadn't been a corner there, the solution would have been easy—I could look down and shoot the son of a bitch.

Flanking him remained an option, but to do so I had to

climb up again to the top of the superstructure. Even though my last try in that direction had ended badly, I decided to give it a chance. The men who'd chased me off the deck above had seen me fall, and the last thing they'd expect would be that I'd climb back up. No one's foolish enough to go back into a place they just escaped from—it'd be like breaking out of jail, only to go around and knock on the front door.

External piping gave me plenty of hand and footholds. I climbed as quickly as I could, then held my breath as I pulled up onto the top deck. The men who'd confronted me earlier were nowhere in sight. I moved to the stern and began climbing down slowly. I aimed to get close enough to whoever was at the corner that I'd have an easy time surprising him, but I didn't want to get so close that I was the one who was surprised.

The problem was, I couldn't see or hear anyone. It almost seemed as if everyone aboard had left the ship. I finally had to lower myself down to the main deck, sucking wind as slowly and silently as possible. Tiptoeing forward, I finally spotted a cluster of shadows ahead that looked humanlike. I pushed back against the bulkhead, and whispered to Trace that I was just about to start.

"Good. Copy," she said.

Polorski chose that moment to come back on the loudspeaker.

"Dick, listen, you've caused me a lot of trouble here," he said. He was calm, but you could hear his anger through his accent. "This is unnecessary. Let's make a deal. We can work together."

The only thing better than a commie who's turned into a capitalist is one who wants to become your business partner. A Russian mobster who already double-crossed me and played one of my best friends and employees—sure, there's someone I would trust as a partner.

I took out the radio I'd grabbed from the sailor earlier and cupped my hand over the microphone.

"Bow," I whispered in Russian. "Forward."

Someone responded immediately, probably demanding more of an explanation or asking who had transmitted. But as limited as my Russian was, I wasn't up to giving out clear directions. Besides, I had other priorities. I checked my weapon, then sprang out of my hiding place. A shot to the back of the head took out the first man, but as I turned the gun to get the second I saw that he had left his position. I walked quickly, not sure where he could have gone.

"*Bystryey!*" hissed a voice from around the corner. "Hurry up."

"*Ya zdyes!*" I answered. "Here I am."

As I turned the corner I put a bullet into the side of his head. He never knew what hit him.

"Trace, smoke!" I yelled over the radio.

I heard the pitter-patter of little feet behind me. But it wasn't the feet so much as the gunfire that got my attention.

"Go!" I told Trace.

I spun around and fired a pair of bursts to give whoever was coming up something to think about. When I turned the corner, Yong Shin Jong was hanging off the railing above.

"Jump!" I told him.

He hit the deck so hard my leg bones shuddered in sympathy. As I started toward him, the deck in front of me bubbled with automatic weapons fire, fired from the deck above. I threw myself against the bulkhead and continued crawling forward. The wind whipped the smoke from Trace's grenade downward, and within seconds I found myself in the middle of a black cloud so thick I couldn't see my own hands or the bulkhead they were feeling along.

"Dick!" yelled Trace over the radio. "Where are you?"

"I'm on the deck."

"Do you have Yong Shin Jong?"

"No. I can't see in this smoke."

I pushed along farther. There was more gunfire than you'd

hear on a Miami street after curfew. Finally I felt a leg that didn't belong to me.

I pulled at the leg and heard a groan. The smoke was so thick I couldn't see the rest of his body, but I grappled him over my shoulder. I knew I was only a few feet from the rail, and that I had a straight path to the water.

I pushed myself to my feet. He was a heavy son of a bitch.

"I got him, Trace. Go! *Go! Jump now. And that is a fucking order!*"

I leaped across the deck to the rail, threw my left foot on the railing, and with Yong Shin Jong on my back tumbled inelegantly toward the water.

PART THREE

FUBAR

"I want to apologize and it will never happen again."

—Kim Jong Il

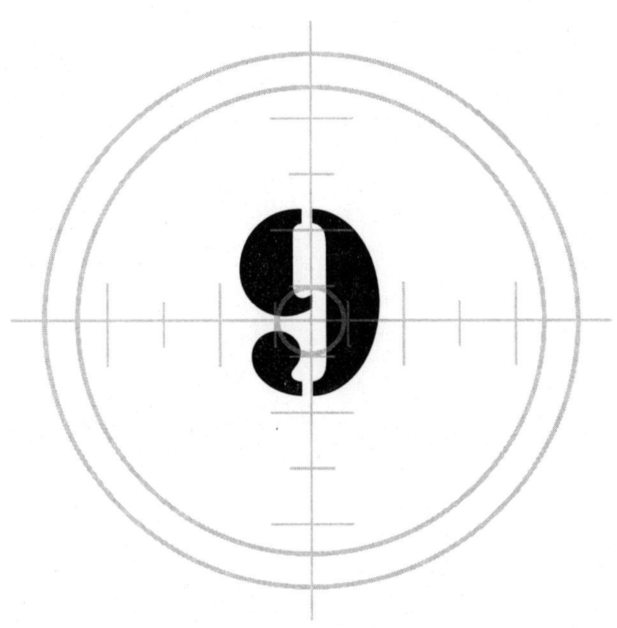
9

[1]

The ocean came up before I had time to do anything more than get my feet together. The cold water sent an electric shock through me. I pushed to the surface and bent forward, slightly disoriented from the smoke and the fall. My "passenger" weighed me down, but at least he wasn't flailing against me or resisting. I slipped around in the water, hooking my arm around him and starting to scissor kick away.

The only progress I made at first was downward. I unhooked my rucksack and let it sink, but what was really weighing me down was Yong, and I couldn't let him go.

I tried not thinking about those giant sucking screws at the stern. If they were shooting at us—and I expect that they were—I couldn't tell. I kicked and paddled with my free arm, willing myself away. An illumination flare shot overhead. I kept kicking, finally pulling away from the ship, either by brute determination or opportune currents.

Back aboard the vessel, Trace waited for the Russians to come down from their hiding places. She'd come aboard to get Polorski, and orders or not, she was damned if she was going to leave without taking a shot at revenge. She guessed that he would come down to check on things himself, and so waited as two sailors rushed by, spraying their weapons in my general direction. Trace was right about Polorski—he was a few yards behind the two men—but she hadn't counted on the fact that Mr. Murphy was even closer.

The smoke from the grenade started to dissipate as Polorski came down, barking at the men. Trace caught a glimpse of him walking toward her to her left; she brought her MP5 up to fire, then lost him momentarily. Stepping away from the bulkhead where she'd hidden, she saw a figure looming in the smoke.

"You son of a bitch," she said, pressing the trigger.

She laced the man with bullets, heard a scream, and stepped forward—probably to kick him in the face and maybe to knife out his balls, though she didn't mention either when she told what happened later on. As she did, she heard a voice shouting an alert in Russian. She didn't know the words, but she instantly recognized the voice. It belonged to Polorski, who had stayed back behind his other men and was now urging them to fire. She saw him, took a step to the right to get better aim, and fired—and simultaneously fell off the ship. Murphy—you can blame it on the earlier gunfire if you want—had removed the lifelines from the section of the deck where she was, something she couldn't tell in the smoke.

She smacked against the side of the ship going down and lost her gun. Hitting the water sideways, she was stunned momentarily, but as she flailed, her hand hit something soft. It was the raft that had fallen when I'd pulled against it earlier.

Meanwhile, I was pulling Yong Shin Jong in the general direction of the cabin cruiser. At least five minutes passed before I heard her yelling to me.

"Dick!"

I altered course toward Trace's shouts. With every stroke, my arms felt heavier and heavier. Back in my salad days as a UDT[25] wannabe, I went through hell week with a severe case of the runs. There have been many times in my life when I've been glad for that experience—it gave me a benchmark to measure my misery by. I thought about it now, and memories of having cold water poured on me just as I was ready to collapse comatose cheered me up. No way this was worse than that. Not even close. My arms were falling out of their sockets, but this was a joke compared to So-Solly Day and the swim I'd had to do, not just kitted up, but with a full pot helmet.

Shit, if I could do that, I could do anything. Which was the idea.

I grabbed on to the raft and pulled myself half up, taking my "passenger" with me.

---

[25] Underwater Demolition Team, the precursor to SEALs. Haven't you read my first book yet?

"God, is he alive?" asked Trace.

"I think he broke his leg when he fell," I told her. "See if there's a medical kit in the raft. He's probably in shock."

I pushed Yong Shin Jong over to check on him.

The only thing was, it wasn't Yong Shin Jong.

[11]

I'd seen Yong jump to the deck. I'd seen where he landed. Yes, it was night and the ship was wrapped in smoke, but it was only thirty or so feet from me. There was nobody between me and Yong Shin Jong. There was no way this wasn't Yong Shin Jong.

And yet it clearly wasn't.

The man I'd towed to the raft was a sailor dressed in a jumpsuit who was about the same weight as Yong Shin Jong, but was clearly Russian. He was also dead. Cursing myself, I unceremoniously kicked his corpse into the water, hoping he'd become what he deserved, shark shit on the bottom of the ocean.

I cursed even louder when I realized the GPS unit had been damaged somewhere along the way, possibly by the fall into the water. The device refused to update itself, then finally went blank altogether—maybe fainting because of my language.

Having gotten rid of my ruck, I'd also gotten rid of the sat phone. We tried broadcasting on the radio, but they were designed for short distances, and it was unlikely that Doc was close enough to hear. (The military's SINCGARS radios are good for about thirty-five kilometers or so. Our units in theory were a bit better—partly because they didn't have to worry about interfacing with analog and what the industry politely calls "legacy" equipment. But their range was limited by design—the farther a signal can go, the more people theoretically who could intercept it.)

By now, we'd moved more than a mile away from the ship, which was continuing toward Korea. We unstowed the oars from the bottom of the raft and began paddling in its direction. I didn't think I was going to catch up, though Trace for one would have welcomed a chance to get back on board. I figured that the closer we were to the ship, the better chance we'd have of being seen in the morning when Doc managed to convince someone to look for us.

Trace looked like she'd spent the past twenty-four hours in the back of a cement mixer. I told her to get some rest. She was her usual compliant self, and being even more cheerful than normal due to fatigue, told me not only that I could "F" myself, but that I could do it in several unnatural positions. She took her oar and punched at the water, no doubt taking out some of her frustration at not having gotten Polorski. If the ship had been a little closer, she might very well have dove into the water and started swimming after it, punched handholds into the skin of the ship to climb up, bulled her way to the bridge, and torn Polorski to pieces with her bare hands.

I let her get her aggression out on the waves while I took stock of the raft's supplies. It was a quick inventory: six bottles of water, a flare gun with six charges, and six signal mirrors. Obviously whoever packed it thought six was a lucky number.

While we were setting a westward course, the *Greenville*'s skipper was headed north, following the GPS signal from the cabin cruiser, whose finicky rudder had steered it back toward Russia. It was roughly an hour before the small boat was spotted, and another half hour or so before it could be recovered and inspected properly. At that point, Doc drew the obvious conclusion, deciding that Trace and I must still be on the merchant ship, or at least nearby. With the help of some other navy assets[26] and an assist from Jimmy Zim, they set a new course and began moving at flank speed in that direction.

Under normal circumstances, that would have brought them to our position just after daybreak. But what is the definition of "normal" in an operational setting?

If you answered "all fucked up," go to the head of the class.

The North Korean navy is not, by any stretch of the imagination, a formidable outfit. The one area where you *might*—emphasis on might—give them a grade of "D-" rather than their

26 Apparently we're not supposed to talk about the satellite system the navy uses to track ships at sea.

normal "F" is in the area of special operations support. They have a number of submarines, from fleet-sized to midgets, which can and have been used for special operations against South Korea and Japan. (The value of those operations is another story, but going into detail here would take us many pages.) They also have a number of small craft that are useful for inserting shooters, including two different types that can be flooded to make them less visible from shore (nothing like arriving at the battle wet as well as bruised) and U.S. made "hand grenade launches," which are extremely fast craft that are closer to speedboats than your run-of-the-mill invasion launch. (The man who managed to procure them for the North Koreans was granted free room and board at a hotel run by Uncle Sam.)

When it comes to conventional ships, however, the North Korean navy is pretty typically North Korean. The vessels are old, beaten to shit, and were never very good to begin with. They have a couple of frigates and corvettes—the latter is the escort-sized baby destroyer, not the Chevy with the big wheels and throaty exhaust. They also have dozens of patrol craft ranging in size from missile gunboats to dinghies with machine guns. Modern or not, they have a lot of them, and it seemed as if nearly every one of them had been scrambled to meet the freighter.

We were too far from the merchant ship to see it in the dark, so our first hint that something was up came in the form of a red flare arcing near the horizon. Twenty minutes later, a pair of jets streaked somewhere overhead. The planes were probably old MiGs or maybe larger two-engined patrol bombers from one of North Korea's air bases near the coast, but of course we had no way of knowing. We kept rowing westward, night giving way to nautical twilight (the false dawn before dawn when the ocean turns from black to purple-gray). Four or five patrol boats came out in our direction. It was unlikely they saw us, either with binoculars or radar; they were probably just running a patrol to screen whatever was going on closer to the coast.

We still couldn't see the freighter, but it wasn't hard to guess that they had arranged a rendezvous. And if the Koreans were getting Yong Shin Jong, then Polorski was getting the nuke.

I had to tell Doc that. I might not have had a working radio, but the Koreans surely would.

It's very possible that the Korean patrol boats would have missed us if we hadn't done anything to call attention to ourselves. It's a big ocean, after all, and they were focused on the freighter. Still, the sun was coming up, there were an awful lot of them nearby, and there were airplanes flying overhead. I'd put the odds at fifty-fifty that they would have spotted something, and sent someone to investigate.

Maybe more like thirty-seventy, but in any event, there was no sense waiting around for it to happen. I took the flare gun and fired off a shot, then another for good measure. One of the patrol craft, and then another, turned in our direction. We dumped the radios and GPS unit, even though it wasn't working, and waited.

"Are you sure you want to do this?" Trace asked as the first patrol boat closed in.

"You forget, I'm a personal friend of the Great Leader," I told her, combing my beard.

The Korean boat that came for us was a 190-ton Russian Project 215, also known as an SO-1 patrol boat. The ship had probably served with the Soviet navy around the time I was in high school. Intended primarily for ASW[27] missions, even with the Koreans, it had a pair of 25mm machine guns as its main armament. The Project 215s were not known for seaworthiness. They would roll in a bathtub, let alone the ocean. The vessel lurched in our direction; it took three tries before they managed to get a line over to us.

None of the crew who waited for us aboard the ship spoke English, which suited me just fine.

---

27 Anti-Submarine Warfare; less formally, pounding submarines into whale piss.

"I need to talk to General Sun," I said very loudly. I took out the card Sun had given me and waved it over my head. "The general sent me on a special mission for the Great Leader, and I must report to him immediately."

The enlisted men who heard me had no idea what I was saying, but they were fairly well programmed to respond to authoritative voices, and even the two sailors armed with AK47s fell in behind me as I marched in the direction of the ship's communications shack. I barked out my intentions as I went, striding quickly through the narrow passageway. Sailors pressed themselves against the bulkheads as I came, then joined our parade; I had quite a little army as I marched into the communications compartment, which was about the size of a phone booth. Incredibly, three North Koreans stood inside, an officer and two enlisted men hunched over equipment so old it probably worked off tubes rather than transistors, let alone circuit boards.

"Contact General Sun, immediately," I told the lieutenant. "Tell him Dick Marcinko needs to speak to him immediately."

The man said something in Korean. I couldn't understand the exact words, but the expression on his face made his meaning clear enough: who the hell are you?

"I'm on a mission for General Sun. I have to speak to the Great Leader. Immediately."

My tone and conviction convinced the man either that I was very important, or very insane. In any event, he decided to do what any C2 officer would do—he began pushing through the crowd to find a higher authority to tell him what to do.

"Here, put me on," I told the seaman sitting in front of the set, taking his microphone.

The other man—clearly an NCO—started to object, but I silenced him with a stare.

"This is Dick Marcinko. I'm reporting to—" I stopped and looked down at the radio operator. "Is this damn thing on? Working? Does it work?"

The man blinked.

"I have to get a message to General Sun," I said, pressing down on the mike's transmit button. "I've located the Great Leader's son aboard a Russian freighter four or five kilometers from here. You might want to check it out. I'd watch the people who have him very carefully. I wouldn't trust them to keep their end of the bargain."

I repeated the message several times, switching through the standard Korean fleet frequencies to the international emergency band to make sure our guys would pick it up. Knowing that the longer the transmission lasted, the better chance the *Greenville* would have to home in on it, I expanded my bit as I went, saying that Trace and I were looking forward to a good breakfast with our North Korean hosts. I'd have thrown in a traffic report if the ship's captain hadn't arrived. With a red-faced shout he ordered the radio turned down and had me taken to his quarters.

The captain didn't speak English, so he didn't know what I said. He clearly thought it wasn't going to boost his career, however, and he went red in the face screaming at me. He was a runt of a man, barely five-two, with arms skinnier than lollipop sticks.

"If I'm causing any trouble, I'll be glad to go," I told him, starting for the door to his cabin.

This provoked even more angry words from him; he began hyperventilating so badly I feared for his health.

I cracked open the door. Trace, and about ten of our escorts, were waiting in the passageway.

"He says we should go," I told her.

We got back out to the main deck before two sailors with AK47s stopped us, standing before us with their rifles in firing position. Our entourage was joined by other seamen; there were enough of us in one place for the patrol craft to list decidedly to starboard. The captain pushed his way through the throng and stared at me for a few seconds, not entirely sure what to do. We now had six other patrol craft of varying sizes and descriptions floating around us. Most of their complements were on deck, some with binoculars, trying to see what was going on. I was the most exciting thing that had happened to the North Korean navy since six sailors had tried to defect to South Korea by stealing a minisub a few years before.

All this excitement brought over the pride of the North Korean fleet, corvette no. 531, rusting—excuse me, I mean rushing—to see what was going on. The ship was armed with two 100mm guns—round 'em up and call 'em four-inchers—and some 30mm antiaircraft weapons, but her main armament were Styx antiship missiles. The weapons were probably more dangerous to 531 than to a potential enemy; the launchers were situated so that the missiles would fire directly over the crowded ship, and one mishap with the finicky missile system would surely sink it. But that's not the sort of thing the Great Leader worries about when he orders his ships equipped with the latest, or almost the latest, toys.

The 531 sent over a launch and a lieutenant who spoke Korean-style pigeon English.

"You come now," he told me after he boarded the patrol boat. "You come to ship."

"How well do you speak English?" I asked.

"You come now."

"I got that part—how well do you speak English?"

"You come now."

"Is that supposed to be a sexual innuendo?" Trace asked.

The lieutenant turned toward her and with a solemn expression said, "You come now."

The members of the security detail that had accompanied him had an even more limited vocabulary, but it was much more eloquent—they showed off their Type 79 submachine guns, clicking the select fire buttons from single round to auto and then pointing them in our direction.

Ugly-looking guns, especially when viewed from the business side of the barrel.

[III]

By this time, the *Greenville* had found the cabin cruiser and was about to head back south. They were still on the surface when I began making my transmission.

Unfortunately, the rest of the navy was listening as well, and apparently sent word of what was going on to the State Department, either to Fogglebottom or some other functionary whose head was positioned where his digestive track should be. A few minutes later, the *Greenville*'s captain received a message telling him that under no circumstances was he to initiate any action that might "provoke or tend to provoke an international incident." The Russian ship was not to be molested in Korean waters. Further orders would be pending.

The skipper immediately ordered the vessel below. As a matter of courtesy, he then went and told Doc what was going on.

Doc's response was anything but courteous. When he calmed down—even Doc realized it wasn't the captain's fault—he asked that he be given an inflatable, claiming he had more than enough people to effect a rescue.

There was no way that was going to happen. The captain said something to the effect that he appreciated Doc's concern and admired his loyalty, but orders were orders. He then turned to the rest of my guys, none of whom had said a word, and declared very loudly that anyone caught staging a mutiny would be shot and disposed of through the torpedo tube. Shotgun raised an eyebrow, probably considering whether getting shot out a torpedo tube would be fun or not, but wisely said nothing.

Corvette 531 was bigger than the patrol boat, but it was also twice as crowded. Sailors were everywhere. Most of them weren't even trying to look busy, a violation of time-honored sailor etiquette that I can only blame on a severe lack of training. They also had the worst fitting uniforms I've ever seen, possibly due to the fact that they were all starving. The crew could have passed for boat people.

"We are very pleased to be honored to invite you aboard," said the lieutenant who met us. "You will surrender your weapons and to be searched."

Trace, always a stickler for proper grammar, objected to being searched by a man who didn't understand the proper use of the verb "to be." In fact, she objected to being searched by *any* male—a problem, since there were only males aboard. The Korean lieutenant appeared embarrassed but firm; Trace was only the latter. The compromise was a hands-off search—Trace pressed her hands against her clothes, proving that they did not conceal any weapons.

The North Koreans managed to be both polite and dictatorial at the same time. Men with stethoscopes and flashlights poked various parts of our bodies, though whether they were concerned about our health or worried that we might be carrying infectious diseases was impossible to tell. We were offered dry clothes. Trace accepted khaki trousers and a shirt that fit her frame reasonably well. Mine were several sizes too small, and so I opted to remain in my combat wet suit.

We were now ready for an audience. The officers' wardroom was probably the most luxurious space on the ship, but it would have embarrassed a tugboat back home. A pair of tables were pushed together and filled the room. All told, there may have been space for a dozen normal men. I'd guess three dozen crammed into the space, and there were more in the passageway outside.

The bulkhead was covered with speckled green melamine board that looked like an artist's attempt to imitate the spatter of finely ground vomit. There was enough of a 3-D quality to the paint job that you almost thought it was the result of projectile vomiting after a meal gone bad. None of the awards or commendations you'd typically find in a Western ship were hung on it. Instead, a pair of large paintings stood facing each other port and starboard—Kim Jong Il and his father, right and left, or left and right, I forget which.

The interior spaces of destroyers and smaller escorts are notoriously and traditionally cramped, but this set new standards. Sacks of rice sat in front of the cabinets at the back of the compartment. Boxes were piled in another corner, reaching all the way to the overhead. A series of pipes also ran overhead. These were used as a storage rack for cans, a few of which were hanging down through their netting. As far as I could tell, there were no labels on the cans; either there was an invisible sorting system in place or the cooks played surprise meal every night—though I suppose it's possible one or more of the pipes carried hot water, and the contents of the cans were being cooked.

Lunch consisted of fish and rice in an oil so smelly it cut through the stench of ammonia and sweat surrounding us. It tasted a bit like seasoned anchovies, with marinated eel gizzards mixed in—not bad, really.

The captain didn't know exactly who I was, but the fact that I had Sun's business card and could refer to the Great Leader as a client clearly impressed him. Even more interesting for him was the fact that, like most North Koreans, he had never seen an American in the flesh before. I was part guest, part prisoner, part zoo animal.

North Koreans are taught two very important things from a young age. The first is that they are members of a superior race. The second is that America is the devil. It committed all manner of heinous crimes against Koreans during the Korean War, which, incidentally, has never ended. Individual Americans are the spawn of the devil. Given the chance, they will gladly cook your children and eat them for dinner.

But being the devil has its advantages. Every culture is fascinated with you. The officers' eyes were as wide as those of a five-year-old meeting Santa for the first time. While I'm sure two or three would have picked up a knife and stabbed me through the heart at a word from the captain, most looked as if they would gladly join the Dark Side if I said the word.

We ate silently, as is the custom in North Korea. The meal concluded with toasts of *soju*, a traditional Korean liquor made from rice. It tastes like a sweet and mild vodka. It's not Bombay Sapphire, but given the alternatives it's not half bad. The captain poured me a drink. Remembering my manners, I rose and bowed as I took the small glass.

"Don't I get any?" asked Trace as the captain passed her by, spilling a small drop from his bottle into the glass of the man next to her. North Korean society is extremely male-oriented, and it probably didn't occur to the captain that Trace would even be interested in a drink. In fact, he may not even have noticed her.

"You sure you want some?" I asked.

Trace looked at my glass and decided she wasn't really thirsty after all.

There's a saying in Korea along the lines of "*il bul, sam so, o ui, chil gwa*"—you can't have just one, three is too little, five's the right number, seven's pushing the limit. The captain went five rounds, him filling my glass, me filling his. The officers' rations got smaller each time, their glasses being filled more for form's sake than inebriation.

As we drank, the captain tried walking a line between interrogation and conversation. He looked old enough to be my father, with big age spots covering both sides of his head. While thin, he had plenty of energy. Veins popped from his neck, and he held himself the way a rooster holds himself when inspecting his henhouse. The lieutenant who had welcomed us aboard acted as translator, engaging in long discussions with the captain before rendering anything into English. He seemed to be a political officer of some sort rather than a member of a specific department aboard the ship. His temples were gray but he was clearly one of the "younger" members of the ship's complement. Even the ensigns were well into their thirties.

"What happened to your ship?" the captain asked.

"We didn't have a ship."

"No ship?"

I shook my head. "I've been following the Russian freighter for a long time."

"You were aboard it?"

"For a while."

"How did you get there?"

"You might say we dropped in."

"You were stowaways?"

"Not precisely."

My answers confused the translator, and it was pretty clear from his reaction that neither he nor the captain believed that an American ship wasn't sailing nearby. But they gave up asking about that, turning instead to questions about the U.S. Navy. I told him again that it had been quite a while since I'd been in the service. I was now a private contractor, working for Kim Jong Il, not the U.S. This, too, they couldn't quite understand; the translator seemed to think we were some sort of defectors.

I tried asking some questions myself, mostly about the trawler, but the response amounted to polite shrugs. Finally, some secret signal passed through the room and the entire company began filing out.

"Do we get a tour of the bridge?" I asked the interpreter.

The captain's face grew grave as the question was translated. On the one hand, showing the bridge to an American devil dog could be considered a treacherous betrayal of the homeland. On the other hand, I appeared to be a friend of the country's most exalted leadership, a man who should be afforded every courtesy and also a very dangerous person to make unhappy. Make the wrong choice, and he could easily face the firing squad. Make the right choice—and he could face it anyway. This was North Korea.

"Maybe I should inspect your escorts instead," I said, rescuing him from his dilemma. "It's an impressive array of ships around us."

This brought immediate relief to the captain's face. Trace and I were soon led to the quarterdeck, where we watched the motley patrol craft zip back and forth importantly for a half hour. We also saw the Russian freighter, now standing completely still to the east.

"Are you escorting the freighter into port?" I asked the captain.

The captain gave the translator a one-word answer; it came to me as a long-winded dissertation on the many missions a navy might have at any one time.

"I heard that speech when I signed up," I said. "What's the freighter doing?"

The translator shrugged, then shook his head.

I watched it for as long as I could. While the patrol boats were near it, it didn't look as if any were actually tied up to it. And there didn't seem to be any larger cargo ships—the sort that would carry a nuclear weapon, for example—coming out to meet it.

North Korea's western navy is headquartered at Toejo Dong, about two-thirds of the way down the coast from the border with Russia. North Korea's biggest port on the west coast, though, is Wonsan, which is closer to South Korea. Wonsan's facilities rival most in Asia, certainly in size. It also has a large collection of old ships and patrol craft, the majority of which are about as seaworthy as the clunker car (i.e., Rent-A-Wreck) in your neighbor's driveway. But if you're a navy buff, calling at Wonsan would probably feel like dying and going to heaven.

If my sources are correct, Corvette 531 was home-ported at Wonsan, and at first I thought that was our destination. But in fact we were going to a much closer and smaller base, Songjin. (Called Kimch'aek on most civilian maps, it's about 220 miles south of Vladivostok.) We reached it an hour after lunch ended, the long arm of its breakwater sticking out a finger to greet us as we approached.

One thing I'll say for North Korea—they have nice beaches. They're sandy and never crowded, unless you count the obstructions designed to prevent an amphibious assault. Take away the minefields, and the beach north of Songjin would be a perfect vacation spot, even if you do have to bring your own beer cooler.

The captain went to attend to business on the bridge, leaving the translator to act as tour guide as we sailed toward the port. He claimed not to know much about the military base or the area, and rather than answering my questions about how I would get in touch with Sun and Kim, told us about local legends involving sea dragons. Without exception, these involved a gorgeous maiden manhandled—god-handled?—by a wayward sea god, who was then put in his place by a hero. The maiden was really a dragon in disguise. The hero had to decide whether to become a dragon himself, or give up the best sex he had ever had. Guess what the hero chose.

The city has an ironworks as well as the military base, but Songjin or Kimch'aek's claim to fame as far as the West is concerned are the mountains nearby: they house a substantial part of North Korea's nuclear arms program.

In 2006, the North Koreans set off a test nuker forty-two miles north of Songjin. Even though the bomb was a dud—it produced an explosion the equivalent of maybe five hundred tons of TNT,[28] about what a good backwoods still would produce if the pressure got too high—it wet the pants of enough diplomats and talking heads to get Kim Jong Il yelled at by the Chinese.

But I digress.

Our ship went straight into the harbor, tying up bow-first at a long, wide cement pier directly below the city, a term that applies only loosely to Kimch'aek. A whaleboat was lowered to

---

[28] Some estimates go as high as two thousand tons, which though generous is still too small to indicate a successful explosion.

bring us ashore. As we approached the dock, a small marching band appeared, arms and instruments swinging in precision. The moment we climbed up the wooden ladder to the pier the band began to play "Patriotic Song," the Korean national anthem. The musicians looked like they ranged from nine to twelve and had the most serious expressions as they worked their way through the number.

Trace and I were led to a spot on the pier where it met the road. A dozen girls in white dresses stepped forward and began throwing red flags around; the show looked like what you'd see if a busload of cheerleaders had been pressed into duty warning people of impending road hazards. When they finished, the band did another number designed to make us feel right at home. Since they didn't know the "Star-Spangled Banner" or even "Yankee Doodle," they played what I believe was "Twinkle, Twinkle, Little Star," the only American song they knew.

When the music stopped, a man dressed in white stepped out from behind the band and began speaking to us in Korean. The translator nodded and smiled encouragement, but didn't bother telling us what the guy was saying.

"What the hell is he talking about?" Trace whispered.

"Got me. Probably welcoming us to Korea and telling us how great the motherland is."

"I think he's trying to sell us insurance," said Trace. "I wish they'd get us some chairs. These crappy boots are killing me."

The speech went on for forty-five minutes. Finally, a pair of troop trucks arrived, followed by three black Hyundai sedans. A company of soldiers mustered from the trucks as a fresh shift of men in Korean proletarian suits filed from the cars. Two little girls from the band were given flowers and sent to the head of the line.

"I have a bad feeling about this," muttered Trace as we took the bouquets.

"We're just being honored," I told her.

"That's what they tell cows before they get slaughtered."

"This is really very flattering," I told the translator, who was smiling next to me. "But I really do have to see General Sun. We do have important business."

"Oh, yes, Mr. Marcinko. This will be done. But you are an honored guest. First you must be welcomed. We must continue."

Two more men approached, followed by the honor guard and the rest of the men who'd come from the cars. One of them carried a small box. I thought by now the only thing left for them to do was to present us with the key to the city, but it turned out I was wrong.

The box contained two pairs of handcuffs. And just in case we didn't understand what they were for, our honor guard locked and loaded.

10

[1]

Going quietly would have been the smart thing to do, both tactically and strategically; resisting wasn't going to help me accomplish my mission. But there's something stubborn in me. Call it fashion sense: I've never been very big on jewelry, especially stainless-steel bracelets.

I shook my head. When the first man approached with the shackles, I expressed my opinion somewhat more forcefully, throwing him into the crowd. I hoisted the next as well, tossing him onto the roof of the Hyundai. Starting to tire, I didn't bother throwing the next man; I just pushed him off the side of the pier.

Just before the man hit the water, one of the soldiers presented me with his AK47. Fortunately, he only hit me in the head. I spun around, intending to grab the rifle out of his hand, but instead found it pointing at my chest. Before I could decide which way to lunge for it, I felt a sharp prick at my neck. The next thing I felt was my knees hitting the concrete. My face followed as my body jerked wildly and I had an electrifying experience—one of the men in the civilian suits had fired a taser at me, and the jolt was so overwhelming that it took a few seconds for my brain cells to figure out what the hell was going on.

They didn't like it very much. But they couldn't do much to stop it.

Trace was undergoing a similar experience, minus the slam to the head. She dove at one of the soldiers, grabbing his gun. The taser hit before she could get her finger on the trigger, but what stopped her from firing was the fact that one of the little flower girls was in the way. Her hesitation allowed the Koreans to hit her with another jolt; at that point she blanked out, and was probably lucky not to have had a heart attack.

The next hour or so passed in a blur. My legs were shackled and I was stabbed with a hypo of something that made me feel as if sacks of cement were tied to every bone in my body. We were placed—dumped might be a better word—in the back of one of the troop trucks. We drove west for somewhere between twenty and forty minutes until we reached a compound used as a military prison and concentration camp, the sort of place where uppity North Koreans were sent to learn their manners. Trace was lifted out of the truck on a stretcher. The guards tried to make me walk. I couldn't quite talk my legs into it, and ended up crawling from the back of the truck to the entrance of a large stone building that served as the camp's processing center and headquarters.

The Kimch'aek Hilton was presided over by the only fat person I saw the entire time I was in North Korea. He waddled out from behind his desk as I crawled in. Putting his hands on his hips, he grinned and leaned over me, muttering something in Korean to the effect that I was a lowly worm.

Even without a full translation, I took that personally.

"Listen, motherfucker," I said. "I have to see General Sun and the Great Leader. And your ass is going to be kicked from here to Pyongyang if something happens to me. Or my assistant."

The translator hadn't accompanied us, and I have no idea whether fatso understood English. His expression didn't change one iota. He said something about clothes, and I was immediately dragged to a room at the side. A set of large pajamas and sandals were thrown in behind the guards as they left. I got changed in slow motion. My body didn't hurt, really, but I felt as if my brain was sending messages to my muscles via tin cans and string. The pants were an inch or too short, but they were dry. The shirt was a size or two too big. The guards came back and zapped me again, putting a spark in my ass that sent me back against the wall like a drunken sailor at fleet landing, almost too late for the last liberty launch. I blacked out, and when I came to I was in a prison cell.

I'm sure the place will be featured in *Home & Prison* next month. Measuring roughly six by eight feet, its back and side walls were made from large stone blocks. The floor was rough concrete, with a good portion of pebbles exposed. There were no windows, and while the place looked older than dirt, there was no sign that anyone else had ever been there—no scrapes on the walls, no hash marks in the cement between the stones. The bed was a thin blanket on the floor. Overhead, a single lightbulb cast a pale light from behind a metal cage. There was a bucket in the corner; that was the bathroom.

Rusted iron bars lined the front of the cell. The walls extended far enough beyond the bars to cut off the view of the corridor. Stones lined the opposite wall, but I sensed there were more cells on my side of the corridor. I couldn't hear anything, except for the occasional shuffle of a guard who appeared intermittently, sneered in my direction, then returned down the hall.

Whatever drug they had hit me with in the truck was still slowing me down. I alternated between trying to get my senses back by doing sit-ups and push-ups, and just lying on the floor in a daze. Twice I was brought a cup-sized tin full of rice, but the rice looked almost black. Even if I'd been hungry there was no way I would have touched it.

I knew things were getting better when I was finally able to count off a hundred sit-ups without losing track. I got up and paced off the cell, then sat against the back wall, trying to adjust my hearing to the sounds of the place. Feet scraped somewhere in the distance. As I listened, I decided that they belonged to a guard walking a patrol in a corridor to my left, probably watching the access point to the section where I was.

When Trace and I had first gone aboard the Korean patrol boat, I figured that sooner or later, someone would tell Sun about me and he'd send someone out to bring us back to him. But now I wasn't so sure. Maybe he had already been told about me, and this was his response. I was reasonably confident that Doc, or someone from the navy, had overheard my transmission and would be keeping an eye on the ship Polorski had boarded. But I knew also that I'd no longer be the priority—Polorski and whatever nuke he managed to weasel out of the North Koreans in exchange for Yong Shin Jong was.

Can you spell "expendable"?

Maybe an hour after my head had cleared, a pair of guards approached the cell. I rose from the floor and watched as they unlocked the door. There were two locks, and each guard had only one key, a good precaution that made it harder to get out by simply overpowering them.

Door open, the men stood back in the hallway. I left the cell, not exactly sure what to expect. The guards weren't telling in Korean, English, or Swahili. They stood behind me as I walked out, then followed as I went down the hall, passing four empty cells before coming to an archway. Another guard stood to the right, blocking off an alcove that was a dead end anyway. I turned to the left and found myself facing an open gate to a courtyard.

Recreation time.

The yard came out of the back of the building. It was narrow but deep, measuring roughly ten feet by nearly a hundred. The sun was about halfway up the sky; I'd lost an entire day.

The weather had turned chilly and I jogged along the fence line to stay warm. The guards stayed by the building, taking out cigarettes to smoke. The drugs and electric zaps had let my muscles relax so much that they no longer felt tired; if the circumstances had been different, I might have asked about getting a supply of the dope they'd used.

An inmate worked on the other side of the fence in the far corner, poking at rocks with a long wooden rake. He was an older fellow, and seemed to ignore me as I jogged. But as I passed, he hissed my name just loud enough for me to hear.

I continued past, pretending to grow more and more tired as I turned the corner past the guards and continued my circuit back in his direction. Gradually I slowed, as if losing my breath, until I was walking with my head hung down and my hands on my hips.

"White rock," whispered the inmate when I came close to him.

I took a few more steps, then spotted the rock he was talking about. I dropped down as if to tie my shoe.

"They don't care," said the inmate, pretending to rake near my part of the fence. His English was heavily accented, and I had trouble making out the words. "Follow the directions."

The directions consisted of numbers—0000—and letters—NE fenc—penciled onto the flat bottom of the rock. Terse, but decipherable: I was to meet someone at midnight, at the northeast corner of the yard or fence.

Or maybe the corner of the compound. Or maybe someplace named "fenc" that I didn't know about.

I started to slip the rock into my pocket.

"Leave it," hissed the inmate. "Go."

I put the stone back and started trotting again. The guards were still passing their lone cigarette back and forth, gazing off into the distance. Obviously they'd been paid off—unless this was a setup. I pumped my legs harder as I considered the situation. Had Trace sent the message? The letters didn't seem to be in her handwriting, but they'd been so faint and small that it was hard to tell. If it wasn't Trace, who was it? Some inmate who had the run of the place? How did he or she know English?

North Korea has a variety of prisons, concentration camps, and villages of exile where people in need of political reform—read, anyone the regime or some other government bully doesn't like—are sent for rehabilitation. Rehabilitation can include the entire family and take a lifetime or two. As you'd expect, informal governments among the prisoners are fairly common, and in some cases are more powerful than the formal structure—until, of course, the guards get the guns out. I guessed that whoever had left the message wanted to meet with me and tell me how things worked. Which was fine with me.

As I completed my fifth circuit of the yard, the guards finished smoking. One whistled loudly, and together they walked toward the entrance to the building, expecting me to follow. I jogged to the building. Just inside I was stopped and searched for contraband by a third man—rocks, presumably.

"I'd like to talk to the woman that came in with me," I told the officer as he patted me down. "I want to see her. Trace Dahlgren."

The man gave me a quizzical look.

"Trace?" I said.

He made a face. I tried gesturing, making the shape of a woman with my hands, but they didn't understand that either. Finally, I just yelled, "Trace!"

This did get a response—the men who'd escorted me to the courtyard grabbed me and threw me against the wall. I pushed one of them away, but before I could get the other one off of me, the man who'd searched me began hitting me with a baton. I started to wrestle it away from him when I felt something prick my side. Before I could do anything else, my body convulsed. I didn't feel any real pain, though, until after I'd hit the floor. Then however many volts they'd tasered me with flashed through my body like a tidal wave, once again rearranging my nervous system.

The rest happened as if it were part of a movie: more guards arrived, men grabbed my arms and legs, and I was unceremoniously pulled back to my prison cell, my butt dragging along the floor though I could barely feel it. The guards left me in the cell and went away, their words the buzzing bees make when you've kicked over their nest. All I could think was that a few more hits like that and I'd be able to give the Energizer Bunny a good run for his money.

[11]

While I was being turned into a human battery, Trace was enduring an entirely different ordeal. She'd been taken to another building adjacent to the one I was in. The first night she spent in a cell similar to mine, also in isolation. The guards stared at her the entire time. She, too, had a pail for a bathroom, and the only way she could get some privacy when nature called was by propping the mattress up against the bars. The guards poked it down. She moved the pail so she could hold it up while she went.

At about the time I was taken out for exercise, a woman arrived with a medical bag to check Trace out. The woman spoke French with a heavy accent that made it sound almost Spanish, which Trace speaks fairly well. She deciphered enough to understand that the woman was a nurse, and was there to make sure she was in good shape and hadn't been abused. Trace decided to cooperate, hoping she might be able to strike up some sort of conversation with the woman to get more information from her.

She also didn't have much choice; the nurse was accompanied by two guards with long, hard-plastic nightsticks. The nurse won some points with Trace when she scolded her escorts and the guards, telling them to go down the hall and shield their eyes while the exam took place. She was entirely businesslike during the exam. Trace couldn't tell whether she understood her Spanish. In any event, the nurse gave no answer to Trace's questions. She checked her over thoroughly, then did what was essentially a cursory rape exam.

"No one has attacked me," Trace told the nurse, in English and Spanish, but the woman didn't acknowledge her. It was likely, thought Trace, that she'd heard that from actual victims, worried that their protests would inevitably lead to more trouble.

The woman packed her gear back into the small case she'd

brought and left. Trace sat back on her mattress, staring at the bars. Unlike my cell, hers had a pair of openings at the back looking out on a yard. There was no glass; they were covered with a chicken wire screen and nailed shut. Prying the wire away wouldn't have been too difficult, but the windows were only eight inches square and there was no way she could squeeze through.

About an hour after the nurse left, another woman showed up; this one was an older inmate who brought a fresh change of clothes and sandals. Trace had been wearing green prison pajamas like mine; now she was given a purple pants suit with a long tunic. Trace tried to shoo off the guards but they didn't retreat; finally she pulled the blouse over her top and then changed her pants, staying behind the woman for cover.

When Trace had finished, the woman led her from the cell. Trace assumed she was going to be put to work. She welcomed the chance—it would give her a better idea of the facility and make it easier to plan an escape. She followed the older woman out to the corridor and then down a short stone staircase, memorizing every footstep.

The building seemed empty; there were no other prisoners and no guards between her cell block and the door to the outside. Painted rocks outlined a path through the dirt to a small one-story building. Trace and the woman were trailed by two guards as they walked around the front and side of the building, then down a hill to a two-story stone building that had a garden and a porch. A sentry stood in front of the steps up to the porch, an AK47 slung over his shoulder and a walkie-talkie at his belt. He kept his eyes straight ahead as Trace and the old woman went to the stairs. The woman hesitated for just a second before reaching to the string tied to a bell at the side of the door. Then she gave it a sharp tug, clanging the bell twice.

A man in a soldier's uniform opened the door. The woman took off her shoes and walked inside without saying a word. Trace did the same, still trying to take note of everything she could. She was so focused on checking out the security—there was no one else in the building, there were no video cameras, no motion detectors, no sensors on the windows—that she didn't guess what was going on until she was shown into a small bedroom on the second floor. A silk print dress had been laid out on the narrow bed.

"Why are you taking me here?" she asked the old woman.

The woman gestured at the dress, then started out of the room. Trace started to follow, but the old woman put up her hand and pointed again at the dress.

The dress was about her size, falling nearly to the ground. It would have covered her entire body, including her arms, but she didn't like the direction this was going in so she didn't bother changing. Instead, she sat on the bed and listened, waiting for the old woman to leave the house so she could reconnoiter. Hearing the downstairs door close, she went to the door to the room, intending to slip downstairs. But as she reached it the sentry who'd been outside came in. A cross look on his face, he jerked his thumb over his shoulder, then turned abruptly and went back downstairs, expecting Trace to follow.

The house's rooms were not very big, but there were a lot of them. A hall several times wider than the upstairs rooms divided the first floor in two. It was unfurnished except for some elaborately decorated vases and two small wooden benches. The doors to the rooms lining the hallway were closed.

The soldier showed Trace to a room near the back of the hall. The room was about twice the size of a suburban living room in the States. It was stuffed with elaborate black lacquer furniture and a variety of chairs. A man sat in one at the far corner of the room. The room was filled with tobacco smoke, and as she followed the soldier toward the chair Trace realized the man was smoking a pipe.

The man in the chair raised his hand, then in English told Trace to come and stand before him. He was the same fat guy who'd checked us in the day before.

"You are an American," he said. "But you are not white."

"What difference does that make to you?"

A dumb little smile appeared on fatty's face.

"I have made a study of the West," he told her. He used the pipe as if it were a pointer. "This pipe is from England."

"That's nice."

"Western women are different from Koreans."

Trace shifted her weight subtly. She decided she could take the soldier first, grabbing his weapon before going for fatty.

"You will cook my dinner. I wish an American dinner," said fatty. "A hamburger."

"What do I look like, McDonald's?"

Fatty didn't seem to understand.

"Are you serious?" said Trace. "You want me to make dinner?"

"Very serious, miss. You will make dinner."

More puzzled than anything else, Trace followed the soldier back out into the hall. I don't want to give you the impression that she's not a good cook, but Trace wouldn't be my first choice behind the stove. We've never seen much of her domestic side at Rogue Manor. Being one of the few women in a mostly male organization, she's careful about not falling into the female role stereotype. Ask her to wash the dishes and she'll usually tell you which part of your anatomy is in need of drastic alteration. And as for cooking at company outings, once or twice she's threatened to treat us to some Apache specialty her great-grandmother taught her, but as they generally involve some variation of marinated armadillo, we've always found an excuse to pass.

The kitchen sat at the end of the hall. The appliances, all German, were upscale and new, the sort that would equip a well-off European home. Opening the double-wide Liebherr refrigerator, she found a bowl of chopped meat. There were vegetables, and some small bottles of condiments, but the fridge looked as if the navy football team had gotten there ahead of her.

Trace set the meat out on the counter and looked over the kitchen. There were no knives anywhere, and no glasses or bottles—in other words, no easy weapons were at hand. She found a medium-sized frying pan, and began cooking the burger.

"We need french fries," she told the guard, who'd been watching her from the doorway. "Potatoes. You can't have a hamburger without fries. It doesn't make sense."

The soldier didn't say anything, nor make any sign that he understood.

"French fries," she said, approaching him. "Potatoes. We chop them up. Chop, chop."

He retreated. Trace ducked below to the cabinets, continuing her search for a weapon. The best she could do before the soldier returned was a large fork.

"You didn't get potatoes?" she said to him, dropping the fork by her side.

He had a plate in his hand and slipped it onto the counter, gesturing at it.

"French fries?" she asked, but the man still didn't understand. "I'm just cooking a burger? No roll, no vegetable, no nothing? What is it, a mono-meal?"

The man shook his head, and kept his distance. Trace finally flipped the burger onto the plate. As she did, the soldier backed out of the room.

"This is fucking weird," she said, taking the plate and following him just up the hall to a dining room. Fatty was already waiting, sitting at the end of the table. Two more guards had appeared, clutching AK47s nervously as she approached.

"You're just eating the hamburger by itself?" asked Trace.

"Hamburger is a very good American meal."

"It's not a hamburger if it's not in a roll," said Trace. "And you need french fries."

She glanced at the guards. Four against one—if she'd had a gun, she wouldn't have minded the odds, but all she was armed with was a fork. She put the burger down and took a step back.

"It really needs a bun," said Trace. "And ketchup."

Fatty smirked. He had a full set of Western utensils on the table.

"You can bake bread tomorrow," he told her.

"You think I'm going to be your cook?"

Fatty laughed and explained to her that he was king here—he used that word—and had complete control over her. And everyone else, for that matter. There was no possibility that either she or I would ever be freed. The best we could do was go along to get along.

Luckily for us, fatty added, he was an all-around nice guy, a rare member of the master race who actually liked Americans. Or didn't despise them as much as they probably should be despised. He believed in knowing the devil, and to that end had not only learned English but had made a devoted study of anything American that he could find. He had an Internet hookup—very rare in North Korea—and had unblocked access to American Web sites—even rarer. He knew that his English needed a little work, and was confident that in the future he would find the time to take some lessons from Trace. In the meantime, she would be his cook, making all Western dishes. She'd have her own room upstairs. If she behaved, she'd be granted special privileges.

"Life here can be very easy," he told her. "You, too, can have horse meat. Not every night, but once in a while."

"Oh, boy."

"Tomorrow, you will make tacos. Then pizza."

"The Great Leader is going to make you a prisoner in your own camp when he finds out that you're keeping us prisoner," Trace told him.

Fatty waved his hand dismissively.

"You better call General Sun," Trace said.

Fatty said something in Korean and the guard who'd showed her in poked a gun in her ribs.

"You will go upstairs now," said fatty. "Good night."

I know what you're thinking: here's the part where fatty follows her and tries to rip off her clothes. We'll have a nice cheesy sex scene, just enough T and A to tease the teenagers—and we're all teenagers when it comes to cheesy sex scenes. Then we'll move on to the real action. Trace will deliver a series of sharp kicks to his intelligence, dispatch the soldier and the other guards one by one, then escape.

But fatty didn't rip off her clothes or make a pass at her. He didn't even go upstairs.

Maybe he was a eunuch.

(III)

While Trace was auditioning as a chef, I was sitting in my cell trying to come up with a way of getting out before midnight. The locks were simple, but I had nothing to pick them with. The only solution was to get the guards to open the door for me.

A few strategic groans, a little foam at the mouth—I'd use one of the oldest tricks in the book, pretending to be sick to get them inside with me. Depending on the circumstances, I'd take them in the cell or on the way to the infirmary. These guys weren't exactly large, and knocking them around would release some tension.

Long years of habit have given me an internal clock that's generally accurate to within ten minutes. I reckoned it was closing in on 1800. But given the stakes I wanted as much confirmation as possible. When dinner came, I asked the guard who pushed it through the slot what time it was. The man didn't answer, or even seem to hear. I took the rice and went back to my spot against the wall. It was brown rather than the usual black—almost good enough to eat. As I scooped up the rice, my fingers scraped against something hard. I took it out, and found a key.

And then another. Someone thought I had an iron deficiency.

I tried to strike up a conversation with the attendant when he reappeared, using my limited Korean to ask what time it was. The blank expression on his face simply became blanker.

"*Myeot soyeyo?*" I repeated.

No answer.

"Time," I told him in English, tapping my wrist.

He shook his head, then grabbed for the bowl. As I gazed at the hall after he walked away, I realized I could see flickers of his shadow. I sat down and began deciphering the gray splotches at the base of the wall. I was seeing the shadows of the two guards out in the corridor. The shadows were extremely faint, reflections of light bouncing off two walls, but I could detect movement as the man who had brought me food walked by them, his narrow gray shadow flickering, then growing steadily fainter. Meanwhile, the other two shadows raised themselves slightly— the guards shifted in their positions, relaxing as the man left.

I now had an early warning system, which I tested a half hour later. I saw the faint gray spots separate, then watched one move toward me. I slid over to the back of the cell and, sure enough, one of my guards appeared, making the rounds.

Seven P.M.

I went back to shadow watching. In another hour, I saw movement again, but this time no one came to my cell. The guards moved on the hours—on the odd hours one checked my cell, on the even hours one walked up somewhere, either to the head of the hallway or a bathroom. Otherwise, they were disciplined enough to remain at their posts with almost no movement and absolutely no chatter. They were as professional as they come.

Armed with the keys, I simplified my plan for escape. I'd let myself out just before the hour and sneak up the corridor, waiting until they split up. As the second man went for his rounds, I'd take out the first and grab his weapon. But whoever had supplied the keys had considered the guard problem as well. Shortly after 2350, the shadows flickered. They grew darker, then disappeared. I waited another minute, unsure whether I was seeing a shift change, then let myself out.

Trace, meanwhile, went up to her room. The two guards she'd seen downstairs came up and took posts outside, standing on either side of the door. She checked her room for bugs and found two listening devices, one in the light and the other beneath the bureau. Both were relatively large; the technology probably dated from the 1970s, which meant they wouldn't be particularly sensitive. Besides the bureau, she had a mat bed and a little table the size of a stool; the only light was an overhead bulb covered by a paper shade. A small windup clock sat on the three-drawer dresser, tick-tocking away like a metronome. The drawers were empty, but an extra set of sandals sat next to them.

There was a window on the east wall of the room. It had been nailed shut, but whoever had had the room before her had loosened the nails. Trace bundled her blankets around the two bugs to muffle any sound, then slid the window open, checking around outside. She couldn't see any guards. Getting down from the second story wouldn't be too difficult—the joints between the stone block were wide enough to provide toe as well as fingerholds—but it was too light to risk it; she decided she'd rest and then go out around midnight. She curled up on the mat and told herself she would sleep for four hours, an amount her Apache forebears had declared proper for a warrior while on the warpath.[29] But she woke up less than three hours later, disturbed by a noise in the hall.

Footsteps.

Trace shifted slightly on the bed, listening as someone opened the door to her room and came in. She knew what was coming, and got ready to spring.

She leaped up as the hand touched her mouth. Her assailant was caught by surprise and tumbled over as she shot her fist into his head. Trace rolled on top of him, kneeing him in the process.

It wasn't fatty. It was the soldier who had shown her to the room. The man's eyes opened wide with surprise—then closed as Trace slammed her fist against his skull several times in rapid

[29] As I understand it, hours are a "paleface" concept, so I'm not sure how they did this. I've asked Trace for an explanation several times and got the Apache death stare in response. If you have any questions, I suggest you take them up with her.

succession, smashing the back of his head against the floor as if it were a basketball.

He was toast, but Trace wasn't quite through. She got up, then dropped her body knee-first into his ribs. The coup de grace was a heel kick strategically administered to assure that he wouldn't be feeling amorous for at least a decade.

She left the soldier on the floor and went over to the door. The soldier had apparently dismissed the other guards, and if the sounds of their assignation had carried through the house, no one seemed particularly worried. She went back and pulled the laces out of his boots, tying his hands behind his back and then putting his feet together. She pulled his shirt off and stuffed it into his mouth as a gag.

All the soldier had on him was a small pocketknife. Trace took it and slipped out of the room, moving down the hall cautiously, checking the other rooms as she went. They were all empty.

Downstairs, fatty had retired for the night. She could hear him wheezing in his bed as she came down the steps. His room was on the west side of the hall, across from where he'd been smoking the pipe. The door was open a crack; she peeked in and saw him sprawled on a Western-style mattress, sleeping completely naked.

Fortunately, she hadn't had anything to eat, or she'd have lost it there.

A pair of guards were posted at the front of the building, standing like guard dogs about ten feet from the entrance, their backs to the front windows. She retreated to the kitchen, and after opening the window and looking outside, saw that the rear of the house was unguarded. She slipped outside.

The perimeter of the grounds was lit by floodlights, but the lights were underpowered and barely illuminated the fence line. Only some of the buildings had lights around their exteriors, and even these were relatively small, so that most of the camp was in deep shadow. While this made it easy for Trace to creep around without being seen, it also meant that she had a hard time seeing some of the guards who were outside—including the two in front of my building whom she didn't realize were there until they were only five feet away.

And training their rifles on her.

(IV)

I left my cell door slightly ajar to make it easier to get back in, then hustled down the hallway. I slipped to the floor, checked to make sure the coast was clear—it's harder for someone to spot you if you're not at eye level—then walked down the corridor, retracing the path I'd taken earlier when I had been let out for exercise.

Anytime something goes this easy, you have to be suspicious. It made sense that anyone who could set up a meeting would bribe the guards as well. But it was also possible—very possible—that whoever had arranged for me to get out of my cell had done so simply to create a pretense for shooting me. While it seemed likely to me that the camp's masters didn't need a pretense, I couldn't be sure. So I tried to check out the situation as much as possible before keeping the appointment. Rather than taking the door at the end of the corridor that led to the exercise yard, I continued up the hallway, looking for another exit.

I found a set of steps to the second story of the building. I crept upward, hugging the side of the wall. The stairs opened onto an empty, unlit hall. Instead of prison cells, the rooms along the corridor were classrooms, complete with blackboards and old wooden desks. The ones on my left had windows; a small amount of gray twilight spilled out of them and into the hallway. I went to one and looked out the window, and found myself looking down at the front of the building. Two men with guns were moving slowly across the lawn.

I didn't see Trace until after I'd decided one of those weapons would be handy. By then I'd already slipped the window open, climbing up so I could jump once they were past.

One of the men shouted to her in Korean, telling her to halt or be shot.

I sprang into action—or more accurately, I dropped into action, landing on the back of the nearest sentry. He crumpled immediately, hardly providing any cushion at all as I, too, hit the ground. Jumping up, I grabbed for the rifle, which lay under his now crushed chest. Trace, meanwhile, threw herself at the other man's midsection, ducking beneath the barrel of his gun. Unfortunately, she did it just as he squeezed the trigger. The bullets missed her. She rolled into his stomach and bowled him over, knocking him down like a flap in a pinball game. But the sound of gunfire was loud and unmistakable, and by the time she caught her breath, sirens were sounding.

"What are you doing out here?" I asked her.

"Looking for you. Come on. The fence is this way."

"No, this way. I have to meet someone."

"Meet someone? Christ, Dick, this isn't *The Dating Game*."

I ran around the back of the building, flanking the yard where I'd exercised. There were several fenced-off sections next to each other, separated by narrow alleys. I followed the alley two yards from where I'd been, intending to come up from behind whoever was waiting for me. Before I could reach it, a pair of floodlights attached to the roof of one of the buildings came on, illuminating the yard where my rendezvous was supposed to take place.

The light didn't quite reach us, but we dove to the ground anyway, unsure whether our area would be illuminated next. A half-dozen North Korean guards ran through the yard to my left. They reached the fence and spread out, taking positions to cover anyone coming out of the back of the building.

"Who are you meeting?" Trace whispered.

"I'm not sure."

"Where?"

"Over there."

"Over there is full of soldiers."

"Yeah."

"They set you up."

"Maybe. Or maybe you screwed everything up."

It seemed more likely the latter. The soldiers had their guns ready, but the detachment didn't look as if it was taking part in a planned ambush. For one thing, they were too easy to see, and clogging the path I would have taken. If I were killing me, I'd have put a sniper in the darkness beyond the lights. He'd have fired when I reached the fence, bull's-eye right through the head.

Assuming I went through the trouble. Most unwanted guests of North Korea commit suicide by shooting themselves fifty times in the back of the head.

As I stared at the rendezvous point, it occurred to me that the spot he'd chosen was easily seen from several vantage points. There was no cover, and even if the guards hadn't been alerted, you wouldn't be able to count on not being seen.

But what if "NE fenc" meant the northeast corner of the entire complex, not the little yard where I'd been during the day? The perimeter was only sparsely lit.

Duh.

"I may have the wrong spot," I told Trace. "Come on."

We backed out of the yard we were in, then moved quickly through the chain-link alley to the open area behind the cottage where Trace had been taken. A small garden ended at another fence; beyond the fence were a dozen or more prisoner barracks, watched over by a guard tower to our extreme right. The northeast corner of the camp lay on the other side of the tower.

The easiest way to get there was by crossing through the barracks area. It was dark and there was plenty of cover, and we wouldn't have to worry about minefields, which were sure to be placed outside the perimeter fence. But just as we started to go, we spotted a man running to one of the buildings, rousting the prisoners for a head count. Figures began spilling from the buildings.

North Korea's shortage of electricity meant that the main barracks area lacked any lights at all. Even though they were now under full alert, the prisoners assembled in the dark. But they must have been used to it, for they moved out silently, forming lines in front of the buildings without speaking. Even the guards and trustees were silent; all we could hear were footsteps against the hard ground.

A set of headlights swung around to our right. An old Soviet-era jeep passed, driving around a perimeter road that ran just outside the fence.

"That's our ride. Come on," I told Trace, jumping to my feet.

"You're nuts," she hissed, following.

The inner perimeter fence was about fifty yards away, and within sight of the watchtower. While it was dimly lit, there was enough light to make anything climbing it obvious. Sixteen feet high and topped by barbed wire, getting over it would take more than a few seconds, which would give even a lazy guard ample time to spot us. So rather than going over it, we wanted to go under it. We moved south along the fence line, staying in the shadows, looking for a drainpipe or some other obstruction where getting under would be easy. We found a culvert a minute or two later. A lot of people had found it before us—the ground on either side was well trod.

Very likely, the guards knew about it, too. The area on the other side of the fence was lit by a spotlight, and would be in full view of the watchtower to our north.

"We'll wait for the jeep," I told Trace. "Just after it passes, we go through. Whoever is watching in the tower will be focused on the jeep."

"How do you know?"

"Human nature."

"I'd be watching the culvert if I knew it was a good spot to cross, especially when a truck passed by."

"You're not in the tower."

The jeep came back about five minutes later, bouncing along on ancient shocks. I've called it a jeep but it was really a UAZ 469B, the Russians' attempt at reengineering a Land Rover. Probably a good forty years old if not fifty, the vehicle was typical of the era it was built in, boxy and tough, prone to rusting and cranky when starting.

But aren't we all?

"Go," I told Trace, pushing her toward the opening in the fence.

She raced to the culvert, slid down the shallow hill with her rifle next to her chest, then pushed through the hole and ran into the darkness beyond. I followed, slipping rather than sliding, and threw myself through the hole under the metal fence.

Which, it turned out, wasn't *quite* big enough for me to get through. My shoulders caught against the metal prongs of the fence, and no matter how I wiggled, I couldn't squeeze underneath. I couldn't back out either.

I pressed my chest against the ground and pushed to the side, edging the rifle I'd taken earlier out from under my body. I was in the light, easy to see. A fish hooked on a line only makes it worse for itself by panicking, jerking its mouth one way and the other to get free. Right now I knew I was a fish, and had to stay calm and work myself out.

Great in theory, hard in practice. Sweat soaked through the thin prison clothes I was wearing. Shifting my mental focus to my shoulders, I relaxed and lowered them as I pushed the gun off to the side. I could see myself in my mind's eye, spotted where I was snagged. I pushed back slightly, then wriggled left, freeing all but one of the metal prongs.

The last one refused to let go. I felt it scrape along my skin. I pushed harder. It dug in.

Sometimes calm doesn't work. I pushed hard, angry. The metal ripped into my flesh—and then I was moving easier, not free entirely but not jammed either. I pulled forward, heard my shirt tear, then felt myself released. I grabbed the gun and scrambled into the shadows. It had seemed like an eternity, but it was only a few seconds; the jeep was just nearing the tower.

"What happened, your head was too big to fit under the fence?" joked Trace.

I growled at her.

"You're bleeding," she added sympathetically. "Your shirt's all ripped. You scraped the hell out of your back."

"Yeah."

A few more scrapes on my body weren't going to make much of a difference. I'd also lost my sandals in the culvert. Even though the soles of my feet have been built up with scar tissue over the years, there's still something annoying about a sharp pebble in the crease under your little toe—especially as you leap onto the back of a jeep.

Not that I can blame the pebble for my lack of balance when we ambushed the two men as they came around the curve in the UAZ ten minutes later. That was entirely Trace's fault—she slipped as she leaped onto the tailgate of the truck and fell against me. I was already in midair, so I couldn't manage much of a midcourse correction. I lassoed my target, wrapping my arms around the driver and pulling him with me as I flew to the ground.

See what happens when you don't wear your seat belt?

The Korean was small and light, but not weak, and even though he'd been taken completely off guard, he fought like a wildcat. I must have had at least 150 pounds on him, and maybe a whole foot of height and reach, but his sheer ferocity matched mine as we rolled in the darkness. Then he made the mistake of biting me on the forearm. That fired up my adrenaline reserve, and I flipped him over my back, stomping his face like an enraged bull and snapping his neck in the process. I can't stand vampires. If I'd had a silver bullet or a wooden stake, I would have put it through his heart.

I grabbed his firearm, then ran back to find Trace and the jeep. The sudden departure of the driver had caused the UAZ to overturn, dumping both Trace and the Korean soldier onto the ground. The jeep rolled down the embankment, landing in the rocks that were part of a drainage ditch used during heavy weather. Trace curled herself into a ball and burst free, bumping and scraping her arms but otherwise not hurting herself. The soldier wasn't so fortunate—he was pinned under the vehicle, which had tipped onto its side. The truck reminded me of a click beetle, its tailpipe sticking out from the chassis like a broken leg.

The UAZ isn't particularly heavy. I reached inside and turned off the engine, then Trace and I pushed it right side up. It was still in the ditch, but it had the good sense to point its nose toward the road. The soldier who'd been pinned underneath had already departed for the Great Workers' Paradise in the Sky. I pulled his body off the road and gave Trace his pistol, an ancient revolver.

"Let's grab their shirts and caps," said Trace.

"Good idea."

We weren't going to fool anyone up close, but from the tower we'd look like soldiers. I had to rip my shirt all the way to the collar to get it on. Then I slouched in the front seat of the jeep as Trace restarted it and drove us up on the road.

By now, it was way too late to make my meeting. So I changed my game plan. We'd drive past the guard tower and find an exit to the complex. Then we would drive as close to the coast as possible. Then . . .

Then we'd figure out another plan.

I got as low in the seat as I could as we drove past the watchtower.

"Intersection coming up on the left," said Trace. "Two guards."

"I can see them."

I positioned the rifle in my lap, ready to fire if necessary. We passed by quickly; the guards didn't react.

"This damn road goes on forever," complained Trace. "You sure we can get out this way?"

"If you want to run across a minefield, be my guest."

A dangerous thing to say to Trace Dahlgren, admittedly. But she stayed on the roadway, passing another guard tower as the road curved. By coincidence, we were at the northeast corner of the complex, where the meeting was to have taken place. The ruins of three old buildings sat on the other side of the fence. The area was in shadows; it would have been a good place to meet.

Or be ambushed in. Headlights switched on in front of us. Trace slammed on the brakes. Before I could raise my pistol, our jeep was swarmed by a pack of soldiers who'd been hiding by the side of the road. I felt the cold steel of several rifles against my neck.

"FUBAR," muttered Trace under her breath. "I knew we should have gone through the minefield."

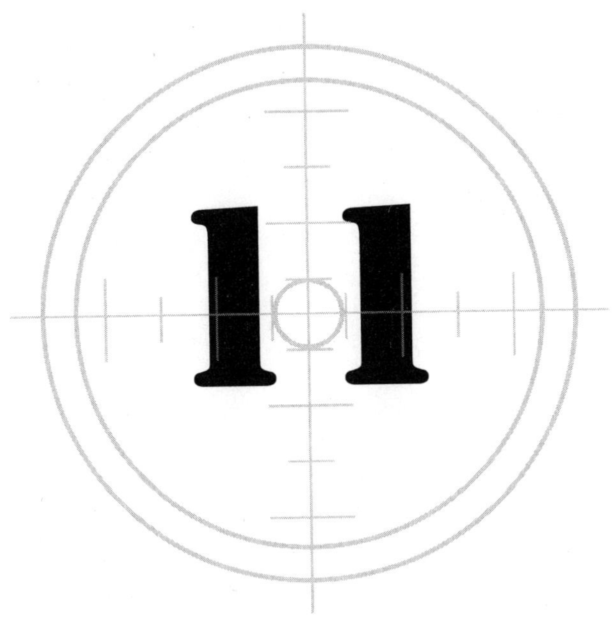

[1]

You're late. What kept you?"

The voice, speaking English, was about the last I would have expected.

It wasn't Doc—it's never surprising to see him turn up when I'm in trouble. Nor was it Kim's goon General Sun. The voice spoke English with a decided American accent.

Jimmy Zim?

The Christians in Action have never been that good.

Sean? Shotgun? Mongoose?

"Junior!" yelled Trace. "What the hell is going on?"

"I was supposed to meet Dick about an hour ago. I've been waiting."

"We were having too much fun to leave," I told him. "Let's get the hell out of here."

The NSA had intercepted communications from the port that indicated we were in custody and where we were going to be held. Junior, monitoring things on Sado-ga-shima, had tried to get ahold of Doc to ask for advice. But Doc was still on the submarine, and incommunicado. So he decided to take things into his own hands. With help from Jimmy Zim—a lot of help—he'd set up a rescue mission. The soldiers who'd swarmed over us were South Korean "hires"[30]—men used to working with the CIA and longtime acquaintances of Jimmy Zim. Zim had also helped Junior make the money transfers that got him hard cash to rent a pair of helicopters, which had dropped them off nearby. He'd also hooked Junior up with a South Korean intelligence agent who had connections inside the camp. He'd used those connections to contact me and set up the meeting.

The agent had also provided a safe house. We set out for it,

---

30 The word "mercenary" seems to have acquired a bad reputation and I promised I wouldn't use it.

boarding a pair of Korean military vehicles Junior had procured along the way.

"That Jimmy Zim is quite a guy," said Junior as we drove toward the safe house.

"Oh, yeah, a real peach," I said, knowing that few Christians in Action had ever done anything out of the kindness of their hearts. Jimmy Zim obviously needed me for something else.

We couldn't have driven more than thirty miles as the crow flies, but the rugged, winding roads through the mountains were so difficult to travel that it took us over two hours to get there. The farmhouse belonged to a prominent government official who had fallen out of favor with the regime nearly five years before and hadn't been heard from again. The Korean agent helping us was his son.[31] I only learned the back story later on; he remained quiet and aloof the whole time he was with us, either brooding or simply being professional.

The North Korean spy network is notorious around the world for its long arms. While many of its operations make no sense to us in the West, they've been able to infiltrate South Korean institutions with relative ease, and have made decent forays into Japan and almost certainly China, though the Chinese don't like to talk much about that. Their South Korean brothers, on the other hand, have a much lower profile. But they have done an equally good job infiltrating the North. They have been helped by numerous recruits like our host, men embittered by the dictator's actions or eager for an end to the insanity that defines life in the Workers' Paradise. As a general rule, greed is the biggest motivator in the spy business, but North Korea is probably the exception that proves the rule. Not that don are ever likely to be refused, even if they are counterfeit.

Yes, counterfeit. And even better quality than the twenties and fifties Kim's father flooded us with back in the nineties.

The Korean agent had his own men watching the place. He

[31] For obvious reasons, I'm not using his name.

was waiting when we arrived. He wore a cap pulled down over his face and dark glasses, even though it was still fairly dark. He let us in, told us we had the run of the downstairs, then disappeared.

"Jimmy Zim wanted you to call him," Junior told me, handing me a sat phone. "He's going to arrange for the boat to pick us up."

Ah, the sound of the other shoe hitting the floor.

While incredibly hospitable, the North Korean agent appeared to be a teetotaler, and the strongest thing I could find to drink was green tea. After two steaming cups my antioxidant level was restored sufficiently enough to survive a conversation with an employee of the federal government, and so I took the sat phone from Junior and went to find a place where I could talk privately. The only place without anyone sleeping in it was a covered patio area at the back of the house. I settled down on the wooden bench and dialed in my new best friend.

Jimmy Zim picked up about midway through the first ring.

"This is Marcinko. What's going on?"

"Ah, Dick. I was beginning to get worried. Matthew is very enthusiastic, but he is still wet behind the ears."

I've never understood exactly what that expression means, but I let it pass.

"Are you okay?" continued Zim. "Were you tortured?"

"It was no worse than sitting down with my accountant and talking about taxes. Can you get us out of here?"

"I'm afraid you're going to have to stay put for a while. We're watching the Russian ship and don't want to tip off the North Koreans."

Jimmy Zim told me that the ship that I had been following was still sitting outside the port, surrounded by small North Korean vessels. The plan was to wait for the exchange, then follow the ship out to sea, where it would be boarded and the weapon confiscated.

"Which is where you come in," he added.

"I've had enough boardings this week."

"Actually, the Pentagon suggested you get closer to the port so you could observe the exchange. They're looking for legal cover."

"Legal cover?"

"The lawyers want something to hang their hat on when the ship is boarded."

"How about we hang the lawyers instead?"

Jimmy Zim snorted. It was the most useful thing he'd said since the conversation began—a snort that spoke volumes.

You think I'm kidding about the lawyers, don't you? You think it's another of Demo Dick's convenient fictional devices, designed to add conflict to an already crowded plot. I hate to disabuse you, grasshopper, but lawyers play a far greater role in military decisions than anyone wants to admit. Every major action is reviewed by a legal staff to make sure it meets muster, not just with the law, but with international standards.

Is it a good idea? Imagine Eisenhower running D-day before Judge Judy for approval.

The CIA is even worse. Reportedly a whole floor at Langley is staffed by nothing but lawyers.

"I thought you had the area under surveillance," I said to Zim.

"We do. In fact, we saw Polorski go ashore."

"With Yong Shin Jong?"

"I can't say. But I'd bet on it."

"Get Yong Shin Jong and I'll cut the same deal Polorski did," I told him. "Simple."

"Washington says we can do nothing officially involving Yong Shin Jong."

"I'm sure the SEALs will be willing to act unofficially."

Jimmy Zim sighed. It was an if-it-were-only-up-to-me sigh, long and full of spit at the end.

"Where did Polorski go?" I asked.

"I couldn't say."

"Couldn't or won't?"

"I do have a Global Hawk following a truck west."

Global Hawks are robot spy planes. Just about everyone knows that we use satellites to spy on foreign countries these days. But there are a lot of misconceptions about that. First of all, it's not possible to keep satellites locked in to position above every part of the world. A geostationary orbit—for us laymen, that's an orbit over a fixed position on Earth[32]—is only practical near the equator. Most of the places we want to look at, North Korea for example, are nowhere near the equator. So the satellites we send up to watch them are always moving. To avoid them, all you have to do is hide when they're overhead.

Satellite paths are extremely predictable; even the satellites that we have that can change their orbits still have to obey the basic laws of physics, and therefore can be tracked through the sky, generally with nothing more sophisticated than a good telescope and a scientific calculator. Probably you could do it with a good slide rule, too, though I haven't seen one of those outside of a museum since my days at Officer Candidate School—aka Organized Chicken Shit.

Even if you don't know when a satellite is overhead—and believe me, even the French can figure it out—the most you're going to be exposed for is ten minutes or so, depending on the satellite and your position beneath its orbit. That makes a satellite great for finding something that doesn't move, but pretty lousy at following a truck.

That's why spy planes are still so popular. One of the most famous aircraft in the U.S. inventory is the U-2—the plane came first, then the band—whose basic design dates back to the Cold War. We also have the SR-71 Blackbird, which is capable of flying three times the speed of sound, good enough to outrun most missiles fired at it. The air farce retired the Blackbird several years ago, only to have to pull it out of retirement in the early 1990s because of an intelligence gap. Last I heard, there

32 Obviously, I'm going to simplify all this. What do you think I am, a rocket scientist?

are still two Blackbirds operational; they're somewhat expensive to fly and are only used for special missions. Still, they're probably the sexiest black birds on the planet.

The real workhorse of aerial reconnaissance these days are robot airplanes—UAVs or unmanned aerial vehicles that can fly halfway across the globe and back without a pilot in the cockpit. In fact, there is no cockpit; the planes are flown from a hangar at Nellis Air Force Base near Las Vegas. They have a lot of advantages over satellites, since they're much more maneuverable and can stay where you need them for as long as you want. And unlike the U-2 and SR-71, if their pilots get tired, they can call the next shift in without having to return to base. The main reconnaissance UAV available is an aircraft called the Global Hawk, which can spend a couple of days "on station" and which flies somewhere around sixty-five thousand feet.

Now one of the main ideas of using robot planes is that people won't get killed if they get shot down or in an accident. (Accidents are actually a lot more common; a number of pilots and mission specialists were killed during the SR-71's heyday just landing the damn thing.) But that doesn't make the aircraft expendable. The air farce really likes its toys, and so has a long list of when and where they can be used. They don't want them too close to missile sites. Even though the Global Hawk is much smaller and stealthier than most airplanes, it can still be seen on radar under the right conditions. Like all shiny toys, it's real easy to break, especially when someone's flinging high explosives and shards of tungsten at you.

I'm just guessing, but it was clear from his pauses and sighs that Jimmy Zim knew the air farce was going to order its toy home as soon as it got near Pyongyang, where the air defenses are designed to shoot down U-2s—higher fliers than the Global Hawk. Zim wanted to make sure someone was still watching Polorski, even though he couldn't directly tell me to do that.

To this day, I don't know exactly how much Zim knew of my real mission; maybe he knew it all, maybe he knew nothing. He told me the Global Hawk had just passed the city of Changghung-ni, heading west along a road that cut through the mountains. We were roughly fifty miles away by air, much farther by car.

"Possibly, they are heading toward Pyongyang," said the CIA officer. "There was a transmission intercepted by the NSA that indicated a Russian and his party should have free passage."

"I need a helicopter," I told him.

"You're not going to go, are you?" Jimmy Zim's mock alarm wouldn't have fooled a deaf man.

"I need a helicopter."

"I don't have one to give you." His voice had become serious again.

"Otherwise there's no way I can catch up."

"They've been stopping roughly every hour. Whoever is with him has a weak bladder."

"So for the record, you're telling me not to go," I said.

"For the record."

That was the end of our conversation. I grabbed Junior and asked if he could find me a map of North Korea. He went one better—he pulled out a small, handheld computer, attached the satellite phone to it, and went online to Google Earth. The view of North Korea was a few years old, but North Korea is not exactly setting records for new development.

I fiddled with Junior's map. The small screen and tiny buttons made it difficult to focus.

"Hey, Junior, what does this look like to you?" I asked finally, handing him the computer.

"Um, a trombone?"

"Can you get it to zoom in closer?"

He tapped the controls. The image remained blurry. Now it was an orange trombone, without the bell-shaped horn.

"Google doesn't use the best technology," he said finally. "I think I could hack into the Russian system and get better resolution if you give me a half hour."

"Not enough time," I told him. "Get your gear."

[11]

What looked like a trombone to Junior was actually the improved area of an airstrip about midway between Irhyang-dong and Namsong-dong. It was a small field, even by North Korean standards, able to support only a few propeller-driven airplanes. That suited me just fine: I only needed one.

Roughly an hour and a half after I killed the sat connection with Jimmy Zim, a company of North Korean soldiers led by a brusque civilian drove through the main gate at the base. The civilian waved dismissively at the sentry who came out to question him, shoved an ID out the car window, then barked an order to the men in the truck to follow him to the headquarters building. The driver stepped on the gas, spewing dust and pebbles everywhere as he swung up the dirt road to the building, which was perhaps fifty feet away. It wasn't hard to identify as the headquarters building; not only did it have a large picture of the Dear Leader above the door, it was the only office building on the base.

"I have important prisoners," said the civilian, bursting through the doors. "We must get to Pyongyang by nightfall."

The man who'd been mopping the floor in the hallway appeared unimpressed, though he did take more interest when three American prisoners were ushered in by a company of soldiers at gunpoint. He pointed down the hall, then grimaced as the troops trampled dirt across his floor.

I was one of the prisoners. Despite the janitor's nonchalance, our arrival was a major event—in fact the *only* event that had taken place at the airstrip all year. The local air force commander, who doubled as the base chief, squadron commander, lead pilot, and quite possibly the stewardess, jumped to attention as we marched in. He bowed deeply and repeatedly, insisting that he was glad to be of service and honored by the visit.

But most air farce officers are cut from the same namby-pamby cloth no matter which country they serve, and when it became clear that we actually wanted this major to *do* something, the protests began. His squadron was currently undermanned. His allotment of fuel was spoken for. His windscreen had just been washed and he didn't want to get any nasty bugs on it.

The civilian—supposedly a member of General Sun's security staff, though you know him better as the spy who'd helped arrange our escape—listened to these objections carefully. Then he answered in the only language that C2[33] officers understand.

"Please spell your name so that when I call General Sun I get it right," he told the officer, a major.

The air farcer turned pale.

"I must get authorization first," he told our spy.

"Of course. Which general should I call?"

The North Korean major swallowed an imaginary brick, then told the spy who to ask for.

Trace and I were in chains—real chains, nice touch—just outside the office. We were being held by the "soldiers," who of course were the hires in their fake North Korean special force uniforms. Junior, meanwhile, was down the hall with two other soldiers, looking for the utility closet so he could cut into the phone lines. Once that was accomplished, he would wire in a new handset and hand the phone over to one of the men with him. That man would pretend to be an aide to the commander's boss. He would order the major to cooperate with us posthaste.

A good plan, except that it depended on the Korean base having a semimodern phone arrangement—modern meaning something dating to maybe the early 1970s. Junior had settled on the closet as the most likely location for the PBX or network box, since it was near where the wire exited the building. But the only thing Junior found in the utility closet were brooms and cleaning supplies. There was literally only one telephone line connecting the base to the rest of the world.

Junior spent some time hunting around before realizing

---

33 Can't Cunt. You ought to know that by now. Obviously, you didn't read the first book.

what he was dealing with. Finally he cursed—I believe it may have been his first good curse while in my employ—and ran outside to cut the wire itself.

In the meantime, our spy got a real operator. Connected with the group commander's office, he found himself talking to a real aide, who demanded to know who the hell he was. Our spy hiccuped a bit, but pressed on—right up until the aide demanded to know why General Sun's office had not filled out form 43-D in triplicate, as the regulations clearly required.

Just on cue, there was a click. Junior had finally connected. Some quick verbal jujitsu—or karate, to use the country-appropriate term—followed.

"I accept your craven apology," said the spy haughtily, handing the phone over to the bewildered major.

The major, who was already standing at attention, stiffened and began repeating "*dwaetseoyo*" (okay) and "*joesonghaeyo*" (I'm sorry) as he was reamed out according to plan. He hung up the phone contritely, bowed deeply, then grabbed his jacket and headed for the flight line.

"Oh, my God," whispered Trace as we marched toward the plane. "Dick, you didn't tell me the Wright Brothers made this plane."

The "squadron" based here had two planes, only one of which had an engine. Not that it inspired visions of the wild blue yonder.

The aircraft was a Y-5 Colt, a Chinese rip-off of the Russian An-2. The Russian version first flew in 1947, but the basic design goes back much further. A biplane, the Y-5 is powered by a single engine at the front. The plane can hold eight combat troops; more if they get out and push.

The Russians originally designed the An-2 as a utility plane to ferry supplies and crops in agricultural areas. What they needed at the time—this was before helicopters caught on—was a plane that could take off and land from small dirt airstrips. That's why they built it with double wings; it could practically take off from a parking lot. All the other qualities you'd like in an airplane—such as the ability to fly high and go fast—are foreign to the plane. On a good day with a tailwind, it might break 150 knots.

Then again, it probably wouldn't.

The pilot immediately began complaining that there were too many of us, and that the aircraft would never get off the ground with the entire company. He was so adamant that I decided we had to believe him. After he went into the cockpit I culled out eight soldiers. The rest got back into the truck and went on the highway, heading west as reinforcements in case they were needed. Their informal leader, a former army captain named Sum Park, would stay in touch with me via a sat phone. No longer needed, our spy went back home, deciding his best course of action for the immediate future was to lay low.

Even with our numbers cut way down, the Colt still had trouble getting airborne. It hopped and tilted its way down the runway, finally bumping into the air rather than leaping. Somewhere in the distant past, the airplane had had bench seats in the rear cabin; we could see the bolt holes in the floor where they had been. But these had been removed. The rear cabin looked like the inside of a cargo container that had seen better days. A few round portholes near the front supplied the only light. A steady stream of air circulated through the cabin after we were airborne, alternating between warm and cold. More than likely the environmental system consisted of a flap of metal over a hole in the fuselage, swiveled into place by the pilot every thirty minutes or so.

Once airborne, I removed my chains and sat near the cockpit so I could hear what was going on. I'd sent one of the hires up front as a lieutenant in charge of the detail, but our pilot grew increasingly skeptical. Something about the flight bothered me, and finally I poked my head into the cockpit. I noticed that the compass reading was heading due south, rather than west.

"Tell him he's on the wrong course," I told our ersatz lieutenant. "This is where he wants to go."

I handed over a printout of the satellite map. And because it's not polite to speak a foreign language in front of someone who doesn't know it, I provided my own translation for the pilot, using universal sign language: I pressed a rifle barrel against his neck.

The pilot pushed the yoke, then grabbed at his chest, screaming in demented Korean as the plane veered toward the ground that everyone in the world was going to die.

That was an exaggeration. Only we were going to die.

And very soon, as the ground seemed to leap up from where it had been hiding beneath the clouds.

Would this be a good place to tell you what Doc and the others were up to in the sub?

Probably not.

Everyone in the cockpit—the pilot, our lieutenant, and myself—began screaming. I made a grab for the controls over the head of our pilot, trying to pull back on the small wheel. At first I thought the wheel was frozen solid, then I realized that the pilot's arms had locked straight out, forcing us into the steep dive.

"Pull us up," I told our lieutenant in the copilot's seat as I attacked the pilot's arms. "Pull back on the wheel. Back!"

The pilot was having a heart attack or stroke. I karate-chopped his forearms, loosening his grip. The brown and green swirl in the window focused into a row of trees on the side of a mountain. The lieutenant pulled back on the wheel with all his might. The plane jerked its nose upward, changing direction so violently the wings made a loud crunching sound. The sound was followed by silence—an odd sensation, since the drone of the fat engine in front of the cockpit had been threatening to drill a hole through my skull ever since takeoff.

The sudden motion of the plane had caused the engine to stall. Our biplane lost its upward momentum, and once more turned into a twelve hundred-pound brick.

As the wings began to spin, the pilot shook his head. Regaining consciousness, he grabbed the yoke with one hand and with the other pounded on the instrument panel. He didn't hit a switch or the throttle, as far as I could tell, just an empty spot on the dash. The engine coughed a few times, then restarted. Once again we lurched forward.

The pilot grabbed at his chest again, screeched loudly, then started to get up from his seat before collapsing.

"Trace, take over here," I yelled. I pulled him out of the cockpit and took him into the back, where two of the hires started CPR. By the time I got back to the front, Trace and the lieutenant had managed to get control of the airplane and were trying to correlate my map with the roads below. Fortunately, there aren't many highways in North Korea. We were south of Songchu. By my calculations we were ahead of Polorski, but I didn't want to land behind him. That meant calling Jimmy Zim and asking where he was.

"Why do you want to know?" said Zim.

"Idle curiosity."

"He's just east of Songchu."

"Thanks," I said, reaching for the end transmit button.

"Dick, the Global Hawk just spotted an aircraft about fifty miles ahead of Polorski, flying along the highway that goes through Songchu. You wouldn't know anything about that aircraft, would you?"

Certainly, Jimmy Zim knew that was us. I suspect that if I had admitted it, he would have done his best impression of Claude Rains in *Casablanca*, telling me how "shocked, simply shocked" he was. But I've never been a big fan of amateur impressionists, so I told him no and hung up.

Even though few people own cars in North Korea, most of the country's highways are several lanes wide. That's because they're intended as landing strips for airplanes the next time there's a war with the U.S. Any strip wide enough and long enough for a MiG can easily handle a Colt. It wasn't hard finding a place on the road where we could land.

The trick was the landing itself. The Colt has fixed landing gear—they're always down—which meant we didn't have to worry about flipping the right switches or compensating for the sudden turbulence the gear induced. But landing an airplane requires a bit more skill than just pointing the nose at the ground. I went into the back to see if our pilot could at least tell us where to set the flaps, but the foam at the side of his mouth made it clear he wasn't going to be much help.

Trace had already decided to use dead reckoning to get us down.

Poor choice of words.

"Seat belts!" she yelled. "We're landing!"

Seat belts would have been an excellent idea, had the plane been equipped with seats. The hires grabbed whatever they could in the back, bracing themselves as the plane descended. Trace tried easing off the engine for a smooth landing. But the power plant was a touchy old geezer; it choked and surged, pulling the airplane forward and then dropping it onto the pavement. Trace cut power completely, and we all hung on as the wheels squealed and then blew, one after the other.

The stretch of highway they'd picked to land was long, straight, and relatively flat. Tires shredded, the plane veered right and then left. Trace tried working the pedals to steer, but the Colt was through taking orders. It rolled over the shoulder of the road, down a slight embankment, and briefly became airborne again before nosing in. Fortunately, we'd lost most of our forward momentum. We were only going five or ten knots when the Colt finally put her nose against the rocks.

One of the soldiers broke his arm in the crash, and there were several bloody noses and bruised ribs. But except for the Korean pilot, who'd died from a heart attack, there were no fatalities, and we were able to get out of the plane without any further adventures.

[III]

While we were scrambling out of the plane, Doc, Shotgun, and Mongoose were in the USS *Greenville*, sitting off the coast of North Korea watching the Russian trawler.

And they weren't too happy about it. They'd been there for more than forty-eight hours, with no indication of what was going on. The submarine had backed off a few miles and raised its radio mast each night to await new orders, but none came. All they could do was sit and wait.

After two days of twiddling their thumbs, Doc went to the SEAL lieutenant and suggested that a clandestine reconnoiter of the Russian ship might be a good idea. The SEAL commander readily agreed, and they mapped out a plan to get aboard the ship. But the submarine captain nixed it. His orders were specific, he said: the ship was not to be molested while in Korean waters.

"I don't want to molest them," said Doc. "Just peek under their dress a bit."

But the sub commander wouldn't budge.

One of the best ways of stopping a truck is by shooting a .50 caliber armor-piercing shell through its engine block. This can actually be done at a good distance with a Barrett sniper rifle, a gun that began proving its worth back in the mid-1980s. The Barrett does have drawbacks—it's long and heavy, about twice as cumbersome as a standard sniper rifle. But its accuracy and efficiency more than make up for them.

Unfortunately, we didn't have one. So we had to come up with an alternative. The most obvious was to set up a checkpoint; we found a good spot between two sets of curves three miles up the highway. The South Korean hires moved double time, trotting forward at a pace that brought a smile to Trace's lips, and more sweat to my bruised and battered brow. I could see her making mental notes as we marched. No doubt we'll have a South Korean branch any day now.

We found a straight uphill stretch where the truck would have to slow down, then set up a simple checkpoint near the crest. Two of the men and our lieutenant stood in the highway with their guns and a red handkerchief we'd attached to a rifle as a flag.

A half hour later, the Korean military truck similar to our army's deuce and a half came lumbering into view. Its canvas back flapped as the driver ground through the gears, climbing toward us. But instead of stopping, he stepped on the gas. I'd stationed four men beyond the checkpoint in case this happened. They shot out the tires, but the truck still didn't stop. It continued for at least thirty yards, shredding its tires, sparks flying from its rims. Fire flashed beneath the truck. It tipped over on its side and slid precariously onto the shoulder.

Did I mention that the North Koreans don't believe in guardrails? Or maybe they were just too cheap to put any here. The truck stopped halfway over the ravine, bright orange and red flames leaping over it. One of our bullets had hit the fuel tank, and the sparks had ignited some of the gas or fumes.

"Stop firing! Stop firing!" I yelled, sprinting to the truck. By the time I reached it, someone was getting out of the back. I grabbed him, checked quickly to make sure it wasn't Yong Shin Jong—he looked Russian, probably one of Polorski's guards—then threw him toward Trace, who was leading the pack of hires behind me. I pushed into the truck, groping for anything that might feel human. I caught hold of something and pulled. It was another Russian. I tossed him aside and went back into the truck. By now the fire was producing thick smoke. I began choking. Seeing was next to impossible. I felt something move next to my left knee and reached down to grab it. Something else bumped into my right side and I threw my arm around it. The three of us tumbled out together, rolling on the pavement. I fished up one of the men, saw it wasn't Yong Shin Jong, and grabbed the other.

Eureka.

Yong Shin Jong coughed and shook his head, sputtering something in Korean. Then he got a strange look on his soot-covered face.

I'd seen that sort of look before. New recruits wear it on their first full gear workout day in ninety-degree heat. I jerked away just as he spewed.

I took Yong Shin Jong by the collar and pulled him as he vomited, trying to get us away from the truck. The fire had reached the cab, and things were starting to pop—small explosions as ammo in the belt of a man trapped inside cooked off. I looked up and saw Trace running toward the truck. I let go of Yong Shin Jong and leaped at her, executing a shoe-string tackle in the black smoke. She started to get up, then yelped as the road in front of us heaved and the truck disappeared, leaving a fireball in its wake. A fresh fireball launched from the engine compartment as it hit the rocks below, an exclamation mark.

Trace got to her feet. "Ike," she said.

"I don't think he got out."

"Damn. I wanted to kill him myself."

Ammo continued cooking off in the truck, and it was a half hour before we could get down and confirm that Tall, Dark, and Polish was now Burned, Black, and Crispy. Half his face was burned beyond recognition, but the other half had miraculously escaped destruction, shielded from the flames by his arm as he died. Trace looked into his cocky grin one last time, then spit on it. She walked back up the hill alone.

[IV]

None of us were going to shed any tears for Ike Polorski, but his demise was inconvenient. I'm not sure how much information he would have volunteered, but whatever passes, map, and radio he was carrying with him were destroyed in the fire.

Besides Yong Shin Jong, two men survived. Both were North Korean soldiers who'd been detailed to ride with the Russian. They claimed they didn't know who their prisoner was, and said they didn't even know where they were going.

How true this was, I don't know. They didn't respond to the South Koreans' standard interrogation methods, nor did they change their stories when promised money and freedom in the South. You can read that any way you want—either they were incredibly loyal and would lie to the death or were incredibly honest and telling the truth.

The truck with the rest of our South Korean hires was about three hours to the east; there was nothing for us to do until it arrived but hide. Junior found a path to a small cave and clearing about a half mile away that appeared to be intended as a temporary rest stop for troops or transports. We scouted the area thoroughly, then searched the cave, hoping it was one of the many depots for explosives, arms, and ammunition that the North Korean government has scattered around the country, just in case the U.S. decides to invade. But it was just a cave.

Yong Shin Jong had been doped up. We made a stretcher from the remains of the truck and carried him to the cave to sleep it off. We also trussed the North Koreans and stuck them at the far end. I suppose if I'd been in a better mood, I'd've arranged for them to come south with us when we left. Even though they would have protested, it would have been the humane thing to do.

The black smoke from the fire dissipated quickly, but I was

concerned that someone might be sent from a nearby village to investigate. I posted a watch to hide near the truck. No one came. It's possible that the area was so desolate that no one was watching, but I think it's more likely that anyone who saw it simply assumed that the authorities had everything under control and there was no reason to do anything themselves. North Koreans are so used to the order imposed by the central government that they believe everything they see makes sense and is somehow under control by a higher power. When you live in a dictatorship that basically says the sun is the moon and the moon is the sun, after a while you stop asking why the sun only shines at night.

While we were waiting for the rest of our men to arrive I had another nonconversation conversation with my favorite Christian, Jimmy Zim. It went like this.

Me: We have Yong Shin Jong.

Zim: Do you have the nuke?

Me: Not yet.

Zim: It wasn't in the truck?

Me: If it was, it would have blown up by now.

Zim: Not necessarily.

Me: No, it wasn't in the truck.

Zim: What are you going to do now?

Me: What everyone does when they visit North Korea. Go see the Great Leader.

Zim: (Pausing, obviously choosing his words carefully) I have to remind you that you are on your own. The government cannot help you. We won't even spell your name right if Korea asks about you.

Me: M-a-r-c-i-n-k-o.

I was actually starting to admire the son of a bitch. Must have been early senility.

Soon after I hung up with the CIA officer, Yong came to. He wasn't as surprised—nor as grateful—to see us as I would have thought.

"Water," he said.

He gulped from the bottle I gave him. There were pimples under his chin, and he blinked like someone trying to get used to seeing without glasses. He drank so quickly water slobbered onto his shirt.

"Slow down," I told him. "You're going to get cramps."

"Thirsty."

"I'm sure. There's plenty of water, though. Take your time."

"Where am I?"

"In your homeland. How do you feel?"

Yong shrugged. "I have a headache. Chains on my feet."

"I didn't want you sleepwalking."

"Am I your prisoner?"

"Not exactly. Do you know what kind of drugs they gave you?"

Yong shook his head. "They shot me up with something in the ship." He shook his head again, possibly reaching a new level of consciousness. Then he jerked back. "I don't want to go to Pyongyang. I can't. Korea is not my home."

"It's not your home?"

"They'll kill me."

"It seems to me that they've had plenty of chances to do that and they haven't. What do they want from you?"

"To kill me."

Obviously there was more to it than that, but I'd have a better chance of tripping over a diamond on the cave floor than getting Yong to tell me the story.

"You're a pretty valuable commodity," I told Yong. "My Russian friend was going to trade you for a nuclear weapon."

Yong Shin Jong scowled. "Kim would never give up a bomb."

"Not even for his bastard son?"

"The Russian was a big talker, but he was a fool."

"He was actually Polish," I said.

"Kim would have had him killed as soon as he arrived."

"What about General Sun?"

Yong Shin Jong didn't get a chance to answer.

"Truck!" yelled Junior, passing the word from one of the lookouts.

"Ours?" I asked.

"Can't tell. Maybe."

"All right, you're with me," I told Yong Shin Jong.

He struggled to get up, but clearly didn't have the strength. I leaned over and hoisted him over my shoulder like a sack of potatoes.

A heavy sack, with a chain that slapped me right across my thigh.

"Trace, Junior, get some AKs. The rest of you—go hide in the cave. Don't make a sound. Go, let's go—I want to make sure these are our guys."

As I scrambled out to the road, I told Trace and Junior to take flanking positions and cover me. They hustled behind the rocks; I waited until they were ready and then went out into the road with Yong.

"Sorry I have to carry you with me," I told him. "But I don't trust you anywhere else."

"I'm not going to run away with these chains on," he croaked from over my shoulder.

"That's not what I'm worried about."

I heard the truck coming up the incline. I raised my AK47. The driver saw me as he came around the bend and slammed on the brakes.

Sum Park, the captain in charge of the hires, jumped from the truck as it stopped. "Dick!" he yelled.

"I got him," I told Park.

"Good," said Park. He had his pistol out. "We can kill him here."

The rest of the company jumped from the truck, their rifles ready.

"We're not killing him," I said.

"He is the son of the dictator and the enemy of my country," said Park. "He deserves nothing but death."

"You'll kill him over my dead body."

"That would be a shame," he said, steadying his pistol.

12

[I]

The fact that I'd anticipated something like this didn't make it any easier to deal with.

The fact that Trace and Junior were standing behind the South Koreans did.

"Yong Shin Jong is just Kim's son," I told Park. "He's nobody."

"You are wrong, Dick. He is responsible for many deaths. He was a member of the special forces and the secret police when he was younger. He led a mission into South Korea and kidnapped several people."

"That was in my youth, when I was a fool," said Yong Shin Jong heatedly. He began speaking rapidly in Korean.

Park answered. Yong Shin Jong shook his head.

"He's a liar," said Park, explaining to me in English. "He claims his father ordered him to do it—a convenient falsehood."

"He may be a liar, but he's my liar," I told him. "Look, Park, we don't have time to argue here. You have to let him go—it's for the greater good."

"Which greater good? So you can get rich?"

"That's not why I'm doing this."

"I know you get much money for your missions, Dick."

"I doubt I'll be paid for this one."

We could have had quite a discussion about patriotism and duty and greed if we'd wanted—and maybe we would have if I hadn't left the other half of Park's force back in the cave where they wouldn't complicate things. But the discussion would still have come down to us two, staring at each other. It was a question of whether he trusted me. And there my reputation—call it fame, call it battle scars—helped considerably.

Or maybe it was the gleam in my eye—and the reflection of Trace's and Junior's guns.

"All right, Dick. I'll trust you," Park said finally. "For now."

He put his weapon away and bowed his head. I bowed in return. His men lowered their weapons.

I will say this for a Korean—if he gives you his solemn word, you can take it to hell and back.

Which is pretty much what I did.

We loaded up the truck and headed west. Sum Park had refilled the gas tank at Songchu, which gave us enough fuel to make Pyongyang without stopping. Since I didn't know what Polorski's arrangement with Kim had been, I decided my best bet was to follow through on my own deal with Sun. Though the terms of Yong Shin Jong's return had not been specified, I interpreted our arrangement to mean that I should bring him back to Kim's compound.

The guards at the outer gate stood at attention when I drove up, not even stopping me. But the second set were much more demanding. The machine guns that flanked the roadway were turned toward me, and a guard demanded in very belligerent Korean that I step out of the truck.

"How do I say, 'No fucking way'?" I asked Sum Park, who was listening over the radio.

He supplied me with a few choice Korean words. Then I told them who I was, and that if they didn't let me through, Kim Jong Il was going to be very angry with them.

That worked with that set of guards, but the final group I met in front of the entrance to the Kim's complex were not persuadable. They surrounded the truck, flashing a variety of weapons, including two grenade launchers and a Minimi, the Belgian cousin of the M243 machine gun. I kept my hands on the steering wheel, and said in very calm, very slow English, that I was Richard Marcinko and had come to see the Great Leader.

They answered in very excited, very rapid Korean that I was a piece of worm shit and should get out of the truck immediately.

"I will get out, if you tell the Great Leader that I am here."

More Korean. More excitement. The grenade launcher was pointed at my face. It's my belief that a round from an RPG-7 when launched at that close of a range will merely blow right through you without igniting, but I decided this wasn't the time to test the theory. The Korean reached to the door and I stepped out, hands spread wide.

More guards arrived. I was poked, prodded, and searched. If I'd been a mass murderer in America, I'd have had one hell of a case against the cops for violating my civil rights. But in North Korea I was an honored guest, and the mass murderer was my host. The Koreans roughhoused me into a low-slung building across from the main entrance to Kim's humble abode, pushing me down the stairs and into a hallway to a windowless room that smelled of rat urine.[34] When the door was closed I was left completely in the dark.

I was there for about a half hour. The place was so dark and quiet that my senses shut down. I stood at the door and began visualizing what was going on outside, trying to project myself out into the corridors. Before I managed to reach the proper state of concentration, the door snapped open. The light practically blinded me.

"Richard Marcinko—you have returned!"

General Sun stood sneering behind the guards who'd opened the door.

"I never renege on a contract," I told Sun.

"Where is the prize?"

"Around."

"Around?"

"An American expression that means we complete the deal to my satisfaction, or you don't get him."

"The arrangement was that we would not kill you if you completed the mission," he replied.

---

34 Yes, I'm sure it was rat urine. Unfortunately, I have the experience to know the difference in several varieties.

"The price has gone up."

"The value of your life has gone down."

"All the more reason to renegotiate."

Sun turned and walked away. I started to follow but the guards blocked my way, then closed the door.

It reopened a minute later. Sun wasn't there, but the guards' attitudes had changed; they were now almost polite, their scowls professional rather than personal. They bowed their heads slightly, then turned without a word. I followed them through the hall, back upstairs, and then outside and across to the main door of Kim Jong Il's palace bunker. Here I was turned over to two sumo wrestler types who frisked me, then took me into the bowels of the underground McMansion. We eventually reached a suite several levels below street level, where a svelte Korean woman greeted me with a silent and discreet nod. Before I could construct any fantasies, she extended her arm, gesturing toward the bathroom.

"You will shower," she said in English. Her accent made her sound as if she were from one of the wealthy London suburbs. "Fresh clothes have been hung on the rack."

"No bath?"

"You may draw yourself a bath, if you prefer," she said, her tone extremely serious.

"Will you draw it?"

"The handles are not hard to turn," she said. "But one of your escorts will draw it for you if you wish."

"They're not going to scrub my back, too, are they?"

"If that is what you wish."

"I'd rather you did."

"I'm afraid that won't be possible." Her tone was so serious she could have been one of my accountants talking about the fine points of depreciating an M16. Then she smiled ever so slightly. "Your reputation precedes you, Mr. Rogue Warrior. You will find me quite on my guard."

Mr. Rogue Warrior opted for the shower, with no back

scrubbing and the door locked. Just in case, I was careful not to drop the soap.

A set of black ninja clothes hung on the rack near the towels, a Korean imitation of SEAL ops wear. They were looser than anything I'd wear on a mission, but comfortable; if the tailor ever leaves Kim's employ, he should start his own clothes business in the West. There were thick socks but no shoes or boots; grip pads on the soles kept me from sliding on the marble floor.

Smelling like the proverbial daisy—the soap was scented—I presented myself to my Korean escorts. They took me to Kim's den, the place where we had had our little drinking contest during my first visit. The Great Leader himself was standing over the snooker table, deep in thought, either contemplating a shot or trying to levitate the balls with mind control. Four or five men, all dressed in military uniforms, were standing behind him. Two waiters with trays of drinks hovered nearby.

"You exaggerate what you write," said Kim without looking at me. "Your stories are exaggerations."

"Usually I leave the really weird stuff out. Fact is always stranger than fiction."

"You should never lie," said Kim, looking up.

It was a true Dr. Phil moment—the world's greatest living scumbag was giving me a lesson in morals.

"I'll try to remember that," I told him.

"Still," said Kim, leaning over to line up his shot, "there must be some truth in what you write. You have done a remarkable job on this trifling business."

He fired the cue ball at its target. The balls rebounded around the table, but none fell. Even so, the others promptly applauded.

"Good shot," I told Kim.

"We both know it was a terrible shot," said the dictator. He smiled confidentially. "They're all just toads."

I glanced over at the men, who didn't seem to mind the slur.

"None of them speak English. But it wouldn't matter if they

did." Kim laughed. "Have a drink, Dick. The Bombay Sapphire is well stocked."

He raised his hand ever so slightly, and one of the waiters stepped forward.

"I believe I will make Bombay Sapphire the national drink," said Kim, laughing. "In your honor."

"Thank you." I took the glass from the tray.

"I always like to be nice to a man on the day he dies."

"I'll be sure to give you a call."

"You misunderstand. Today is the day." Kim turned back to the snooker table. "We're never ready, are we?"

"It'd be a shame if I died before telling you where your son Yong Shin Jong is."

Kim frowned, but I think his reaction had more to do with where the balls were lined up than what I said. As he stared at the table, one of the bookcases on the far wall moved, revealing a passage. General Sun entered through it, went to Kim, and whispered some sweet nothing in his ear. Kim nodded, then took his shot. One of the red balls fell and the assembled stooges gave another round of applause.

"So you have brought my son," said Kim, looking up. "Where is he?"

"I have him available. I'll turn him over once we work out a deal."

"In that case, I will change my mind. You will not be shot until after dinner."

[11]

While the Dear Leader and I were spending some quality time together, Doc and the others were still sitting on their thumbs aboard the *Greenville*. The submarine was sitting a few miles from the Russian merchant ship, just at the edge of North Korea's territorial waters. They'd been there long enough that the captain's suggestion that he would shoot them out the torpedo tube was starting to look like an offer rather than a threat. But before Shotgun could finish measuring his shoulders to see if he would fit, the *Greenville*'s captain received new orders.

With Polorski now neutralized—polite Washingtonspeak for being fried to shit—Jimmy Zim had convinced his superiors that now that the deal had been squashed, it was safe to take over the Russian merchant ship and inspect it. This was actually a cover-your-ass move—if the exchange had already been made and the ship got away, the CIA would naturally be blamed. Saying the ship should be inspected shifted all potential blame to a much larger organization—the navy, which of course would have to carry out any such boarding.

But this fell afoul of the State Department's earlier concerns about screwing up the nuclear treaty. Some bright bulb at the NSC realized this and referred the matter to State as an "advisory." In less time than it took to put a red "Eyes Only" sticker on the paper file, word came back from a State Department lawyer that the matter had to be reviewed at the highest level. This of course was the nuclear bomb of CYA statements, shifting the matter up through the food chain to the political sharks at the top. And in good political shark fashion, the matter was then sent for "input."

To the CIA.

I'll spare you the rest of the back and forth and around. In the end, the action was approved—provided "international legal concerns" were satisfied. These concerns could be boiled down into a single sentence for us laymen: don't seize the ship while it is in North Korean waters.

Goodness no, why would we do that?

Maybe to grab any sort of incriminating evidence before the people aboard had a chance to destroy it? Or grab the people themselves before they realized there was a problem and escaped? Or just to stop fooling around and get the damn thing done?

Nah.

The *Greenville*'s captain held a conference to discuss the situation. The Russian ship was about a half mile inside the territorial limits. Once it moved over the line, the SEALs could take it over.

He looked at Doc as he said this. He didn't have to say it twice.

"Captain, I've been wondering if we could arrange for some extended PT," said Doc. "The boys and I are getting a little restless, and obviously we can't be running laps through a nuclear submarine."

"And what would you have in mind, Chief?" asked the captain.

Once a chief, always a chief as far as the navy is concerned.

"A little swim, just to get the blood flowing."

Their blood was flowing pretty well a few hours later as they slipped out of one of the SEAL Delivery Vehicles and began a leisurely underwater stroll in a direction that just happened to take them to the Russian ship. As they swam, lo and behold, they happened to come across a large chain in the water.

Odd, a chain in the water. Definitely something to investigate.

Like Jack and the Beanstalk, Doc, Sean, Shotgun, and Mongoose climbed up the chain. But instead of finding a castle in the clouds, they discovered a ship, sitting at anchor. Being curious souls, they decided to investigate.

Mongoose figured that with his relatively recent service as a

SEAL, he had pride of place in the detachment: he wanted to be point man. This amused Shotgun and Sean no end, but not nearly as much as Mongoose's curses when he reached the top of the anchor chain.

Even Sean wouldn't have been tall enough to reach to the ship's railing from the hole where the anchor chain came through the hull, and there was no room to crawl in through the opening to get aboard. So they had packed the large suction cups I mentioned earlier as an alternative ship-boarding device. Mongoose had placed his too close to the chain and now couldn't get it to budge so he could move it higher.

You couldn't blame this on Mr. Murphy. Ol' Murph had been snoozing soundly so far, and was still cutting Z's when Mongoose began hammering on the release tab to get the cup undone.

"What the fuck is going on up there?" growled Doc, several links below. "Let's go, Shitforbrains."

"I'm fuckin' working on it, Chief. Crap."

"Don't crap me. Just get the damn thing done."

"You think I'm jackin' off up here?"

"Maybe that would help," suggested Sean.

Shotgun, who was right below Mongoose, thought this exchange was the funniest damn thing he'd ever heard. Of course, he couldn't laugh out loud, so instead he clamped his mouth shut and pressed it against his arm, shaking so hard he practically laughed himself back into the water.

"You take over," said Mongoose finally. "Use your f'ing cup."

The only way for Shotgun to get into position was to climb up and over Mongoose, which naturally added injury to insult. He stuck his suction cup into place, gave Mongoose a wide ass grin, then stepped on his shoulders and climbed over the side of the ship.

With their prize gone and half the North Korean Navy—such as it was—nearby, the Russians had posted a minimal night watch. There was no one on the forward deck, and the nearest man in fact was sleeping, though of course Shotgun didn't know that as he boosted himself over the gunwale and rolled onto the ship with a splat. He groaned, then sprang to his feet, pulling his MP5N out of its waterproof bag and taking a last look around before giving the all-clear.

"Yo, Blankethugger—you stepped on my hand on the way up," said Mongoose once he was on board.

"Want me to kiss it and make it better?"

"Shuddup and get with the program," said Doc. "Shotgun, take care of that anchor chain. Sean, Mongoose, you're with me."

The Russian ship was oriented almost perfectly perpendicular to the Korean coast. All it had to do to get into neutral water was to "drift" backward exactly a quarter mile. It would drift a little faster if the engines were on and the screw turning in reverse. Losing the anchor would help even more.

Doc and Sean followed Mongoose at point. They got inside the ship without being seen, stopping near the ladder as a pair of sailors passed by, one deck below. Mongoose slipped down after them, but they'd turned the corner and were gone.

There should have been an officer or at least some sort of watchman in the engine room near the control station on the compartment's upper deck. But either he was sleeping somewhere, or hiding, because neither Doc nor Mongoose could spot him as they snuck down the passage into the space. The overhead lights were off, and the room was filled with a reddish glow cast from the night lights and instruments. Though the ship was probably twenty years old, whoever owned it had retrofitted it with new engines and controls within the last few years. While its exterior was covered with thick rust, the diesel-electric motors and apparatus below practically sparkled in the dim light. A large computer screen sat at the left end of the panel; this showed the operator the status of the systems at a glance. The propulsion controls for the ship's two screws were at the center of the board, their black ball-topped handles looking like Tootsie Pops standing above the wheels.

"Tell Shotgun to cut the chain," Doc told Sean, studying the panel. "And hold on."

Doc stared at the panel. Had this been a vintage sixties control system—or even the original one put in the ship—he would have been fine. But Doc and computers don't completely mix. Whether that was a problem or not, he had trouble getting the engines cranking.

Meanwhile, Shotgun was running into his own problem up at the anchor chain. The plan for taking out the anchors was simple—a dab of plastique on each, ignited by remote control. A certain level of skill was involved, of course: Shotgun had to be fairly judicious in measuring out the explosive, since too big a blast would put a hole in the bow. But otherwise the job was fairly easy. As the last man up, Sean had applied the first charge when climbing aboard; all Shotgun had to do was put the charge on the other chain and push the button on his igniter.

It was at this point that Murphy decided to wake up the watch hand who'd been snoozing earlier. Then he whispered in his ear, sending him forward to check and make sure that the shadows he saw near the bow were just shadows.

There was very little room for a normal person to hide where Shotgun was, and even less for someone Shotgun's size. Shotgun raised his gun to pop the man, then heard someone calling to him from the distance. Deciding now that hiding was his best option, he hid in the only place available—on the anchor chain over the side.

Unfortunately, he forgot how far it was between the gunwale and the anchor. He was already hanging over when he realized it; thinking he could grab the chain as he fell, he let go.

They don't teach you much in the army about ships, and apparently even less about gravity. The latter pulled him down so quickly there was no way for him to get a handhold and he plummeted into the water.

Shotgun surfaced right next to the anchor chain. Unsure whether he'd been seen or not, he began shimmying up the chain, climbing up to a good spot to leave the explosives. He strapped them in place, then continued topside. But having used his suction cup earlier to help Mongoose, he was stuck below the rail.

As Shotgun contemplated his situation, he saw lights flash on the nearby North Korean ships. His first thought was that they had spotted him; then he realized they were moving away. General Sun had alerted the North Korean Navy that there was no longer any point in watching the Russian merchant ship; the deal was off and the navy could go home. Shotgun didn't know this, of course, but he did realize that the Russian ship would start moving soon as well. He pulled up the microphone to the SEAL radio he'd borrowed and contacted the others to let them know what was going on.

"Shotgun to Doc—yo, the other ships are moving."

"Clarify?" said Mongoose. All four of my guys were on the same circuit.

Knowing Shotgun, he probably made some comment about Mongoose suddenly using big words. But in the version of the story I heard, all he did was explain what he meant.

"Screw that," said Doc, who at this point hadn't gotten the controls to work. "Are the anchors blown or what?"

"I'm working on it."

"Blow them now! Jesus."

Shotgun, being very religious about demolition work, wanted to comply. The problem was, the explosives were less than ten feet away, and simply pushing the button would bring him face-to-face with the Creator quite a bit sooner than he wanted. So he took the detonator in his hand and jumped off the chain, pressing the little red button just as he hit the water.

Below, Doc was pressing buttons as well. In fact, he'd graduated to combinations, frantically hitting them in any order he could think of. Finally, he remembered his chief's training and did what any old salt would do when faced with a similar situation: he unleashed a string of curses the like of which had never been heard in the Eastern Hemisphere before.

Possibly, some random combination of computer screen tappings and switch shoving overrode the computer safety protocols that had kept Doc out of the automated system. But I prefer to think the computer simply wilted under the weight of the chief's personality, as many a seaman and lesser officer had over the years. The ship's engines sprang to life.

Doc threw the levers to full astern and the ship immediately began to respond. As soon as he was sure it was moving in the right direction, he put a small explosive charge on the engine controls, set the timer for two minutes, then began trotting over to Mongoose.

"We got company!" yelled Mongoose as a crewman appeared in the passage. He raised his gun to fire, but the sudden, unexpected movement of the ship knocked his target off balance. The Russian fell behind a piece of machinery, blocking Mongoose's shot.

Alarms began ringing. There were shouts in the distance. Mongoose fired a few rounds to knock out the lights in the nearby passage.

"Come on, door number two," said Doc, leading the way to the nearby catwalk. "We have a minute and a half before my bomb goes off."

They crossed over the engine room, pausing in the middle of the steel bridge to send a burst of gunfire toward the passage, beating back a crewman who'd foolishly thought of coming in. They then continued across to a second catwalk above the motors, where they found a ladder leading upward.

Mongoose once more took point. The passage was part of an auxiliary piping space, barely wide enough for Doc—Shotgun couldn't have squeezed through. It was also pitch-black. Mongoose continued climbing hand over hand until finally he came to a hatch.

A locked hatch. Where's OSHA when you need it?

"We'll have to blow it," said Mongoose.

"No time. Shoot the hell out of the latch."

"The ricochets will kill us."

"Not if you close your eyes."

Mongoose held the gun up to the metal, closed his eyes, and fired. The 9mm slugs, designed for doing maximum damage to human flesh, did a workable job on the Russian steel. Mongoose levered the submachine gun's snout into the space and pushed up into fresh air.

"Up, up, up," said Doc, encouraging Mongoose to explore the open deck.

He was grabbing the nearby railing when the bomb on the control panel blew.

Shotgun prided himself on using just the right amount of explosives for a job. Doc was old school—he'd never seen an explosion too big. He had prepared the explosives for the control panel, and his explosion didn't just take out the controls—they turned most of the engine room into a mangled mess of blackened metal and burnt plastic.

Wind from the blast flew up the hatchway they'd just escaped from. Debris showered over Mongoose and Doc, who covered their heads and ducked. When the ship finally stopped spewing, Mongoose rose and took the GPS locator beacon from his vest pocket, activated it, and attached it to the side of the railing, making sure that it had a clear view skyward. As he turned around to see where Doc was, something whizzed overhead.

"If I didn't know any better," he said, "I'd think that was a 37mm cannon going by."

"Fifty-seven millimeter," said Doc, pointing in the direction of the Hainan-class patrol craft a short distance away. "The bastards are shooting at us."

I'm not sure whether Sun's orders had advised that the Russian ship could be sunk, or the North Korean captain in charge of the escort fleet had decided to make his play for admiral. In any event, the effect was the same—the Russian vessel was taking heavy fire. The automated control system shut down the engines once Doc's bomb went off, but by then the ship was already moving astern at a good pace. Fast enough, in fact, that less than a minute after hitting the water, Shotgun found himself a good distance from the ship.

Coming up from the engine room, Sean took out the man on watch. A few seconds later, the explosives went off. Sean was baffled when he couldn't find Shotgun or get an answer to his hail on the radio. He began searching the deck in vain, looking for a hiding place that didn't exist.

Shotgun is not a weak swimmer, but with all due respect to my friends in the army, even a good land soldier doesn't compare to a poor SEAL. He'd been chosen to cut the anchors because Doc figured Mongoose's naval background would come in handy if something happened to him on the way to the engine room. It was a logical choice, but Murphy loves making hash of logic. Weighed down by his gear, Shotgun began to tire. He finally had to rest—not an easy feat in the ocean, even after inflating his faithful UDT SEAL life vest—drifting and bobbing rather than continuing to swim. This just made things worse; in the darkness, he lost sight of the Russian ship.

The cannon fire should have given him a clue. Doc and Mongoose scrambled to the other side of the ship as the nearby Korean patrol boat continued to pummel the superstructure. Another zeroed in on the Russian's retreating bow, lobbing 37mm shells just over the railing. They were close enough that Sean could have read the serial numbers on them as they passed.

The Russian captain, realizing that the North Korean ships were not going to accept a surrender, gave the order to abandon ship. Two sailors ran by Doc and Mongoose without stopping or even seeming to notice them, scrambling over to the lifeboat. With the help of four or five other men, they began lowering it to the water. They'd only gotten a few feet when a shell splintered one of the davits. The men were spilled into the waves; two were killed by shrapnel and a third drowned.

The SEALS chose this moment to arrive. They'd left the *Greenville* via an Advanced SEAL Delivery Vehicle, surfaced just inside international waters, and crowded into inflatable raiding crafts to bide their time. As the Russian ship drew next to them, they shot lines to the railing and pulled themselves up, securing the ship exactly as planned.

Except for the shelling. That wasn't planned.

The young bloods fanned out throughout the ship, one detail heading to the engine room. Despite the fact that Doc had been a little too enthusiastic in his application of the explosives, one of the SEALs with a mechanical bent managed to get an engine back online and jury-rigged a system to control it. Meanwhile, a prize team took the bridge and began steering the ship deeper into international waters.

Sean hadn't found Shotgun, but he did turn up a Russian heavy machine gun. He set it up near the bow and began firing toward the nearest North Korean ship, doing enough damage to turn it away, though the others continued to blast their guns.

Our new generation of SEALs are a raucous, can-do bunch, but even they wouldn't have survived the onslaught had it continued. Fortunately, the commander of *Greenville* decided to intervene.

The captain's orders directed him *not* to attack the North Korean vessels, and it's likely that had he *followed* those orders, no one above him in rank would have blamed him no matter what happened to the SEALs or my men.

Not that he would have made the SEALs or my men happy. But then dead men tell no tales.

The captain had two Korean-speaking specialists aboard, and he was just about to order one of them to tell the Koreans to stand down or be sunk when he had a more creative idea.

"Tell them we're Korean sub 409 and we're going to sink the ship for the glory of the homeland. Tell them to stand off while we take our position."

The sailor looked at him cross-eyed, then complied.

"Tell them this Admiral Ku. Use that name," said the captain. "Go ahead."

Ku and submarine 409 were real Korean units, which the captain knew from his briefings. His transmission gave the commander of the small ships pause, though only for a moment. He requested the submarine's identifier codes.

The *Greenville*'s captain checked the location of the Russian ship, which was now moving at about six knots away from Korea. He ordered the *Greenville* to surface between the Koreans and the ship, and then prepared his torpedoes to fire.

Let's face it. Submarines are nowhere near as intimidating as capital ships, which can make a hell of a show swiveling guns and missiles in an enemy's direction. But the *Greenville*'s sudden appearance took the Koreans by surprise. The sun had just set, and in the dusk it's likely they thought the *Greenville* really was their comrade: no American would be nuts enough to surface so close to this many enemy ships; the lawyers would never allow it. The Korean commander ordered his ships to immediately stop firing at the Russian vessel.

If it had been me, I'd've fired the damn torpedoes and told the C2 commanders above me what they could do with their orders. But some people say I have trouble with authority. By the time the Koreans realized that the *Greenville* had no intention of sinking the Russian ship—it's not clear that they ever realized it wasn't on their side—the SEALs had taken the vessel well out of their range. A flight of Super Hornets from the aircraft carrier *Abraham Lincoln* came on the scene a few minutes later. Just like aviators, always late even for sloppy seconds. A pass or two convinced the lingering Korean ships that their fuel supplies were low and had best be checked back at base.

While the SEALs took care of the injured Russian crewmen,

Doc, Mongoose, and Sean looked for Shotgun. With him not answering their radio calls, they feared the worst.

"That no good son of a bitch. If he died, I'm going to kill him," said Mongoose.

Shotgun's radio gear included an emergency GPS locator beacon, but the system had not been activated. Bad news. The ship was searched and secured without finding him. Worse news.

Search and rescue assets from the *Lincoln* were rallied, and an aircraft with infrared gear, along with escorts, was ordered up and vectored over to our area. Mongoose borrowed some night goggles from the SEALs and began scouring the nearby ocean. By that point, I'm sorry to say, everyone was convinced they were looking for a dead body. Their eyes swept the ocean back and forth, back and forth, without seeing anything.

Until a green blip appeared in the distance, stroking a bit unsteadily.

"Doc—look," yelled Mongoose.

"You sure that's him?"

"Has to be. The head's too square to be a normal human being."

A rigid hulled inflatable boat set out from the sub to investigate. As they neared the figure, one of the crewmen reported hearing an odd sound rising above the waves. At first he thought it might be the baying of a very lost sea lion. Then he realized the voice was human, and it was singing.

"Sir, the words to the song appear to be, 'I keep a close watch on this heart of mine,' " the sailor reported back.

"Johnny Cash," said Sean.

"That's Shotgun," Doc told the sailor. "Pick him up—but you better make him promise to stop singing before you do."

[III]

Meanwhile, I was having dinner with the world's last true communist pinko slime. Rather than having me shot as promised when we finished, Kim took me back to his lair for a final game of snooker. It was just him and me; the sycophants had been dismissed, and Sun was off seeing to whatever latest evil required his attention. Kim played well, and probably would have won even without his special house rule enabling him to take his opponent's shot as his own by decree.

After he'd beaten me for the fifth straight time, he had a pair of full bottles of Bombay Sapphire placed on a table in the center of the room. Opening them, he poured me a drink and offered a toast to my health. I poured him one and offered a toast to his health. We traded shots back and forth until the bottles were half full . . . or were they half empty? General Sun came in with some sort of update for Kim, distracting him long enough for me to switch the bottles. To my great surprise, his bottle had been filled with gin as well.

We bantered a bit more when Sun left. I offered another toast to his health, then asked how his cancer was.

"Oh, that. It turns out the doctors got it wrong," he said. "I don't have cancer at all."

"So you really don't care about seeing your bastard son?"

"On the contrary—seeing him now is more important than ever. General Sun's men are bringing him over as we speak."

"I doubt that," I said, taking my cue to line up a shot.

"It is a fact. When he arrives, I will have you killed. Since I am a great admirer of yours, I have decided to allow you to choose your method of death."

"Old age."

"More Rogue Warrior humor. Very funny. Not." He did his best impression of a snarl. It made him look like a woodchuck that has had its front teeth knocked out. "You are wondering about your country's agreement to disarm, no doubt. I'm not interested in going through with it, now that I know I'm not going to die. There's no sense. I was interested in peace only if I didn't have to suffer through it. War is more interesting."

"Can't argue with you there."

I took my shot, sinking a red ball, then a black. I ran through the rest of the colored balls, but I left the pink for him.

"I'm not interested in world peace either," I told him. "I just want the same deal the Russian got."

"Which Russian?"

"Polorski. General Sun didn't tell you about that?"

"General Sun tells me many things," said Kim, his voice so haughty that it was obvious he hadn't known about it.

"Polorski and his mafiya crew were getting a small warhead in exchange for Yong Shin Jong. I would have thought Sun would tell you about it, since it was your nukes he was giving away."

Kim missed his shot.

"As a matter of fact, Polorski interfered when I grabbed your son. I had to go through considerable trouble to get him back. If it weren't for Polorski, we would have been here days ago."

"You go," said Kim, pointing to the table.

I smiled, and lined up a fresh shot. I was about five balls into the run when Kim stepped up and silently elbowed me away. He blew the shot. He took another and blew that one, too. Finally he looked up at me.

"The way I have it figured," I told Kim, "is that Yong Shin Jong has access to money you want. General Sun wants it, too. So he worked out a deal with the Russian to get it."

Kim had a funny look on his face. I wouldn't call it disbelief.

"Maybe we can ask him the next time he comes back," I added.

As if on cue, the bookcase behind Kim moved. Sun stepped out—followed by Trace and Junior, and three dozen of Kim's security people.

13

[I]

While I had been letting Kim snooker me, Trace and Junior had been conducting a sneak and peak of the dictator's grounds. Yong Shin Jong had helped considerably, mapping a gap in the video camera coverage of the perimeter walls, and telling them the security codes for one of the service entrances. He also diagrammed a good portion of the underground complex, though his knowledge was limited to the main house and part of the security area, including the bunker and hallways where I'd been taken when I first came in. But one look at their faces and I knew that they hadn't found the warheads.

"Your people were looking for you," said Sun. "They seem to feel you are in some danger."

"*Moi?* Danger?" I took a sip of the Bombay. "I've just been here with my friend and employer."

"It was an assassination plot," said Sun, turning to Kim. "They came to kill you."

"He'd be dead by now if that were true," I said. "It's been fun, but it's time to stop playing around. Tell me where to find my nuke, and I'll tell you where to find Yong."

Kim looked at Sun. "Why did you promise the Russians a warhead?"

Sun said something in Korean that made Kim's face turn the color of a plum that had been squashed on the pavement and baked in the summer heat for a week. He raised his hand and opened his mouth. I could practically see the words forming on his lips: "Arrest him."

But I saw nothing—the lights went out.

(II)

I could take credit for having planned out and executed a perfect mission. I could claim that everything that followed was part of a carefully considered, meticulously planned, exquisitely executed plan.

If someone else is buying the drinks, I may just do that. But to be honest, twenty-five percent of what happened after the lights went out was due to training, planning, and execution.

The rest was due to luck—good, bad, and cockeyed.

People began yelling and shouting in Korean. Guns fired. Grenades exploded.

Grenades—where did those come from? Who would set off grenades in a crowded room?

Three guesses, and the first two don't count.

The grenades were miniature flash-bangs that Junior smuggled in his boot heels. Little more than overgrown firecrackers, they were just enough to stun everyone while we made our escape.

"Go!" I yelled, catching an AK47 Trace tossed over after grabbing it from a guard. I lassoed the person to my left—Kim Jong Il—and dragged him with me into the passage behind the bookcase. As soon as I was through, Trace pulled down on the metal bar at the side of the door, manually closing off the opening. Then she jammed her rifle into the mechanism and left it so the door couldn't be opened from inside the room.

"Did you find the storeroom with the bombs?" I asked Trace and Junior.

"No—and we checked all of the corridors where Yong Shin Jong said they might be," said Trace. "The CIA's information must be wrong."

It wouldn't be the first time the Christians in Action had screwed up, but I suspected we just hadn't looked hard enough yet.

Yong Shin Jong's map showed a route to the utility area where Trace and Junior had come in. The corridor was lined with a backup battery light system, activated by light sensors and not connected to the complex's main power grid. But only about half of these were working, and their dim yellow lights filled the concrete hallways with as much shadow as light. After I'd gone about ten feet, a gun loomed ahead. It was Junior, who'd gone ahead. I just barely kept myself from firing at him.

"This way, Dick," he said, waving.

"I got it, Junior," I told him. "Go."

Kim Jong Il grunted beside me, waddling rather than running as I pulled him along. The dictator was wheezing and cursing in Korean. He wasn't resisting me exactly; he was just out of shape. He seemed dazed, not sure what was going on, though he must have known it wasn't good. I doubt he had expected Sun to turn against him, but he wasn't so delusional as to think I was on his side.

When we reached the first intersection in the passage he tried to resist. He jerked to the right—we were supposed to go straight, according to Yong Shin Jong's map—and tried to get out of my grip. When that didn't work, he pushed against me and spun, attempting to twist away.

I whacked him on the side of the head with my rifle, sending him to the floor with enough topspin to bounce his head two or three times against the wall.

"Up, asshole." I grabbed him by the collar and dragged him after the others.

"Just shoot the mother and be done with him," said Trace.

Tempting advice. But at that point, I thought that if I took it we wouldn't get out alive.

And let's face it—being able to say you kidnapped the world's biggest despot is pretty heady stuff. It's the ultimate fuck-you to all the people in Washington and everywhere else who think I'm over the hill.

"I'm not shooting him—not yet, not unless I have to," I told

Trace before turning back to him. "Where are your nukes? They're down here, aren't they?"

Kim glared contemptuously—a little too contemptuously, I thought, but he insisted haughtily that he had already told the U.S. and UN everything.

"You think you are smarter than everyone else," he said finally. "But you are always just guessing—I've read your books."

"You'll have a lot more time to read them from now on," I told him, pushing him to walk with us. "And in hardcover. No more bootleg Chinese editions."

"I'm not going," he said, bracing his feet and refusing to move.

"If you don't come with us, Kim, General Sun will have you flayed. Don't you see that he's in the process of overthrowing you?"

Reminded of his henchman's treachery, Kim became a bit more compliant, though he didn't exactly lead the charge as we continued down the corridor. The walls were made of concrete, lined with a million scratches in what the masons call a fancy "broom" finish so they can add twenty percent to the bill. At its peak, the rounded ceiling was eight feet high and dissected by a metal conduit chase. Fluorescent lights were hung every fifty feet or so off the conduit; the emergency lights were spaced irregularly at the sides of the ceiling.

We were a good fifty feet below the earth's surface, if not more. The tunnel got its air from the facilities it connected to, and even though it didn't have fans or a ventilation system, we could feel a decent breeze in the hall as we moved. Because of the circulation, the air wasn't quite fetid, but it did have the faintly stale smell of an unused men's room whose door and windows have been closed all day long.

According to Yong Shin Jong's map, we had to turn right at the next intersection. We stopped about ten feet short of it, listening to hear if we were being followed, or if there was someone coming from the other direction. Yong Shin Jong had said no one was stationed in the tunnel itself, but it wasn't entirely unprotected. The tunnel connected to the sentry room that I'd seen during my brief incarceration upstairs, as well as to a secure situation room on the other side of the complex and reserve guardroom where at least a dozen soldiers were on duty at all times.

The way seemed clear. Trace went to the corner, peeked around, then signaled for us to follow. We ran another thirty or forty yards, then came to a second intersection. Yong Shin Jong had marked the cross tunnel as unfinished; it was narrower than the main passages, and I could see the end of the tunnel on the right. The one to the left was completely in shadow.

Kim Jong Il hesitated as we went through, glancing down the corridor to the left before coming with me.

Bingo.

"Trace, did you go down the tunnel on the way in?"

"We didn't get this far."

"They're down here, aren't they?" I asked Kim, gesturing to my left.

The Great Leader hesitated; for just a moment he looked like he'd been punched in the stomach. Then he scowled, looking at me like I was a total ass.

"Take him out," I told Trace, pushing him toward her.

"Where are you going, Dick?"

"To find the warheads."

"We're going with you," said Trace.

"No, you take Kim and get out."

"That wasn't the plan."

"It is now."

"Dick, are you sure it's in that direction?" asked Junior. "Yong Shin Jong said the tunnel was supposed to connect to the guardroom but was never finished."

"Kim says they're here. Don't you, Kim?"

The dictator scowled again.

"Maybe they're in one of the tunnels near the power generators," said Junior.

"No, they're here," I said.

I considered the possibility that Kim was deeking me; it was possible that the tunnel had been connected to the guardroom as Yong Shin Jong believed was intended. But having played snooker with Kim, I believed I had a good sense of his gamesmanship and ability to bluff. Some people would have preferred poker, but it's harder to lie with a cue stick.

"I'll catch up to you," I told the others. "Go."

"If you're going, we're going," said Trace. She yanked Kim. "Come on, pudgeball. Get the lead out."

We moved down the tunnel, through a series of sharp curves. The passage angled downward. There were no emergency lights for about fifty yards, so we were moving in real darkness until we finally found a stretch lit by battery-powered red lights dimmer by half than those you'd find in a blackened theater. We half walked, half trotted another hundred yards before coming to a gate made of wood and thick plastic bars. The gate marked the entrance to a much wider open area. It was impossible to tell what its dimensions were because it was so dark.

The gate's dead bolt worked from our side. I turned it and swung the door open, entering what turned out to be a level hall wide enough for two trucks to pass. To my left sat a large machine, covered with dust. I had to get close to examine it, and even then had trouble making it out. It looked like a stripped-down bulldozer. Instead of a blade at the front, a cone-shaped nose extended to the wall. It must have been some sort of tunnel digger, though the wall it sat before was covered in concrete.

A thick wooden door about the size of a double garage filled the wall on the other side of the machine, our right.

"This is it?" asked Junior as I checked out the door.

"Behind the wooden door. It's wood because the amount of metal in this whole area has been carefully calculated in case a magnameter is used to try to detect an underground passage. That's a tunnel digger, right, Kim? That's how you get the nukes out if you need them. Because it's sealed off from above and you can't get a truck down that corridor. If there's a problem, you can flood the tunnels with water from the nearby lake, or maybe you just blow out the ceiling supports. Don't want the inspectors finding this room."

I couldn't see the dictator's face in the poor light, but I imagine he wasn't smiling.

"You should have sealed it off," I told him. "For security. But you probably couldn't resist taking a peek at your treasure, could you?"

A pair of sophisticated digital locks held the door against the floor. It worked like an old-fashioned solid-piece garage door, lifting and flipping up from the bottom.

"What's the combination?" I asked Kim.

He made a snorting sound. I swung my rifle around and aimed it at the lock.

"If the lock is tampered with, it will explode," he said nervously. "The roof will cave in and we will be buried alive."

"Then you better give me the combination."

Kim shook his head.

"Try his father's birthday," said Junior.

It didn't work.

"Translate it to the Korean calendar." Junior came over. "Let me."

I rose and went to Kim, leveling the rifle at his chest. The locks snapped open behind me.

"You're not going to get out of here alive, Marcinko," said Kim Jong Il. "You're a dead man."

"If I die, you die."

Not much of a clever comeback, I know, but I had other things on my mind. I helped Junior open the door, swinging it gently as I tried to figure out whether it was booby-trapped or not. It didn't appear so—or at least nothing went boom.

"You guys stay there," I told them.

"What if it's a trap?" said Trace.

"Then get the hell out."

"What about laughing boy?"

"Kill him if you have to."

"With my bare hands."

I had to duck to fit inside the room. It was pitch-black, and the ceiling angled downward sharply, as if the space were a wedge removed from the center of a cheese wheel. Three steps in and I was hunched over about halfway. It was so dark I couldn't see my hand as I reached out in front of me. I took a step, then got into a crouch. I pushed forward another few feet, hands out, until finally I felt something cold and round—the metal jacket of a bomb, sitting on a wooden cradle.

I used my fingertips as eyes. There were four bomb-shaped metal casks, each about the size and shape of a stubby torpedo—longer and thinner than I'd seen in the briefing. The cylinders were flat on both ends, with what felt like screws and sockets, presumably the plug-ins for the detonators.

Were they nukes? The truth is, I had no way to tell for sure. I had no instruments to test for radioactivity, and I couldn't even see them. But what else would Kim hide here?

I reached behind my right earlobe and dug my fingernail into the small flap of skin, retrieving half of the locator device Admiral Jones had given me back in the States. My fingers were so wet it slipped to the floor.

Murphy, you son of a bitch.

I thought I was going to puke. I dropped to my knees, patting around the floor for the damn thing. All sorts of ideas flew through my mind, none of them very nice. I was mad enough that if the nukes had had triggers on them, and if I had known how to set them off, I would have blown up the whole bunker right then.

A calmer alternative had just presented itself to me when my fingers found the tiny little pimple of an integrated circuit. I picked it up gingerly, then placed it in the only safe spot I could think of while I retrieved the other half—my tongue.

Take your thumb and first two fingers on your left hand,

and put them against the thumb and first two fingers of your right, and then try and triangulate them all together. Line them up precisely so that the nails of all six fingers form a perfect hexagon.

Got it?

Good. Now close your eyes and do it again. And by the way soak one of them in spit and make sure people are shouting at you to hurry up because the fate of the free world hangs in the balance.

It took forever to get the two little buggers together. Finally there was a little pop between my fingers. I twisted, pushed with my thumb and forefinger to make sure the connection was solid, then put the unit, still no bigger than a ladybug, on the cradle of the bomb next to me.

(III)

Mission accomplished, right? Break out the champagne, strike up the band, roll the credits. Dickie's done. Adventure over.

Right?

Oh, yeah. Fuckin' A. In the movies, maybe. In the real world where I lived, we actually like to get out from wherever the hell we are and live to brag about it. Or write about it, as the case may be.

"Dick! Let's go," said Trace. "What are you doing in there? Praying?"

"Very devoutly," I answered, feeling the lock mechanism for the explosives Kim had warned me about. The locks themselves were small, no bigger than decks of cards, and at first I thought Kim had been lying. But then I felt a slight bump of a wire running from each up through the wooden panel of the door. I followed the wire with my fingernail, tracing it up into the hinge and across to a dugout shelf at the side of the room. There was a large brick of explosives there, along with a detonator.

Was it enough explosive to set off one of the bombs at the back?

Surely not, or it never would have been put there. On the other hand, if it went off now, it would keep the warheads nice and safe until Uncle Sam's bunker busters could find them.

"Junior, you're wearing the watch Doc gave you, right?" I shouted.

"Um, yes."

"Come here."

By now, my eyes had adjusted so well to the darkness that I could see the screws that connected the wire from the door locks to the explosive. I teased the wire strands from the crevice they had been pushed into, then put my teeth into one and broke it off.

As I did, the thought crossed my mind that a clever demolitions expert would have set up the detonator to blow as soon as the circuit was broken.

Luckily for me, whoever had set up the booby trap hadn't been that clever. I bit off a second wire and stripped the ends with my teeth as Junior walked down into the bomb room, his hands feeling the space before him like a blind man.

"Dick?"

"Here, Junior." I reached out and grabbed him. "Give me your watch."

"But—"

"Not now, Junior."

He slipped it off. I'd noticed it when we first met; it did everything but open beer bottles. Probably his belt buckle did that.

"How do you get the alarm function?" I asked.

"Hit the bottom left-hand button twice. What are you timing?"

"Nothing. I want to use it as a timer for the explosives."

"I haven't been able to get it to time more than ten minutes in years."

"Ten minutes will do. How do I set vibrate?"

"Vibrate or vibrate and beep?"

"Either one." I took the watch and pried off the back. Timers from watches can be used as part of a bomb circuit, but even your basic geek watch didn't come ready to be used for one. My idea was much simpler. I hooked the back of the watch through one of the wires, then perched it precariously over the other wire. When the alarm went off, the vibrations would knock it from the ledge. The wires would cross. Boom.

"Ten minutes?" I asked Junior, who was still standing near me in the dark.

"You got it, Pops."

I laughed, then set the watch down and backed away. "Come on. Out of here."

Kim Jong Il leaned against the wall of the tunnel on the other side of the gate, frowning in Trace's direction when we joined them. Trace frowned back. Given Kim's enlightened attitude toward women, I'm sure he found it humiliating to be guarded by her. Then again, given Trace's attitude toward scumbags, she probably felt more than a little put out to be guarding him rather than shooting him.

"We have nine and a half minutes," I told them. "Let's go."

There were noises in the tunnels as we ran back toward the intersection where we'd turned down. I got ahead of the others as we reached the intersection, looking down both ways to see if it was clear.

It wasn't. A knot of men was running up from the direction of Kim's den. I saw them before they saw me, which meant I was the last thing they saw—six North Koreans fell over in a clump as I shot through the AK47's magazine.

"Go, let's go!" I yelled. "Come on."

We headed straight down the passage that Yong Shin Jong had marked for us for the exit. We were about seventy-five yards from the manhole that led upward when the lights came back on.

"Uh-oh," said Junior.

I didn't share his apprehension until I saw something drop from the ceiling ahead. Something big, and with a gun.

Something else dropped behind it.

"Junior, give me your gun," I said, grabbing his AK47.

"But—"

I pulled the weapon up and fired, point-blank, into three Korean soldiers.

Or would have fired, had it been loaded.

"It-it-it's out of ammo," stuttered Junior.

Doom on Dickie. Doom on us.

I twisted around. There were more soldiers coming up behind us.

"Dick," said Trace.

I turned around. The three soldiers had formed a line in the corridor in front of us. Right behind them was Yong Shin Jong.

Who was pointing an MP5 at us.

"Even better than I hoped," said Yong. None of the soldiers with him were the hires I'd left with him outside.

Kim Jong Il said something in Korean to the effect of "Here you are." I couldn't make out Yong Shin Jong's answer, but I'm pretty sure it wasn't "Oh, sweet daddy, I'm so happy to see you."

Just to make the party complete, several more soldiers and General Sun came up behind us. Rifles bristled; the conversation continued in loud and rabid Korean.

Trace, Junior, and I were in the middle of a three-way standoff. I was holding Junior's AK47 at Kim's head, but this didn't have much of an effect on the other two men, who clearly wanted him dead. In the meantime, Junior's clock was ticking away. The explosives it would set off were clearly not enough to make the tunnels collapse. The air shock from the explosion, however, would blow through the complex, and I couldn't be sure how forceful it would be. And I really didn't want to find out.

"Listen, I'd love to stay for your party," I said loudly. "But I've radioed in the position of your nukes and they're about to drop a pair of bunker busters on them. If we don't get the hell out of here, we'll all be buried alive."

Everyone was so busy threatening each other, they didn't hear a word I said. The Koreans now were arguing bitterly, Kim probably calling the others rat-faced traitors, the others no doubt calling him a slime of the worst sort. I couldn't have disagreed with any of them even if I'd known how to speak their language.

Sensing time was running out—my internal clock had drained to thirty seconds—I shouted a second warning.

"I radioed in the location of the Great Dictator's nukes," I told them. "An American B-2 bomber is circling overhead, about to drop a pair of bunker busters on them. There'll be two bombs, one right after the other. The second's a nuke. We'll be fried, sizzled, and roasted, and not in that order."

Sun turned from the others and looked at me.

"A bluff," he said. "Typical American horse shit."

"Mr. Rogue Warrior is so full of shit his eyes are brown," said Yong Shin Jong.

Very nice use of an American idiom, but we'll save the compliments for his English teacher.

"I have read Marcinko's books," Kim said, looking at me. "This is not the part where he bluffs."

They started to argue again in Korean, this time about me. I glanced at Trace, swinging my eyes up toward the manhole and our escape route, then did the same for Junior.

"We have to go!" I shouted emphatically.

At that instant, the timer went off. The watch buzzed, the wires fell together, and the explosion sent a shock wave through the tunnel.

[IV]

It's surprising how powerful air can be. Push around enough of it, and a locomotive can leap up off its tracks and sail halfway across a station before setting down again. There were no locomotives in the corridor when the bomb exploded—a good thing, because the force of the wind shock would have thrown it against us. As it was, all of the Korean soldiers and leaders, along with Trace, Junior, and I, were blown against the far wall of the tunnel like pieces of paper. Trace, Junior, and I were the ham and cheese in a Korean sandwich, but our spot in the middle of the scrum probably protected us from much greater injuries—those closest to the bomb spray were peppered with concrete splinters and other debris loosened by the explosion, and those farthest were smashed directly against the wall, absorbing most of the impact.

The explosion knocked out the lights again, this time taking the emergency lamps as well as the regular overheads. I pushed my way through the pile in the darkness. Trace had been right next to me when the explosion went off; I felt her elbow in my rib and pulled her free from the tangle. As I did, I nearly tripped over a Korean I thought was probably Kim Jong Il.

He was too good a prize to pass up. I grabbed him and started hauling him up over my shoulder.

"Dick, where's Junior?" yelled Trace behind me.

Good question. I called for him, yelling over the moans. As they pulled themselves to their feet, the Koreans began to panic. They thought the explosion was just the first of two, and the next would be a nuke.

"Junior, where the hell are you?" I shouted again.

"Dick, the ladder is over here. Get Junior and let's go!" yelled Trace.

A heap of bodies lay next to me on the floor. It was still dark, and the only way to identify Junior was by touch. To do that, I had to let go of Kim Jong Il.

I tossed him aside, then began pulling bodies from the pile.

Finally I heard a familiar moan. I grabbed Matthew by the shirt and threw him onto my back.

He was a hell of a lot heavier than he looked. I staggered through the Koreans toward the ladder. The soldiers who hadn't been injured by the blast were pushing and pulling at each other, trying to get their bearings and get away. Finally Trace tugged my shoulder, moving me to the ladder. With one hand on Junior's back, I started climbing.

Trace kicked one of the soldiers aside, grabbing his rifle as he fell. The gun wasn't necessary though—the Koreans were all running for their lives, heading toward the perimeter fence. I hesitated for a second, thinking maybe I would go back and grab Kim Jong Il. But Trace's shouts convinced me to forget about him and just go.

Our truck with the Korean troops should have been waiting for us near the entrance we had used to get in. But claiming to have received a message from me, Yong Shin Jong had dismissed the men, sending them into the city to wait. We looked around and spotted something nearly as good—a Land Rover belonging to one of Kim's lackeys.

It took me exactly thirty seconds to hot-wire the truck. We got in, Junior in the back, Trace riding shotgun. I revved it toward the utility entrance. We were just about to the main road when the ground began to sway. Before I could say the words "holy shit," the ground dropped and then rose, as if it had suddenly become liquid.

"Dick?" said Trace.

"We're out of here," I told her, stepping on the gas. I held on as the road jerked beneath me. The Rover pitched hard right, the wheels leaving the ground, but I was able to get it back on all four. Then a fissure opened up in front of us. There was no way I could stop in time—I put the gas pedal all the way to the floor and held on as the Rover flew over the gap in the pavement. Within seconds I was veering left and right, ducking rifts and small asphalt mountains in the highway.

A fresh tremor threw the vehicle into the air. Had this been a road back in the States, we would have come down in the middle of a pile of rubble. But the highway had been engineered to withstand bombing attacks, and it remained in one piece. I drove on, passing men running to defensive positions as air-raid sirens screamed.

My original escape plan called for us to head to an airport north of the capital, where a chartered Russian airliner (with a filed flight plan to Vladivostok) would take us to Japan. But given what was going on, and that Yong Shin Jong knew of the plan, I realized we had to find an alternative.

And one presented itself at the end of the road.

"Trace, you up to flying that helo?" I asked.

"What helo?"

"The one in front of us," I said, jerking the wheel onto a dirt fire emergency road behind Kim Jong Il's private helipad. There were two brand-new Sikorsky S-92 helos—pretty civilian helicopters of the same basic type as the president's helicopter, Marine One.

"Shit yeah," said Trace. "Those new Sikorskys? I've never flown the type but we trained on an S-70.[35] Very sweet. They practically fly themselves."

"Not that one. One of the old Russian crates," I said, pointing the Rover toward a pair of Hind helicopters at the far end of the small field.

"God, Dick, they look older than you."

"Thanks for the compliment."

The Korean helicopter crews were mustering with the alert. The newer ones—Sikorsky S-92s—were Kim Jong Il's personal aircraft. The Hinds—and Trace was right about them being older than me—were escorts. I chose the older aircraft for two reasons. First, I figured that Kim would be much more upset about losing his shiny new toy than he would be an older aircraft.

35 The S-70 is the civilian version of the Blackhawk.

Second, and more important, the Hind had weapons and the Sikorsky didn't.

The Hinds were very early models, more primitive than the ones we used on the raid with the Russians earlier. Their configuration was different and more complicated. The cockpit was larger and bulkier, looking more like a greenhouse than the two-level, one plus one arrangement that became standard in the later aircraft. In this version, the gunner sat in front of a pilot and copilot, and there was a hell of a lot more room to work the weapons. And while they didn't include a kickass cannon beneath the nose, there was a nice array, including rockets, antitank missiles, and a 12.7mm four-barrel machine gun that made a hell of a noise when it was fired.

Which I found out when two Korean troop trucks came toward us across the tarmac just as Trace powered us up. The gun blew out the engine compartments of both trucks. Soldiers swarmed out and began returning fire.

"Get us out of here!" I yelled as the helo spun around on the ground.

"I'm trying!"

The engines kicked into some higher gear, drowning out the machine gun. We taxied forward, picking up speed but not altitude. Losing my angle on the Koreans, I sat back and strapped on my restraints, hoping to enjoy the flight. Sitting in the nose of an aircraft can be picturesque—except when all you're seeing is an eight-foot steel fence held in place by thick girders.

"Up!" I yelled. "Get us the fuck *up*!"

Trace pulled on the stick or the collective or whatever the hell it is you pull on to get a helicopter into the air. We jerked into the air, scraping the fence but still going.

Pyongyang stretched out below us—though not far enough below us. Antiaircraft batteries were coming to life all over the city, throwing streaks of red in our direction. More of a problem was the row of buildings directly in front of us as we flew. They weren't very high, but neither were we.

"Up, up, up," I yelled. "Trace!"

The helicopter jerked hard to the left—toward a hail of tracers.

"We have to broadcast to them and say that we're on their side," yelled Junior, picking an excellent moment to regain consciousness. We'd thrown him in the back when we'd climbed aboard. "They think we're the enemy."

Junior got into the copilot's seat and began hitting switches to turn on the radio. The kid certainly had the right idea, but since none of us spoke Korean, there was no way to follow through on it. Saying "Don't fire at us" in English wasn't going to do it.

A stream of bullets ripped through the right side of the helo as Trace jerked out of the way of the latest spray of flak. Shrapnel exploded through the cockpit; I felt a familiar hot pain in the shoulder and neck as slivers of metal bounced past the seat and hit me.

"Get us going south," I said, probably only to myself. "Get us over the border."

Trace was already working on that, ramming the Hind's throttles into overdrive. Junior was yelling on the radio, using the odd bits of Korean he'd managed to pick up. For all I know, he was asking where the restrooms were, but either his messages worked or we finally outran the outer ring of defenses, because the gunfire gradually stopped. Our low altitude—we were still barely at treetop level—may have helped; we were too low for most radars to pick us up, and by the time the antiair gunner realized we were there it was too late to fire.

The shrapnel had torn some nice holes in my flesh as well as my shirt, but the fact that I was still conscious told me that nothing important had been cut. Even so, I was still losing a decent amount of blood; the entire left side of my chest was covered with it. I tore off the right sleeve of my Korean ninja shirt, wadding it up to use as a bandage. I pushed it against my neck and then wedged my head back against the seat, compressing the wound. As I leaned in, I felt a sharp tweak of pain—the metal or whatever the hell it was still inside. I grit my teeth and stuck my fingers in the wound, trying to fish it out.

Don't try that at home, kids. My fingers were dirty as hell; despite the flowing blood I probably infected the wound. I got the metal, a little frag no bigger than a paperclip. For some reason I thought it was important and slipped it into my pocket. Then I put the wadded shirt back and pressed on my neck. My head was swimming, starting to zoom around in circles above my body.

A stream of fresh tracers off the port bow told us we had a new problem—the other Hind helicopter had scrambled into the air and was trying to shoot us down.

Now it was Trace's turn to shout at me.

"Dick! He's coming around to the right! Nail the son of a bitch. On three."

Trace counted three, then pushed the helicopter to the side, trying to give me a clear shot. I was so dazed I couldn't aim the machine gun for shit. I grabbed at the gun control and fired the trigger, watching in vain as the bullets flew to the right when I wanted them to go to the left. I pushed the gun but it was too late. The Hind ducked away, circling to try to get behind us. Trace wasn't about to let that happen. She jinked hard left and pushed our nose toward the ground, sending what was left of my blood sloshing to the roof of my skull.

If you've ever sat in the front car of a roller coaster and tried firing a machine gun at a passing seagull, you know how I felt. I gripped the trigger of the Hind's forward machine gun, firing wildly as the other Hind danced in front of us, then disappeared. We whipped back and forth as tracers flashed through the sky. Then the other Hind appeared so close on my right I could have opened up the window and shaken the pilot's hand.

I pushed the machine gun to the right, but couldn't get a shot. My eyes lost focus; there were suddenly six Hinds in front of me.

"Dad! Shoot the rockets when Trace kills the throttle. The rockets!"

Dad?

Junior?

My head felt as if someone had sliced it into three parts, then put them back out of order. The rockets had to be armed before they could be fired, a simple two-step process, if you knew the sequence . . . if you knew where the panel was . . . if you knew how to turn the damn thing on.

The controls were to my right.

"Fire!"

Fire?

I jammed my hands on the panel, then felt something helping me, something from above.

Not the hand of God, but the hand of Junior, pushing the buttons.

"Fire, damn it!" I yelled, and the rockets shot out from the winglets in a surge of red, turning the sky in front of us into a huge red ball of flame.

Then the small part of the world that wasn't twisting into darkness gave up and joined the rest, swarming me in a black hole of unconsciousness.

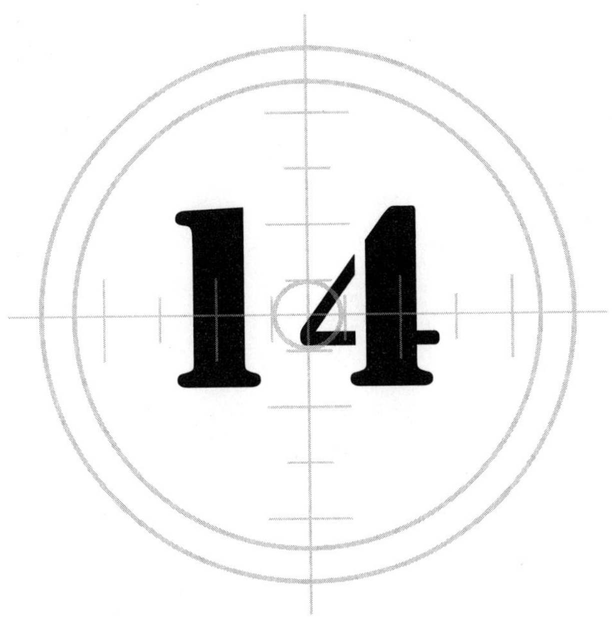
14

[1]

I woke up in Tokyo General Hospital, feeling as if I were at the tail end of a three-day hangover. As a matter of fact, it had been three days since I'd been conscious. I'd lost a lot of blood in the helicopter. Rather than just going straight to Sapphire, the doctors refilled me with blood, which probably explained why I was out so long.

Karen was sitting in the chair next to me, a sight for sore eyes and battered bones. She looked over at me, smiled, and told me to relax and go back to sleep.

"What's going on? Where's Trace? What about Junior?" I asked, pushing myself up in the bed. "And Doc—where's Doc?"

"Dick, you have to relax."

"I am relaxed. What happened?"

"Trace is fine, and so is Doc, Shotgun, Mongoose, Sean—everyone is fine." Karen sighed. "I'll tell you the whole story if you just lay down in bed and relax."

"Come into bed with me and help me relax."

"Now I know you're going to be okay."

Bit by bit, Karen told me what happened. A pair of South Korean F-16s had arrived soon after Junior and I shot down the other Hind. After some expletive-laden exchanges over the radio, Trace managed to convince them we were on their side. They escorted us over the DMZ and into South Korea. Junior and Trace had a few cuts and bruises, but otherwise had come through the battle OK.

The Russian cargo ship had sunk from the battering administered by the North Koreans—that and some strategically placed explosives that were ignited by the SEALs when their inspection was complete. Their search didn't turn up a nuke, nor did they find any members of Polorski's Russian mob aboard. But it did turn up two computer laptops, as well as some leads on the gang's financial connections. Other members of the gang are still at large. The last I heard, the hard drives on those computers had been studied by six different U.S. agencies, and shared with at least three foreign governments. With that many people in the mix, you can judge for yourself what the results are likely to be.

As you've probably guessed by now, the air farce—*our* air farce—dropped a pair of bunker buster bombs on Kim's secret stash of nukes soon after I activated the homing signal. The warheads on the American bombs were specifically designed to be exploded underground against bunkers.[36] The resulting explosion was powerful enough that it was recorded as an earthquake centering around a previously unknown fault just north of Pyongyang. Some scientists believed it was actually a nuclear test by Kim Jong Il's government, a final experiment to make sure his technology was sound before surrendering his bombs.

Kim Jong Il has been notably silent on the matter. Nor would he comment on rumors that elements of the government and army had tried to overthrow him. The official North Korean news agency announced that he was looking forward to continued cooperation with the world community regarding nuclear weapons and the related treaties, and if you've been following the news lately, you'll see that he has. More or less. Sometimes a lot less, but given that he no longer has any nukes hidden away, American authorities are no longer quite as concerned about how long the process takes.

I didn't know that the bombs were going to be dropped. I said what I said to the others as a bluff. True, I'd expected something would happen. I knew Jones wouldn't have gotten me involved if he wasn't serious, and I realized the old-warhorse-dying-with-his-boots-on comments he'd dropped at our meeting weren't idle musings. Personally, I would have wanted a bit more of an interlude between the time the locator was activated and the bombs were dropped. You might draw the conclusion that

---

[36] Were they nukes? Ask your congressman.

whoever ordered the attack was not very concerned about me making it out alive. You might even conclude that they didn't want me to get out alive.

You might.

Of course, the timing might simply have been a result of standard bureaucratic screwups . . . or the air farcers flying the planes may have wanted to knock off work early.

Both Yong Shin Jong and Sun have disappeared from public view. You can read into that what you want. One thing you can't do is find any mention of them anymore in any official or unofficial North Korean document. In fact, all memory of them seems to have been erased; they're not even mentioned in Wikipedia anymore.

As for yours truly, the doctors had a long list of arteries and veins that the shrapnel had supposedly nicked, cut, and contorted. Some nerves, muscles, and bones had been abused as well. The list reminded me that every square millimeter of the body has a fancy Latin name, which is how doctors justify their high prices when they patch you up.

"You know, Dick," said Karen, who'd snuggled up to me as the tale progressed, "you're getting too old for this. You can't keep abusing your body and expecting to walk away with a smile."

"So I limp away," I said. "Where's the harm in that?"

"You know what I mean."

"Not really."

I stifled her complaint with a kiss, but before we could get into a more thorough discussion, there was a knock on the door.

"Go away," I said.

"Always joking," said Jimmy Zim, coming in. "Commander Marcinko, Admiral Jones sends his regards."

"Tell him to fuck himself."

Jimmy Zim wasn't sure how to take that, and I didn't explain. He told me roughly the same story that Karen had, filling in a few of the blanks and apologizing for the C2 officers above him who had made things so difficult.

"You lived up to your reputation," he said when he was done. "I hope we work together again."

"Fuck you very much."

Zim smiled—the first time I'd seen him smile since we met. "Fuck you, too."

He left. I pulled Karen closer and asked her to explain a few things.

"Like?"

"Why are your lips so sweet?"

"I put honey on them."

She pressed them against mine. There was a knock on the door.

"Go away," I said.

"Um, okay." It was Matthew Loring. "When should I, um, come back."

"Never."

"Uh, all right."

"He's only joking, Matthew," said Karen. "You should know that by now."

"Should I really go away?"

"Give us five minutes," said Karen.

Five minutes? Let's get to work, I thought, but she got up from the bed and went over to the chair where she'd put her pocketbook.

"It's going to be hard to inspect your lips from this distance," I told her.

"I have to show you something before Matthew comes in."

"No kidding."

"I'm not making a joke, Dick."

Karen dug into her pocketbook and retrieved a small packet of papers. She had an odd look on her face as she handed it to me.

I unfolded the papers. It was the security report on Matthew Loring.

Bright kid—he'd won a scholarship to MIT. Graduated in three years. Been a counselor in some sort of Outward Bound program. Won a rock-climbing competition in the Smoky Mountains. Star high school soccer player.

"Nice stuff," I told Karen. "I'm going to offer him a permanent position. Not as a computer guy—Shunt's got that handled. If we can get some more meat on his bones, I think he might make it as a shooter. He's a little eccentric, but I think he's got great potential."

"He ought to," said Karen. "Read the last page."

I flipped over to it. It contained information about his early childhood. He'd been to a parochial school in northern New Jersey, just outside of New York. I'd gone to parochial school myself, though several miles away.

"Does he have a phobia about flying nuns attacking him in the dark?" I asked.

"Read the entire thing."

Junior's mother's name was Marian Mahon. She was a single mother; father recorded as unknown on the birth certificate. His date of birth was 1986.

That was not a great year for me. My marriage had already gone to hell. My navy career died. And the government was in the process of inviting me to spend a little time in one of their no-charge hotels thanks to the hurt feelings of a few admirals I'd embarrassed during Red Cell exercises.

I couldn't place a Maria Mahon, and couldn't even remember being in a situation that would have led to Junior. But I couldn't rule it out, either. She lived in the town where I had holed up for several months. She was dead now, having passed away two years before after an unsuccessful fight with breast cancer. But one of her surviving friends, interviewed during the security check, claimed that Matthew was the product of a one-night stand with a famous naval officer—yours truly.

The only "proof," if you could call it that, was a collection of newspaper and magazine articles about me that dated to 1986. Maria had also bought every book I ever wrote.

"You think he's my son?" I asked her.

"I think it's a possibility. Don't you?"

Physically, he didn't look like me at all, not even when I was a kid. Personality-wise, he was quiet where I was loud, he was thoughtful where I charged ahead, certainly at that age. And yet—he did have definite Rogue Warrior tendencies.

"Does he know about this?" I asked.

"I haven't asked."

As I've gotten older over the years I've gotten pretty close to a lot of the shooters and other people who have worked for me at Red Cell International and in various other jobs. Sometimes I think of the younger ones almost as my kids: prodigal, for the most part, but I definitely felt affection toward them. But confronted with the possibility that Matthew might be my son, I didn't know what to feel or do.

I was still trying to figure something out when he knocked on the door again.

"Come," I said.

"How are you, boss?" he asked.

"Still in one piece."

I pushed myself up in the bed to take a good long look at him. He'd been eating since I saw him last. Not that he'd really filled out; he couldn't have gained more than three or four pounds. But he looked a lot less like a scarecrow, and more like a kid who'd just gone through a growth spurt and was about to fill out.

I'd been like that when I joined the navy.

"Are you all right?" I asked him.

"Fine. You were the only one hit when the flak got the chopper. There was a ton of blood all over the place. I thought you were a goner."

"I've taken it in the neck plenty of times."

Junior opened his mouth as if to say something. I waited. No words came out.

"Well, I just wanted to see if you were okay," he said finally. "I mean, I figured you were but, you know, just to check it with my own eyes."

He started back from the room.

"Hold on just a second," I said.

Junior turned around quickly. He had a look in his eyes, something I hadn't seen there before. It was fear.

Was he afraid of being my son?

"I want to offer you a permanent job," I told him. "If you're up for it. You'd have to go through real training. Trace would bust your butt."

"She already is," he said. He was suddenly beaming. "She's got me running five miles a day, and that's just before breakfast."

Maybe at that point I should have said something, given him an opening in case he wanted to talk. But I didn't. Partly, it was because I was still confused about my feelings, and unsure whether he really was my son or not. I wasn't really ready to talk about it, even theoretically.

And partly it was because I didn't think he was ready either. There was no sense spoiling the moment.

"Don't let her run you down. Take two weeks off, then report to Rogue Manor," I told him. "We'll get you airfare."

"Yes sir, thank you sir. Thanks, Dick—you won't regret it."

Junior practically ran from the room before I could say anything else.

"You're not going to talk to him about it?" asked Karen.

"Eventually," I told her, putting my arm around her and pulling her close to give her a kiss. "In the meantime, I have other family business to take care of."